CHAIN

— OF —

COMMAND

CHAIN

— OF —

COMMAND

WALTER GOFF II

WORD PUBLISHING

NASHVILLE

A Thomas Nelson Company

Library of Congress Cataloging-in-Publication Data
Goff, Walter B., 1945–
    Chain of command / Walter B. Goff, II.
        p.   cm.
    ISBN 0-8499-1454-X
    I. Title.
PS3557.03228C48   1998
813'.54—dc21   98-26700
                                                                              CIP

Printed in the United States of America.
8 9 0 1 2 3 4 5 9 BVG 9 8 7 6 5 4 3 2 1

This book is dedicated to my wife,

Sandy,

with all my love on

our twenty-fifth wedding anniversary.

The car door swung open abruptly in front of him, blocking his way. A raspy whisper demanded, "Get in, Dr. Chandler."

All he could see was the cavernous end of a revolver pointed directly at his chest. He looked around for help, but there was none. Reluctantly, he slid into the backseat. The door closed, blocking the morning sunlight. Staring at the black hole of the gun barrel, he wondered momentarily what it would feel like to be shot.

"You've caused Mr. Jarvis a lot of trouble, Doctor. I don't think he's going to be very happy when he sees you. There are many other things he would rather be doing than chasing you around the country," the man sneered.

"Well, he sort of screwed up my vacation too," Chandler rebutted.

No one could possibly see in through the blackened windows of the limousine as it nosed its way through traffic and turned up the George Washington Parkway on the Virginia side of the river. Potomac was an easy drive from Crystal City. Bill silently prayed Holly had gotten away and was able to meet with Ken.

The day was spectacular. The leaves, still covering most of the trees, displayed a multitude of color. They had been washed clean by the rain the night before, and the droplets of water magnified their pigment. It was the kind of day when he would have enjoyed walking the streets of Georgetown arm in arm with someone he loved.

Suddenly he realized he might never see Georgetown again. Just as abruptly it occurred to him that he had fallen in love with Holly.

I wonder if Sandy somehow knows, and if she knows, does she approve? he thought.

The car swerved sharply onto the brick drive to the mansion's entrance and brought him back to reality. It was hard to believe that only twenty-four hours had passed since he and Holly had been in this house together; that all seemed like a different world in a different time in a different life.

His escorts pushed him ahead into the great room. If this house was supposed to give the impression of a fortress, it was well designed. Jarvis stood at the far end of the room, watching with an amused grin as Chandler was tied into a straight-backed chair and then pummeled several times by one of his thugs.

"Where's Holly, Dr. Chandler?" Jarvis finally asked.

"I don't know," Chandler spat out defiantly.

The impact of the back of Jarvis's hand snapped Chandler's head sideways. Blood ran from the corner of his mouth.

"Don't make this unpleasant! Where's Holly?" Jarvis demanded again.

Chandler licked the blood from the corner of his mouth, smiled slightly, and said nothing.

"Holly, where's Holly?"

"The last time I saw her she was on her way to the ladies' room. Did your thugs try there? Maybe she has a bladder problem." Chandler wanted to hurt Jarvis, but all he could do was make bad jokes.

A feeling of dread swept over Bill Chandler as he saw Jarvis step back. One of the escorts from Crystal City methodically began to beat him. Each impact was expertly executed. This was clearly a man who was good at what he did and who enjoyed his work. The blows were not hard enough to break anything vital, and Bill fought to remain conscious. They were delivered and placed hard enough to hurt, but he was determined not to go easily into oblivion. He wondered if they would beat him to death or execute him with a bullet to the brain. Finally, feeling consciousness slipping away,

Chandler's last thought was that he would probably never wake up.

Who knows? he told himself as another blow landed on the side of his face. *Maybe I'll see Sandy.*

1

DAY ONE:
ENCOUNTER WITH DARKNESS

Hey!"

Silence.

"Hey, anybody down there hear me?" the man shouted louder.

"Yeah, we hear ya. Whadda ya want?" another man snarled as he leaned over the massive oak railing and looked up the spiral staircase.

Suspended high above him, the ornate crystal chandelier reflected opulence and grace, in opposition to the uncouth and rugged appearance of the man standing on the top landing. Dressed in faded jeans and a pullover sweater, the harsh blackness of the turtleneck accentuated his jutting chin, pockmarked face, and slightly crooked nose. His voice was loud but somehow intimated the kind of authority handed down from a superior. It was evident he was not in charge.

"Mr. Jarvis wants the girl upstairs . . . now!"

Silence again.

"Did you guys hear what I said? He wants her up here *now!*" He raised his voice to emphasize that the order must be obeyed.

"Yeah, right, give us a minute. We'll get her right up there."

1

The surly man turned and walked the length of the downstairs hallway with a deliberate slowness in his steps, a gesture of defiance to the one giving the order from the second floor. Entering the kitchen, he moved around the woman tied to a chair in the center of the large room. His black eyes surveyed her as only a man with lust flowing through his heart can stare. She was either asleep or had passed out. He shook her roughly by the shoulder; her head rocked like a rag doll's. She moaned softly and coughed as her eyes opened.

Holly fought to comprehend where she was . . . and who was this man with the foul breath who wouldn't leave her alone? The room was spinning, out of focus, and her head throbbed. A sharp, stabbing pain pierced Holly's right temple. She tried to reach up to rub her face and then remembered that she was tied into the chair. Her hands felt numb, and her feet tingled from being in one position so long.

"OK, lady, the *man* wants you, so get your sweet self out of that chair," he said as he untied her.

Every muscle ached, and her legs felt like rubber when he whipped the last rope away from her ankles and pulled her to her feet. Holly swayed unsteadily as the room's spinning slowed, her private merry-go-round coming to a tedious stop. Her head throbbed with increasing intensity, and her lower lip felt swollen as she tried to moisten it with her tongue.

"Can I wash my face first?" she asked.

"Ah, I don't know . . . I guess it'll be OK." The man roughly took her arm and half led her, half dragged her to the small bathroom just to the right of the main hall.

Walking down the hall had restored the feeling in her legs. The man released his hold on her, but only after shoving a gun to the side of her face and threatening, "Don't try anything funny."

Holly shut the bathroom door, leaning back against it, and stared at her face in the mirror. Dark circles ringed her eyes, not just from the smeared mascara but from the bruises, grim reminders of the rage Jarvis had unleashed at her announcement that she was leaving him.

"I'm sorry, Sid, but I just can't go through with it." She recalled those fateful words. Holly had mustered all of her courage preparing for the encounter with Sidney Jarvis. But no amount of courage would have been enough.

At first he had controlled his rage. "Holly, Holly, you're just upset. I know we've been busy lately, but there will be plenty of time to plan the wedding," he had purred confidently.

"It's not that!" she had shouted, fighting back her tears. "It's . . . it's you, your business, what you really are . . ." The sentence was interrupted by the slap from Jarvis's hand that had sent her sprawling to the floor.

"Yes, Holly, and what am I?" She remembered her fear as she had looked up and saw him glaring down at her, saw the menace in his eyes.

Holly had forgotten her well-rehearsed speech and screamed back, "You know what you are, and *I* know what you are. I'm leaving, Sid! And you aren't going to stop me. I have everything I need to show the *world* just who and what you are. . . ." That fateful sentence was lost as he hit her again, this time with his fist. . . .

Now, alone in a bathroom in Sid Jarvis's oceanside mansion, she rubbed her hands together nervously, trying to restore circulation. *This is no time to panic,* she told herself.

Slowly dropping her hands, she looked around. The room was tiny. It wasn't even a full bathroom, more of a powder room. The wallpaper, tastefully done in a subdued stripe, now looked like the thin bars of a dungeon. Yesterday, Holly would have said it was the latest motif.

She slid back the curtain, exposing a small window; beyond the glass, the blackness of the night glared at her like the throat of an evil monster. The window was high and narrow. *But maybe,* she thought, *just maybe it's big enough.*

She had to try. Several hours of sitting, tied to a chair, had convinced her of one fact. There was little time left. Holly was certain the only thing Jarvis could do with her now was kill her. She knew too much.

As the doorknob started to turn, she quickly snatched her skirt up to her waist and sat on the commode, then allowed the slightest delay before she viciously kicked the door shut again, so her captor would be sure to see her sitting there.

"Can't I even have a little privacy in the *bathroom*?" she yelled sarcastically, twisting the lock. There was little security in the sound of the tumblers falling into place.

"Sorry, just following orders," the embarrassed man said. "But hurry it up in there. Mr. Jarvis ain't gonna wait all night."

She twisted the latch on the window. After a slight hesitation and a gentle push, the window opened. The sound of the ocean filled the room, so she flushed the toilet and turned on the water in the sink, trying to drown out the noise from the surf. Holly slipped off her high-heeled shoes and quietly set them on the floor beside the sink. Then she stepped up onto the toilet seat, put her shoulders out the window, and pulled herself through, dropping feet-first onto the soft sand below.

The wind rushed through her hair, and she felt the thrill of freedom. Staying in the shadows to avoid the spotlights at the corners of the mansion, her flight began. She knew the gate leading to the beach would be open. Sid always left it open when he was at Cape Fear.

• • •

"You 'bout done in there?" the man asked.

No answer. Just the sound of running water.

"Hey, you in there, you 'bout done?" He tried the door, but it was locked. He shoved on it, but it wouldn't give. Finally, in panic and desperation he took a step back and kicked the door with his foot. The lock gave, and the doorjamb splintered. The sight of the empty bathroom with the water still running in the sink and the curtain billowing out from the open window brought a gasp of anger and fear.

"She's gone!" he shouted as he ran back to the kitchen where the others were waiting. "She's gone! The woman's gone!" he shouted up the empty stairwell.

● ● ●

As Holly ran down the beach, the wind tore at her hair and clothes. Terror prevented her from feeling how cold it really was. Her eyes watered until the world looked blurry and the stars and lights had little halos about them. Her lungs ached, and her heart felt as if it would explode. The sand slipped underfoot with each step, threatening a fall that could end her desperate flight for liberty. Running was easier on the wet sand, so she angled toward the sound of the waves. Behind her, she now heard the sounds of her pursuers.

She imagined herself as having become a small red fox with the hounds at her heels. The scene was from an old British movie, and if these human hounds caught her they would tear her to pieces. She wanted to cry . . . to scream . . . but no energy could be spared for that, and furthermore, on this deserted beach there was no one who would hear, no one but the hounds.

Then, in the distance, several large, dark shapes suddenly loomed out of the darkness and came down the beach directly toward her. They were silhouetted by the spotlights from the development beyond the pier. She could hear voices.

"Unit one, unit one, do you see her yet? Over," the voice crackled from the walkie-talkie.

"Negative, but we started far enough up the beach for a clean sweep. She has to be between us. Over," one of the shapes panted into the radio as he struggled through the sand.

Holly turned away from the ocean as soon as she came to the

pier. Scrambling over the sand dune, the razor-sharp dune grass cut easily at the sides of her legs through her torn nylons. Pausing to lean on the stairs leading up to the pier, she scrutinized the dark beach behind her. Desperately, she tried to catch her breath and look for somewhere to hide. Several vans, their searchlights sweeping the dunes, now cruised slowly up and down the street in front of her.

Looking under the pier, Holly could see its blackened, weathered wood, rotted and splintered, jutting out into the ocean like a black runway slowly tapering into the gloom. Numerous Atlantic storms had taken their toll on the once-elegant structure. Turning back toward the street, she saw the vans make another pass, closer this time. The shadows moving on the beach drew closer too; the hounds were relentless.

Holly turned from the street and quickly ran up the stairs onto the darkened platform; the boards beneath her felt cold and inhospitable. She wished she'd not left her shoes in the bathroom as splinters pierced the soft flesh of her feet, making walking painful. But fear blotted out the pain and drove her down the long alley into the unknown.

There was no moon, but a million stars shone in the expanse of blackness above the cold, ominous ocean. The lights on the pier had been turned off for the winter, making it difficult for Holly to see, but the darkness afforded her some protection from the search parties below.

As her eyes adjusted to the darkness, the vague shape of a deserted bait house came into view, standing its lonely vigil at the far end of the pier. It might afford a hiding place until the search ended. She ventured out onto the pier; the beach began to retreat behind her into the shadowy gloom of night. Holly crept along, slowing her pace slightly in order to catch her breath. Suddenly a raised plank snared her foot and she fell to her knees. A ragged board tore the supple skin of her right knee. A small cry escaped from her throat into the icy air. It should have been inaudible, but somehow it seemed to reverberate from one end of the beach to the other, even above the roar of the surf. Holly held her breath and listened. Kneeling beside the railing, the only noise she heard was the endless rush of the water against the pilings below.

For Holly, time was suspended in space with only the sound of the waves crashing in the darkness. As she neared the end of the pier, the startling screech of a sea gull, scared from its perch on the bait house roof, made her pulse race. Shivering uncontrollably from a summation of fear and cold, she tried the door; it was locked. Cautiously she rounded the corner and lifted up the shutter. It was loose enough to allow her to crawl inside, where she wriggled across the counter and dropped to the floor. A stool blocked her path in the darkness; she stumbled against it, knocking it over and almost falling.

Then the waiting began, waiting for the hounds to lose the scent and move off into the darkness. The seconds slowly, painfully, became minutes. Those minutes seemed more like hours. Crouched in the corner, praying that the covering shelter would encompass and hide her, breathlessly, she waited. On the beach, the hounds milled about, sniffing for the lost scent of the fox.

Holly pressed her eye against a crack between the boards. Suddenly, far down the pier, a light was switched on, its yellow beam exposing the ebony creosote of the planks and pilings. The light swept back and forth, as if alive, becoming the sense of smell of the hounds that had been at her heels on the beach. Closer and closer the light came, its menacing circle growing in a logarithmic fashion until finally it stopped on the door of the bait house.

The door rattled, then silence. Holly heard heavy footsteps circling the building. The edge of the shutter lifted and a small piece of fabric torn from her skirt fluttered in the flashlight's beam. Holly's stomach began to churn and she shook with fear as the footsteps quickly rounded the small building again and the weathered wood of the locked door began to splinter apart. The door burst open and the light blinded her temporarily.

A man stepped forward, sweeping the small shelter with his flashlight. She watched from the shadows, not daring to breathe, crouched like a cat, balancing on the balls of her feet. Then Holly sprang to the right in an attempt to get past him. His large hand hit her shoulder and knocked her to the floor. She started to rise up; he placed a foot on her back and shoved her down to the floor and held her there.

With sobs emanating from her raw throat, Holly looked up into the gleaming eye of the flashlight and felt completely defenseless and exposed. Had her escape been so short-lived that she was now lost? she wondered.

He took his foot from her back, reached down, and pulled her into a sitting position. It took several seconds for her eyes to adjust to the brightness of the light. Then the lower portion of a man's face came into view. He was smiling, but the grin was more of a sneer. He obviously needed a shave, and the stench of his sweat was more pungent than the salt in the air. A front tooth was either missing or rendered invisible with filth.

"Mr. Jarvis is disappointed in you, Holly," he growled. "He wants you to come back to the house *now*. He didn't like it that you ran away. He had plans for ya this evening." Laughter gurgled in his throat.

"No! I won't go back! He'll kill me," she spat defiantly.

The man started toward her again. "Mr. Jarvis, well, he's real mad. You shouldn'ta done what ya did. And then running away and all. Well, you know I gotta take ya back."

"No, please don't!" This time she pleaded, irrationally hoping for the man to show mercy.

"Don't have no other choice, ya know. And . . . well, Mr. Jarvis said he don't care what happens to ya now, just as long as he gets ya back. So ya know, I was thinkin' that first we could have some fun," he taunted.

That was what was needed. The stench of her captor, the sneer from his unshaven face, and his foul breath coupled with his threat made Holly reach down deep inside herself to that inner stamina and instinctive cunning that can produce survival.

Slowly, she stood up with renewed determination, knowing that her life depended on the next few seconds. Purposefully, her hand smoothed the front of her torn skirt; seductively, she placed her other hand on her chest and flirted with the top button. He followed her hand with the beam of the light, and it reflected on the whiteness of her skin exposed above the lace camisole.

Holly tried desperately to control any panic in her voice. "If . . . if we could work out a deal," she whispered, "I could make it lots better for you." The words came hard, because her throat was dry, her head was pounding, and the thought of what she was suggesting was totally repulsive to her.

He grunted. "A deal . . . yeah, you make it special, honey!"

As he stepped forward, the smell of stale cigarettes nauseated her. He was still panting with exhaustion from his run up the beach. Holly could hear his dank breath exit from the sides of his mouth through clenched teeth. Saliva was starting to trickle from the corner of his lip and run down his grisly chin.

He turned off the light and grabbed her, forcing his mouth down on hers and roughly pawing her with his free hand. She felt and heard her blouse rip from her shoulder.

Another wave of nausea swept over her. She fought it back as the acid taste of her own stomach juices surged into her throat. She had to keep control as he pushed her against the counter and pressed his body to hers. . . .

She tilted her head up slowly toward his face—then suddenly bit his lip, her teeth clamping together viciously. The pain made him jerk back, stunned and enraged.

"You . . . you . . . !" he snarled as he dropped the flashlight and grabbed her around the neck and began to choke her.

Holly felt her throat closing off and her lungs burning as the carbon dioxide started to build up. She knew she would soon be unconscious. With one last effort, she brought her knee up. He had been standing with his legs apart for balance, leaving him vulnerable. As her knee rammed into his groin, he screamed and let go of her neck. He pitched forward, hitting the floor and rolling onto his side with his knees up. He noisily wretched and vomited.

Holly stood frozen for a moment, massaging her throat. Then she heard the sounds of other men running on the pier planking toward them . . . could see their lights bobbing up and down through the shattered doorway. Without a second's hesitation she jumped over the man moaning at her feet, ran from the bait house, climbed onto the rail at the end of the pier, and jumped.

In the darkness, the fall seemed eternal as she plunged toward the crashing swells below. The water was frigid, and she let out a gasp as she sank deeper and deeper into the swirling black Atlantic, propelled downward by the momentum of her fall. Then she began to kick and struggle upward.

Her mind told her it was better to drown than to be mauled by that pig up on the pier, but the impulse for living made her pull intensely toward the surface of the water. Just as she knew she couldn't hold her breath any longer, her head broke through the surface. She gasped for air. A wave crested and threw her against one of the pilings. Her mouth was filled with seawater, and she coughed uncontrollably. Holly felt the jagged edges of the barnacles tearing at her back, and she fought against the waves to free herself from the entanglements of seaweed and wood. To stay against the piling meant sure death, if not from the crashing waves then from the men above. Using what strength was left, she pushed off from the pier. As she swam away, yellow beams of light from multiple flashlights skimmed the water's surface like pesky insects darting this way and that, but none could locate her in the vast darkness of the ocean. Each stroke her arms cut through the water brought her a renewed sense of deliverance. Over the roar of the water she could hear muffled shouts and unintelligible voices from the pier above.

Holly knew the euphoria she felt was from her sense of freedom.

She did not realize the extent of her exhaustion or recognize the symptoms of shock as the icy Atlantic continued to deplete her body temperature.

Somehow, though, she managed to continue reaching arm over arm, struggling to swim northward against the current. Her arms ached, and her feet felt numb as they churned through the ocean. A large wave crested and filled her mouth and nose with burning saltwater, causing her to cough and choke. Continued swimming seemed impossible, but there was nothing else she could do . . . except drown. If she just closed her eyes for a moment, she fantasized, she'd have renewed energy. The icy water was taking its toll.

It's funny, she thought. *The water doesn't even feel so cold now.* As her unconscious mind began to take control, blotting out her pain and fear, Holly slipped into the black envelope of death. . . .

• • •

A picture of a little girl on a swing projected itself onto the screen of her mind. A warm wind was blowing through her hair as the girl swung back and forth under the oak tree in her backyard. A melody filtered from the kitchen. Her mother's voice repeated the words over and over, "There will be peace in the valley for me someday." The song kept time with the swing.

Amazingly, the smell of Sunday dinner now drifted on the wind. A feeling of tranquillity completely overwhelmed Holly as the swing began to float on the gentle breeze, moving through the air like the pendulum of a giant grandfather clock. Each arc of the swing took her higher and higher into the atmosphere. She felt like a bird, gliding from cloud to cloud as she floated through the summer sky.

Abruptly, the branch holding the swing broke, and she was falling. The ground rushed up at her. She was in the vortex of a great whirlpool with no escape. . . .

• • •

Holly was intensely aware of being rolled over and over as the sand dug into the cuts in her back, reopening them and allowing the salt and sand to sear the edges of each wound. Another wave hit her, and she rolled over again. Sand clogged her mouth, and saltwater burned her eyes. With her last ounce of strength, she crawled and clawed her way out of the water and up onto the sand. Finally, the water no longer crashed over her, and she collapsed, completely losing consciousness again.

She was unaware of the raw October wind blowing across her torn and drenched body. She didn't feel the tiny drops of blood coagulating in a nonsensical pattern on her serrated back. She lay there, silent and cold, exposed to a dropping temperature whipped on by a cruel north wind. With each minute this brutal side of nature was bringing her closer to death.

Meanwhile, the hounds were confidently assuring Jarvis of her untimely death, promising to retrieve the body at first light.

2

GHOSTS OF THE PAST

Bill Chandler watched a line of pelicans fly past, each one following the same course as the leader. The surf crashed and ebbed, and a sea gull screeched.

The tumult of the sea echoed in Bill's head, the sounds that once had accompanied so much happiness were now sending his spirits plummeting. He and Sandy had spent so many good times at the shore. Now . . . now, the sounds of the ocean seemed so lonely, so forlorn.

As Bill stared at the shoreline he realized there is a partnership between the water and the land, and yet intense competition exists between these partners. He watched the waves rush onto the beach, bringing their fortune of shells, seaweed, driftwood, and pollution. Where the foam washes and rewashes it, the sand turns from stark white to a deep tan. The land accepts the litter from her mate, and then her mate tries to take it back.

Life is like that, Chandler thought, watching the waves. *We are in partnership with life. We accept what life gives us. Then, as soon as we are comfortable with those gifts, life takes them back.*

The beach had been so much a part of the life he had loved, the life *they* had loved. They had walked together, lived as one, until she was taken. Now the beach seemed so lonely, as lonely as life itself.

He watched the waves roll a broken shell up and down the sandy bank until it was ultimately deposited above the high-water line. Cracks marred the shell's elegant finish, its brilliant colors had been dulled with time, and its edges had been chipped off, ruining its symmetrical beauty.

Like that shell, his life was rolling up and down the bank of time, aimless and broken. He thought, *I feel like I'm awaiting that final wave that will leave me stranded . . . the final wave that will leave me bleached and lifeless on the hot sand.*

"Oh, God, I'm so lonely!" he groaned aloud at the circling sea gulls. Visions of earlier days swirled in his consciousness. . . .

• • •

"Billy!"

"Yeah, Mom?"

"Have you finished your homework yet?" he heard the petite woman shout from the kitchen.

"I'm going up to do it now." The blond-haired teenager rushed through the kitchen and headed for the stairs.

"I told you to get your homework finished as soon as you got home! What have you been doing?" Bill knew his mother was not really mad. He was a good student and had caused her no problems since his father had been killed five years earlier.

Billy yelled from his room, "Sorry, Mom, I had to get the new cat settled in. . . ."

"New cat?" she responded. "What new cat?"

"Well, ya see, there was this cat, more like a kitty. It isn't very old . . . ," he stammered. "Looked like it had been left all alone and . . ."

"William J. Chandler! I thought we had an agreement, NO MORE ANIMALS!"

"I know, Mom, but I couldn't leave it there to die, could I?"

They were both playing out a recurrent scenario.

Bill had been bringing lost and injured animals home since he was old enough to walk around the block. Their house had been the hospital and home to almost every kind of creature that could be found in the central plains. This new addition would be nursed to health and, if all went well, a suitable home would be found.

But he knew the last thing his mother wanted was another cat underfoot.

Bill walked up beside his mom. She'd been peeling a potato and had shredded most of it into the sink. "Not much left of that one, Mom," he said with a disarming grin.

She smiled back at him and ruffled his hair. "Another cat! Are you going to spend your life looking after the helpless cats of the world?"

"Nah. Cats are okay, but what I really want to do is build things . . . important things. What's for supper tonight? I'm starved."

● ● ●

Now sitting on the balcony of the condominium overlooking the Atlantic, Bill discovered what he'd been hiding from himself for the last year and a half. *I am in pain . . . so much pain, and it's been bottled up for so long. I didn't expect to feel it. I didn't want to feel it.* But the sound of the ocean had reopened the lacerations of the past two years. And now, with each successive breaker, his very lifeblood seemed to be draining away. He felt he was emotionally bleeding out as fast as the water retreated from the shore.

Bill looked out at the endless ocean, wishing he could talk to his mother about the pain, the emptiness. But she had died during his first year at Iowa State. Heart failure, the doctors had said—a bad heart valve from the rheumatic fever she had contracted as a child.

Now he felt as if he were dying of heart failure, too, but it was emotional failure, not physical. Sure, years ago he had brought home injured and helpless animals. But that was kid stuff. As an adult there was only one rescue that would have counted . . . and that one time there was simply nothing he could have done. He looked down at the floor between his feet, bleached boards stained with sand and dirt, and he saw it again, the sight that would never go away . . . the severed hand with the wedding band he knew only too well.

The anguish in his soul and the loneliness of the day caused his mind to wander again. Less than a week ago his best friend and boss Ed Harris had walked into his office. It was anything but a social call.

• • •

"Bill, we have to talk."

"Sure, but can you come back later? I'm busy."

"No!" Harris said, raising his voice. "I will not come back later! This is something we're going to talk about now. It's something I should have talked to you about six months ago. Here it is, short and sweet: If you keep on like this, you're through!"

"Through! You mean fired?" Bill answered, stunned.

"Yes, I mean fired! I might put up with you because I knew you when you didn't have a bad temper, when you didn't go around here with your petty ranting and raving, when you were a top-notch researcher—not playing the part of some spoiled, eccentric professor!"

Bill looked at Ed in disbelief at what he was hearing. Had he been that difficult to get along with?

Ed went on in a little gentler tone. "I'm only telling you this, Bill, because I'm your friend. But the rest of the people working here aren't—and they won't stand for it any longer. I hope you hear me, Bill, it's time for you to have a rest."

"A rest? You call firing me a *rest*? What on earth's gotten into you, Ed? Am I not doing a good job? Have you ever caught me sleeping on company time? What do you mean, busting in here like this and telling me I'm through?"

"Look, I know you've been under a lot of pressure with this research deadline—"

"You're right I have, Ed! And you're the boss; it's your lousy company. Do you want this project done or not?"

"Bill . . . I . . ."

"You know if I don't get the final paths worked out soon, the money's going to dry up. And then who's going to complete your precious Tel-Ray system?" Bill paused and walked over to a table. A ceramic dish-shaped object sat on a stand looking like a piece of modern art incongruously displayed in a warehouse. "Do you have anyone else with the ability to get as far into it as I have? I'll tell you the answer to that, Mr. Ed Harris, Mr. *Boss*. No way! I'm the best you've got. Maybe the best there *is*!"

Ed Harris sighed as the truth of Bill's statement sank in. "That may be true for now," he admitted, "but remember what you your-self have said: There are a lot of bright boys out there. It may take a while, but I'll find one, and *it will get done*." He drew out the last four words, emphasizing the threat and the promise they contained. Ed took a long breath and continued. "And it'll get done with or with-out you, Bill. Listen . . . the company has a condo down on an island on the Outer Banks of North Carolina; you have a choice. You can take a couple of weeks off, go down there and get some R and R, then come back with a decent attitude . . . or you can clean out your desk. And the way you're acting, I don't care which!"

Bill turned back and saw Ed looking at him. There was under-standing in his eyes; he knew Ed was aware of the shock Bill had had to deal with. The death of Sandy, his wife, had been traumatic to them all. Ed and Ann had been friends of theirs for years. Bill knew Ed understood on one level, but he also knew his friend could not truly fathom the impact of his loss.

As Ed waited silently for his decision, Bill saw something else in his friend at that moment—a look that said unequivocally, "I'm not kidding!" Bill realized that Ed was not going to let one man— even a good friend—ruin everything he'd worked for all these years.

The scuttlebutt was that some of the other engineers were going to quit if he didn't get his act together; he'd heard the rumors whispered around corners and at cafeteria tables. No one was indispensable, not even William Chandler, Ph.D.

"Bill, I want this project to succeed, and I know how important it is to you," Ed said, his tone now more appeasing. "It's important to me too. But quite frankly, sometimes I think it's too all-fired important. You've lived and breathed it since you got back from London. It's destroyed your sense of humor, it's caused three secretaries to quit in as many months, and it's affecting the entire output of the company. I like you as a friend . . . I love you like a brother . . . but hear me, Bill, and hear me good: As the boss, I'll fire you to preserve the company. That's the extent to which you're disrupting things! Now, you think it over, and you go to the beach, or *you're* beached . . . permanently!"

• • •

The words echoed painfully as Bill now sat watching the breakers roll onto the beach. He marveled at how that argument with his best friend—and if he was really honest with himself, he had to admit that Ed was one of his *only* friends—had made him realize how out of control he really was. He wondered if his life would ever have any semblance of order again. But, for the first time in over a year, he began to let the thoughts of London reenter his consciousness. He could still see Sandy's face as he walked through the door of their apartment with the airline tickets.

• • •

"M'lady!" He smiled from ear to ear and extended the gift with a slight bow. "For you!"

"Why, sir, what could this be?" She curtsied, playing her part, as she took the letter from him.

"It's an invitation to see the queen."

"You're kidding!" Her eyes were wide, and she laughed as she carefully opened the envelope and spotted the tickets. "Oh, Bill! After all these years, finally we're going to London!" The excitement in her voice was real.

"What we have here are two tickets to England—for the honeymoon we never had," he said as he kissed her, holding her in his arms.

"Bill, I can't believe it. Can we afford it?"

"We can't afford not to. The tickets are nonrefundable. So let's celebrate!"

The next month had raced by like a whirlwind, packed with the details of obtaining passports and collecting last-minute items Sandy had thought necessary for the journey. The day arrived almost too quickly.

They had been ecstatic as they walked down the jetway from the 747 into the terminal at Heathrow Airport. Neither of them had really slept on the flight over because of their excitement.

After clearing customs, they took a taxi into downtown London.

"The Rochester, please," Bill said.

"The Rochester, you say?" the driver of the classic black London cab asked.

Bill fumbled for the paper that held the address, "Yeah, uh, 60 Saint Vincent Square. Does that help?"

"Right. Don't know where it is for certain, but we'll find it, right along." The driver launched his taxi into the maelstrom of traffic and headed toward the heart of London.

As they watched the traffic move swiftly along on the "wrong" side of the road, he and Sandy had felt the exhilaration of having discovered a whole new world, where fortunately they spoke the same language. Their exuberant anticipation must have been very similar to Lewis and Clark's as they explored the Northwest Territory. This was new territory for Bill and Sandy, and they tried to drink in every new sensation.

The Rochester was a small hotel located just off a neighborhood park. It looked more like an apartment building than a hotel, but the sign beside the door said ROCHESTER HOTEL.

A large brass birdcage elevator ran up the center of the building with a stairway winding around it. The rooms were large and spacious with all of the creature comforts taken into consideration. It was certainly a place in which memories could be made.

It was more than a honeymoon, because they were more than newlyweds. After many years of marriage, Bill was finally taking the trip of his life with his wife. Thus far their life together had been goal-oriented toward completing their education. Vacations had been few and far between. Now they were both moving up professionally and could take some time just for each other.

Eighteen years earlier, during their sophomore year of college, he had met Sandy at a friend's party. Their immediate attraction to each other had slowly grown from casual friendship into something much deeper. They had often talked over coffee in the Doghouse, the small cafe in the student union. When the weather permitted, they took walks together, and generally enjoyed each other's company.

Sandy was short, only five feet two, pert and lively in her approach to life. She had long, straight black hair, and she didn't wear the customary hippie uniform of the day, preferring more feminine styles. She had a spontaneity that enhanced any conversation.

Their desire for each other was a combination of physical and emotional appeal. Physical for her because he was a man who had continued to play sports to maintain his trim, muscular appearance, and physical for him because she had a bewitchingly proportioned body and slender, enticingly curved legs. Her style was to wear kilts or short skirts that highlighted her figure and legs perfectly.

Emotionally, their attraction had at its nucleus a restful comfort they found in each other's presence. As they became better acquainted, he knew she was the girl for him.

They were married before finishing undergraduate school. The honeymoon, if it could be called that, was short, just a weekend, but memorable. It was short because they both had class the following Monday; it was memorable because he had never experienced the exciting fusion of untouched virginal passion coupled with the total oneness that only happens in the marriage bed.

Each day and night they spent together as husband and wife intensified their love with an escalating enthusiasm. Marriage served to strengthen their individual goals. True, there was give-and-take, but it did not alter the singular plans each of them had. They set their own goals and the order of priority to achieve their success. The first order of business for both was to finish college. Sandy worked days and attended classes at night; he went to school days and worked nights. It was a whirlwind existence, but they thrived on it.

After college, he started a career as an electrical engineer with a small radio manufacturer centered in the thriving CB industry. Sandy went to graduate school. Following the successful completion of her master's degree, she started a career in marriage counseling while he returned to academics and eventually acquired a Ph.D. in electrical engineering.

Next came the move to Washington, D.C., and new jobs for both. Bill's academic research in electronic communication led to the job with Tel-Ex and his research on the Tel-Ray system. Sandy found a position with a psychiatric hospital in suburban Maryland.

They lived an existence framed by the pressures of society, Madison Avenue, and the media. They left for work in the morning before it was light, returned after it was dark, ate at the best restaurants, and kept in shape at the best health clubs. They were bright, upwardly mobile people who thought they knew what they wanted.

What they really wanted, though, was to be normal. They wanted to take vacations, have 2.5 kids, two cars (one a Volvo station wagon), and a mortgage. What they had instead were two careers. But one day they realized they were finally in a position to shift gears and fulfill the dream that had kept them going so many long nights when discouragement had rested on their shoulders. The fulfillment began with the trip to England.

Bill and Sandy had spent many long hours during their undergraduate years discussing every detail of the trip they would someday take. When the plane finally lifted off across the Atlantic, they knew the rest of their dream was sure to follow.

They spent their days in London sightseeing and visiting the quaint shops on the back streets. They made it a point to avoid the tourist areas and the British equivalent of a Gray Line tour. The nights were devoted to dinner, dancing, and making love. Their ten days were quickly exhausted as they tried to make every memory last, not just for the moment, but for eternity.

• • •

I never realized how close eternity would be, Bill thought as he watched the clouds build over the North Carolina coast. The wind had come up and chilled the air. Bill rose and stretched, leaning over the balcony railing and glancing up the lonely, deserted beach. He went into the condo and selected a down-filled jacket, then returned to the porch and sat back down, propping his feet on the railing and leaning back in his chair. His thoughts drifted back to London. But he paused a moment. Was he prepared to face this part of his life again?

Yes, I have to. . . . He relived his last night in London with Sandy, tenderly yet reluctantly calling up the memories, physically flinching as the ache in his heart returned.

• • •

Though they were sad to leave London, the trip had been all they had hoped for, and more. The wonderful second honeymoon had given them confidence that the future they had dreamed of was starting to fall into place.

They shared a quiet dinner in the hotel dining room, the background music filtering lightly though the heavy air that lacked circulation. The dark oak walls were dimly illuminated by twinkling crystal chandeliers. The light from the candle on the table sparkled into the diamond brooch hanging from Sandy's slender, elegant neck. Her eyes flashed with delight as the waiter, dressed as a coachman, served a succulent roast beef with the traditional baked Yorkshire pudding smothered in gravy. Afterward, they walked in the park across the street, where a small lake provided refuge for a family of ducks. As the birds swam in a line toward the shore, Sandy said, "Bill, they're so cute. Look how the babies follow the mom. They seem to do exactly as she says."

She turned to look at him. "Do you suppose our little duckling will do the same?"

"What do you mean, our little duckling?" he asked accusingly.

"Oh, nothing," she said, looking down and pretending to examine her fingernails, toying with him. "But, if you wanted to take me back to the hotel . . . well . . . I might be willing to explain." She smiled provocatively.

• • •

Sandy came out of the bath and glided across the floor to the bed. The dim light of the bathroom had silhouetted her form as she approached. The thin veil of the negligee did little to obscure her beauty. He held the blanket up as she gracefully slipped between the sheets.

She lay back, her soft hair spilling over the pillow, Bill leaned down on one elbow and kissed her tenderly. He crossed his leg over hers and gently stroked her calf with his heel. Their fingertips began a slow, sensuous mapping of each other's contour. His breathing became faster as she seductively wiggled to remove the gossamer-thin negligee. . . .

The next morning Sandy and Bill sat in the TWA waiting area listening to the boarding calls and reflecting on their vacation. He watched her out of the corner of his eye, remembering how good it had been to stroll with his arm around her waist along the Thames, to sit in a sidewalk cafe and look into her eyes, and to feel the warmth of her body against his in the night. Now, catching a whiff of her fragrance, he remembered the nights, especially last night, and he longed to be beside her in bed again.

"Bill, I'm going to get a magazine. I forgot to pick one up at the hotel before we left."

"OK, but we're supposed to start boarding in about twenty minutes, so keep your eye on the clock. I'd hate to leave you here in England. I don't know who'd do all of this laundry when I get home!" he teased.

She smiled and kissed him lightly on the cheek. "I'll be right back," she promised.

At partings, people say things out of habit, sometimes just to be polite. Occasionally they make promises they cannot keep. For Sandy, this was one of those times.

He watched her walk down the corridor, smiling, thinking how much he loved her.

● ● ●

Events in the world continue at a breakneck pace with no thought of one individual over another. While Bill and Sandy had been eating dinner and making love the night before, somewhere deep in the back alleys of a London suburb three men and a woman had toiled over a small package. While the world was going about its business of everyday life, four sticks of dynamite had been fashioned into a bomb.

Carefully wrapped together, this was, by modern standards, an old-fashioned weapon of death and destruction. This particular bomb was assembled to promote the independence of Northern Ireland. The dynamite sticks lay side by side on the table, each measuring about an inch in diameter and six inches long. In an odd sort of way, the bomb was a connection of the past with the present. Its purpose was simple—to kill. In many ways it was just a more efficient version of whatever Cain had used to kill Abel.

Carefully, magazines were stacked and then cut, leaving a hollow well in the middle. The explosives with the detonator and nine-volt battery were then carefully laid into the well. Four more magazines were placed on top, and the deadly bundle was meticulously tied with twine. The detonator was then wired to the twine to trigger an explosion when the cord was cut.

In the same way a doctor unleashes a new life into the world when he cuts an umbilical cord, the political statement of these four patriots would be unleashed by the hapless person who would cut their deadly cord.

A delivery truck stolen from a local vendor was parked at the curb in front of the busy international terminal at Heathrow Airport, its lights left flashing as the driver hurried in to make his delivery to the selected newspaper stand. The clerk was busy with customers as the package was placed between the stacks of daily newspapers and the driver headed back to his truck and sped away. He knew that by the time the mayhem was unleashed and the investigation begun, he would have safely abandoned the truck in the English countryside and wiped away all fingerprints.

• • •

"I'd like this magazine and a Cadbury's please—that one, over there . . . ," Sandy said, pointing at the candy bar on the second shelf. The clerk turned and reached for the chocolate. And at that same moment, her coworker in the tiny shop reached for the stack of magazines. The cord was severed.

The blast wave tore through the airport corridor like a freight train. The plate-glass windows in front of Bill were blown out, and glass fragments and shredded aluminum showered the plane that was to have taken them back to Washington. He was dazed from the concussion.

The explosive power of the dynamite used in the London blast was more than sufficient to obliterate the newspaper stand with a killing radius of fifty yards.

Others lay dead besides Sandy—the clerk, the worker who opened the magazine bundle, and an old man on his way to his granddaughter's wedding. Twenty-four other people in the vicinity were critically injured. The group that claimed responsibility said it was another victory for the freedom of Northern Ireland.

• • •

Now, sitting on the other side of the Atlantic and thinking about his dead wife, Bill couldn't see how her death had done anything for the freedom of Ireland. He wondered if the relatives of the other victims felt the same way. His mind kept repeating over and over, *What's the point?*

Gradually his thoughts became even more despondent. *Is there any real reason to live? It all seems so useless. . . . It hurts so much . . . and I feel so alone.*

He wanted to scream at no one in particular and everyone in general. He wanted desperately to kill the people who had ripped Sandy from him, but he didn't even know who they were. His chest felt empty, as if his heart had dissolved.

The sun was down by the time he realized he'd been sitting

with the sounds of a deserted beach and hungry sea gulls as his only company for several hours. *I must have slept,* he thought, startled to discover the missing hours. *That's good. Maybe for a while I didn't think.*

As he got out of the chair he felt stiff and hungry. Picking up his keys and a billfold, Bill walked down the open stairwell. Bypassing his car, he ambled onto the sand and began striding up the shore toward the lights of the old boardwalk of Carolina Beach. The night was cool. A breeze from the north brought the full ambiance of fall upon this part of the country, and winter would not be far behind. The wind that had come up earlier had blown the clouds away, and now the stars seemed magical, shining so clearly without a moon to subdue their light.

He left the sand when he reached the boardwalk area and turned onto a deserted street bounded on the left by summer shops and on the right by the expanse of beach leading to the water's edge. The shops were locked, some with windows boarded against the onslaught of the Atlantic during winter. Others had windows whose only protection was the year's accumulation of dirt and grease.

Bill stopped and tried to look into the window of a bar. The dirty blur made the dark interior as much out of focus as his life felt. He stood there, peering into the window, the wind stinging his face with small bits of sand as it whipped around the buildings. Chairs were stacked on the tables, and shadows danced nervously around the deserted room from the swaying streetlights along the boardwalk. On the bar stood a single bottle of beer, obviously left or forgotten by the last one out at the end of the season. He felt as if he had a lot in common with that bottle.

He turned from the window and continued down the street. The lights ablaze in a small diner in the next block brought a feeling of relief. Not only was hunger a major driving force, but by now Bill was cold. The sign over the door was weather-worn and faded, announcing the name of the establishment as the "Atlantic

House Restaurant." Bill thought it a rather grand name for what appeared to be an ordinary diner.

At first the warmth of the diner was soothing as he walked through the door. There were no customers, just a slightly overweight man wearing a stained white apron and standing behind the counter. Walking over to a stool, Bill sat down and nodded a greeting without words.

"Hey, buddy, whatcha gonna have?" the man asked cheerfully.

Bill studied the menu on the board behind the cook for several seconds. The heat he had at first appreciated now began to feel stifling as the smells of the ancient diner permeated his senses.

"Let's see, I'll have a hamburger and a beer—anything light," he answered.

The restaurant (definitely a misnomer, Bill decided, considering the establishment's gastronomical history) had too many years of grease, cigarette smoke, and spilled beer to be appetizing. But it came highly recommended this night. It was one of the few eating places open during the off-season. The man behind the counter— waiter, cook, and probably the owner—also looked as though he'd had too many years of grease, cigarettes, and beer under his belt.

A radio blaring in the background was finishing Waylon Jennings's latest hit when a news bulletin began.

"At 4 P.M. today, the body of an unidentified man washed up on the shore at the south end of Pleasure Island. The body was badly decomposed and has been taken to the medical examiner's office in Wilmington for examination. There has been no identification at this time, and the cause of death is unknown.

"Elsewhere, in Washington today there were new allegations of more top-secret defense plans appearing in Eastern Bloc countries. . . ."

The cook set the hamburger and beer in front of him. Bill's mind wandered from the radio as the cook said, "I wonder if some snowbird headin' south for the winter got washed off his boat. Those guys would be a lot better off if they either hired a captain or stuck to the Intracoastal Waterway to git them yachts down to the sunny South."

"Huh?" Bill didn't realize the man had been talking to him.

"That feller that washed up on the beach. The town cop was in here talkin' about it earlier. Guess the body was in real bad shape."

"Yeah, I guess so," Bill replied without really thinking about what he was saying.

Then it suddenly occurred to him that he had just heard his own voice for the second time that day. It almost sounded strange, yet it was a relief to talk. *Maybe I am crazy,* he thought.

"You're new down here, ain'tcha?" The cook was obviously tired of his own company.

"Yes, I came down last Wednesday."

"Where ya from?"

"Just outside of Washington, D.C. A little town in Maryland. I doubt if you've ever heard of it," Bill replied.

"Try me. We git a lot of you folks down here in the season. I'll bet I've heard of almost every town up that way." The cook seemed genuinely interested.

"Derwood . . . Derwood, Maryland." As Bill said it, guilt swept over him like a breaking wave. He should be up there, working in the lab right now.

"Nope, you're right. Never heard of that one. Say, why'dya come down here this time of year? The season is over. It's gonna git cold and nasty any day now. This place is nice in the summer, but fall and winter here is—well, let's say you'd better not be a monkey, if ya know what I mean." He grinned with yellow-stained teeth and winked, enjoying the company and obviously proud of the analogy he'd come up with.

"I get the picture. By the way, my name is Bill Chandler." He held out his hand.

"They call me Cookie," the man said as he wiped his hand on the dirty apron before taking Bill's.

Bill ate in silence, paying attention to the fact that when you eat alone you tend to rush and not really enjoy the meal. He wondered if that would affect one's digestion. Then he decided it probably didn't make a lot of difference anyway in his case. He was certain he was destined for heartburn from whatever was eaten here.

"Thanks for the food and the company," he said when the hamburger was gone. As he reached for his wallet he asked, "How late do you usually stay open?"

"Till ten most nights except Thursday; then I close at six. I bowl in a winter league on Thursday. Do you bowl?"

Bill shook his head with a smile, paid the check, and headed out the door into the nippy autumn air.

The air seemed colder on the walk from the boardwalk back toward the surf. The heels of his shoes slipped as the soft sand pulled at them. In just a few minutes his eyes were watering from the sting of the strong wind blowing in from the ocean. The tears spilled over and ran down his cheeks and caused him to see little halos around the security lights of the vacant buildings along the beach.

The tide was in, forcing him higher up on the sand. Most of the houses were dark, and only an occasional light shone from a window. The nagging thought that he should be back in the lab in Maryland pounded in his head.

Suddenly, in the shadows about fifty yards ahead, he saw someone or something move. It was low to the ground, crawling up the sand. Instant fear welled up inside him, that deep-seated gut-wrenching fear that can only happen on the darkest of nights. The knot in his stomach turned the hamburger and the beer sour. An icy chill pierced the nape of his neck.

Bill fought the urge to turn and run back up the beach toward the safety of the boardwalk and the comfort of another human being. *Come on, old man. This is small-town America,* he thought. *There's nothing to fear on this beach, even if it is nighttime.*

He walked on, cautiously driven as much by curiosity as the urge to help someone in trouble; a few more steps, and he'd be where the shadow was. His heart beat faster and seemed almost audible over the sound of the waves crashing on the shore. Sweat beaded on his forehead, sending a chill throughout his body as the wind raced down his collar.

Like a fog lifting from a deep valley, the shadows began to clear as his eyes focused. The thing stirring was a body, it was . . . human. Someone was lying facedown on the sand, moving slowly in an attempt to rise. Bill slowed his pace and cautiously approached as if the shape would suddenly levitate and devour him. The news report he had heard in the diner swept back over his mind. *"The body of an unidentified man . . . badly decomposed . . ."*

But this was a woman. If Cookie was right and a yacht had gone down, maybe this was another victim. He knelt beside her, his hand shaking as he slowly reached out and touched the exposed arm.

The flesh felt cool, and he thought at first he'd touched a dead person. But then the body moved slightly, a breath of air lifting and lowering the torso. He rolled the body over and saw the smooth but sand-caked features of a young woman.

She gave a soft moan.

"Lie still. I'll get help!" The words sounded shallow as he said them.

"No . . . no . . . please . . . let me go!" Her voice pleaded so softly he could barely hear it over the sound of the wind. He leaned down to hear her better.

"What? I couldn't hear you," he said.

"Please . . . have to go . . ." Her voice trailed off again.

Bill felt the sting of the cold October wind and knew she would be dead shortly if he didn't help her. He had to get her off the beach. Putting one arm under her back and one under her thighs, he lifted her up.

"No . . . oh, please . . . no!" She was trying to scream, but the words were barely discernible.

Her head dropped to one side as she fainted.

Carrying her back toward the condo was surprisingly easy. She couldn't have weighed much more than a hundred pounds. After climbing up the stairs, he fumbled for the key, finally got the door open, and carried her into the warmth of the condo.

Her lips were blue, and she was shivering as Bill took her into the bedroom. Quickly he removed her wet clothing and wrapped her in a wool blanket, then checked her pulse and breathing. Sitting down on the side of the bed, he studied her in the dim light. She was about thirty or so with long, dark hair. Her face was deathly pale, and he knew he ought to call an ambulance, but something about her restrained him.

Was it her voice? he wondered. What she said? Or was it his own need to rescue someone—to be the only one to help her survive? To get it right this time.

Pull yourself together, Chandler, he chided himself. *This isn't like taking in a lost or injured kitten as a boy. What if she dies?* These thoughts ran through his mind at light speed. He fumbled about the bedroom to find where he had laid his cellular phone, but he stopped when she made a sound.

She moaned once, thrashed her arms about, then resumed quiet breathing. A few minutes more and she stopped shaking, finally settling into a deep sleep. He decided not to call anyone. Maybe she was in trouble. She probably just needed to rest . . . to stay warm . . . drink hot liquids. He could take care of her.

Bill lost track of time as he sat beside her on the bed, watching her. In some respects it probably was a childlike reflex action left over from all those years of rescuing unwanted animals. He repeatedly checked her pulse and listened to the quiet rhythm of her breathing. When it seemed obvious that she was going to sleep quietly, he left the bedroom and walked into the kitchen to put on a pot of coffee.

The clock on the stove showed 11:30.

As the coffee perked, he ventured out onto the deck overlooking the beach and stared into the darkness. Now the earlier thoughts about his life and wife were replaced with a growing curiosity about the woman asleep in his bedroom. The lone running light of a fishing boat was bobbing far off in the blackness. He wondered if the skipper of that boat was hoping for a safe port for the night or if he was going to spend the night on the frigid dark Atlantic.

What was a woman doing on the beach by herself at this time of night? She had obviously been in the water. Did she fall, was she pushed, had she tried to commit suicide?

As the light from the boat faded from sight, the questions haunted him.

Several times during the next few hours he looked in on his unexpected guest. She seemed to be sleeping well. Her breathing was regular, and her pulse was strong each time he checked it.

Why didn't I call an ambulance?

The thought ran through his mind, but then he remembered the almost hysterical pleading in her voice as he had picked her up.

Who was she, and why was she on the beach in this condition?

3

Day Two:
Mystery Woman

Jarvis leaned against the leather back of his desk chair, his hands clasped behind his head. He pushed back from the desk and spun the chair effortlessly with a tap of his foot. This was the best time of the day. He stared at the heavy draperies completely obscuring the east wall of his den.

Jarvis touched a button on the desk and watched the curtains noiselessly slide into the corner, exposing a large expanse of glass that formed the front wall of this room. From here he could watch the sun slowly creep over the edge of the world. It began as a small, faintly pink haze that separated the black ocean from the black sky on the horizon. Slowly the glow extinguished the stars as if spraying water on them, one by one.

He reviewed the events of the last few days. Something wasn't right, but he could not put his finger on it. Whatever it was, it had caused him to lose a full night's sleep.

The premonition had started four days ago with the arrival of Ed Harris.

• • •

"Hey, Jarvis, how's it going?" Ed asked as he strode through the door.

Looking up from his desk, Jarvis's cold, icy stare met the pupils of Harris's eyes and killed any hint of camaraderie. Without a word, he stood and extended his right hand, not so much a gesture of kindness or friendship as a reflexive act.

"Sit down. I'll be with you in a moment," Jarvis murmured.

He continued eyeing the paper before him as Harris sat quietly in front of the massive desk, moving uncomfortably as the silence chilled the room. Finally Jarvis reached over and pressed a button on the intercom.

"Holly, come in here!"

"Yes, Mr. Jarvis," the reply echoed off the window behind Jarvis.

The secretary walked through the door and approached the desk.

"Get some coffee . . . uh, do you want anything to eat?" He looked at Harris.

"No . . . no, thank you," Harris replied awkwardly.

"Just coffee then." He never looked at Holly or took his stony stare from Harris.

Holly left the room, and Jarvis's next words bounced off the walls. "Well, do you have it or don't you?"

"It isn't that easy," Harris protested.

"Easy, easy! I don't pay for easy. I pay for results, and Ed . . ." He paused for effect. "I pay you very well." The silence between his phrases hung in the air like a sword to let the meaning soak into Harris's consciousness.

"Yes . . . yes, sir . . . you do. And I've always delivered, haven't I?"

"I don't pay for past work. I pay for what I need now. You were supposed to have the plans for the Tel-Ray project to me last week at the latest. I could tell from your voice on the phone you weren't going to bring them. Where are they?"

"It's been a much more difficult project than first anticipated. I have my best man on it, but . . ." His voice trailed off.

"But what?" Jarvis roared.

At that moment Holly opened the door, returning with the coffee. The question seemed to snap through the doorway and reverberate down the long hallway. She walked over to the large credenza and set the tray down. Carefully, she poured the coffee, adding the correct amount of sugar to Ed Harris's without asking. He had been a frequent visitor over the last year, and Holly made it her responsibility to know the desires of Mr. Jarvis's business acquaintances. She carried the cups to the desk and set them down.

"Will there be anything else?" she asked.

"No, that's all."

As she neared the door, Jarvis spoke again. "Yes, Holly, there is something else. Tell James to have the boat ready at two today. I think it might be a good day to do some fishing." He paused. "What do you think, Ed?"

Harris nodded mutely, one eyebrow raised. Holly closed the door.

They drank their coffee in silence. When there were no more distractions, Harris continued. "You see, not only is the project difficult, but the man responsible for it has had a lot of stress."

"I don't care what problems you're having. I want *results*. Now, this afternoon we'll go fishing. Maybe you can think of a way to speed up production."

• • •

Jarvis concentrated on the remembered scene, revisiting his recollections surrounding Harris's arrival as the sun climbed above the level of the ocean and penetrated the room with its brilliance. He focused carefully on all of the events of the last few days. No, there had been nothing unusual but something was just not right. Then he asked himself out loud, "So why did Holly feel like she had to leave me?" There had been no warning, no inkling that she was dissatisfied. His mind drifted back again to that moment.

● ● ●

"Mr. Jarvis."

"Holly, what's this Mr. Jarvis nonsense? There's no one around."

"Sid . . ." She hesitated. "We . . . er, I . . . I can't do it."

"Can't do what?"

"I can't marry you. And I can't work for you any longer. I'm going to leave."

"Leave. LEAVE! What do you mean you're going to leave? After all I've done for—"

She cut him off with a slight raise of her hand. "Sid, you've done too much for me. You've been too good to me. I just can't do it. I can't live your kind of life . . ." Her voice nearly broke, but her eyes were hard, resolved.

"Holly, sweet Holly, if you understand 'my kind of life,' as you call it . . ." He smiled and studied her eyes. They were warm but also conveyed fear, her fear of him.

Good, he thought. *Now she'll understand what I'm about to tell her.* He walked up to her and put his hands around her arms and held her with a firm grip. *She's going to have to understand there's only one way out of this organization—no matter where you are in the chain.*

"You know I can't let you do that, Holly. You do know that, don't you?" he mocked her as he continued to apply pressure to her arms.

"I'm sorry, Sid, I can't go through with it." She tried to pull away, but he only squeezed tighter. "Sid, you're hurting me!"

That was when he hit her. And he hit her hard.

● ● ●

These thoughts played and replayed in his mind as Jarvis stood staring out across the deserted beach through his den window. He could feel nothing but seething rage at her rejection. *No one crosses Sidney Jarvis*, he thought. *No one!*

The sun was now high in the morning sky, reflecting brilliantly off the blue waters of the Atlantic. *I wonder if her body has washed up on shore yet.*

Carolina Beach

Bill slept fitfully on the couch and was up early. Sunlight erupted through the sliding door and landed directly on his face. It was going to be a clear day, but the night chill lingered in the air. The coffeepot was still hot; he'd forgotten to turn it off. He was too tired to make a new pot. Unfortunately, the coffee fell into the cup, almost as thick as a glob of hot tar. He took a couple of sips anyway—just to wake himself up.

He put on his boat shoes and pulled a dark blue turtleneck sweater over his head. The crumpled slacks he'd slept in seemed to symbolize the pounding in his head. After looking in on the girl, he went out on the deck, hoping the smell of the ocean in the early morning would clear his jumbled thoughts.

The beach was almost deserted except for two joggers. They passed just below, heading down the beach. He thought it strange that they both wore the same blue jackets with matching emblems on the left front and pants with the same white stripe. They ran in a cadence as if they had spent a lot of time running together. He waved as they glanced up.

About a quarter-mile down the beach was the old pier, where a group of men had congregated near the refreshment stand. This was the most beach activity he had seen since he had arrived. Maybe the fish were running. Or maybe it had something to do with the boat that went down . . . or maybe it had something to do with the girl in his bedroom.

Tossing the undrinkable coffee on the sand below, he turned

around to see his guest staring at him through the sliding-glass door. She was wrapped in a blanket.

He walked into the living room and with each step he took, she slowly backed away, deliberately and carefully placing one foot behind the other. Her balance didn't appear to be too good. She had beautifully haunting eyes that were large and dark, almost unblinking; the pupils were large, trimmed with a thin rim of deep blue. She was obviously having trouble focusing against the glaring sunlight. Even without makeup, her prominent cheekbones stood out. Her lips were sucked in tightly against her teeth, and her face showed small lines of apprehension and fear. She was much more beautiful than he'd realized the night before.

He could see by her expression that she was in a sustained emotional and possibly even physical shock. Again Bill wondered if she wouldn't be better off in a hospital.

"Good morning. I'm glad to see you up," he said warmly. He was standing still, poised as though coaxing a frightened kitten.

She gave no response.

"You were pretty wet and cold when I found you. Why in the world did you go for a swim at that time of night? A person could die in that water, as cold as it is."

He stepped toward her, and she backed farther away.

"You . . . you found me?" Her voice was soft and shaking slightly.

"Yes," he replied.

"I remember the sand . . . I think . . ."

"You were lying on the beach, very wet and cold," he told her.

"You brought me . . . here." It was more of a statement of fact than a question.

"Yes. I'm Bill Chandler. What's your name?"

"Holly . . . Holly James," she replied.

"Do you live around here, Holly? The phones are turned off here for the winter, but I've got a cellular phone somewhere. Or I'd be happy to walk to the pay phone and call someone for you—let 'em know you're all right."

"No! Don't call anyone! Don't tell anyone! Please!" The tone in her voice was somewhere between a panicky plea and full hysteria. Her eyes flitted over the room, trying desperately to find a path of escape. She looked around like a caged animal.

At that moment her eyes drifted upward, and her knees gave way. He caught her before she hit the floor and carried her back into the bedroom. Although her breathing was steady, she was completely incognizant. Unwrapping the blanket and putting her under the covers, he noticed a bruise on her neck; it was apparent something tight had been placed about her throat. The bruise had not been visible last night in the dim bedroom light. Then he noticed dried blood on the sheet. Carefully rolling her onto her side, it was astounding to see that her back was raked with small cuts and clotted blood.

He went to the kitchen and returned with a pan of warm water and a soft cloth, then carefully washed her back as gently as possible. She moaned several times but never fully awoke. Afterward, she seemed to be sleeping peacefully again, so he covered her again and quietly crept out of the room.

He ambled into the kitchen, lost in thought, and absent-mindedly began making himself some breakfast. Why had this beautiful woman, this Holly James, been on the beach in that condition? And what caused the strange bruise on her neck? More important, he wondered why he hadn't called the police. Then he remembered the urgent pleading in her soft voice, the terror in her eyes.

No, it was right not to call the police . . . not yet anyway, he reasoned with himself. She hadn't wanted him to. But there was another reason. The reality was that he was lonely and had a desperate need at that moment to be needed. That, he knew, was the real reason he had not called anyone.

The remainder of the morning he checked her frequently, listening for her respiration, taking her pulse. Those two activities completely exhausted his Boy Scout first-aid knowledge. The rest of the time he spent staring at the unsettled ocean. Then, sometime about noon, he heard her murmur softly. That gave him an excuse to confront her again.

Carrying two cups of coffee and a plate of sweet rolls into the bedroom, he softly swung the door against the wall to announce his entrance. She opened her eyes at the sound.

"I thought you could use some coffee and sweets. Not much of a selection. You managed to be rescued by someone who doesn't fancy himself a gourmet. I hope you're not too choosy." He noticed that her eyes seemed to have more life in them now.

She grimaced in pain as she tried to smile politely.

"Are you sure you're OK?" Bill asked.

"I think so. What do they say? It only hurts when I laugh. It seems to hurt the most when I breathe, move, or think about doing either. My back feels like a thousand pins are sticking in it."

"I washed the cuts off the best I could. None were too deep, so I don't think you need stitches. But I'm no doctor."

"Did you say you had something to eat?" She obviously wanted to change the subject.

"Yeah, I bought the kind with all three major food groups—sugar, cholesterol, and preservatives." He handed her a plate with a Danish on it.

"Thanks, I'm kind of hungry, and I'm not a gourmet either," she said, taking a bite.

Holly sat up, pulling the blanket up to her neck but somehow leaving one shoulder bare. He handed her a mug, and she sipped its steamy contents.

"Are you feeling better?" he asked.

"Yes, thanks," she replied.

They looked at each other silently, then both seemed to concentrate fully on the sweet rolls. The quiet was broken only by the call of the sea gulls searching the beach for food. Bill broke the awkwardness of their silence by clearing his throat and reaching for his coffee.

"I was pretty worried about you last night. You didn't look too good when I got you inside." He wanted to say more but didn't quite know how to get into it.

"I guess I haven't thanked you for . . . saving . . . my life." She stopped, apparently unable to think of what to say next.

"Well . . ." He smiled, hoping to lighten the gloom that was rapidly engulfing the room. "My mother taught me to always clean my plate—you know, because of all the starving children in India—and to never leave a person dying of exposure lying on the beach."

His attempted joke fell flat. They stared at each other again in silence.

"Shoot! This polite chitchat isn't getting us anywhere, Holly. What were you doing on the beach last night?" he asked.

"That's none of your business," she replied in a sharp tone and turned her head away from him to look out the window. He watched as she took a long drink of coffee. The profile of her nose was perfect, and her hair fell in tangles across her shoulders.

"Since I probably saved your life, I have a right to some kind of an explanation. Try to see it from my point of view. First, I find a woman unconscious, facedown on the sand, soaked to the skin. Second, there's a bruise on her neck like she's been choked, and her back is cut like a furrowed field ready for spring planting. Third, I don't call an ambulance because she begs me not to, even though she's half-dead and should be in a hospital. She spends the night in my bed so I have to sleep on the couch. Then I wake up with a stiff back, and this mysterious woman tells me the whole thing's none of my business. I'm sorry, I'm entitled to some kind of an explanation! It's not like I picked you up at a party and brought you here for a night of frolic." He found himself getting angry out of frustration.

"I'm sorry, you were . . . er . . . you are very kind." She smiled a demure smile. "And I do owe you my life. But it would be best for you, ah . . . I know you told me your name before I fainted but I can't remember it," she stammered.

"Bill . . . Bill Chandler," he replied, having calmed himself some.

"It would be best for you, Bill Chandler, if you just forgot you ever saw me and let me leave. By the way, where are my clothes? I assume you were the one who undressed me." Her eyes darted quickly away from his, and she looked slightly embarrassed.

"First, I have the right to choose what is or is not best for me," he argued. "And second, yes, I undressed you. However, rest assured no impropriety took place. And I used to be married, so I can testify that you have nothing different from my late wife." The words burned his throat, and he suddenly wondered why he had said them. He had not been able to talk about Sandy to a stranger since the explosion in London. Now his eyes burned as tears welled up in them.

Seeing the hurt on his face, Holly's tone immediately softened. "I'm sorry. I didn't mean to imply you might have done anything improper. I just don't know if I can trust anyone anymore. And I don't want you to get involved in something you would be sorry for later. So, it would just be best if you gave me my clothes and let me go."

"Your clothes have dried, but they're too ripped up to be of much use. The holes are in all the wrong . . . or *right* places, depending on your point of view." His attempt to lighten the conversation met with a suspicious look from the woman.

"Look, if you'll write down your sizes I'll go into town and get you something to wear," Bill offered, grabbing a pencil and paper to cover his embarrassment. "But first, let me put this antiseptic on your back. I found it in the bathroom."

As she turned onto her side, he pulled the blanket back and again was impressed with the numerous small, jagged tears in the formerly flawless skin.

She tensed as the spray of red antiseptic seeped into the cuts but said nothing. "Until I get back, put this sweatshirt on." As he spoke he went to the dresser, pulled out his old Iowa State University sweatshirt, threw it to her, and walked out of the room.

A moment later she emerged from the bedroom, supporting herself on the casing of the doorway. The sweatshirt went halfway down her thighs and, he had to admit, it had never looked that good on him. She eased onto a chair as Bill set their coffee on the table. Then once again they looked at each other in silence.

Apparently remembering her assignment, Holly wrote down her sizes and handed the paper wordlessly to Bill. He asked no more questions, but as he stood to go, the mystery of her appearance gnawed at his stomach.

4

A Return of Feeling

About an hour later he came back with what he hoped would be appropriate clothing. There wasn't a great deal to choose from in the off-season. During the fall and winter months, most of the natives went to Wilmington for their shopping, and few of the local shops were open. He'd gotten blue jeans, a white blouse, and a blue sweater as well as tennis shoes and a medium-weight jacket. The salesclerk picked out the necessary underwear, giving him a questioning look as he bought such a complete outfit.

To break the embarrassment of the moment he said, "The airline lost her luggage. They promised to deliver it yesterday, but you know how that goes."

"No, I've never been on an airplane. Got no reason to go traipsing all over the country!" the clerk replied coldly.

Bill left the store without further comment.

Holly took the bundle and disappeared into the bedroom. She carefully pulled off the sweatshirt and looked into the mirror. The bruise at the base of her neck now extended down to the top of her collarbone, a stark distinction to the pure whiteness of her breasts below, flawed only by a scratch on the right breast where the thug had grabbed her. An icy shiver ran down her spine, and small goose bumps suddenly appeared, brought on by the memory of the nightmare just past.

Next she turned around and peered over her shoulder and was shocked at the multitude of tiny red welts and cuts. They appeared much worse now because of the antiseptic that had been applied. Her back burned with pain as she put on the brassiere and sweater, but Holly reminded herself she was lucky to be alive . . . at least for the moment.

While Bill had been gone, she had straightened up the condo, washed the dishes, and started a load of laundry.

"Thanks for the maid service," he joked when he returned.

"It's the least I can do. I lost my purse last night, so I can't even pay you for the clothes right now, but I will, as soon as I get everything taken care of," she said.

His attitude and voice had softened, but his curiosity had not. "Holly, I think I deserve an explanation of what happened last night."

"Yes . . . I know you do . . . ," she responded.

Just then came the sound of footsteps on the stairway outside the condo and a knock at the door.

"Don't go to the door!" Holly whispered with panic in her voice and fear in her eyes as she frantically looked around the condo for a place to hide.

The knock was repeated, louder and more persistent.

Her eyes pleaded with him not to betray her.

"Go into the bedroom and stay out of sight," Bill whispered. He thought to himself as he went to the door, *Now she has me acting kooky too.*

A man of about forty faced the door and leaned on the banister. Noticing his blue jogging suit, Bill thought he might be one of the two blue-clad joggers he had seen on the beach earlier in the morning.

"Yes?"

"Pardon me for bothering you," he began, "but I wonder if you can help me out." His speech had a thick southern drawl, but it wasn't North Carolinian. Maybe Texan.

"I don't know, but I'll try. What's the problem?"

"I'm a-lookin' for a young woman who disappeared last night. She was staying with a friend down on the lower end of the island. She . . . well . . . ya see, she's been, well, kinda sick. I mean, she was in an institution. Had a nervous breakdown, ya know what I mean?" He pointed at the side of his head with his finger twirling in a rotary motion. "It's not . . . well, ya see, she's not really dangerous to anyone or anything like that. But she gets confused, loses touch with what's happening around her . . ." He paused, waiting for a response.

Bill smiled and nodded but said nothing. The silence hung in the air like a drifting cloud of fog.

Finally the man continued. "It's real important that we find her." He seemed to be genuinely concerned for her welfare. "They said she tried to commit suicide once. That's why she's been in the hospital."

"Why did you stop here?"

"Well, there ain't many people down here this time of year, and I saw you this morning when I was looking for Holly. Holly, that's her name. So I thought I'd stop and ask if you might have seen her walking on the beach early this morning."

Bill wasn't sure why, but he didn't trust this stranger at his door. Maybe it was the fear he had seen on Holly's face at the sound of his knock, but there was also something about the man himself that Bill did not trust. Whatever the reason, he found himself lying without remorse.

"No. The only person I've seen today is you and some folks uptown when I went to get some things. That's one of the reasons I came down here this time of year, so I wouldn't see anyone."

The stranger's body language said he really wanted to come in but he wasn't going to push the point. He tried to look into the living room over Bill's shoulder as they talked. Finally, he took a piece of paper and a pen out of his pocket and wrote down a phone number.

"If you do see her, would you give me a call?" he asked.

"Sure. By the way, what did you say her name was?"

"Holly," he replied.

"What did you say Holly looked like?" Bill was interested in finding out if his guest was who this man thought she was.

"About five feet three inches tall or so, a hundred, maybe a hundred ten pounds, long dark hair, dark eyes, high cheekbones, real nice figure . . ." Then he added, "You know, one of those model types . . . nice legs, if you know what I mean?"

"Yeah, sure thing." Bill smiled and took a step back from the door, preparing to close it. "Sounds like I'd like to see her. Too bad I haven't. But it's probably too cold for bathing suits anyway."

As the man walked away he stopped and looked back. "I'd sure appreciate it if you could help me. So would the fellow she was staying with."

"Sure. If I see her, I'll give you a ring. By the way, what's *your* name?"

"Most folks call me Buck," he answered.

"OK, Buck, I'll call if I see her."

After shutting the door and locking it, Bill leaned against the wall and stared out at the restless sea, considering what he'd just done. It was all so out of character for him. Then, slowly, he turned and walked into the bedroom.

"Who was that and who are you?" he demanded.

"You didn't tell him I was here!" She sat on the bed and breathed deeply, her long white fingers trembling as she raked them through her hair. "I guess all I can say is thank you. But I have to get out of here. He'll be back. I know him. He'll be back!" There was terror in her voice.

Holly got up and paced the floor quickly like a trapped and frightened animal.

"Now, just hold on, Holly. First, I'm not sure you're strong enough to get out of here, and second, I'm not the world's greatest liar, so your friend in the blue suit is probably watching the building. Third, my car is the only one downstairs, and the beach is wide open. So, unless you can sprout wings and fly, you're stuck here with me for a while."

As he spoke he took her by the shoulders and made her look at him. The deep blue color of her eyes in the morning light was captivating. They looked at each other silently, searchingly. Bill wondered what he was getting into—and why.

She shook herself loose from his grasp and collapsed onto the bed, turning away from him. He could again see the bruise at the side of her neck.

"OK, Holly. If you want my help and if you don't want me to go look up that fellow who was at the door, you had better tell me what's going on. He said you just got out of a mental hospital, and I'll have to admit, you *are* acting a little weird," he said. He wondered if she could tell he was not at all serious about turning her in. Indeed, he was fascinated with this strange woman who had suddenly touched his life.

"Could . . . could I have some more coffee?" she asked.

As they sat at the table, she reluctantly began. "That man at the door, works for . . . well . . . my fiancé. I also worked for him—not for Buck, for my fiancé. His name is Sid Jarvis. I've worked for him for about two years, and I was engaged to him until last night. We had postponed the wedding several times because of his business. Then, last week, he wanted to rush out and get married. I told him I wasn't sure I wanted to marry him now. He became furious and wouldn't let me leave. Last night I finally got away from him. Now if I can just get away from this island I'll be OK. I can go back home."

Tears were running down her face as she finished. She nervously licked them from her lips and brushed them from the side of her cheek with her palm.

"That's all well and good, Holly, but when I found you last

night, you were soaked from being in the ocean. That doesn't fit." He continued, "I might believe you're trying to get away from a jealous lover, and I might even believe you're already married and you're trying to leave your husband. But that doesn't explain the rest of it."

When he finished speaking, the silence between them hung in the air with the staleness of a smoke-filled pool hall.

"OK, I tried to kill myself! Is that what you wanted to hear? I started swimming out into the ocean, but I couldn't go through with it. Only, I almost did die . . . and I would have died if it hadn't been . . . been, for you. I suppose—no, I *know* that I sound crazy, like he said, but I'm not. You have to believe me." She sat looking at Bill with pleading eyes.

There was another long silence, then she raised her eyes to his and said, "I have no right to ask, but . . . will you help me?" She took a breath then hurried on. "If I can just get off the island . . . everything will be all right. If you could just help me do that, then I'll go away . . . and everything will be all right." Her last words were more for herself than for him. She was trying to believe she could survive this nightmare.

He thought for several more minutes while she sat and looked at him with those large, dark eyes. She looked like one of the lost kittens he had brought home as a child, the kitten that had been caught in a culvert during a thunderstorm. Her story sounded good, except—and it was a significant exception—there was still that bruise on her neck and the scratches on her back. Those didn't fit with either her story or with the story that fellow Buck had told.

Maybe it was the mystery of finding an unknown woman on the beach, or perhaps it was the lack of orderliness in explaining all the facts to his scientific mind, or it could have been the look of terror he had seen in her eyes earlier. But whatever the reason, he found himself saying, "All right, Holly James, I'll help you. I have a hunch I'm going to live to regret this decision, but I'll help you."

He looked out the window at the blue sky and suddenly, for

the first time since Sandy was killed, he started to feel something inside. Strangely, he noticed that his hands were shaking. He set down his coffee cup, then stared at it as he thought to himself, *Maybe my soul didn't die in London with my late wife.*

Holly took a long drink of the steamy black coffee, tilted her head slightly, and smiled for the first time. There was a small dimple at the corner of her mouth, and she had the most beautiful teeth he'd ever seen.

5

COOKIE

They waited until dark. Holly had slept off and on during the day, and when Bill had gone out to the store about 3:30, he had noticed a dark van with two men inside that was parked facing the stairs up to his condo. The van was still there when he returned. The two men seemed more than mildly interested in the coming and going of his car.

He hoped the bag of groceries made him look much more innocent than he felt. Climbing the stairs, he saw a man out on the beach in front of his place. The man was pretending to be surf fishing, but Bill was willing to bet he didn't even have a hook on the line. What he did have was a small earpiece attached to a wire that disappeared inside the collar of his jacket, and Bill had a feeling he was not listening to the top ten songs on the hit parade. Suddenly, for the off-season, it was getting very crowded here.

Stepping inside the condo, Bill set down the groceries, found a screwdriver, and began loosening one of the grates covering the heating duct in the living room. "Bring me your old clothes. If you're right, your friends will eventually check this apartment. If they find your clothes, they'll know I'm helping you." He pulled the louvered grill from the duct. "We might need all the time we can get," he added under his breath.

Holly looked at Bill with an icy stare. "They're not my friends."

• • •

Finally, night settled over the island. The soothing sound of the waves rolling onto the beach was in high contrast to the tension that enveloped the man and woman inside the condo as they hurriedly prepared to leave. If it was possible to get Holly out of here, this was the time.

The first problem was the condo's lighting system. The stairways and parking lot were as bright as if it were noon. He had seen the main circuit breaker near the Dumpster and thought that, if he could get to it, he could make things dark enough for Holly to get down the stairs unseen.

"Holly, turn out all the lights," Bill said as he headed out the door.

"Why? What are you doing?" she asked.

"I'm going to throw the circuit breaker for the outside lights. When they go off, come out the door and go toward the street on this level. There's a stairway at the other end. Come down those stairs, and I'll be waiting for you there." He felt a little foolish, like a commando giving instructions to his men.

"Bill, be careful. Sid was pretty mad when I left," she cautioned. "He tried to kill me. I don't think he'll like anyone helping me."

"Finally, you've said something I'm willing to believe," he answered, a wry smile creasing his face. He squeezed her arm slightly. "'Careful' is my middle name."

He turned out the light over the deck outside the bedroom then climbed over the railing, clinging to the pilings. It was twenty feet down to the sand, and the surf sounded like it was breaking right under him. The darkness was as black as any night made for

Halloween goblins, and the wind struck him with the kind of bone-chilling cold for which there is no protection. So he found it ironic to feel sweat trickling down his neck.

Stretching, he could just touch the underside of the flooring of the deck above his. He climbed, spiderlike, to a point where his fingers could not quite reach anything to grasp then leaped for one of the two-by-fours of the railing above. He pulled himself up to get one of his arms around one of the slats of the upper balcony. As his legs swung wildly in the air, he wondered briefly what bones sounded like as they broke. If that board he was holding on to came loose, he would probably find out as he plunged twenty or more feet to the ground below.

His jacket caught on a bent nail sticking out from the main support beam, and the muscles in his arms trembled with exertion as he pulled forcefully against the fabric snared by the rusty hook. Finally, the cloth ripped, and he was free. By the time he pulled himself up to the rail and his feet were firmly planted on the upper deck, he was panting and sweating as if he'd run two miles. His throat was dry, his eyes burned, and his heart was fluttering crazily. But at the same time, he felt strangely exhilarated and alive.

There was a clamor of metal on metal as the door of the deserted condo slid open. The lock was easy to jimmy with the screwdriver he had brought along. Passing quickly through the living room, he slipped out the front door. Staying close to the wall and crouching to stay below the level of the railing, he easily made his way along the upper corridor and crossed to the inside of the building. There an enclosed stairway hid his descent.

By the time Bill arrived at the main electrical box, he was out of breath and his heart seemed ready to explode, but most important, he had not been seen—at least he hoped he hadn't. He cautiously peered around the corner, ready to step out to the circuit-breaker box, and realized he was now behind the dark van he'd seen earlier in the day. Two figures sat in the front seats, their main focus apparently out the front windshield. He saw their heads tilt backward occasionally as they lifted long-necked bottles to their mouths.

Silently, Bill moved to the electrical panel. He forced the door open, grabbed the main switch, and pulled it down, plunging the entire complex into darkness. Even before the huge parking-lot lights had completely dimmed, he was racing over the pavement, staying as close to the building's pilings as possible. He arrived at the stairway just as Holly descended. She was silhouetted against the red exit light, hesitating as if wondering which way to go. He grasped her arm and put his other hand over her mouth. She stiffened in his grasp, trying to pull away from him.

"It's me!" he hissed. "Don't make a sound. We have lots of company out here tonight."

They crouched down behind a piling as the headlights from several cars moved quickly toward the parking area under the end of the building nearest the beach.

"All right, now, stay low. We're going up the street two houses then we'll cut back toward the beach," he whispered.

"You check those condos at that end!" a voice with authority yelled out. "Hank, you watch the street over by the 7-Eleven. I'll check the beach."

A man carrying a flashlight trotted by the other side of the piling that hid them. The light beams bounced from ground to deck as he hurried up the stairway Holly had just descended. An adrenaline rush filled Bill's head with a tremendous roar, and Holly's pulse was pounding in her ears.

Quickly, he led her up the alley running north from the complex. They reached the second house and turned into the yard; he pulled her onto the sand, and they lay motionless beside a hurricane fence, the sharp, razorlike dune grass pressed against their faces. He wondered if it was too late in the season for sand crabs.

A car drove slowly up the alley, shining a large spotlight into the deserted yards and parking spaces. The light flashed over their bodies as they pressed themselves into the sand and held their breath.

The car was quickly gone, and he whispered, "We certainly can't stay here much longer. Let's head up the beach on the other side of the dunes. Keep low."

When he took her hand to help her up from the sand, her palm was cool and clammy. She stumbled as they started up the dune. He grabbed her around the waist to keep them both from falling and felt her body trembling. "Bill, I'm scared. What if . . ."

"Yeah, well, I'm scared, too, so let's not play what-if. Come on, let's go," he answered in a low whisper.

Moving in the shadows of the deserted summer homes and staying close to the sand dunes, their passage up the beach was slow and terrifying since every shadow could hide the enemy. It seemed to take hours, but only fifteen minutes had actually passed when they reached the boardwalk. They brushed the sand off their clothes, then he impulsively put his arms around Holly, pulling her close.

"In case we meet anyone, act like we're lovers and we belong here," he said, only half joking.

He was momentarily distracted by a faint stirring as something deep inside him responded to the warmth and softness of her body next to his.

"They'll wonder why we're here. What'll we say?"

"I'll tell them everyone's got to be somewhere," he quipped.

Just as they reached the midpoint of the boardwalk, a man in a dark coat with the collar turned up against the wind stepped out of an alleyway. Holly's body tensed against Bill's.

"We're lovers, remember?" he said.

Holly buried her face into his shoulder and nuzzled his neck as the man approached with deliberate slowness. When he drew into hearing distance, Holly said, "Oh, darling! I'm not really hungry. Let's go back to the condo. There's lots more exciting things there." She paused, then seductively slipped her arms around his neck. "Nothing's even open on this dirty old boardwalk anyway."

The smirk on the man's face as he passed them indicated he had heard every word.

After the man had gone by, Bill whispered, "It seems a bit crowded on the boardwalk tonight. Let's go in here." He guided her in the door of the greasy spoon where he'd eaten the night before.

They sat down at the counter, and Cookie, wearing the same soiled apron, turned toward them.

"Ya must've really liked that burger last night, huh?" He flashed his big toothy grin of assorted cigarette and coffee stains.

"Just a couple of coffees, please," Bill said, returning the smile.

Cookie poured the coffee and set it in front of them.

"Sure I cain't gitcha somethin' else? Got some pie left over, was fresh this mornin'." He smiled again.

"No . . . no thanks, this'll be fine. Just something to take the chill off," Bill replied as he laid the money down on the counter.

The restaurant door opened, and a man in the all-too-familiar blue jogging suit walked in. He sat down at the other end of the counter and stared at them for a couple of minutes. Cookie walked over to him and asked, "What'll ya have, mister?"

Mr. Blue Suit stared at them a little longer. "Uh . . . nothing. I don't want nothing."

He got up and left. The door banged shut, and Bill had a very bad feeling he wouldn't be gone long.

"Ah . . . say, Cookie," he said to the man behind the counter. "Uh, I have, er . . . we have a slight problem."

Holly looked at him, startled.

"Yeah, what's the trouble?" Cookie answered.

"Did you see that guy who just came in here?" Bill asked.

"Yeah, he sure looked you two over good," he replied.

"Well," Bill said, leaning over the counter. "This lady wanted to go out with me tonight"—he motioned toward Holly—"and, well . . . you see, she used to be his girlfriend. And, well . . . we just walked up the beach from my place at the Villas. Unfortunately, we left my car down there. Do you know where that is?" he asked.

"Sure, that big condo complex 'bout a mile down the beach," Cookie replied.

Bill continued. "It's a long, dark walk back down the street. I don't think that guy's any too happy with either one of us tonight, if you know what I mean." Bill looked over at Holly, then back at Cookie and smiled.

Cookie's face lit up. "Want me to go git yer car fer y'all when I close up?" he asked.

"That's a great idea. But he might get tired of waiting before then and come back in here. I sure wouldn't want a scene. Could we meet you somewhere?" Bill asked.

Cookie quickly drew a rough map on a paper napkin and handed it to him. Then he said, "Tell ya what; I live on Route 27 toward Wilmington. You take my car out back, and I'll go get yours when I close up, and we'll meet at my house." He beamed with pride at having come up with the idea Bill had hoped for.

They quickly traded car keys.

Bill could hear voices approaching from outside and knew time was running out. He said, "My car is the only one parked at the Villa tonight. It's a Pontiac Grand Prix, parked at the north end toward the ocean."

The voices were getting louder, closer. Their "friends" were returning.

Cookie motioned toward the back door.

"I'll see ya in 'bout an hour and a half," he said, holding the door open.

Seeming nonchalant, Bill and Holly pulled away from the back of the diner in a rather bedraggled '77 Ford just as two men walked through the diner's front door. They paused and looked around the room, now empty of customers. The larger one said, "Where did they go?"

"Where did who go?" Cookie asked. "Been kind of busy tonight."

"The man and woman who were sitting at the counter just five minutes ago," the second man snarled.

"Oh, the lovebirds. They went out just before you two came in. I'm surprised ya didn't pass 'em on the street. Who knows? Maybe they went the other way." Cookie turned away and began to clean his grill. "The way they was lookin' at each other, I don't think they particularly wanted any company, though."

"Jarvis isn't going to like this one bit," the taller man said to his companion as they turned back toward the door.

"Say, these folks you're lookin' for," Cookie said. "Whadda ya want 'em fer?"

"They stole some money from our boss," the shorter man said.

"Is that so? Well, you oughta report 'em. The police station is just two blocks over and one block to the right," Cookie said. But his words bounced unclaimed against the door as it swung shut.

He closed fifteen minutes early. Not that it really mattered—there hadn't been any more customers since the pair in the blue suits had left. He went out the back door and headed down the alley toward the Villas, thinking things through as he walked.

Something didn't add up. He wasn't the smartest man on earth, but his two tours in 'Nam had schooled him in sensing danger and foiling a trap. About a block from the Villas, he cut through a yard to the beach. Walking in the sand was harder, but there was comfort in being away from the streetlights and closer to the sound of the surf.

As he approached the condos, he was surprised to see them cloaked in darkness. Usually this place was lit up like a Christmas tree, even though only a few condos were rented this time of the year. He was creeping through the high grass on the dunes when suddenly all of the lights in the complex came on. He felt like the only person in the middle of a football field surrounded by stands packed with spectators.

Dropping instantly to the ground, he cautiously peered over the dune he'd rolled behind and saw ten men, all in the same kind of blue jogging suits, milling about in the shadow of the building. A single car, Bill's late-model Grand Prix, was parked between the pilings at the northeast corner of the building.

Cookie nervously fingered the key in his pocket. 'Nam had taught him to be patient in the bush. He settled in quietly on the sand. After an hour or more the men left the parking lot and climbed into three vans parked out on the street. He listened as they started their engines and drove off.

When the last van had pulled out, Cookie slowly crept forward. Keeping low and using the pilings for cover, he made his way to the Grand Prix, slipped the key in the lock, opened the door, and slid behind the wheel. It was a rental car and still smelled new. He put the key into the ignition and turned it.

Cookie never heard the blast. The car exploded into a mass of flaming metal and fire. The explosives had been placed against the gas tank so the fuel would add to the fury of the initial explosion.

The blast shattered two pilings, causing the corner of the building to sag, and the flames rising out of the white-hot metal ignited the condo above the car.

By the time the Carolina Beach Volunteer Fire Department and the town's police officers arrived, the building was beyond saving. The firefighters were only able to control the flames to keep them from spreading to the summerhouse next door.

6

ESCAPE FROM CAROLINA ISLAND

W ho authorized you to put a bomb in his car?" Jarvis almost screamed as he slammed his fist down on the desk.

"You said if we find 'em to make 'em inoperable," the tall man replied. "I'm sure he was helping her. I know he was the one we saw at the diner."

"I didn't want them *killed*, at least not yet. You didn't even know who he was. And anyway, we don't know for sure that Holly was with him." Jarvis was clearly frustrated. "I don't like the way this affair is going. It's been screwed up from the beginning."

He began to pace around the room, using his anger to hide a smoldering cancer of fear growing inside him. Somehow things were not quite right. He just couldn't put his finger on it, but something was not fitting into place. The thoughts raced through his head at a breakneck pace. *First Ed Harris comes down without the Tel-Ray plans, and when a little pressure is applied, he dies. Then Holly pulls her stunt and gets away. Now we've had an accident that might not have needed to happen.* Jarvis had no problem with eliminating anyone, but . . . he just couldn't put his finger on what was bothering him.

There's something wrong with the way it's all happening . . . too many dumb mistakes. This isn't that difficult an operation. He stood glaring at the men in the room.

All of these men had been with Jarvis for many years, some of them since the organization was started. They could sense his frustration, and they respected and feared Jarvis because of his temper. Each had seen what he was capable of when he was enraged. One thing none of them wanted was to be the target of his anger.

"I don't like it. This whole thing is getting too sloppy. Too many accidents—Ed Harris dying, Holly . . ."

"Hey, Mr. Jarvis, I'm real sorry about Mr. Harris. We hadn't even laid a hand on him. He was just standing at the side of the boat, lookin' out at the water. He just kept staring at the water, kind of shakin' his head.

"You told us to take him out and make sure he understood that you needed those plans now. We were just startin' to, uh, *talk* to him about not fulfilling his promise to you. I took hold of his jacket, and he just keeled over, dead. He grabbed his chest and turned a funny color, and that was it. I guess he had a heart attack or somethin'. There wasn't nothin' we could do; he just died. We had to throw him overboard. We couldn't come back into port with a stiff on board."

The man was nervously stammering on, trying to explain why things weren't going so well.

"Well, gentlemen." Jarvis slowed his speech, enunciating each word distinctly. "Listen and listen well. We need Holly back . . . if she wasn't killed in that car. And we need the rest of the information on the Tel-Ray project. Now, I'm leaving for Washington in the morning to find that scientist Harris was talking about. If Holly wasn't killed in the blast, I want her found and brought to me. If she was killed," he said, hesitating, "I don't want it traced to us. Do I make myself clear?"

Jarvis wearily sat down and rubbed his hand across his face. Then, in a calmer voice, he said, "John, get your men out there and find her. She knows some things about us that must be kept quiet.

Find her, and don't hurt her if you don't have to, and for heaven's sake, keep the men in line. If one of your goons hadn't tried to rape her, we'd have her back now. Are there any questions?"

"Yes, sir, Mr. Jarvis. I mean, no, sir . . . Don't worry, we have the airport and bus station covered, and she doesn't have any money or credit cards because we still have her purse. We'll have her by morning for sure. She can't get off the island. Don't you worry, Mr. Jarvis, we'll have her by morning."

● ● ●

"Cookie's late," Bill said.

"That's the fourth time you've said that in the last fifteen minutes," Holly answered.

"This whole thing doesn't feel right." Bill paced nervously while watching the moon dodge between the clouds and pine trees. Ever since they had crossed the Intracoastal Waterway from the island, Bill had felt uneasy. Now as he looked out at the landscape he saw the moon's rays were playing tricks with the brown earth and the black shadows on this lonely stretch of the Carolina coast. It made it feel like something out of an old Boris Karloff movie. "I don't like being here, and I'm not sure I like the story you told me."

His anger was a charade, an attempt to make up for the fear he felt in his gut. Bill dug the toe of his shoe into the soft, sandy soil, then kicked a large dust cloud into the still night air. Suddenly he raised his head and let loose a stream of brief but potent profanity.

"Feel better?" she asked coldly.

"What do you think?"

"What do you want me to say?" Holly replied, her voice rising slightly.

"The truth, woman. We could start with at least part of the truth. First, why did I find you half-drowned on the beach last night? And then tell me the truth about that bruise on your neck that looks like someone tried to strangle you. Next I'd like the truth about why some rather unpleasant men are chasing us around North Carolina."

He paused, looking at her steadily.

"I'm listening, Holly, but I'm not hearing a thing." His anger was rising again.

Holly raised her hand to her throat, gently probing the bruise, and looked down at the ground in silence.

"Holly, you're a very beautiful woman. I also think you're a nice lady—maybe a little crazy, but nice. But I'm not real happy with the people who are chasing you. They seem to have a different set of values. Their norm isn't like Little League on Saturday morning with the family—it seems to run more along the lines of murder, rape, and pillage.

"Now, if I'm going to continue playing James Bond, I'd sure as heck like to know why. Up to now, I'm convinced I haven't a clue about what is going on." He paused again for several seconds and then continued. "I'll tell you this: If I don't get the truth now, I'm going to walk away from you and this whole mess. I mean it." By now Bill was yelling furiously and had grasped Holly by her shoulders.

"Stop! You're hurting me!" she answered him. "And please don't yell. I've heard Jarvis yell like that. It frightens me." She straightened her back and took a deep breath in anticipation of the rest of their conversation. "Okay, if you want the truth, I'll tell you the truth, but no more yelling." Holly's voice was much more subdued than his was, and it was remarkably under control.

She was without a doubt one poised and elegant woman, he marveled, releasing his grip on her. She rubbed her shoulders to ease the pain from his fingers. It was only then that Bill realized how tightly he had held her.

"Sorry, I guess I'm not very good at this sort of thing."

As her eyes came up to meet his, Holly took a deep breath and began. "Some of what I told you before is true. I am, or was, the personal secretary to S. E. Jarvis. And we were supposed to be married. The wedding was to have taken place last May but had to be postponed because of his business. That much is true." Holly was talking in almost a monotone now, though her breathing was still exaggerated.

"Fine, but normal people don't resort to murder just because they're late to the altar," he said.

"Well," she responded slowly, "you have to understand his business."

"All right." Bill paused and looked up at the sky, dotted with stars. "I'll try to understand his business. What is it?"

"It's not as simple as you might think . . ." She paused to collect her thoughts. "He has an import-export business with offices in Washington, New York, and San Francisco. He imports from Asia mostly—clothes, shoes, and things like that."

Listening to her, Bill decided she might actually be telling the truth for the first time since he'd met her.

"But there's more to it, isn't there? After all, your average clothing importer doesn't go around terrorizing people when he's been jilted. What did you do, take his favorite Jordache jeans when you left? Tell me more, Holly, or this trip is just about over." He tried to sound angry without raising his voice. But the truth was that he was fascinated by what she had to say, and his anger waned.

"Don't be a smart-mouth!" she responded.

"Sorry."

"Well . . ." She drew in a breath and tried to continue, but her voice began to falter. "Like I said, he also exports . . ."

"OK, he exports! Exports what?" he asked impatiently.

"Things . . ."

"Holly, you're doing it again. What things? No tricks, no double-talk. What does Jarvis export?" he asked.

"Guns, ammunition, secrets, high technology . . . things," she stated. "I really shouldn't be telling you this." She turned away and folded her arms across her chest.

He should have been stunned by the revelation, but somehow he wasn't. Her pursuers had not identified themselves as law officers, so he had long ago concluded that they must be some kind of bad guys. The silence enclosed them like an ominous shroud.

"Right, so he's an exporter. Guns may not be my favorite thing, but people have a right to buy and sell them. He's an exporter. I suppose now you're going to tell me he's an *illegal* exporter, right?" The sarcasm was creeping into his voice again.

"OK, Bill, I don't blame you if you don't believe me. It sounds too Hollywood to be real. Sometimes I don't believe it myself."

"So who are his clients? The other crazies of the world?"

She still had her back toward him. He looked at her mane of long, dark hair and had to deliberately fight a sudden urge to touch it. Her shoulders were slightly drooped, and she nervously shuffled her foot in the loose sand.

"Yes," she said in a small, matter-of-fact voice.

"So, you're telling me that I am mixed up with someone who's in trouble with the *mob*?" There was a hint of panic in his voice. "Who are you, Holly? And how on earth did you get mixed up with the Mafia?"

"Bill, please believe me! I didn't know for a long time," she protested. "I just learned about it a little at a time. At first, I only dealt with the legitimate side of his business. Then, after he fell in love with me, he felt he could trust me with . . . more of the details of the other side. As I found out more and more of what he really did, I decided . . . I knew . . . that I couldn't marry him. Then when I finally told him I was going to quit and that I wouldn't marry him, he thought I might go to the authorities. Killing me was the only way he could be sure that I wouldn't. That's why you found me nearly dead on the beach."

"I want the whole story, Holly. How did you wind up in the ocean, and how'd you get that bruise on your neck?" he asked.

Still calm and reserved, Holly walked back to the car and sat on the front fender as she spoke. Nervously, she pushed her hair back from her face, brought one knee up to her chest, and wrapped her arms around it as if she were trying to strengthen her resolve to tell the story. "Last night I told Sid I was leaving. But he wouldn't let me go; he had me locked up in his house down the beach from where you found me. I don't think he had decided yet what to do with me, though I'm sure sooner or later he would have had to kill me . . . *has* to kill me." She paused a moment, sniffed quietly, and wiped a hand over her mouth.

"You see, I know too much. I have too much dirt on him and his operation. But I got lucky and climbed out a bathroom window when his men weren't looking. They chased me down the beach and out onto the old pier just down the beach from your condo. One of them was going to rape me because he said Jarvis just wanted me dead anyway. I bit him, and he started choking me, but I got loose and jumped into the ocean. I thought it was better to drown than to let them have me. I would be dead now if you hadn't found me."

Now the dam burst. Holly sobbed uncontrollably, drawing both her knees up to her chest and rocking side to side. "And maybe I'd be better off!" she moaned.

Bill gently put his arms around her, pulled her close to his chest, and held her for several minutes, until the crying stopped. Her hair smelled sweet. Another part of his memory that had been closed for a long time began to slowly reopen, allowing a small whiff of fresh air to swirl through a gray and musty room in his mind.

"OK, well . . ." Suddenly he felt awkward, as if he had violated her, forced her to do something she hadn't wanted to do. He cleared his throat. "Thank you for finally being honest with me."

They were silent a moment, then Bill continued. "So . . . the current situation is . . . Cookie is not here. That means either he took my car and left for Brazil, or one of your friends got to him. In either case, we can't stay here."

"They *aren't* my friends!" Holly nearly screamed at him.

"I'm sorry; it's a figure of speech." Properly chastised, he felt guilty for having said it a second time.

They got into Cookie's old Ford and headed back to the island. *Maybe Cookie stayed open late. Maybe there was a sudden rush of customers, maybe . . .* There were a thousand maybes, none of which fit into the carefully partitioned rooms of his engineering mind.

In the distant sky, a pink glow appeared as they drove east. It was much too early for sunrise, but instinctively he looked at his watch: 11:32. As the car crested the top of the bridge over the Intracoastal Waterway, they could see a fire glowing ahead of them in the distance, somewhere on the island.

"A whole block must be on fire," Holly said.

"Yes, and it looks like it's just about where my villa is." His stomach felt as if someone had just turned on the acid valve.

"Surely that's a coincidence . . . isn't it?"

Bill didn't reply.

The street was blocked by fire equipment, so he stopped the car about two blocks from the blaze. The overwhelmed volunteer fire department was making a desperate attempt to keep the flames from spreading to the adjacent buildings. The street was awash with locals who had been pulled from their sleep by the blast. Right now Jay Leno was speaking to a lot of empty living rooms on Carolina Beach. Bill stopped the car a half-block from the edge of the crowd.

"Holly, stay in the car and keep out of sight. I'm going to try to find out what happened," he said.

"I'm coming with you! I don't want to be alone . . . what if something happens to you out there?" she replied.

"Nothing's going to happen to me. I probably won't be recognized in the crowd, but you might be if any of Jarvis's goons are here. Anyway, with both of us together there is too much of a risk of being spotted."

He had Holly lie down on the floor of the old Ford and threw his jacket over her. Slowly, he got out of the car and merged into the crowd at the north end of the street. He could see his car, or what was left of it, in the parking space under his apartment. The building now sagged toward it since the supporting pilings had been blown away. Bill prayed silently that Cookie had not arrived before the building caught fire, but somehow he knew that prayer was probably too late.

Turning to a man near him, he said, "Do you know what happened?"

"Nope, just heard an explosion, an' when I ran out of my house over there," he replied as he gestured in the darkness toward his house, "I saw the building on fire. Nothing like this has ever happened here before. I just knew if they kept on building these dad-gum condos, something like this was gonna happen. I just knew it." He looked back at the inferno and said to no one in particular, "We ain't able to handle this kind of thing."

For a few more minutes Bill watched the futile attempts of the volunteers, most of whom were fishermen, mechanics, and store clerks. Then he made his way back to the car. Opening the door, he slid in. Holly was about to get up off the floor when he saw . . . no, rather he *felt*, the stare from a faceless shadow by a nearby telephone pole.

"Stay down!" he whispered coarsely, leaning down toward Holly. "We're being watched, I think." Bill was beginning to realize coming back to the island had been a substantial mistake.

He looked back in the direction of the pole, and the shadow was gone.

"I guess I'm seeing things, but anyway, stay down on the floor until we're off the island."

During the off-season, when the ferry shuts down at dusk, there is only one way off Carolina Island in the middle of the night—a wide, four-lane bridge arching gracefully over the Intracoastal Waterway, the bridge they had crossed twenty minutes earlier. As they neared it, the cars in front of them were stopped.

"What's the matter?" Holly whispered. "Why are we stopping?"

"I'm not sure. Just stay down in the shadows," he replied.

Bill pulled up behind a BMW, and a man with a flashlight came up to the car.

As Bill rolled the window down, the man said, "Sorry, you can't get over the bridge right now; the road's blocked. Darnedest thing, a truck jackknifed and spilled its whole load of lumber, boards, and nails everywhere. Probably be a couple of hours before we can get a lane opened up. Too bad . . . those firemen could have used some extra help with that fire." He casually shined his light into the backseat before walking on to the next car in line.

"Too bad," Bill mumbled under his breath. "Is this more of your boss's work?" he asked with disgust in his voice, mostly to hide his growing fear.

"Jarvis is not my boss! At least he hasn't been for the last two days. I quit, remember? Yes, I used to work for him, but . . . Oh well, forget it. You won't believe me anyway." No tears this time, not even anger, just a resigned tone to her voice.

"Right. I guess I should've said your *former* boss."

"Bill, if we're going to keep up this sparring, I'm getting out."

"You're right, no more sparring. I'm sorry, but I've never been in the middle of espionage, international intrigue, and attempted murder, so I'm a bit nervous. We need to think. We have to get off this island before we're spotted, and that means before sunrise. Do you have any ideas? I figure we have about three and a half hours, maybe four, at the most," he said, feeling foolish for having brought them back here in the first place.

"The ferry doesn't start running until eight in the morning, and anyway, to get to it we'd have to go right past Jarvis's compound."

"Great! You don't happen to own a boat, do you?" he asked with irony in his voice.

"No, but . . . Jarvis does; he has a boat down at the marina."

"Great, let's go and see if we can borrow it," Bill replied.

"He keeps the crew on it all the time," Holly said.

"Fine! You go to a phone, call him up and say, 'Uh, Jarvis, I know you're looking for me, but could I use your boat to get away from you?'" He eyed her sarcastically.

"You're crazy," Holly stated flatly.

"Maybe the only way to do this is to be a little crazy. Now, listen. Call Jarvis and tell him you're tired of running, that you're scared. Tell him you'll come back if he promises not to hurt you. Tell him you'll meet him at the fire," he said.

"What good will that do?" she asked.

"It will take most of his men to cover all the people at the fire. Maybe he'll pull the men off the boat to help find you." He spoke with a lot more confidence than he really had that the plan would work. The power steering on Cookie's old car whined as Bill slowly turned the car around, backing and turning repeatedly until the wheels were headed straight toward the median. Then he floored it. The front end bounced, and the undercarriage banged loudly as the muffler and frame dragged over the lane divider. It was all Bill could do to regain control as they headed back toward the center of the island.

He stopped the car within a half-block of the marina and switched the lights off. Well hidden behind a small bait shop, the two cast anxious glances up and down the deserted street, then cautiously crept around the end of the building. In the distance they could hear the dull roar from the fire. A phone booth was located beside a ticket office for sportfishing charters. The shadows of the surrounding buildings concealed them as they crossed to the phone, and Bill nervously watched as Holly dialed the number. The idea of them standing in the light provided by Ma Bell was contrary to his idea of good order and common sense. *Why do lights never go out when you want them to, and why do they never work when you need them? The universe is full of those deep philosophical questions,* Bill thought grimly.

The phone rang several times, and finally someone answered. "Let me talk to Jarvis," Holly said.

During the pause that followed, Bill thought he saw shadows moving in on them from every angle. The closest noise was the water lapping quietly at the sides of the many fishing boats docked at the town's marina. Bill had never experienced such fear.

Get a grip, buddy! he ordered himself.

There were no lights on the boat that Holly had pointed out as the one Jarvis owned. It was a forty-five-footer with a flying bridge, rigged for deep-sea fishing. He spotted the name on the transom and chuckled at the irony: *The Getaway.* He hoped the boat would live up to its name.

"Hello, Sid." The silence of the night was broken. "Listen . . . please listen for a minute, Sid, I . . . I'm tired . . . I can't run anymore. I want to talk . . . no, I mean it. Yes, I'll come back if . . . Sid, please promise you won't hurt me! . . . No, I ran away because . . . because I was afraid. I still love you, Sid. I don't know why, but I was afraid . . . I don't want you to hurt me, please." Holly was really pleading, and Bill wasn't sure she didn't mean it. Or else she was one great actress, and if she could act for Jarvis, was she acting for him too?

"No, I'll come to you . . . I'll meet you at the fire. I want other people around when we meet. No, I'm alone." She sounded less convincing as the conversation continued. "No . . . he helped me get out of the condo, but he didn't go along. . . . No, I said! I don't know who he was, just a man. . . . No, I don't know where he is. His condo's burning; maybe he's in the fire." He hoped the hesitancy in her voice would work to their advantage. If Jarvis thought she wasn't alone, maybe he would muster all his forces, including pulling the crew off of his boat.

"Thirty minutes? Yes, that will be fine. I can make it there by then. . . . I *said* I'd be there," Holly insisted. Then she added, "I'm sorry, Sid, I love you. . . ."

She carefully hung up the phone. Then they stepped back into the shadows and watched the boat for signs of activity.

A few minutes later a light came on inside the boat's cabin, then a second. Finally, after what seemed like an eternity, two men hurriedly left the dock, got into a small Toyota pickup truck parked nearby, and drove off.

After watching the men pull around the corner, Holly and Bill stepped from the darkness and hurried down the street toward the ramp leading to the boat dock.

"Uh, Bill, I know this might be a little late. And I know we are kind of making this up as we go, but I have two questions."

"What are they?"

"First, can you run one of these things? And second, how are we going to get it started?" Holly asked.

"If I can't drive one, then we've picked a lousy way to try and escape, now, haven't we?" he replied.

"And getting it started . . . ?"

"If the keys aren't there, I guess I'll have to hot-wire it, a vice commonly practiced by electrical engineers." He winked.

As they cautiously walked down the ramp leading to the dock, Bill stooped and picked up a piece of a broken two-by-four lying loose. It felt good to have something to hang on to, just in case a straggler had been left behind.

Moving slowly and quietly, they proceeded down to the dock and crouched low as they went past the portholes of *The Getaway*. The two steps up to the boat's deck were covered with rubber, but the deck was wet with the dew of the damp ocean air. With the gracefulness of a ballerina in a barnyard, he hopped onto the boat. The door to the deck house was unlocked. The men obviously had been in a big hurry when they left.

Bill stepped through the opening and paused to listen. There was no noise but the sound of the water lapping against the hull. Painstakingly, he descended the ladder to the lower level. The galley was to the right and a small navigation desk to the left. A single red navigation light shone over the chart table. The gauges indicated the boat was hooked to shore power, and the batteries were fully charged.

Just then he heard the noise of a toilet being flushed in the captain's cabin, aft of the chart desk. His heart began to pound so loudly he was afraid it could be heard through the eerie red silence.

Bill quickly stepped back into the galley so the passageway to the aft cabin was clear. He picked up a metal salt shaker from a rack above the stove and dropped it on the deck. The noise was deafening as it crashed to the floor and rolled away from him.

"What the—" The rest of the crewman's words were lost as the two-by-four crashed down on the back of his head and he crumpled to the floor. His blond hair started to glisten with a dark wetness in the red light of the cabin. A small scarlet rivulet began to snake slowly across the deck.

Without hesitation, Bill surveyed the aft cabin as well as the forward compartments of the boat and found them deserted.

"All clear, Holly," he called softly.

The young deck hand had not moved. Bill wondered if he had killed him; as he stooped over him, he heard the man moaning softly. Bill found a piece of rope and tied his hands and feet. Turning the light on in the cabin, he could see the coagulating blood in his blond hair.

Holly looked down the ladder and asked, "Did you kill him?"

"I hope not," Bill answered under his breath. Then he called in a half-whisper, "Unhook the shore power and untie the ropes from the dock."

As she hopped onto the dock, he sprang up the ladder to the flying bridge. The key was in the ignition. He gave it a quick turn, and the port engine roared to life, throwing a steamy foam up over the transom. Next the starboard engine reverberated with a deep throaty sound. Bill checked the gas gauges, noting they were full. Holly jumped back aboard the boat and climbed the ladder to the bridge as he put the boat into reverse and eased it out of the slip. The backward motion was checked as the starboard engine was switched into forward and he spun the wheel. The bow of the boat swung toward the channel between the rows of moored boats. Then he gently eased the other engine into forward, the vibration under his feet increasing as the power of the propellers began to tunnel into the water. The heart of the boat beat faster, its potency stirred as the black water behind the fantail turned white and foamy.

She leaned close to him and murmured, "We're going to make it, aren't we?"

"I certainly hope so," he answered. Then, only in his mind, he added, *I hope you're telling the truth, lady.*

Violating all the rules of navigation, Bill did not turn on the running lights or maintain a no-wake status inside the boundary buoys. Instead the boat headed out of the marina and shot into the channel between Carolina Island and the North Carolina shore. He laid the wheel hard to the right to enter the Intracoastal Waterway and headed north. In the distance he could see the buoy lights marking the channel. He aimed the bow toward the blinking light that signaled their path to freedom.

"Which way are we going?" Holly shouted over the wind.

"I hope we can head up the Cape Fear River to Wilmington, but we're going to give the island a wide berth," he replied. "I have a feeling when Jarvis finds out that you aren't coming to the meeting and deduces we borrowed his boat, he's going to be pretty mad."

The boat rounded the point at the northern end of the island. With the bow turned east toward the open sea, Bill envisioned the blockade-runners of the Civil War. Here, on this windswept region of the eastern shore, daring seamen had been eminently successful in thwarting the enemy. They had victoriously outrun and outsailed more Union ships than anywhere else in the South. Looking up into the dark sky, he wondered what the brave Confederate sailors had thought as they tried to avoid the Union ships that patrolled this region. With their memory in mind, he said a silent prayer that some of their success was still available. The thought also clouded his mind that at the bottom of this channel lay many hulls of the less fortunate ones, probably with the remains of their crews still inside.

With the bow now piercing the waves gracefully, he signaled for Holly to take the wheel.

"Hold this course while I check the map below," he said.

Holly took the wheel with some reluctance and eased back on the throttle. The dual power plants' low rumble and pulsating vibrations gave her a sensation of strength and security.

Heading toward the chart room, Bill observed on the eastern horizon a pink glow as the sun began its climb over the Atlantic. A nagging question haunted the recesses of his mind: *Once we get away from Jarvis, what then?*

• • •

"No, Mr. Jarvis. That's right, we can't find her anywhere. The men have covered the whole crowd. Over." The man spoke into the transmitter. "No sir. She has to be on the island; the truck is still blocking all the traffic, just like you figured. Over."

"Where is she? What kind of game is Holly playing with me?!" Jarvis's outrage was seething. He was not angered that Holly would have to be eliminated; it was the sloppiness of such a simple operation that infuriated him. Control, that was it; he had lost control, and the fact made him furious.

One woman, one simple, powerless woman. How could one woman create such a problem? When necessary, he had had whole villages eliminated, but look at the mess this had turned into. Why had he ever let himself get emotionally involved with her anyway? All these years he had just used women, considered them only a convenience. He had never had an emotional attachment to any of them—well, with one other notable exception. Until Holly, women were only a diversion, an object for entertainment, to be used at will and discarded. There had never been a problem before. Now, for the first time since Istanbul, he had let himself become emotionally involved with a woman, and it had caused nothing but trouble.

"James, get in here!" Jarvis yelled.

"Yes sir, Mr. Jarvis."

"Is there any other way to get off of this island that we haven't covered?" Jarvis asked. He wanted all the possibilities assessed as usual. Jarvis always had all of the angles and probabilities covered. He played life on his terms on his field. And he was always the victor.

"No, sir. The ferry doesn't start to run until eight A.M., and anyway, we have men down there. So unless she becomes a fish, I don't think there's any way she can leave," he replied. "She has to be holed up somewhere on the island."

"Unless . . . unless . . . someone is helping her," Jarvis mused.

The telephone rang.

"Hello, this is James. Okay. . . . Is that right? No, stay there. I'll get back to you." James hung up the phone.

"Who was that?" Jarvis asked.

"Uh, Brink . . . Brink, down at the boat." James paused. "I think . . . there's a good possibility that she *is* off the island after all, Mr. Jarvis," he said. "And I'll bet someone is helping her."

"Oh? What makes you think so?" Jarvis responded, raising his eyebrows slightly in an overt sign of disapproval.

"Brink said that your boat is missing from the marina. The crew just got back there, and it's gone. And I'll bet she didn't take it by herself," James said.

"Why wasn't the crew on the boat?" Jarvis fumed.

"You said to have every available man cover the fire so there would be no chance of her escape, sir."

"Holly's resourceful; what makes you think she didn't take it by herself?"

"When we sent the crew to the fire, they left one man on board. He had been drinking earlier. They figured he wouldn't be much help. Either he's helping her, or someone else is," James replied.

"As soon as it's light, I want the plane up, and I want that boat found. Do you understand?" Jarvis barked.

I wonder just how much Holly can prove? Jarvis thought to himself. *It really doesn't matter, but still, if she did happen to make it to the authorities, how much could she truly prove?*

7

DAY THREE:
AT SEA

The boat was pitching forward with a steady, pulsating rhythm. Bill went below. By now the man he had clubbed was awake and fighting his ropes.

"Whaddaya think you're doin'?" he demanded. Then, without waiting for an answer, he growled, "When I get loose from here, I'm gonna kill ya!" He spat out a torrent of vile language with all the vengeance he could muster.

Bill ignored his curses and switched on the light over the chart table. The eerie red glow of the navigation light gave the cabin a sinister quality. He flipped the switch on the overhead light, then blinked, squinted, and rubbed his eyes impulsively as its much brighter beam flooded the space. Coupled with the fatigue that had set in from too little sleep, the light almost blinded him.

Gradually his eyes adjusted, and he studied the map for several minutes. The cadence of the boat rushing forward brought a growing sensation of freedom. Suddenly, he was reminded why he and Sandy had loved the sea so much. They had enjoyed its sense of eternal freedom arising from its inability to be controlled or subdued.

This is no time to get sentimental, he thought, shaking off the memories. But the sudden thought of Sandy and remembering why he was in North Carolina sent a flood of emotions rushing over him. A sharp pain stabbed his stomach as if he had been pierced with an icicle. He could still see her walking down the airport corridor. The way her hair bounced as she hurried away. That final walk that had never ended for him. Bill stared at the map for several seconds without seeing anything. Finally he looked up.

"OK, mate. If you cooperate, I'll put you up in a bunk so you'll be more comfortable," he said.

"Don't do me any favors," the crewman snarled.

"Suit yourself. But I'll bet Jarvis doesn't give bonuses for discomfort," Bill replied, smiling at him.

He climbed the ladder up to the flying bridge and stopped on the top step. The sun was moving over the horizon, and the boat was heading straight for it. For a moment he gazed at the way Holly's hair, highlighted by the rising sun, was blowing back in the wind. She held her shoulders rigid as she clutched the steering wheel, which formed a partial oval frame of her slender silhouette and gave her a statuesque appearance.

Suddenly he felt very isolated from the world, and he longed for a woman to need him. *It is not good for man to live alone.*

The old verse echoed unexpectedly through his mind. It had been a long time since he'd set foot in a church or read a Bible. Not since he was a kid. He wasn't sure anymore if there really was a God, although he certainly prayed when he thought it might help some. But what kind of a God would have allowed his wife to die?

Bill quickly turned his attention away from such confusing thoughts, determining in his mind to deal with them in the future, and looked back at the fading coastline. A dark shadow of the tree-lined coast still held the eerie light of the fire, the smoke still visible in the southwest as a reminder of why they were out on the ocean this morning in a stolen boat. He watched the white wake fade from the stern of the boat in a patternless yet mysteriously ordered configuration. It seemed to be going nowhere, yet it was going somewhere. In many ways it resembled the two of them.

Holly turned and looked at Bill. "Are you OK?" she called over the noise of the wind.

"I'll take it now," he said. "Yeah . . . yeah, I'm OK."

"Where are we going?" Holly asked as she moved away from the wheel.

He stared at the compass. It still pointed due east.

"We'll go east until the island's out of sight, then turn south. If we cut by the south end of the island we can make the channel of the Cape Fear River up to Wilmington. Once we're in Wilmington we can ditch the boat and get out of North Carolina."

"I don't think that's a good idea."

"Oh? Why not?"

"Jarvis's house is on that end of the island. We'll have to go right past it."

"Well, it's the same path the old blockade-runners used. They had to go right past a Union fort with guns. If we can get there before we're spotted, I think we have half a chance," he shouted back at her. "By the way, does Jarvis have any shore batteries?"

Holly gave him a very condescending stare. She didn't seem to be in tune to his humor. "Just remember one thing, Bill."

"What's that?"

"The South lost the war!"

"No problem!" he shouted confidently. Then he thought to himself, *But that is a lot of IF'S, isn't it?*

For more than an hour they traveled in silence, lost in their own thoughts, before Bill started a slow turn to the south.

"Do you know the name of his house here?" Holly asked.

"What?" he yelled over the sound of the wind.

"Cape Fear Manor. It's a very appropriate name." She stared at the mansion standing arrogantly on the tip of the island. It seemed so small from that distance but no less fearsome.

The fishing boat moved easily now at ten knots in a very gentle, rolling sea. Had they been doing anything else but trying to escape with their lives, it would have been a perfect day to head out to sea.

The sunrise had given birth to a full day. The clouds were light except for the dense black smoke that rose like a furnace from hell where the apartment had been.

"There it is!" Holly yelled into his ear as she pointed with her finger.

"There what is?" Bill hollered back.

"Cape Fear Manor. That's it, the big white house."

A pair of binoculars hung beside the steering wheel console. He raised them to his eyes and saw a southern mansion with large Greek revival columns. Porches graced the lower and upper levels. The lower porch appeared to wind around both sides. There was a low white wall with black posts and some supporting lights that still blazed despite the daylight. It looked like a scene from *Gone with the Wind*.

The southern end of the island came into view off the starboard rail. The mound of dirt that made the wall of old Fort Fisher stood high on the edge of the island. Thinking again of the blockade-runners, Bill realized how protective those guns had been for them. They kept the Union navy's ships at bay while allowing the Confederate heroes to bring their cargo to the port upriver. How he wished they had some protection like that. Their run past the island and up the river today would be unprotected . . . and dangerous.

He eased the bow toward the red buoy marker that marked the channel to the river. The trees on the end of the island grew larger as they neared the shore. Bill tried to imagine what the blockade-runners of the Civil War must have felt when they made this same turn. Maybe they had felt the same as he did now. *And maybe . . .* he thought, *every generation and every man has a blockade to run in life.*

As they approached the mouth of the Cape Fear River, the

Southport Ferry and several fishing boats appeared, coming toward them. The tide was on its way in, and he had to throttle back some to decrease his wake so as not to draw attention to themselves. It was probably strange to see a fishing boat returning at that time of the morning. Bill hoped the boat would not be recognized by any of the locals.

"Go gag our friend down below," he ordered Holly. "Be careful. He's not real happy about us borrowing his boat. If he acts up, quiet him anyway you can. But if we have to pull into a dock, I don't want him drawing attention to us."

When Holly returned, they were well up the channel. Intermittent openings appeared in the tree-lined shore. The ferry and fishing boats were moving off into the distance behind them as they began their graceful swing into the river. An occasional fishing shack could be seen, nestled in the trees along the bank, as the river started its serpentine course from the ocean. In the distance, large cranes for unloading freighters thrust their robotic arms into the morning sky along the southern edge of the river. He began to feel they had a chance of evading Jarvis, whoever he was, and his mood began to brighten.

As the wind and the speed of the boat had decreased, the noise from the engines had settled into a low, synchronous vibration that could be felt more than heard. It was then that Bill became aware of a new sound . . . a menacing sound. Far away, yet threatening, it escalated slowly, conveying the notion that a large, roaring animal was approaching. Its low growl sounded a warning as a giant jungle cat does just before pouncing on its hapless prey. The sound grew louder, moving closer and closer. Then it hit him like the two-by-four he'd laid upon the mate's head.

"Does your boss, er, ex-boss, have an airplane?" he shouted.

As Bill turned around he saw the silhouette low on the horizon, a scant hundred feet above the water but moving rapidly up the channel they'd just left and heading straight for them. The plane was much too low to be anything other than a spotter plane.

"Yes, he has several," Holly gasped.

"Quick, get below. Maybe he hasn't recognized us yet." He urged Holly down the ladder, but the plane was over them and gone in a moment.

Inside the cabin it was much easier to talk. "I suppose it doesn't make any difference if they saw us; they'd probably recognize the boat anyway." He shrugged. "I guess it's time to go ashore."

They rounded a bend and saw a small cove lined with weeping willows dipping their slender branches into the water. Bill slowed the boat and eased it toward the bank. It stopped abruptly as the bow settled into the soft river mud about four feet from the bank. He shut down the engines.

With little effort Holly nimbly jumped to the shore from the bow of the boat. He threw her a rope, and she tied it to a tree.

"Just a minute!" he yelled.

Bill ran back in to search the cabin.

He paused by the crewman and checked his ropes. They were secure. The bound man glared at Bill with contempt in his eyes.

"Your friends should be along soon to let you go. I'm sorry I had to hit you." Bill stood looking at him for a minute, then shook his head and continued to scan the cabin. He wondered why he'd said that.

He didn't turn up a gun as he had hoped, but he found a fishing knife, a flare gun, and some flares. Bill had no idea what he'd do with the flares, but once in an old movie he had seen them used very effectively. Wrapping the items in a tablecloth, he joined Holly on the bank. Just then the plane made another sweep over the boat, this time coming back down the river. They ducked under the trees as they watched it head for the open ocean beyond the river's mouth.

Who is this man Jarvis? Bill wondered.

● ● ●

Nebraska, 1944

"Well, what's going to happen to Sidney now?" she asked.

"Edna! Don't talk in front of the boy," he responded.

Five-year-old Sidney Jarvis looked up at the strange adults with a questioning expression on his face.

"When's Mommy and Daddy coming back?" he said.

The adults looked at each other in horror, both afraid to speak.

"Mommy said she'd be back soon," he continued. "I want my mommy and daddy." He was scared and wanted to cry, though he wasn't sure why. All he knew was that late yesterday his parents had left him with Mr. and Mrs. Olsen while they went to Omaha to see some friends. He thought he remembered his mother saying they would be back the next night. Now it was dark out, and worse yet, everyone was acting strange and whispering around him. Just then there was a knock at the door.

"Reverend Thomas . . . oh, thank goodness you're here. We just don't know what to say to Sidney," Mrs. Olsen said.

"I came as soon as I got the message," Reverend Thomas replied.

"We just don't know what to tell the boy or what to do with him. Oh, this is just awful . . . ," Mrs. Olsen rambled.

"Come here, son," Reverend Thomas said.

Sidney slowly walked up to the tall man in a black suit with a funny white collar around his neck. He was fat, and the rolls of flesh in his neck hung over his collar in an odd sort of way. One massive hand held a black hat; the other lay gently on Sidney's shoulder as the preacher walked him over to a large chair. Reverend Thomas sat down and laid his hat aside. He put his hands around Sidney and lifted him effortlessly onto his knee. This still did not bring them eye to eye, so he leaned forward at the waist. As awesome as his size and appearance were, Sidney did not feel fear with this man. There was extreme kindness in his eyes. And with the innocence of a young child, he looked into those kind eyes.

"Sid." That was the first time anyone had used the shortened form of his name. "I'm Pastor Thomas," he said. "How old are you, son?"

"I'm five and a half, but I'll be six in June," Sid answered.

"That's good, Sid. You're old enough that I can talk to you man to man. Sometimes things happen in the world that we don't understand, Sid. One of those things is when young people go home to the Lord."

"What do you mean?" Sid asked.

"When people go to heaven to be with God," Reverend Thomas answered.

"I don't understand," Sid said, becoming more apprehensive about this conversation.

"Sid, your mom and dad were killed in a car wreck on their way back from Omaha today. They are now up in heaven with God. And that is a good thing. It's really the best thing, but it means they can't be down here with you," he answered.

Sid began to cry. He knew he had lost a very important part of his life.

On the day of the funeral, Sid still did not understand every-thing completely. He knew he was lonely, and he knew he wanted to lay his head on his mother's arm and listen to her read him a story. Instead of that, he was standing on the windswept hill out-side of town. The sky was gray, and the prairie grass was still brown from the long winter. There were two large holes in the ground with wooden boxes being lowered down into them. Someone said his mommy and daddy were in those boxes. Sid just wished he could be in the one with his mommy. A tear ran down his cheek, and a lump swelled up in his throat.

"The Lord is my shepherd . . . ," Reverend Thomas was saying.

Sid looked up as a light, cold mist began to fall. "Mommy, please come home. I'm lonely," he said out loud.

Muffled crying drifted across the desolate prairie.

For a few weeks after the funeral, he lived with the Olsens. It wasn't as good as living at home with his mom and dad, but there was a routine and Sid wasn't always lonely. One afternoon when the weather had turned warm, he was playing outside, glad not to be cooped up in the house. Wanting a ball from the small box of toys in his room, he skipped inside the house and headed up the stairs. As he walked into his room, he found Mrs. Olsen packing his suitcase.

When he asked where he was going, she said nothing. She carried his suitcase down to the car, Sid following. No one told him to follow, but he knew he was supposed to. They drove to an orphanage outside of Omaha, and Mr. Olsen took him in. There he met a lot of other boys who didn't have parents, and Sidney Jarvis began to learn what it meant to be alone.

They treated him kindly at the orphanage, but Sid's loneliness continued to grow until he learned to read. Suddenly, through books, he discovered a whole new world. There were knights and villains, ladies and kings. He read about faraway places and made new friends who never left him. Sid found he could escape the loneliness in books, and he began to read voraciously. When he was old enough for the Saturday movie matinee, another world opened to him, and Sidney E. Jarvis was on his way to high adventure.

Turkey, April 1966

"Hey, Lieutenant, where ya goin'?" The sergeant gave a toothy grin as he leaned on the dusty Jeep.

"Istanbul. I'm taking a few days off; gonna get a hotel room with a real bathtub and forget this hellhole." Lieutenant Jarvis laughed.

"Better be careful, Lieutenant. I hear the hotel rooms have hot and cold running maids as well as hot and cold running water," the sergeant chided.

For four months Sid Jarvis had been stationed in a communications station, another name for a listening post, near the Russian border. In that amount of time he had not been outside the camp's perimeter. Day after day the electronic gear swept the horizon over the Union of Soviet Socialist Republics. Day after day the soldiers recorded messages and contacts. Day after day was the same on the bleak northern perimeter of Turkey.

Finally, another officer had shown up, so now Jarvis could take some leave. Vietnam was using up most of the replacement officers, so getting R and R away from a noncombat station was at best difficult and usually impossible.

"Well, Sergeant, if I don't take some leave soon I'll end up losing some. And you know it's against army policy to lose leave," Jarvis said.

"Don't ya think ya should have a bodyguard down there in the big city?" the sergeant probed.

"I'll tell you what, Rod. All my life I've waited for a trip like this. It's going to be the trip of my life—and it's one I have to do alone. Maybe later we can take some leave together. But not now." Sid knew it was not a good idea to call the enlisted men by their first names. It could lead to undue familiarity. However, this was a special day, and he considered the sergeant his best and only friend at the small outpost.

"Well then, have a good time, sir," the sergeant said as Jarvis drove out of the camp. "Don't forget to come back!"

Sid Jarvis had dreamed of visiting places like Casablanca, Tripoli, and Istanbul ever since he'd seen his first Humphrey Bogart film as a kid. An exotic trip for a kid growing up in that orphanage on the outskirts of Omaha, Nebraska, was going across the river to Council Bluffs, Iowa.

He had enrolled in college and joined the ROTC program with the express idea of seeing the world. Now he was really on his way, headed toward a city of ancient history and intrigue, a city that had lived through the ages, where men of old, both famous and infamous, had lived and died as they tested their wit and skill. He was going to be a part of it, if only for a short seven-day leave.

As his Jeep bounced over the ruts that formed the trail from the outpost to the main road, he marveled at the countryside. So desolate, yet so beautiful in its own rugged way. The landscape had witnessed so much of the world's history. He wondered what stories these hills could tell. This was the land of Mount Ararat, where the ark of Noah had come to rest. It was from these very rocky slopes that civilization had begun to rebuild the world. He tried to imagine how it must have looked as Noah and his family descended down the mountain to a world wiped clean.

Sid thought about his assignment and concluded that the way things were going there would be no civilization to rebuild after the next devastation.

His mind wandered next to the stories of the Trojan wars, and he began to feel that Ulysses really had existed and had ridden chariots along this very rocky trail. He could almost hear the sound of Alexander the Great's army thundering by. Yes, this was the reason he had joined the army and volunteered to become a spy. He knew he would probably meet Bogart in one of the dingy bars of Istanbul. Even if he learned no secrets to bring back to the Allies in his World War II fantasies, he knew in reality this was where he belonged.

Istanbul bustled with activity. Its sights and smells were almost overpowering after Jarvis's four months in the deep desert. With difficulty, he found the hotel where he had booked a reservation.

"May I help you?" the Turkish desk clerk asked in perfect English.

"I have a reservation: Jarvis, Sidney Jarvis," he replied.

"Yes, Mr. Jarvis. You will be in room 407. It overlooks the courtyard and has a magnificent view of the straits," the clerk said with pride in his voice.

An elevator that looked like a birdcage took him to the fourth floor. The corridor was dimly lit, thickly carpeted, and smelled foreign. Sid loved each new attack on his senses. Even his room held intrigue. It was more than he had imagined during the long winter nights of dreaming as he grew up in Nebraska. The bed was brass with mosquito netting hanging from the ceiling, and an ornate double door, as high as the ceiling, led onto a small porch enclosed with a black wrought-iron railing. The bathroom had porcelain fixtures, including a bathtub large enough to swim in that stood on legs resembling the paws of a lion.

After a long hot bath, a shave, and a change into civilian clothing, Sid was ready to see the city. Stopping at the front desk, he asked, "Where's a good place to eat—not too expensive and no American food?"

"What you want is the Cafe Istiklal. Turn left at the second street; it sits on the edge of the cliff overlooking the Bosporus Straits. I'm sure you will enjoy it," the clerk replied. "Tell them Amin recommended it."

Sid found the cafe poised on the hill as promised. What the desk clerk hadn't told him about was its next-door neighbor, the famous spice bazaar. He stood at the entrance and watched women come and go, buying spices, cheese, and staples for their families. Finally, hunger won the battle with his curiosity, and he entered the restaurant.

● ● ●

"Are you sure that's the one?" The woman gestured toward the man sitting alone at the edge of the patio.

"Yes, he's the one Blaine fingered for me. Blaine's had him under surveillance since he left the desert," Michael Jardeen answered. "Remember, it has to look natural and not like a—"

She cut him off with a cold icy stare from the depths of her black Asian eyes. "Don't try to tell me my business. You're paying for a service, and you will get what you pay for." She walked calmly away from him without another comment.

Now that he was in Istanbul, Sid was living out every fantasy he'd had as a kid. Here he sat overlooking the straits, not understanding a word that was spoken around him. But that made it all the more exciting. Suddenly the most beautiful woman he had ever seen approached the table. She wasn't tall, maybe just over five feet two. She had long, straight black hair that set off her dark olive skin. A crimson dress was positioned low on her slight shoulders, its skirt swaying sensuously around her narrow hips as she walked toward him. Her dark eyes snapped as she spoke to him.

"May I sit down?" she said.

"I've been in the desert too long. I'm hallucinating!" he replied.

"Pardon me? I don't understand," she responded.

"Uh . . . excuse me. What did you say?" Sid stammered as he rose from his chair.

"May I sit down?" she repeated.

"Yes, certainly. Please do." He fumbled as he helped her with the chair.

"You're an American, aren't you?" she began.

"Yes. Does it show that badly?" he answered.

"Not at all. You look like you belong here."

"Oh, how is that?" he queried, enjoying the stroke to his ego.

"You don't look like the typical tourist. How long have you been in Istanbul?"

"I got in this afternoon, and it's my first visit. If I'm not a typical tourist, what does one look like?"

"Striped Bermuda shorts and a camera, with a slightly overweight wife, I guess." She laughed.

"Well, I left my shorts and camera at my room back at the Angora," he responded.

"And the wife?"

"None . . . overweight or otherwise." He stared at her

haunting eyes. "I'm curious; why did you pick my table?" Now his mood was more serious.

She smiled; her eyes sparkled. "I saw you sitting alone, and I thought it did not speak well for our Turkish hospitality. And besides, it is very unlucky for a stranger to have to watch a sunset such as this alone in Istanbul." She gracefully waved her arm toward the setting sun, a diamond bracelet dangling from her wrist.

"I'm Sid Jarvis from Omaha, Nebraska," he said.

"My name is Maria Clifton from Istanbul," she replied.

"Strange, you don't look like a Maria Clifton from Istanbul. I would think you'd have a name I couldn't begin to say properly, much less spell," Sid remarked.

"My father was English. My mother had a name like you refer to."

"Could I get you something to eat or drink?"

"That would be very kind of you. I would like a little white wine," she said.

Sid held up his hand and motioned for a waiter.

"I think your story about not wanting a stranger to watch the sunset alone is romantic, but why, Mrs. Clifton, did you come to my table?"

"It isn't Mrs. Clifton, it's Miss, and please call me Maria." Her eyes sparkled in the light of the candle on the table. "Well, the truth is, I was supposed to have dinner here with an old friend. He called and left a message that he couldn't come. I hate to eat alone in a restaurant and had no reason to go home. And you were the only single man in here. Personally, I thought a story about a Turkish tradition sounded very good," she said quietly, her eyes laughing. "However, if you don't want me to stay . . ." She started to get up.

"No, please, don't go. I'm sorry," he apologized. "I guess I was just taken off guard."

"Well, let's talk of Turkish nights and start over. I'm Maria. Welcome to Istanbul." She smiled seductively.

They sat at the table long after sunset while Maria told Sid about the sights of the city and what it was like to live in Istanbul. As she got up to leave, Sid said, "Would you like to show me around your city sometime? I'll be in town for a week."

"I would like that very much. I'll call for you at your hotel tomorrow afternoon. Say, around three o'clock?" Maria said.

● ● ●

The next day was bright and as pleasant a spring day as Sid could remember. The heat rising from the cobblestone streets had no effect on him while he wandered through the Grand Bazaar, where merchants sold everything from live animals to dressed meat and vegetables. Baskets and porcelain sprang up from every cart, and Persian rugs of indescribable color and intricacy graced the walls of each shop. Sid wandered from street to street, swept along by the tide of humanity that lived on this edge of the world. He did wonder momentarily how his life might have been different if his parents had lived.

Just before three, he returned to his hotel to meet Maria. He sat nervously in the lobby, which was ornately decorated with Greek and Roman scenes and the ever-present fans whirling gently overhead like a flock of silent birds.

"Maria, I'm glad to see you," Sid said. "I was a little afraid you might not come."

"Now, why would you think that?" she replied.

"I was afraid I had just dreamed you up last night and that you really weren't real," he answered.

Maria was wearing a simple flowered skirt and a white blouse with sandals and no nylons. Sid took all of this in as a man is prone to do when confronted by a beautiful woman. She looked real enough to him in the daylight.

"Well, Mr. Sid Jarvis from Omaha, Nebraska, if you take my hand you'll find I am real and so is Istanbul. Are you ready to see it?" She laughed.

As they drove through the streets, Maria kept up a running narrative about the spectacle and the history of this city that had stood at the crossroads of mankind for so long. Sid paid attention to all she said. As she drove, her skirt rode up her leg, exposing her thigh above her knee, another fact that didn't escape Sid's attention.

"Did you know the city has had a number of different names, depending on who happened to control it at the time?" Maria said.

"I know the Persians called it Deri-Seadet, the Italians called it Cospoli, and the Greeks called it Constantinopolis," Sid replied.

"You seem to know quite a lot about our country."

"When I was younger, I read all I could about Turkey and most of the other countries around the Mediterranean Sea."

They crossed the Gallate Bridge and ventured into the old part of the city, called Stamboul. Holding hands, they walked along the high walls that separate Stamboul from the rest of the metropolis. They enjoyed lunch in a small cafe where, twenty-five years earlier Nazi and Allied agents had stared at each other from tables across the room.

Later they visited a museum that had served as a palace during the Ottoman Empire, and they toured the famed Castle of Seven Towers, which had been the official house of execution during one period of history. Sid's fascination with the city never waned, and his fascination with Maria steadily grew.

As they walked through a courtyard, Maria asked, "Would you like to come over to my house tomorrow?"

"Certainly! Where is it?"

"It is on the other side of the straits. If you take the ferry over, I'll meet you at the landing," Maria said.

"That's fine for tomorrow, but what about tonight?" Sid responded.

"I'm afraid I have a prior engagement, but that will only make tomorrow sweeter," she said.

"Sweetness should be savored, never just consumed. Like a good wine, it should never be rushed." He took her in his arms and pulled her close to him, looking deeply into the black pools of her eyes. Her lips parted slightly, and he felt the warmth of her embrace as they kissed longingly under the colonnade of the palace and said good-night.

• • •

The next morning when Sid Jarvis awoke, Maria was gone—not that she had been there physically. She was gone from the beautiful dream he had been having. Sid lay alone in the massive bed in his hotel room, listening to the sounds of the street below his open window. The dream melted from his thoughts but not the anticipation of his next rendezvous with Maria.

After breakfast he crossed the Bosporus Straits on the ferry. He stood on the top deck and savored the salty air as it blew past him. As the boat approached the dock, he could see her standing at the back of the crowd awaiting its arrival. He thought of the dream and wondered if . . . if the superstitious people of the world were right. Would his dream come true?

"I'm glad you decided to come," she said.

"Wild horses couldn't have kept me away. You look beautiful today," he remarked.

"So do you," she said.

"Men aren't supposed to look beautiful," he said, laughing.

They joined hands for the walk to her car as if the touching of their hands could renew the magic generated in their parting the day before.

Riding up to her villa, Sid was unprepared for its spectacular, stark beauty of Eastern architecture with a modern accent set against the rugged hillside. In some respects, the villa seemed to be a medieval castle that time had forgotten. Yet in other respects, it was straight out of the twentieth century. Its gleaming whitewashed walls reflected the full force of the sun so brilliantly that it was difficult to look at them, even wearing sunglasses.

She ushered him into a room with couches and chairs arranged to take advantage of the magnificent panoramic view of Istanbul and the straits afforded by the large picture window. Maria excused herself, and Sid wandered around the room admiring the furniture, pictures, and pottery. As he examined a small urn on a table, he felt more intrigued than ever with Eastern culture. The house reminded him of one of the museums they had visited the previous day.

Maria returned, and as Sid watched her walk, she seemed to flow through the room. She was wearing a white cotton dress with a tight collar, highlighting the dark skin of her neck and face. The thin fabric did nothing to hide the shapeliness of her legs as she passed in front of the window.

"Would you like something to drink?" Maria asked.

"Please. Seven and seven, if you have it," Sid said.

"I have something very close," Maria answered. She turned and said something in Turkish to a servant, who quickly and quietly departed.

Taking Sid by the arm, she led him up the stairs to a large hall with several heavy oak doors. They walked to the far door and opened it. Inside was what seemed to Sid like another complete house. A moderate-sized sitting room was connected to the bedroom by way of an arch. A thin veil of fabric served as a door that fluttered delicately in the soft breeze. Sid watched as Maria glided through the curtain and disappeared behind the arch. She stopped and turned back toward him, her hair flowing across her shoulders as she tilted her head and smiled.

"It's much cooler in here during the heat of the day."

"We should certainly avoid the heat as much as possible," he answered as he walked up to her and pulled her to him. He rested his hand on the nape of her neck and kissed her gently on the lips. As they kissed, he unbuttoned the buttons on the back of her dress. She let the fabric slide down her arms, and with nothing to restrain it, the dress fell unencumbered to the floor at her feet.

Sid lifted her effortlessly and carried her to the bed.

"I want you more than I have ever wanted anyone," he breathed.

"I know, and you shall have me. But you said yesterday that sweetness should be savored, not rushed. Let's relish the moment," she whispered as she unbuttoned his shirt.

Her embrace was warm and exciting, and they burned with an unrestrained craving that has driven man and woman from the beginning of time. The heat of the Mediterranean afternoon waned as the setting sun's gentle rays lingered in the afterglow of their desire.

• • •

When he awoke it was dark, and there were no lights in the room. Maria was gone from the bed, but he knew this time his memories of her had not been a dream. He could see thousands of stars and a new moon through the open window. A gentle breeze from the straits drifted into the room. He stood at the open window, looking out into the night sky and enjoying the fresh smell of the ocean. Suddenly, he felt Maria behind him; she put her arms around his waist, her body pressed tightly against his.

"And this," she said softly, "is how to enjoy a Turkish night."

"I love you," Sid said, turning to kiss her. He kissed her again and again on the mouth and neck.

"Don't talk and don't think, Sid. Just take me back to bed," she replied, and he was only too happy to comply.

• • •

The next morning they took a drive through the country north of the Bosporus Straits. The roads were winding and narrow, but Maria expertly handled the red Porsche convertible. Late in the morning she parked on a narrow lane, and they walked down through the woods to a small meadow. Sheep could be seen grazing in the valley below. The azure sky was infrequently broken by small puffs of white clouds. It made Sid imagine that wool had been plucked from the sheep and slung into the heavens.

"It's a perfect place for a picnic, isn't it?"

"Absolutely perfect. I know. I've been here before," Sid replied.

She looked startled. "You've been here before? I thought you said you'd never been to Istanbul before."

"I've been here many times . . . in one of my books."

"One of your books?" Maria questioned.

"I told you I grew up in an orphanage in Nebraska."

"Yes," she responded.

"Well, I spent most of my free time reading books about this part of the world—history, adventure, even romance. It didn't matter. I just wanted to know about it and be a part of it." He paused and looked out over the valley, his eyes shining.

"And now you are . . . you have also conquered a part of this world, just like one of your books," she said as she leaned over and kissed him lightly on the lips.

They ate bread and cheese and drank wine while they lay in the warm sunshine, talking for hours.

Late in the afternoon Maria and Sid started back toward her villa. Instead of turning in, she drove straight to the ferry.

"Sid . . ." Her voice held a very sober tone. "I want you to take the ferry—*now*. Go back to your room, get your things, and get out of Istanbul. Return to your base . . . I don't care where you go. Just go."

"Why? I don't understand," he protested.

"Just do as I say. Go now, and don't ever try to see me again. *Ever!*"

He looked at her with bewilderment on his face. "I'm sorry. What did I do? I don't understand!" His voice betrayed both his hurt male pride and his anger. "For the last twenty-four hours we have had nothing but fun. I made love to you; don't you remember that? Or doesn't it count for anything?"

"Just do as I say!" Her voice was curt and cold.

"What's the matter? You already have an ol' man or something? Is that it? I'm not going to let it drop like this. Maybe you don't owe me an explanation, but I want one!"

"Sid, you had an adventure—an Arabian night, if you want to call it that, just . . . just let it end here." Her jaw was clenched with emotion.

Maria looked down at the steering wheel. She paused for several seconds, then with no hint of emotion, she said, "Yes, Sid, I already have an 'ol' man or something,' as you call it. *Now get out!*" The emphasis in her voice was somewhere between a plea and an order. She pushed his back as he got out of the car, then she sped away.

Sid stood staring at the receding car in utter amazement. Her mood had changed in an instant. What had gone wrong? He walked down the ramp and started to board the waiting ferry, then stopped. *NO!* he thought. *I can't leave like this.* He had to have an explanation. Quickly, he turned around and headed up the street toward Maria's house. As he neared the gate he noticed two cars in the driveway, neither of them Maria's red Porsche. He knocked on the door. Maria opened it and stared at him in shock.

"Who's there, Maria?" a man's voice with an American accent echoed from the interior. Michael Jardeen quickly got up from his chair.

Before she could answer, the man was at her side.

"Well, this must be Sid, the one you've told me so much about. Bring him in, I was hoping I would get a chance to meet him. Come in, come in," he said as he took Sid's arm and escorted him into the house.

Maria looked at Sid in bewilderment and pain. Reluctantly she took Sid's hand, guiding him out of Michael's grasp. Together they walked out onto the patio. Much to Sid's surprise, there was a second American sitting at a small table. As Sid and Maria approached, the second man stood up.

"Randolph, this is Sid Jarvis, the man I told you I met the other day at the cafe. Mr. Jarvis, this is Randolph Blaine. His assistant, Michael Jardeen, you met at the door," Maria said, her face solemn.

Greetings were exchanged, and Sid was disappointed he wasn't the only American at Maria's house.

"What do you do, Mr. Jarvis?" Blaine asked.

"I'm in the army," he replied.

"Are you in Istanbul on business?" Jardeen asked.

"No, I'm on leave for a few days, just seeing the sights," Sid replied.

The conversation was light and friendly; Maria's servants quietly moved among the gathering, serving drinks on silver trays. The primary subject was the beauty and history of the country, especially Istanbul.

Gradually Sid felt the voices starting to run together. The world about him seemed to be slowing and weaving as if he were on a very sluggish roller coaster. Faces, pictures, and furniture started to blur in his vision.

"Are you OK, Sid?" Jardeen asked.

"I don't know . . ." The words were difficult to form. "I don't . . . think I . . . feel . . . too . . ." His sentence was unfinished as he slumped out of his chair onto the patio floor.

"Michael, it isn't right with this one. Please! There must be some other way," Maria said. "I can't go through with it, not with him. . . . Please!"

"Maria, you aren't going to start getting sentimental on us now, are you? We've waited too long to find just the right person and start setting this plan up," Jardeen said. "We now have the beginning of the perfect system for the profitable sharing of information in the world to come. Right, Randolph?"

Randolph looked the other way and did not acknowledge Jardeen's comment.

Two of Maria's servants carried Sid's unconscious body to the basement of the house.

"All right, Randolph, I'll take care of things here. You go back to the hotel and clear out Jarvis's room. Wipe it down so there are no fingerprints. He has to disappear, clean and completely, until we are ready for him to reappear."

"What are you going to do with him?" Blaine asked.

"If you don't know, we'll probably all be better off," Jardeen replied curtly. "Just do as you're told and say all the right things when you're asked. We won't meet again until Mr. Jarvis resurfaces. Do you understand?"

"Yes, I know," Blaine answered and hurriedly left Maria's villa.

Blaine drove quickly to the landing and boarded the next ferry. He swiftly walked to the upper deck, elbowed his way to the front railing, then stood, staring at the skyline of Istanbul the entire ride across. He never looked back at the silhouette of Maria's house perched high on the hills behind.

He used the hotel's service entrance, then took the stairs to Jarvis's room to avoid being seen. The gloomy stairwell and poorly lighted back halls made the excursion simple. The purpose for Blaine's visit was uncomplicated, and the task was easy. Blaine used Sid's key to open the door, then gathered up all his belongings, cleaned the room thoroughly of fingerprints, and left. His exit through the same dingy corridors was unobserved and effortless.

He caught a taxi several blocks from the hotel and went straight to the airport. A standby ticket had been purchased some days before. He had no problem getting a seat on the plane and was relaxing on the BOAC flight to London by six o'clock. Once in England, he disposed of the worldly remnants of one Lt. Sid Jarvis in an incinerator in the basement of the rented house where he was staying. Clothes, passport, papers, and all other identification were burned completely. As the flames swallowed up his belongings,

Sidney Jarvis of Nebraska vanished completely from the face of the earth.

• • •

After Blaine had left Maria's house, Jardeen walked down to the basement. Maria's two servants were watching over Sid Jarvis, who was laid out on the floor. Jardeen calmly shut the door then pulled a 9 mm model 951 Beretta pistol from under his coat and attached a silencer to it. He took careful aim between Sid's eyes and pulled the trigger. Almost noiselessly, the gun jumped in Jardeen's hand.

Maria's servants looked on without emotion at the blood running across the floor from the back of Sid's head where the bullet had shattered the skull. They were so engrossed in watching it coagulate into a thick, lavalike river they did not see Jardeen change the aim of his pistol. The gun jumped two more times, and the man on the right grabbed his chest in horror as he was slammed back against the wall. Blood oozed out between his fingers as his heart emptied itself of its contents from the holes made by the projectiles. The second man tried to run but had only taken two steps sideways before Jardeen's accurate aim sent a piece of lead through the left side of his skull. As the bullet exited the right side it left an evil, twisted artwork of the man's life spattered on the gray stucco wall of the basement. The man was dead even before his body landed on the floor in a grotesquely twisted position.

Jardeen looked around the small room. The air was filled with the smell of spent gunpowder mixed with the sickening, sweet stench of fresh blood. He smiled, knowing this was the first step in the quest for fame and fortune he'd planned for so many years.

He closed the door behind him before climbing the stairs.

"Is everything all right?" Maria asked when she saw him emerge from the basement.

"No trouble," he replied.

"What will you do with him?" Maria questioned.

"Let's not worry about that right now. There is something I need to talk about with you. You were going to double-cross me, weren't you? You were taking him to the ferry instead of bringing him here. That was not nice, Maria."

"I . . . just couldn't . . . ," she stammered.

"No one crosses me, Maria. Never. Do you understand?" Jardeen snapped. "Besides, you have something else I want."

Maria was now angry, her eyes flashing. "You tried that once before, you're not—"

The rest of the thought was lost as Jardeen slapped her.

"You have a very nice business with your contacts in the U.S. and Russia. And I know the profits have been good," Jardeen said.

"How do you dare say such a thing?" Maria screamed.

"Maria, don't play dumb with me. Remember, I work for the Company. It's our job to know those things. How do you think I knew you were the right one to seduce him and bring him out here? How do you think I knew Sid Jarvis was the one we had been waiting for? I had to have someone who could disappear and have no human on earth ever come looking for him. He also had to have a top-secret clearance. Otherwise, after he is officially dead and forgotten, I might have trouble assuming his identity. You see, when a dead man starts selling the things I'm going to sell, it will be almost impossible to track him. Now, what I need, Maria, are your contacts," Jardeen said softly.

"Just why should I give you these contacts, as you call them, if they even exist?" Maria asked.

"Because it is the only way you will leave this house alive," Jardeen calmly answered.

Maria jumped up from the chair, but Jardeen grabbed her before she could get away from him. He hit her hard on the mouth, and she felt the salty, hot taste of blood as two teeth fell out and she experienced the agony of a broken mandible. She wanted to scream, but strangely her teeth did not fit together anymore. Jardeen dragged her into the living room and held her in front of a large mirror. She was shocked to see the ashen color of her face, her beautiful olive complexion now a pale gray. He then pulled a knife out of his pocket, the silver edge gleaming as it snapped into position at the touch of a small button. He laid the blade along her right cheek just below the eye. She almost felt as if she were in a dream, watching the scene from afar, as shock slowly engulfed her being.

"Now, Maria, the list of contacts. If I cut your face across the cheek I'll cut the facial nerve. That's the one that lets you smile; it's also the nerve that keeps you from drooling out of your mouth constantly. Would you like to walk around drooling all the time, Maria?" Jardeen said coldly.

"Please! Please! Help!" she screamed as best she could.

"No use calling for help, Maria. They're all dead," Jardeen replied.

A look of resignation came over her. Her shoulders drooped, and she let her head sag.

"You win. The list is in the safe in my bedroom," she said.

"I know I win. I always win!" Jardeen said emphatically.

Jardeen dragged her up to the bedroom and let go of her. Maria staggered over to a wall safe behind a picture and opened it. She pulled out a small, dark blue book and handed it to Jardeen. He eagerly thumbed through it. Maria had collapsed onto the bed and was sobbing softly. The blood was now dried at the corner of her mouth, and as the terror of the situation wore off, the pain in her broken jaw was becoming unbearable.

"Help me, please," she begged.

"Sure, like you always help your competition," Jardeen replied as he walked over to her.

Maria's eyes dilated with fear as he calmly took out the Beretta. He shot her in the side of the head. The bullet severed the midbrain from the cerebral cortex, and she died instantly. Jardeen then wrapped her body in a sheet and carried her to the basement.

He piled the four corpses into a stack and went to his car. Returning to the basement, he soaked the bodies thoroughly with gasoline, then poured more of it throughout the basement as well as up the stairs and throughout the first floor of Maria's villa.

Next he retrieved two kilos of heroin from his car and carried them to a small gardener's shed about fifty yards from the main house. There he pried off a loose board from the wall, carefully hid the drugs behind it, and replaced the board, being sure the pry marks were visible.

He returned to the house and threw a match into the hallway. The gasoline ignited with a rush. The fire quickly devoured the liquid, racing down the stairs and exploding with a thunderous roar as the flames embraced the vapor.

He then got into his car and drove away from the house, away from Istanbul. There was no one along the road as he wound his way down the mountain. The back highways were empty, and he saw no one the rest of the day as he drove toward Greece.

He who lives by the sword will probably die by the sword—but not you, Jardeen thought, smiling to himself.

• • •

The newspaper account of the murders parroted the police report. The fire and murders at Clifton Villa were probably linked to a smuggling and black market problem. Maria Clifton had long been suspected of smuggling and dealing in drugs. From a moderate amount of heroin found in the garden shed, it was believed this was a drug deal gone awry. The bodies were burned beyond recognition, but there was one female, thought to be Maria Clifton, and three males, probably her employees or possibly smugglers. The police spent little time investigating the murders. Such activity was not an unusual event in this part of the world.

Lt. Sidney Jarvis never returned to his post and was declared a deserter after thirty days. Seven years later the army could find no trace of him, and he was declared dead. There was no one to notify. As a deserter there was no serviceman's life insurance. The only thing slightly out of the ordinary was a single request regarding his death, or presumed death, by someone in the spy organization commonly known as "the Company."

Cape Fear River

"Cape Fear base . . . Cape Fear base . . . this is aerial one. Over," the pilot said.

"Aerial one, this is Cape Fear base. Over," came the immediate reply.

"I took a second pass over the boat. It stopped along the bank about one and a half miles up from the mouth of the river just west of the south tip of Carolina Island. I'm sure it's Mr. Jarvis's boat, but I don't see any activity on it. Do you want me to circle it? Over," the pilot asked.

"Aerial one, wait one, over." Static cracked in the pilot's ears as he slowed his air speed another notch. "Aerial one, do you see anyone on the ground? Over."

"Cape Fear base, the trees are too thick. You couldn't see a yellow caterpillar tractor from up here. Over."

"Aerial one, this is Cape Fear base. Negative, return to the airport. Ya did good. Over." The radio clicked off.

8

MICHAEL JARDEEN

It had been a long and frustrating night for Sid Jarvis, and the sound of the phone ringing was both ominous and welcome.

"This is Jarvis," he said, his voice indisputably edgy.

"Mr. Jarvis, we spotted the boat. It's tied up along the bank of the Cape Fear River about a mile and a half from the mouth." Jarvis welcomed the news. He stood holding the phone and looking out over the beach at the clear skies and the rising sun. He knew his night of apprehension was over.

Now, like a military operation, it was time to mop up. He would deal with Holly, soon. Jarvis had spent most of his life in a paramilitary organization, and his organization was similar. He liked it that way. It gave a good, clean chain of command to handle problem situations like this.

"Get some men up there now! And no mistakes this time. Do you understand?" Jarvis was starting to feel as if he was in control again. His dark mood began to dissipate, the fatigue from the sleepless night lifted as the morning sun lifts the fog from the land.

• • •

"Mr. Jarvis," James said as he opened the door. "Mr. Jarvis, they're here. Do you want me to bring them in?"

"Not today. I forgot they were coming." He paced back and forth in front of the window. *But I guess I don't have any choice,* he thought to himself. Jarvis paused and studied a sea gull that had landed on the fence outside his window. *Oh, how I'd like to be like that bird!* Then after a moment's hesitation he said, "Never mind, James. Yes, please *do* bring them in. And bring a pot of coffee and some Danish for all of us."

Jarvis still had a business to run, even if there was an occasional complication. And, he reasoned, it would be good to have an alibi if Holly and whomever she was with met with an unfortunate accident. Obviously, someone was helping her. Maybe she convinced the deck hand on the boat to help her get off the island. If he would, Holly could certainly offer what every young drifter might want in payment for a favor like that. Even without money and credit cards, he was sure she could be resourceful, and every woman he had ever known would sell what she had in a pinch. He smiled to himself at that thought.

"Mr. Jarvis, I'm Glen, Glen Johns from Wolfson International. I'm glad you could see us today on such short notice." Three men walked into the study. The one who introduced himself as Glen Johns was obviously American. The other two wore western suits but were without a doubt from eastern Europe or the Middle East, not Arabic but somewhere north of the desert. Neither one offered his name, nor his hand.

They sat down in the large leather chairs around a coffee table that featured a globe in the center. Jarvis had often remarked that his organization was like the wooden table encircling the globe. The world would spin within the confines he wanted. The coffee service was brought in and served. After James left, the four men looked at one another.

"When can we expect delivery on the item?" Johns asked.

"We have already shipped most of the electronic hardware we discussed at our last meeting," Jarvis answered.

"When do my clients, whom these gentlemen represent"—he gestured toward the silent men across from him—"get delivery on the entire package, including Tel-Ray?"

"There's a slight delay on the final shipment of that package," Jarvis answered.

"What's the problem, Jarvis?" Glen Johns asked. "You told us you would have the complete specs on the Tel-Ray project by now. My clients are getting anxious to complete it. They have timetables that require that equipment. They don't like to be kept waiting." The threat in his voice was not veiled.

"Well . . . there has been, as you say, a slight problem. But it will be resolved shortly," Jarvis said in an arrogant manner.

"A problem. That sounds like sloppy work to me. A great amount of money has been spent for the initial system. And you know the system is of no use to anyone without the Tel-Ray component. My clients don't like to deal with people who do sloppy work. Now I can tell you that either this matter is concluded shortly or my clients will take their business elsewhere. You will no longer figure in the competition. Do I make myself clear?" Johns said.

Jarvis listened quietly; with a calculated slowness in his movements, he braced his hands on the arms of the leather chair and leaned forward, his upper body stretched over the globe. He hissed through almost-clenched teeth, "Don't think you can walk in here and start threatening me!" Jarvis paused. "There is no one else who has any chance of ever producing that piece of equipment or the programs to run it. So tell your clients to sit back and wait . . . or forget the deal altogether! They deal with me, or they deal with no one."

Jarvis rose from his chair and stood over Johns, glaring down at him. "Do I make *myself* clear?" Jarvis knew there was no one else they could turn to for this information; they would have to do things his way. He could feel the cold, emotionless stare of the silent pair as they watched his display of machismo. He knew from his past experience with these people that they were very unforgiving of failure. However, he was sure he was in the driver's seat. He smiled to himself. These arrogant jackasses were no match for him. Still, there was always something about the coldness of their piercing black eyes that made him uncomfortable.

Glen Johns stood up. His two partners did likewise.

"Jarvis, you above all people should know that my clients don't threaten. They just expect results, and as you already know, they pay well for those results. They have been up-front with you and made the payments on time. Now they expect you to keep your end of the arrangement." Without waiting for a reply, the three men turned and left the room.

Sure, I know your clients don't threaten—they expect results, Jarvis thought. "What they don't realize," he said aloud to himself, "is that I've been dealing with people like them for years."

Jarvis walked out of the study and onto the broad porch that encompassed three sides of Cape Fear Manor. There was a bite in the wind as it blew in from the Atlantic Ocean. It reminded him of another time when there had been a problem and he had produced results.

• • •

"So, Michael, now you're ready for the field," the mentor said as they walked to his car. "We've taught you everything we can here at the 'Farm.' The rest you will learn out there." He let his hand sweep across the horizon. "You joined the Company after a good tour in 'Nam. What you learned in the jungle will serve you well as long as you remember you have never left the jungle." With that he turned and walked away.

Michael Jardeen was now a trained field agent for the Central Intelligence Agency, ready to take on the aggressor the Soviet

Union. He'd majored in political pcience in college, joined the marines, and was given a rank of second lieutenant and sent to Vietnam after intelligence training.

In 'Nam Michael distinguished himself as a masterful tactician in the art of ambush, and he displayed a ruthlessness unsurpassed in his unit. If you wanted someone taken out quickly and efficiently, you gave the assignment to Michael. He should have had two or three times the decorations on his uniform by the time his Marine Corps duty ended, but too many of his operations were not reportable because of their severity and political incorrectness. But that never bothered Lieutenant Michael Jardeen. He learned early on that he liked to be in control, he liked the power of life and death, and he liked killing. He also learned during those days that a good operation could only be conducted by an organization that had tight command and control, and the chain of command was the most important part.

Jardeen was posted to Naples, Italy, for his first assignment. He was a political analyst at the U.S. Consulate, which fit well with his degree from college. In the evenings he began an infiltration of the Italian Communist Party cell. It was there he became friendly with Roberto and Christiana. They were brother and sister who shared an intense dedication to the communist beliefs and the party.

Over a period of time Michael and Christiana became more than friends. Their love affair introduced a major problem when Michael was ordered to eliminate Roberto. Over time Roberto had become politically active in Naples and was likely to win a seat in the Italian government at the next election. That was not felt to be in the best interests of the Company. Michael was given the assignment in April. He had ample opportunity but procrastinated for the first time in his life. On the fifth day of May he had a visit from his mentor, Lindsey.

"Michael, good to see you again," his old mentor said as he walked into the room with his hand extended.

"Always a pleasure, but what brings you to Italy? I thought you'd never leave Virginia again," Michael answered.

"Let's go for a walk."

They walked out onto the street and headed toward a small park about a block from the consulate, rarely used except on weekends. Right now it was deserted.

"Michael, they sent me to tell you it's taking too long." Lindsey smiled a beguiling smile.

"There have been problems," Michael answered.

"Problems. You were brought into the community because it was assumed you never had problems." Lindsey laughed.

"Well, the right opportunity . . . ," Michael started to explain.

"Jardeen, you are paid for results. And just because you happen to be making it with the target's sister is not a concern of the Company." He looked out at the bay. Across the water, Capri could be seen as a bluish haze. It was a beautiful island of which Lindsey had many memories from his earlier years when he was a field agent like Jardeen. "You see, Michael, in our business we have no room for circumstances, for problems, for situations. There is nothing wrong with an affair with the enemy. Sometimes it may be a good cover or just good business. However, when it is time to complete a task, you can't let personal feelings interfere. What we do is too big, too important." He paused. "It is time for a solution." He stood up and started to walk away. "The next time you see me, Michael, you won't."

The mentor slowly walked toward a waiting car at the end of the block.

Michael got the message. There would be no more problems. No more procrastination.

Late that night he stood in the shadows outside Roberto and Christiana's house. There was a light in her bedroom window. He knocked on the door.

"Buonasera, Michael!" Christiana said as she gave him a kiss.

"Is Roberto home?" Michael asked.

"Yes, but it's late. Can't it wait until tomorrow?" she asked.

"No, I must see him now." He looked at her with the cold, steely eyes of a jungle assassin. "Now."

She wrinkled her forehead as she let go of her lover and looked at the deadness reflecting from the depths of his eyes. This was a side of Michael she had not experienced before. His laughter and zest were gone, vanished. In their place was an intensity that produced a feeling of fear deep in her heart. She pushed away from him and started up the stairs to Roberto's bedroom.

Michael slipped the Walther 9 mm short *polizei pistole* from the shoulder holster. He had installed a silencer before he left his apartment. Quietly following Christiana to the staircase, he raised it to the back of her head and pulled the trigger. A small pop was the only sound as he swiftly dispatched her. As she fell he caught her to eliminate any noise from alerting Roberto. He laid her gently down on the floor and looked at the beautiful face that had been so full of life only seconds before. A momentary pang of guilt ran through his veins, chased away by the threat from his mentor.

Michael Jardeen then slowly and carefully climbed the stairs, opened the door, and assassinated Roberto as he lay sleeping. He turned off the lights in the house and quietly left by the back door. No one saw him come or go.

The newspapers reported the Mafia had been involved in the killing of Roberto and Christiana to prevent Roberto's possible election. Suspects were brought in for questioning, but no one was ever charged with the double homicide.

Several days later Michael Jardeen was transferred to a new posting in Istanbul, Turkey, where he met Randolph Blaine. Blaine was then working for the Department of Defense at the embassy in Istanbul. They became instant friends. It was at the posting in Turkey when he realized the pay and benefits from the Company were pennies compared to what could be made at the right time with the right organization. He began to plan for a more profitable future. "Who knows? The Cold War might not last forever," he once told Blaine as he explained their prospects for a lucrative partnership.

● ● ●

Thinking back on that part of his life always helped put the present in perspective for Michael Jardeen—now known as Sidney Jarvis.

Jarvis walked back into his study and sat down in the high-backed leather chair. It had taken several minutes before the rage and fear had calmed. Thinking of the past always helped. He poured a cup of coffee, propped his feet up on the desk, and stared out the window.

"Just a small problem that will be solved shortly," he said out loud to no one. Then he thought, *It's too bad she has to die.* He had just started to grow fond of her. If she had married him, there would have been no problem. *Oh well, I can't let myself get sentimental over one woman.* He smiled to himself. *I never have before.* Probably the only reason he had considered marrying her was to enhance his image as a respectable businessman. In all likelihood, he would have tired of her in a year or so anyway. But all that was irrelevant now.

9

THE ROAD OUT

They walked away from the river for several minutes. A primitive path took them between the tall, thin Carolina coastal pines. The accumulation of years of fallen needles were soft underfoot. Eventually they came to a dirt road.

"Which way?" Holly asked.

"Let's try downriver. They might not expect us to double back," Bill responded.

The road was dusty, and there was litter from discarded tires and refrigerators, but the cool fall day made walking easy. They were silent, both lost in their own thoughts as much as they felt lost in the North Carolina countryside. About fifteen minutes later, Bill was starting to feel more confident. Then he heard two men talking around the next bend in the road. He grabbed Holly's hand and pulled her off the road and into the trees. They crouched down in a small thicket. Once again his heart began to race, and his hands became clammy. He strained to hear what was being said.

"You cut over to the river and work your way up along the bank. I'll go about a mile up and work my way down. The plane said the boat was between those two points. Keep your eyes open.

Remember, Jarvis wants the girl and whoever is helping her, even if you have to take them out on the spot."

"Yeah, Dean, I know my job," the second voice replied.

"I'll check in with you every ten minutes on the radio."

A car started up and drove slowly up the road. The sun glared from the car's polished surface as it passed within a few feet of them. The driver, a man in his early twenties, was scrutinizing the edge of the woods as he drove. They waited in the thicket a few more minutes and then began to move parallel to the road in the cover of the trees. The tangled underbrush made for painfully slow going, and Bill suspected that reinforcements were on the way. Just as he was considering moving back onto the road, they came to a dirt bike path leading away from the river.

"Come on!" He took Holly's hand and started to run. As they ran down the path away from the river, he could hear more cars on the road. They ran until neither had any breath left and then began to walk with purpose.

It seemed like an eternity, but it was only about thirty minutes later when the silence of the North Carolina pines was broken by the sound of steady traffic up ahead. Carefully, Bill and Holly approached the edge of the protective forest and peered out on a small crossroads town bustling with the usual morning activity. On their side of the road was a service station shaped like a Spanish hacienda with gasoline pumps left over from the fifties. At one time the building had been white, but that was years ago; now it was somewhere between dirty gray and pitch black. When the pumps were new, the station might have been the main attraction in town. Maybe back then there had been something in this town to attract visitors. Unfortunately, time had long since passed it by. Across the road was a small diner with a large clientele whose pickups filled the parking lot. Several ramshackle houses ringed the two businesses, making the crossroads complete in a depressing sort of way.

"Let's go in that gas station and clean up a bit," Bill said, looking at Holly. She had dirt on her cheek. His eyes scanned her appreciatively. She was beautiful, even with dirt on her face.

"I can't put on a new face, but I'd like to wash this one," she responded. "You wouldn't have a comb, would you?" Holly asked. Bill reached into his pocket and pulled out a small black comb.

They approached the station from the back and slipped unseen into the bathrooms. Bill tried the hot water; it didn't work. However, the cold water helped wash the fog from his head. A hard night without sleep was starting to take its toll.

Somewhat more refreshed and, he hoped, looking more respectable, he stepped out beside the gas station and stood looking at the small diner across the street. His stomach was starting to tell him it had been a long time since he'd indulged it.

"There. How do I look?" Holly asked as she stepped out of the women's room.

Even without makeup she looked terrific. She had combed her hair and allowed it to drop around her shoulders in a natural and graceful spiral that gave her face a much softer appearance. Her smile was contagious.

"You look wonderful, Holly," he said with a little more enthusiasm than he'd intended.

She detected his embarrassment. "You men are all alike." She laughed.

"You hungry?" he asked, trying to change the subject quickly.

"Starved," she replied.

"I know this great restaurant." He chuckled, pointing across the street to the diner.

The atmosphere seemed lighter as they crossed the street, but the traffic speeding by also left Bill with a naked feeling—he had revealed too much about his interest in this woman. What would Sandy think if she knew? He was very glad when they were inside the diner. They took a booth where they could watch the door.

"Hi, folks, what'll ya have?" the waitress asked.

"Two eggs over easy, toast, and coffee," Holly said without hesitation.

"Coffee and a roll for me," Bill replied.

"A good breakfast is the most important meal of the day," Holly said, trying to sound authoritarian.

"The way things are going, I'm not sure I'll live long enough for it to make any difference," he responded. Besides, food just hadn't held too much interest for him since Sandy died.

"I'm sorry I got you into this," Holly said. "You can just get up and walk out now, Bill. You've done enough."

"And then what is your plan?" he asked. "Where are you going to go? Who are you going to get to help you? What are you going to use for money?" He paused. "Anyway, in the last twenty-four hours, I've committed assault and battery, grand larceny, and who knows what else." Then he looked around to see if anyone had heard him. Bill was sure guilt was written all over his face.

"I don't know," she replied. "I don't know." She looked down at the table as if she didn't want to see what the answers to those questions were.

"Leaving you is not an option right now. What we need is transportation," he said, thinking out loud.

"Transportation to where?"

"Who knows? First, transportation. Then we'll figure out where we want to go."

The food arrived, and they ate in silence. Nothing was coming to mind, and a darkening depression was descending upon both of them. The rain cloud named Jarvis had started to dim this cloudless day. Always in the movies a great plan suddenly occurs to the hero, but at the moment this hero couldn't think of a thing.

"I know we can't stay around here, but honestly, I don't have anywhere to go," Holly said.

"What we need is some time. There is an answer to everything, given the time to work out the problems," Bill said, thinking out loud.

"Does every problem have a solution?" Holly queried.

"Well, they all have up to now," Bill replied with more optimism than he had felt in many months.

"I'll make you a deal. If I can get us transportation, you have to decide where to go." Holly smiled. "Deal?"

"Not a problem. We would go to the airport at Wilmington. From there, the world is ours," Bill replied.

Holly sat staring out the window for several minutes, then suddenly she turned to him and said, "Pay the bill and meet me outside."

She was up and out the door of the diner before he could say a word. He left a tip and walked to the register.

"That'll be four-fifty," the waitress said. "Was everything all right?" Then, without waiting for an answer she said, "Y'all come back now, hear?"

Bill met Holly outside.

"I got us a ride to the airport!" she said excitedly.

"How? Where?" he stammered.

"That guy in the gravel truck at the edge of the parking lot. I told him I was running away from my husband with you. He agreed to take us that far. He said he'd take us out toward I-95 if we wanted."

"No, I think the airport will be just fine," Bill answered.

As they walked to the truck, she grabbed his arm and held him close to emphasize that they were lovers.

"I told him my husband beat me. Well, it's almost the truth." She laughed.

The truck bounced and belched out of the parking lot as the three of them sat in an uneasy silence. The North Carolina countryside slid slowly by as they avoided eye contact. Finally the driver said, "Ain't none of my business, but how come y'all don't have a car? I know ya don't live around the truck stop."

Holly looked at Bill with a look that said, *This one's on you.* Bill fumbled a chewing-gum package from his pocket before replying. "We had a car but had to leave it on the island last night. You heard about the fire, and the truck that was wrecked on the bridge. We had to walk or face her ol' man."

"Y'all walked from Pleasure Island? That's one heck of a walk." He sounded doubtful.

"No, we hitchhiked most of the way. What did you think about the fire?" Bill tried to change the subject.

"That must have been some kind of a burn! We could see the sky light up clear over to our place."

The explanation seemed to at least temporarily satisfy the trucker's curiosity. *In a way, it's not really a complete lie*, Bill thought.

The ride to the airport took about an hour and was uncomfortable, but Bill felt safer than he had for the last twenty-four hours. The driver stopped in front of the terminal at the far end of the building.

"Hey, buddy, thanks for the lift," Bill said.

"No problem. I just hope whatever you two's runnin' from don't catch ya," he replied. Obviously, the story didn't wash completely.

They got out of the truck and had started toward the building when Bill saw two men watching the crowd intensely. He wondered if they were police or more of Jarvis's thugs. Holly was waving at the departing gravel truck as the men turned to look at Bill and Holly. Suddenly Bill grabbed Holly and kissed her. She resisted at first then relaxed and responded to him. When Bill opened his eyes, the men were gone.

"They have the airport covered," he said quietly, whispering into her ear as he nuzzled her nose. "Go into the ladies' room and wait fifteen minutes, then walk into the long-term parking lot like you're going to your car." His voice said *No questions*, and she didn't ask any.

Fifteen minutes later, as Holly walked out into the middle of the parking lot, Bill pulled up in a rented car and pushed the door open.

"Get in and duck down!"

She slid into the car and immediately crouched onto the floor of the passenger's side. Bill looked down, and their eyes met for an instant. Hers said thanks; he was not sure what his said.

"Where are we going?"

"How about to the police?" Bill replied.

"No . . . we can't!"

"And why not?" he demanded. "It's my opinion that when someone is trying to kill you, that's the best place to go."

"Just how are we going to prove they're trying to kill us? You yourself said we *stole* Jarvis's boat. And you beat up his deck hand. Jarvis is a respectable businessman down here. At best, they won't believe us, and we'll probably get locked up for grand larceny. At the worst, they might hand us over to Jarvis." She sounded convincing. "This whole thing would be our word against his, and we don't look too believable right now, Bill."

"OK, fine. Then we're going to my place. We can find someone there who will believe us. I know I can count on my boss," he responded.

"Bill, I'm sorry I got you into this. You should have left me on the beach."

"Well, first off, I couldn't have left you on the beach, and second, well, I'm not sorry, and third, stop saying you're sorry," he replied.

They drove along in silence for some time, trying to make some sense out of what had happened over the last forty-eight hours. Finally Holly said, "I really don't know very much about my rescuer. Tell me about yourself."

"There isn't much of a story. I'm just an average knight on a white horse."

"Oh, I don't believe that. As a damsel in quality distress, I wouldn't be rescued by just an average knight, nor would he own an average white horse." She laughed. "I know you have to be a high-quality knight."

There was an awkward moment of silence between them.

"OK, I work for a company called Tel-Ex. It's a communication research group that handles mostly defense contracts. It's one of the beltway bandit companies preying off the government. I do some research there," Bill said.

"Tel-Ex?"

"Have you heard of it?" he asked.

"Jarvis has done business with that company."

"That's hard to believe," Bill responded.

"What about Mrs. Chandler?" she asked, trying to avoid a confrontation.

"I'm a widower. My wife died . . . last year."

"I'm sorry," Holly responded. She paused a moment and then asked, "Do you have any children?"

"No. My wife was . . . well, we had just found out she was pregnant when she was . . . when she died." The words came out hard, and the emotion welled up in his throat. He had not been able to say those words since it had happened. But relating the story to Holly seemed to have a purging effect. She listened sympathetically without comment as Bill told her of their life before London and of his life since. After that, they were both quiet for some time. Eventually Holly fell asleep with her head against the door of the car.

Bill reached the limits of his endurance at Richmond and pulled off I-95 at a Holiday Inn. He checked them into the last room the motel had left. He was too exhausted to look for another motel.

He returned to the car, "They only have one room left . . . and I said that would be OK. I'm sorry."

"I'm not," she replied.

While Holly went into the bathroom to freshen up, Bill collapsed onto the bed without even undressing. When she emerged, he was snoring.

Bill slept better than he had for a year. When he awoke it was dark, and Holly was resting in the recliner, looking at him.

"I'm hungry," he said.

"You slept soundly," she replied. "I hope you don't mind, but while you were asleep, I took your credit cards and went shopping."

Several shopping bags lay on the dresser. Then he noticed she was wearing some new clothes. She had on a long-sleeved blue-green blouse with a collar that framed her face. It was tucked into a pair of belted khaki pants. She had also purchased some makeup and had flawlessly applied it to accentuate her high cheekbones and slightly prominent lips.

"I hope you bought me a razor," he said, rubbing a two-day growth of beard.

She produced not only a razor but a new shirt, slacks, a full shaving kit, underwear, and socks.

"I had to guess at some of the sizes. I hope they fit," Holly mused.

He looked up, smiled, and said, "You are most definitely the most expensive damsel in distress I've ever rescued."

"Yes, well, I had no trouble using your credit cards, so you must be a white knight with good credit," she retorted.

Bill staggered into the bathroom and looked in the mirror. His eyes had dark circles under them, and his beard was longer than he could ever remember. A murky fog had settled over most of his brain, and it seemed like he should be waking from a bad dream any moment.

The water in the shower was hot, and though it created a white haze in the bathroom, it cleared the one in his head. He dried off and wiped the mirror so he would not cut his throat when he shaved. He wrapped the towel around his waist and began to attack the grisly stubble on his face.

The door of the bathroom opened as Holly walked in. Bill turned from the mirror to look at her. He knew this was not the time to say anything. She gazed at him for a minute and then wrapped her arms around his chest and held herself close to him. Some of the shaving cream rubbed onto the top of her hair.

After a long moment he jested, "Hey! Can't a man have a little privacy when he shaves?"

She pressed her face against his damp chest and said, "I just couldn't be alone. Don't say anything. Just hold me . . . please."

He laid the razor down and tenderly held her in his arms. The moment was a peaceful interlude in the midst of a tempest. Slowly she relaxed her arms, and he let her back away. Neither of them said anything. She sat down on the edge of the tub and watched him shave.

Following a meal in the coffee shop, they both felt like different people. They walked back to their room holding hands. Once inside he put his arms around her and held her close. As she laid her head on his shoulder, Bill stared up at the ceiling, listening to her breathing.

"Oh, Bill. I'm so confused and scared."

"Now, don't worry. We'll get this worked out," he responded while thinking to himself, *Men are supposed to always say something reassuring; our fathers teach us that. It's expected.* But in truth he was scared to death.

As he felt the warmth of her close to his body, he wondered to himself just what it was that they were really trying to work out. This whole Jarvis situation seemed like a nightmare, something unreal that couldn't be happening.

Her body was soft and delicate against his, and he had the yearning to make love to her. He sensed intuitively that she wouldn't resist, but he knew it wouldn't be right. He would be taking advantage of her fear, not giving and taking from her love. His life with Sandy had taught him what true love was. He had no desire to spoil the memory of their marriage by falling into an affair with a woman he'd found on the beach. He hardly knew Holly!

As he struggled with his feelings of rightness concerning this beautiful woman beside him, there began within him an awakening of long-neglected emotions—his need to love and be loved by another human being, his desire for the intimacy of two bodies becoming one. They were the first such feelings he'd had since London. *Blasted morals!* he thought with growing frustration. Why did he have to care so much? But then the realization dawned that if he didn't have a conscience, where would he be in life? *When morals get in the way, then I guess they're doing their job.* He remembered his mother telling him that. He smiled to himself.

"Let's not complicate this any more than it is for the present," he said gently, holding her away from him and looking deeply into her eyes. But inwardly, he felt real joy in wanting a woman again. Though he couldn't tell Holly, several times Bill had imagined her without clothes, locked in a passionate embrace with him.

He motioned for her to take the bed for the night, while he grabbed a pillow and blanket and curled up in the recliner. *No sense in tempting fate,* he decided, and they both slept soundly until morning.

10

DAY FOUR:
POSITIVE IDENTIFICATION

Bill awoke first in the morning and went out to get some coffee. When he got back to the room, Holly was coming out of the bathroom.

"You're famous, and I'm dead," he said.

"What are you talking about?" she replied.

He held up a newspaper. The headline read, "Woman Sought in Death of Scientist." Below the headline was a picture of Holly and a smaller picture of the burned-out condo and Bill's rental car. The article went on to say that the body found in the car was believed to be William Chandler, Ph.D., though positive identification was pending a check of dental records.

"I guess that's why Cookie never showed up at his house," he said sadly.

"Oh, Bill! Poor Cookie . . . Bill, I told you Jarvis is a powerful man. Now what am I going to do?" Holly appeared shaken.

"Well, it won't be long until it's not just you but it will be *us* they'll be looking for—as soon as they find out that the body in the car is not me," he replied.

When they checked out of the motel, he wondered if the clerk had read the paper that morning and would recognize the name on the credit card. Bill felt only temporarily safe as they headed north up I-95 toward Washington. He'd made up the license plate number on the registration card so it would be harder to spot them on the crowded roadway.

"I hope we can make D.C. before we're recognized," he said, thinking out loud. "I suspect the police will check the rental car agencies soon enough."

"Do you have any great plan yet?" Holly asked.

"I have a friend with some connections who may be able to help us," Bill said but offered no more explanation. Holly didn't ask any questions.

Tension in the car was high, but the road from Richmond to Washington was so crowded they were relatively safe. At the next exit past the Quantico Marine Corps base, Bill pulled into a gas station and went to the phone. After dialing, the phone seemed to ring for an eternity before it was finally picked up. Without waiting for the traditional salutation, he said, "Ken—oh, hi, Sally. Is Ken there?" he asked. "Yes . . . it's me. Yes, I know I'm supposed to be dead, but I'm not. Now calm down, and please let me talk to Ken."

"Ken?" he said into the phone.

"Is that you, Bill? What . . . where . . . ? Who in the world was killed in your car?" he stammered.

"We need to talk but not on the phone," Bill said. "I need your help. I need a friend right now, and I can't come to your house. It wouldn't be safe for you or me. Meet me at the Vietnam Memorial. The woman is with me. Ken, you just have to trust me for a little while. Come alone in about an hour. And, Ken, as my friend, please don't talk to anyone—I mean *anyone*—until we meet. Please!" he said desperately.

"OK, Bill, you have my word . . . until we meet."

Bill hung up the phone and went back to the car.

There was enough traffic that they blended inconspicuously

into the rush of tourists and bureaucrats that threatens Washington with gridlock every day. They crossed the Fourteenth Street Bridge, found a parking spot several blocks from the river, and parked the car. It was early, but the crush of tourists had already taken most of the available parking, forcing them to walk several blocks farther than Bill wanted. Being out on the street, he felt like an endangered species, sort of like a rabbit on the first day of hunting season.

They crossed onto the Mall behind the Lincoln Memorial. Bill took a circuitous route around the memorial, taking the time to go up the steps. He didn't know for sure how to spot a tail, but he kept glancing back anyway. They stood at the foot of the statue and looked up at the face of the man who had saved the nation a hundred years ago. Somehow Lincoln had been able to pull off a very difficult situation.

"Mr. Lincoln, where are you when we need you?" Bill muttered.

"Did you say something?" Holly asked.

"Uh, no . . . just thinking out loud," he replied.

Walking up the path through the trees to the Vietnam Memorial, he hoped they looked like tourists. Ten minutes later, FBI agent Ken Jenkins walked into view. Fortunately, there were no other people around the entrance to the Wall. Ken saw them at the top of the walkway and sprinted toward them.

"Bill, what is going on?" Ken demanded.

"Ken, this is Holly James," Bill said.

"Yes, I recognize you from the picture. You're supposed to have killed Bill," he responded. "I guess the news story was wrong."

"Sit down, Ken, and listen," Bill said.

Slowly, he began to recount the last three days, beginning with his finding Holly on the beach.

"Ken, you're the only one I know in the FBI," Bill said. "We need your help."

Holly turned white and jumped to her feet. "Bill, you . . . you traitor! I trusted you, and you've turned me in!" She was almost screaming.

"Holly!" he shouted, grabbing her by the shoulders. "Settle down! We need help! Ken is the only person I know and trust right now. Do you have any better ideas?" He held on to Holly as if he were afraid she was going to run off.

"I'm not going anywhere," she said angrily, shaking herself loose from his grasp.

"Bill, Holly, I don't want to interrupt any lovers' spats, but all of this doesn't make a lot of sense. You do know Ed Harris is dead, don't you?"

Ken's words hit Bill like a slap in the face. "What? How?" he stammered.

"Accident. He fell overboard from a boat while he was fishing. Must have gotten caught in the prop. It took two days to identify him; he was pretty messed up. I'm surprised you didn't know. It happened just off Wilmington close to where you were . . . uh . . . where you were supposedly killed," Ken replied. "Bill, just what in the world is going on?"

Several birds suddenly flew from a nearby tree with a startlingly screeching sound as his mind furiously tried to comprehend what was happening. Bill nervously looked around.

"Let's walk," he suggested.

They slowly walked toward the reflecting pool, Holly sandwiched between them. The water in the pool reflected the gray autumn sky. A chilled breeze was beginning to kick up.

"This man . . . Ed, I think you said, Ed Harris, who was killed . . . did you know him, Bill?" Holly asked, having regained control of herself.

"He was my boss and best friend at Tel-Ex," he replied.

"There was a man visiting Jarvis two days before you found me on the beach. Later I heard one of the men saying Jarvis wasn't very happy because the guest had not brought the information he was supposed to. They said Jarvis was going to use some leverage on him. I assumed it was just a routine business deal," Holly said.

Bill pulled a picture out of his billfold. It showed Ed and his wife, Ann, with Sandy and him at a ski slope in Vermont three years earlier.

"Did you see this visitor?" Ken asked Holly.

"Yes, just for a few minutes when he first got there," she replied.

As she looked at the picture, she said excitedly, "That's the man. That was the visitor last week. In fact, now that I think about it . . . he has visited several times over the last six months."

"Holly, are you sure?" Bill questioned.

"Yes . . . yes, Bill, I'm positive. He came down for meetings several times, starting in the spring."

Ken and Bill looked at each other in disbelief at what they had just heard.

11

TRAPPED

Mr. Jarvis, we got some information," the man said, shifting uncomfortably from side to side.

"Well, what is it?" Jarvis demanded.

"She's traveling with a man. They're using William Chandler's credit cards—he's the man who died in the fire at the villa," the messenger stated. "They rented a car at the Wilmington airport, then spent the night at a Holiday Inn in Richmond and bought some new clothes there. Best guess is they're heading for Washington."

"Okay, so let's assume she's probably gotten to Washington by now," Jarvis thought out loud. "Now where will she go? They're using Chandler's credit cards. . . . If Chandler was killed, who's helping her?"

Jarvis paused. He needed to think. "If Chandler was killed . . . what if . . . what if Chandler *wasn't* killed? They haven't gotten a positive ID on the body from the fire yet." Jarvis slowly paced back and forth in front of his desk. He stopped and picked up a small brass cannon and studied it for several minutes, rotating it deliberately in his hand.

Pivoting slowly to face the messenger, he said, "Now, listen.

Find out all you can about Chandler—where he lives and works, his family, what kind of a dog he has. I want to know everything, even what he likes for breakfast . . . and find out quickly." He envisioned the trap beginning to close around Holly like a noose.

She's caused me a lot of trouble and expense, he thought. *I will enjoy her removal.*

Jarvis looked thoughtfully out the window at the ocean. A storm had passed, and the water was a beautiful royal blue. He could almost feel the chill in the air coming through the window. Fall was his favorite season, and Cape Fear was his favorite place on earth. He felt good.

Two hours later, another man came into the study. "Mr. Jarvis?"

"Yes, what is it?" Jarvis responded.

"If Chandler is the one helping her, we've hit the jackpot," the man said excitedly.

"Why is that?" Jarvis said.

"William J. Chandler, forty-one, Ph.D. in electrical engineering from MIT," the man read from the paper in his hand. "His main interest, his doctorate, was in the area of instant communications. He's a widower. His wife was accidentally killed in a bombing in London thirteen months ago, probably by the IRA. He lives in Derwood, Maryland, just outside of D.C. And get this: He's the head of research for Tel-Ex, Inc., and believed to be the primary researcher on the Tel-Ray project. It's his work that Harris was peddling. He's the one we need to complete our deal with the current client."

Jarvis stared intently at the walnut-paneled wall and bookcases. "If Harris had been more cooperative, he would still be alive, and we would have Dr. Chandler's work in our hands! However, it may just work out for the best anyway," Jarvis said, slamming his fist on the desk.

"Now, listen!" he said. "Let's have some coordination this time. Get a team to Chandler's house and to Tel-Ex. I want him and

Holly, and I want them alive. I will supervise this myself. If they arrive before I get there, just keep them under surveillance. Don't try to take them. Dr. Chandler has the information we need. And I'll want to personally take care of dear Holly. She is going to regret the day she was born," Jarvis vowed. "Have the plane ready. I'll be ready to leave for Washington within the hour. I'll stay at the Potomac house—we'll take them both there when we get them. When the time is right, Dr. Chandler will give me what I want, and so will Holly."

"Mr. Jarvis, the car is ready now."

"Thank you, James," Jarvis said with a smile.

As the car drove past the burned-out villa on its way to the airport, Jarvis smiled. *I don't know who died in that fire, but I'll bet it wasn't Dr. Chandler.* He leaned back against the seat and closed his eyes. *I think I'll take some time off after this affair; maybe I'll go to the Med and have a vacation.*

Washington, D.C.

The wind was escalating its efforts to blow away any remaining hint of Indian summer. Leaves swirled across the Mall in small whirlpools as Ken, Bill, and Holly walked. Ken was questioning Holly again.

"This Jarvis, you say he has an import-export business. Where is his office?"

"He has offices in New York, Washington, and San Francisco, but mostly he works out of his house in North Carolina. He calls it Cape Fear Manor. It's in Carolina Beach," Holly answered.

"I don't know for sure if I believe you or not. By all rights, I should just take you both in right now, but . . ." He paused.

"But what?" Holly demanded.

"I've known Bill here for a long time. I don't like what you're telling me, but if he believes you, then I have to check it out. I'm going to the bureau and see what we know about him." Ken

139

turned to Bill and asked, "Do you and Holly have somewhere to stay out of sight?"

"If they think I'm dead we can go to my place," he replied. "I need to get some things anyway. I can't afford to keep traveling the way I have been."

Holly laughed and Bill winked knowingly at her, thinking of the two times in the last three days when one of them had gone shopping for new clothes.

"Where do you want to meet?" Bill asked Ken.

"Let's meet at the Farragut North Metro station, Silver Spring side, in eight hours. That will be six o'clock," Ken said.

They walked as far as the Museum of Natural History together. Ken left the Mall first. Holly and Bill watched him cross the street, then they turned around and walked to a park bench nearby and sat down.

"Ken must be a good friend of yours, huh?" she asked.

Bill had been staring into space, not really focusing on anything. For several seconds he said nothing, then he noticed Holly waiting for his reply. "I'm sorry. You said something, but I didn't get it."

"I said Ken must be a good friend of yours."

"I guess you could say that. . . ." He paused.

She waited in silence before asking finally, "Well, are you going to tell me, or do I have to charm it out of you?"

"Depending on how you plan to charm me, I might wait," he joked. "No, really, Ken and I do go back a long way. We met in college. His wife and Sandy were roommates. We're the godparents of his kids. We used to do everything together—take vacations, spend Sundays. We went out to dinner or a movie together every week or so. While he was in 'Nam, Sandy and I spent a lot of time with his family. I never had a brother, but if I had, well, I guess I would want him to be like Ken."

"I like him."

"I'm the one I can't figure out right now," Bill replied. "I seem to be out of step with the world."

"What do you mean, 'out of step'?"

"I was just thinking about our last few days. I rescue you like a white knight, have a chance to make love to you—a very attractive and inviting thought—and I don't. Furthermore, I think I'm glad I didn't. I can't adapt to modern times."

"Bill, I think I'm glad you didn't too—not that I might not have wanted to also. But if you're out of step, then I must be out of step too." She smiled at him and moved closer so that their shoulders would touch. They sat quietly for several minutes.

"Will this nightmare ever end?" she whispered, trembling in the chilly air. A tear ran down her cheek. He drew her close and, gently tilting her face up to his, kissed her.

"Ken is a good man and a good friend. He'll help us get out of this," Bill replied.

"But neither one of you knows Jarvis," she said. "He's a very powerful man. He has a lot of friends . . . very important friends."

After sitting quietly with their own thoughts for awhile, they left the Mall and crossed the street. Taking a circuitous route, they made their way back to where they had parked the car. Rounding the corner, Bill squeezed Holly's hand. A police tow truck was pulling away with the rented car. They quickly recrossed the street and turned their faces away from the uniformed and plain-clothes police standing in the gaping hole in the wall of cars where theirs had been parked. Somehow the quiet, tree-lined street did not seem as quaint and safe as it had when Bill had parked there.

"Soon they'll know I'm not dead. We need to hurry if we're going to get anything from my place," he whispered.

They turned at the next corner, then Bill guided Holly onto the Mall again and headed for the Smithsonian Metro stop. During the fifteen-minute walk, neither of them said anything.

There was security in the cool dimness of the underground station as Bill bought two Metro cards. They rode to Metro Center, got off, and mixed into the crowd waiting for the next Red Line train to Shady Grove.

It's easy to look ordinary except when you need to, Bill thought with a growing sense of panic as their train pulled into the station and they stepped on. For the next thirty minutes, Bill supposed every schoolgirl and old lady with a shopping bag was going to recognize them. Passengers filed on and off. The congestion finally began to diminish as they sped northward into the suburbs of Maryland. A man next to Bill stood up, leaving a section of the morning *Washington Post* on the seat he'd just vacated. Bill quickly buried his face in the paper. By the time they arrived at Shady Grove, he had read the same stories and ads about six times.

The parking lot at the station was a sea of cars, but very few commuters had gotten off the train at this stop. Just beyond the parking lot lay the safety of his apartment. The complex bordered a small lake. He took Holly's hand and hurried her across the bridge and around the lake. The sky was maintaining its barren gray cast and threatening rain as he let them in the back door of the stairwell with his key. They went up to the second floor without being seen. Bill had started to open the fire door when his hand froze on the knob. There, through the window of the door, he saw a man with his back to them wearing a jogging suit.

Bill stood motionless out of fear and confusion. Then slowly the man turned toward them and pushed the fire door open. He looked intently at them both before walking down the stairs and through the door leading outside. Bill looked out the window, and as the man began doing some stretching exercises in preparation for running, Bill felt like laughing and crying at the same time.

"Holly, I don't think I'm much good at this spy stuff," he said as he turned the knob on the fire door with a trembling hand. His heart was racing, and sweat was running down his neck.

They walked down the carpeted corridor. Bill let them into his apartment. A feeling of safety returned as he noiselessly closed the door. He turned the bolt on the lock and rested his head against the door.

"Hello, Dr. Chandler. My name is Jarvis," said a man with a sadistic grin as he walked into the living room from the kitchen.

12

SECRET FILES

Ken logged on to the computer terminal at his desk in the Hoover Building.

"A little late coming in today, eh, guy?" one of his friends quipped as he passed by.

"Too nice a day to work," Ken responded with a laugh. "Much better day to stay home and play with the kids . . . or their mother." The agent was gone with no further comment.

Ken brought up the program for personal information and typed in GD.

A NAME window flashed on the screen.

"Jarvis, Sidney E.," he typed.

Sixteen "Sidney Jarvis" listings appeared. He then typed the numeral 6 to expand the first listing.

DOB 7-12-16. DECEASED. IF FURTHER INFORMATION IS NECESSARY ACCESS DECEASED FILE.

Then he typed in 7.

Jarvis, Sidney E.

DOB 12-12-66

SSN 406-32-4759

REGISTERED WITH SELECTIVE SERVICE 12-15-84

16714 LONGWOOD LANE

CHARLESTON, SOUTH CAROLINA 29407

(803) 359-8112

Before it went any farther, Ken typed cancel. He then entered 8.

Jarvis, Sidney E.

DOB 6-18-40

SSN 456-84-3187

FURTHER INFORMATION CLASSIFIED A-I-D.

He sat there in stunned silence. He almost didn't hear the approaching footsteps, but just as two fellow agents walked up to his desk, he pressed the escape key, and the screen went blank.

"Ken, we just got a call from the D.C. police. They said they found the car that Holly James used to get out of North Carolina. That puts it in our jurisdiction. The ol' man wants it checked out. It's in the impound lot. We're on our way over. Do you want to come along?" Dirk Anderson, a man about Ken's age, asked.

"Uh . . . no . . . no thanks. I have a report due day after tomorrow I need to work on for the attorney general's office. I don't think you need three of us to look at that car. By the way, they didn't happen to pick her up *with* the car, did they?" Ken asked.

"I don't think so—at least they didn't say anything about having the girl," he answered.

"Say, Dirk," Ken asked as he was walking away.

"What?" Dirk answered.

"Is the computer on the fritz?"

"I don't think so. Why?"

"I was just running some routine personnel data and got something I've never seen before."

"Oh, now what's the brain up to?" Dirk quipped.

"Have you ever heard of a file being classified A-I-D?"

"A-I-D. I heard once about a few people who are very important in the intelligence community, NSA or CIA, who have that designation. But they're very important people we probably would never come across." He put a special emphasis on the last three words. "Only the director and a couple of the top people have access to the information on them. What name were you looking up?" Dirk asked.

"You wouldn't believe it. John Jones; it was number 475. Who would have thought?" Ken lied.

When the two agents were gone, Ken dialed Bill's phone number. After ten rings he hung up. He got up from his desk, took the elevator down to the parking garage, and headed north up Wisconsin Avenue toward the Maryland line. Traffic was moderate by the time he had reached the beltway and exited onto the 270 spur toward Frederick.

The trip cost him about forty-five minutes, but traffic being what it was, there was no quicker way. And, at least for the moment, he couldn't trust anyone else with the information that he he'd had the opportunity to arrest a wanted murderer and didn't. His only thought as he drove into the parking lot was that Bill and this girl Holly had better be telling the truth.

Everything was quiet around Bill's apartment complex since most of the residents worked in the city during the week.

It's like a daggone morgue around here, Ken thought, then grimaced at his own bad analogy.

As he raced up the steps to Bill's apartment, he was afraid of what he might find. He tried the knob; the door was locked. He knocked; no answer. He knocked louder; no response.

Ken then went down to the manager's office and pulled out his identification badge.

"Ken Jenkins, FBI."

"Howdy. What can I do for you?" the manager replied.

"I need to get into Dr. Chandler's apartment," Ken said.

"I don't know," the manager countered. "Do ya have a warrant?"

"National security matter," Ken said. "I don't need one. Now, are you going to let me in?"

The manager eyed him suspiciously. He didn't seem too willing to cooperate.

"Look, we can go down to my office and talk about this right now if that's the way you want to play." Ken paused. "Obstruction of justice carries a pretty heavy penalty, you know." His voice was getting harsher.

"No, no, I don't want no trouble," the manager stammered.

He let Ken into Bill's apartment with the passkey. It was as orderly and clean as one might leave it when going on a trip. In fact it looked like a showplace, with not a pillow out of place. Ken quickly and professionally went through the bedroom, dining area, bath, and kitchen. There was no indication of anything amiss. *Maybe Bill and Holly hadn't gotten here yet*, he thought.

He was about to leave when he noticed the dishwasher door slightly ajar. He opened it and pulled out the rack. There were six glasses upside down in the top rack. All six were wet.

"Who else has been in this apartment today?" Ken demanded from the startled manager.

"No one," he protested.

"How long has Dr. Chandler been gone?" Ken asked.

"'Bout a week, maybe more," he replied.

"Get your coat!" Ken ordered.

"Why? I don't have to go nowhere with you," the manager said defiantly.

"Whether you'll be charged as an accomplice or as the only perpetrator remains to be seen," Ken responded, putting the pressure on.

"Perpetrator! Perpetrator of what?" the man squealed.

"I think Dr. Chandler was here, and now he isn't. Therefore, I have probable cause to think that he may have been kidnapped," Ken said.

"I never was in this apartment today. I didn't have anything to do with those other guys!" the manager cried.

"What other guys?" Ken demanded.

"Them guys that was here earlier. All of them seemed pretty nice, except the older fellow. Anyway, they said they was friends of his. And they was going to play a trick on Dr. Chandler."

Obviously, fear had set in; the man was starting to run his words together.

"Slow down!" Ken said. "Tell me what happened here today, from the beginning."

"Well, about two hours ago, four fellows, three of them were younger than the boss—"

"Describe the boss."

"He was an older guy in a business suit."

"How do you know he was the boss?"

"Mister, when you've worked for someone else as long as I have, it's pretty easy to know who the boss is," the manager said.

"OK, go on, three men and a boss. What happened?" Ken stared intently at the manager, trying to find a crack that might indicate the man was lying.

"Well, they gave me twenty-five dollars and said they were friends of Dr. Chandler. They said he was due back from his trip today and they wanted to play a trick on him to try and cheer him up. Ya know, he's been real lonely since his wife died. They said they were just going to have a little surprise party for him. So, well, I let them in to his place. They seemed like real respectable people." He hurriedly added, "Ya won't tell Dr. Chandler, will ya? I really need this job. Please, mister . . ." The manager's bravado was gone, and he was now pleading for his livelihood.

"Did Dr. Chandler ever show up?" Ken demanded.

"I never saw him, but I was working in the other building until just before you came," the manager whispered and pointed off into space. Then he added, "That's the truth, mister . . . honest!"

Ken took down the information and wondered, *Could Jarvis, whoever he is, have caught Bill and Holly this quickly? Most people wouldn't have known Bill was still alive, let alone know where he lived.*

"This is a matter of national security," Ken cautioned the

manager. "I'll be back later if anything else comes up. In the mean-time, if you think of anything you might have left out, call me at this number." He handed the man a card. "And it is very impor-tant that you don't talk about this to anyone."

As he merged onto the interstate heading back toward the District, he thought, *I guess all I can do now is see if they show up at the Metro station tonight.*

13

PRISONERS ON THE POTOMAC

The drive from Bill's apartment to Jarvis's mansion took about twenty minutes. Not a word was spoken by any of the occupants.

Finally the car carrying Jarvis, Holly, and Bill pulled up a long driveway in a secluded area of Potomac. It stopped in front of a large English Tudor home overlooking the Potomac River. Trees completely shrouded the estate from any prying eyes.

Bill and Holly sat in the backseat, staring silently at the back of the driver's head. Bill's mind was racing from one thought to another, but none of the ideas had any merit in freeing them.

Jarvis turned to them and said, "You two lovebirds were certainly silent on the way over here."

"What do you want with us?" Bill demanded.

"Now, Dr. Chandler, I'm not stupid, and neither are you. You have two things I've been after for some time. In fact, I've wanted both of them very badly. Of course, you have only *one* thing I want now; you see, now I have Holly." He looked at her sadistically, then asked, "What has my little Holly told you about me?"

"She just said she used to work for you, that she was in some kind of trouble and needed to get away for a while," he lied.

"She must have done something very convincing to get you to steal my yacht and assault one of my hands," he sneered.

"So I'm a thief, and you're a kidnapper. Does that make us even?"

"No, Dr. Chandler, we're not even. You see, I now have what I was after, so I win."

Ignoring the implication, Bill looked out the window at the array of colors that made up the backdrop of nature in Maryland during the fall. In a setting so beautiful, such problems should not be happening. He said nothing.

"Well, aren't *you* the hero to the damsel in distress?" Jarvis accented the phrase as he got out of the car. "Now, get out of the car! Both of you!"

They followed Jarvis into the house, guarded by his clones. Bill thought one of them looked like a cat that had cornered a couple of mice and was determined to play with them before killing them. They reached the living room. It had a high vaulted ceiling with darkly stained beams running the full expanse of the width. It was furnished lavishly with country French furniture. There were several floor-to-ceiling windows, but they were curtained so heavily the room had a shadowy cast that made it seem like twilight.

"Sit down . . . please," Jarvis said. "Bring something for our guests to drink. Are you hungry?" he asked.

"No, thank you," Bill responded. Holly said nothing.

They sat on a tufted leather sofa facing a fireplace that took up most of the wall at the end of the room. A fire crackled as the flames licked at a pile of logs. *It could have been a cheery setting under other conditions*, Bill thought.

"Dr. Chandler, you have caused me a lot of undue worry over the last few days," Jarvis said as he slowly paced back and forth like a caged lion in front of the fireplace. Sparks ascended and the popping of the wet logs burning on the grate added emphasis to each word he said.

Who are these people? Bill asked himself. "I'm sorry, Mr. Jarvis, but quite frankly I've found you to be a pain in the butt. So I don't really care if you've been worried," he replied, looking straight at Jarvis.

Unruffled, Jarvis went on. "And Holly, my dear Holly . . . how disappointing you have been. I had such plans for you. Plans for us. There were so many things I was going to give you. But, alas, after all this . . . I'm afraid it's too late."

She was silent.

"What do you mean, 'too late'?" Bill challenged.

"Dr. Chandler, you are in no position to ask anything!" Jarvis snapped. "Anyway, Holly knows what I'm talking about. She knows I like people to be reasonable. In the past, Holly was reasonable, but she also knows that lately she has been very unreasonable. And if she hasn't told you, I'm sure she knows what happens to people I find unreasonable."

"Do you mean people like Ed Harris?" Bill asked, hoping he would deny even knowing Ed.

"Ah, my dear Mr. Harris. We had a long and mutually profitable business relationship. Unfortunately, one of the precepts of business is production leading to profitability. Well, Mr. Harris became unable to produce and, therefore, he became unprofitable . . . at least to me. Do you understand, Dr. Chandler?" Jarvis smiled. The way the corner of his mouth drew up, Bill could almost imagine a long fang protruding. These people were definitely in a different stratum of society than he'd ever been exposed to before.

He drew up his courage. "You mean you *killed* him?" Bill said.

"*Killed* is such a melodramatic word. I'd rather say I divested him from my service. Actually, it was an accident. I had not intended Mr. Harris to have such an untimely demise," Jarvis quipped. "And Holly"—he looked over at her seriously—"I'm afraid I will soon have to divest you from my service also."

"Jarvis, you lay one hand on her, and I'll—" Bill snarled as he started to get up from the couch.

Just then a hand on the back of his shoulder slammed him down onto the seat.

"Dr. Chandler," Jarvis's tone was mocking, "you're not in any position to threaten anyone. But if you cooperate in a pleasant manner, we might negotiate something that involves Holly. After all, I am a businessman. You know, I was very glad to find out you weren't killed in the fire down on the island. I was afraid for a while one of my people had made a grave mistake putting that bomb in your car. You see, we really didn't know who you were at the time. And, unfortunately, my employee was . . . well . . . he was just trying to tidy up a small matter. . . ." Jarvis continued pacing back and forth in front of them. He then stopped and stared out the window for several seconds.

"Well, anyway, let's forget the charades and get down to business. I want you to give me all the technical data on the Tel-Ray project. If you do, maybe we can reach an agreement like I had with Mr. Harris, and as I said, we might also be able to negotiate for my former fiancée." There was something in his tone that told Bill, as far as Jarvis was concerned, Holly would never be a negotiable item.

"Jarvis, working with you would be very difficult. I don't think I like the way the air smells when I'm around you. It's hard to breathe, and I have grown accustomed to breathing," Bill said.

"Don't be rash, Dr. Chandler. I don't want you to become unprofitable too early in our relationship."

He never finished the thought because the telephone rang.

"Mr. Jarvis, it's for you," said a man who appeared to be a butler.

"Hello, Jarvis here. . . . Is that so? . . . Well, I see. That may make a difference only in the immediate time frame. Long term, the deal will be the same with both clients. I want you to go down right now so we can move forward on this. I have the key to the information in a safe place," Jarvis said, looking at Bill and Holly. He hung up the phone.

Quickly he dialed another number. "This is Sid Jarvis; is your boss available? . . . Thanks, I'll hold. . . . Hello, oh fine, how about you? . . . The wife and kids all feeling good? . . . Wonderful. Say, there have been a few developments in the project. I think we need to talk. . . . Sure, I can be there in forty minutes. See you then."

"Howard!" he called.

"Yes, sir, Mr. Jarvis?" The butler appeared almost instantly.

"Put the guests in a comfortable but safe place for a while and have the car brought around. I have to go downtown for a meeting," Jarvis ordered.

Holly and Bill were roughly herded out of the living room and upstairs to a bedroom. The door was shut and locked from the outside, but Bill did not hear the footsteps recede. He put his finger to his lips and said nothing. Looking out the window, he could see the same three Jarvis men who had met them at his apartment get into the car with their boss. He knew he should be afraid, but right now he was too mad at himself for allowing them to get caught.

Pulling Holly close, he whispered, "We're going to get out of here. I'm not about to negotiate with him, and I'm certainly not going to let him hurt you." He hoped his words didn't sound as hollow as they felt.

They heard the car drive out of the compound. Bill looked out the window of their prison and thought he could see Jarvis in the backseat. Slowly, he took stock of their surroundings. The room was a large bedroom with French furnishings, much like the living room had been. The bed was tall, requiring a stepstool to climb onto it; an elegant canopy stretched overhead, and the ceiling was easily six feet above that. A large stone fireplace filled one end of the room, its mantel overshadowed by the large head of an elk. Bill had no ambition to have his head mounted beside it.

On the dresser was a crystal vase with fresh flowers. The guy had taste anyway. Coordinating this house had obviously been a decorator's dream come true. The pictures were either original oils or first-rate reproductions of the French impressionists.

Bill opened the only other door in the room and found a closet with no clothes. Somehow the emptiness seemed out of place. A designer worth her salt should have put clothes in the closet for realism. But this house was beginning to feel very unreal anyway.

Bill whispered to Holly to throw the vase against the wall on his signal. Grabbing the brass candlestick holder from the mantel, he positioned himself behind the door. On the signal, Holly threw the vase; it crashed against the wall and sounded like a window breaking. He heard the key turn in the lock, and the door burst open as the butler rushed into the room. Bill tripped him, and as Howard fell, he brought the candlestick holder down on his head. The man landed on the carpet with a soft thud and didn't move. They searched him quickly and found a gun in his shoulder holster. Bill put it in his pocket, and they cautiously stepped into the hall.

He held her hand for security—his if not hers. They crept to the top of the stairs and peered over. Downstairs it was quiet. Cautiously he stepped onto the landing. The front door opened, and voices drifted up like smoke rising from a bonfire.

"So what's the plan with the guests upstairs?"

"Don't know for sure, but Jarvis mentioned something about going back to Cape Fear tonight."

"That's a good idea. Things can be done much quieter down there. Not as many nosy people around."

Holly and Bill jumped back and flattened themselves against the wall. They waited as two of Jarvis's men walked past, their footsteps echoing on the flagstone.

Carefully, they descended the stairs. At the bottom, Bill peered down the hall and saw the kitchen at the far end. They could hear bottles rattling in the refrigerator. The front door was ahead of them, the living room to the right. The door to the left was closed; Bill motioned toward it, and Holly opened it slowly. They stepped inside the library and silently closed the door. Several minutes passed as they stood, breathlessly listening. Bill pressed his ear against the door; all was silent in the hall. His hastily conceived plan called for them to make a quick, silent dash for the front door and freedom. Suddenly, like thunder crashing before a rainstorm, footsteps rang out in the hall just as his hand was turning the knob. Bill froze. They both held their breath while the sound of the footsteps gained in intensity, then passed by and headed up the stairs. Bill frantically looked about the room they were in. It was time for a new escape plan.

"Let's go to plan B," he whispered.

He grabbed Holly's hand and pulled her toward a door leading to a terrace and the yard with trees beyond. It seemed an eternity as he fumbled with the lock. Finally it turned, and the door swung free. Bill and Holly ran out across the terrace and yard, heading for a low stone wall at the tree line. They jumped over it and discovered too late that the bank dropped sharply away on the other side.

Bill swore as he and Holly began a very uncontrolled descent down the bank. The dried bushes and fallen leaves did little to impede their progress. When they stopped they were lying beside the old C & O Canal—now only a few small pools of water overgrown with underbrush and intermittently sprinkled with fallen trees along its once-grand course.

"Are you hurt?" he asked Holly.

"*That* was plan B?" she sputtered. "I'm not sure. I don't think anything is broken," she whispered as she tried to brush the leaves out of her hair.

Bill helped her to her feet, then they scrambled up to the trail along the levee and started to run as fast as they could away from Jarvis's prison. The trees alongside the levee became a blur of orange and yellow separated by brown and black trunks that glistened with moisture from the rain. Heavy mud caked their shoes, causing extra exertion for each step. Bill and Holly were alone with only the gasping of their lungs piercing the silence of the woods. They ran until Holly was exhausted.

"I've got to rest a minute!" she pleaded.

Bill bent forward panting like a dog and rested his hands on his thighs. Their bodies were sweat-soaked and caked with mud from their fall. A light, chilling mist was starting to descend from the darkening autumn sky. For several minutes they stood, winded, supporting themselves against a tree.

Finally, Bill said, "We have to keep moving. I'm sure they're looking for us by now. From what I saw of Jarvis back there I'll bet he's not going to be happy when he finds us gone."

"You may be the king of understatement," Holly added.

Walking along the canal, it seemed to Bill that the world had suddenly become a foreign place. If he wasn't a criminal already, he soon would be. He was sure the police would know by now that Cookie had been killed in the fire at Cape Fear, not him. So he would soon be an accomplice to the famous Holly James. And if that wasn't bad enough, people he'd never met were trying to kill them. This was not supposed to happen to an ordinary guy like Bill Chandler. He wasn't a hero; he hadn't even gone to Vietnam. Right now he was just tired, cold, and scared.

This was the USA, for heaven's sake, and they were only ten miles from the nation's Capitol. He felt as if he'd suddenly landed on a foreign planet. *I wonder if Scotty could beam me up!* he thought.

About an hour later, somewhere below Seven Locks, Bill looked at his watch. It was 5:15. They had agreed to meet Ken at the Farragut North Metro station at 6 P.M. They had to get there somehow, and they had to get there in time.

They turned off the canal path at the next street. After waiting just a few minutes, a cab came along.

"Where to?" the driver asked, curiously eying his two passengers in the backseat. Holly thought he was probably trying to imagine what they'd been doing to be so disheveled—and wondering if he would get paid.

"Farragut North Metro Station," Bill replied.

Holly was shivering, so he drew her close.

"Cold or scared?" he whispered.

"Both," she whispered. "It's such a nightmare. I want to wake up and be a little girl back home again. You know, I had a dream when I was in the water after I'd jumped from the pier down in Carolina Beach."

"Tell me about it," he urged.

Holly gazed out the side window, searching for the right words. "I saw myself as a little girl, swinging in my yard. Mother was in the kitchen. I could even smell the pie she was baking. There was such a peace there that I felt safe. Who knows? Maybe I was on my way to heaven. . . . Things are just so mixed up now. *I'm* so mixed up now. . . . Maybe it would be better if Jarvis killed me and got it over with. At least then I wouldn't have to run anymore," she whispered.

"Don't say that. Don't ever say that," he whispered softly as he gently held her.

Riding through the rush-hour traffic, Bill held her close. Her warm breath on his neck gave him that special tingling between his shoulders that only the sensual breathing of a woman can produce in a man. She felt small, curled into his arm as he held her softly. He looked down at her. Holly's lips were parted slightly; even without lipstick, they stimulated his desire. He shifted slightly on the seat, turned her face up to his, and kissed her gently. She responded with a soft purring in her throat.

The rain increased in intensity to match Bill's growing hunger, though gloom spread around them in the concentric circles of a vortex for a few moments. With their lips pressed together, they were in another place, another time.

14

BLANK PUZZLE PIECES

The rain had slowed traffic. Cars were bumper to bumper, and tempers were just as hot. Bill and Holly were ten minutes late arriving at the station.

Ken was standing conspicuously at the center of the platform. He nodded to them, and when the next train stopped in front of them, they boarded the same car from different doors. As they rode along in the jam-packed train, Bill watched Ken. It was easy to hide in the crowd. The train was filled with secretaries and midlevel bureaucrats on their way home after a day like all the other days at the factory called Government. Hairstyles that earlier in the day had been combed to perfection now hung loose and disheveled on the women. The crisp white shirts and unwrinkled neckties of the morning were now wrinkled and haphazardly slung around the necks of the men. The commuters all had the same, mindless expression and disinterest in everything going on around them. Bill felt lost in the crowd.

At Gallery Place, Ken left the train; Holly and Bill followed about fifty feet behind. They took the escalator down to the lower level and boarded a train toward National Airport. Two stops later they disembarked. They followed him up the stairs at a safe distance, careful not to look at anyone as they walked along. He entered the plaza building and went through a basement door marked AUTHORIZED PERSONS ONLY.

They followed, but by the time they were at the bottom of the stairs and their eyes had adjusted to the dark, Ken was gone.

"Bill, where did he go?" Holly whispered.

"Bill! Holly! Back here," Ken said coarsely.

They turned and saw Ken in the corner under the metal stairs. The shadows cast an impression of a headless man in a trench coat. Bill knew his mind must be going into overload and he would soon lose touch with reality.

"I guess you were late for a reason," Ken remarked as he sized up their appearance.

"Today made for an interesting day at the office," Bill said sarcastically. "Ken, with your cloak-and-dagger actions I guess you believe Holly's story now. Am I right?"

"Something strange is certainly going on. But I don't know what it is yet," Ken answered. "Bill, what happened at your apartment this morning? And why do you both look like you've been dragged through a mud hole backward?"

Bill looked at Holly; she almost gave the appearance of a bag lady. He guessed he probably looked as bad.

"Jarvis was waiting for us when we got there," he said.

"I'm not really surprised," Ken responded.

"He took us to a house in Potomac. He was going to kill us both, but he got a call and had to go to a meeting downtown. It sounded like he wanted to kill Holly right away, but I think he had planned on saving me until I gave him the final schematics on the Tel-Ray project," he said.

"The what project?" Ken asked.

"Tel-Ray, something I've been working on at Tel-Ex. I think it's the reason Ed's dead," Bill concluded.

"That doesn't surprise me, either, after what I found out about him today," Ken said.

"What did you find?" Holly asked.

"That's the whole trouble," Ken said. "I couldn't find out *any-thing*. His information is in a super-secret locked file in the computer. I may have tipped my hand by even trying to have a look at it."

"I'll tell you something else. He killed Ed Harris," Bill said grimly.

"How do you know that? I thought Ed's death was ruled a boating accident caused by a heart attack."

"That was the official reason," Bill said. "But it seems Ed had been doing business with Jarvis for years. Then all of a sudden he couldn't deliver on something, and Jarvis was applying pressure. I don't know if he had him killed or if Ed was simply scared to death. Jarvis is one rough player!" Bill shook his head, then hastily added, "I think it was my Tel-Ray project Ed couldn't deliver on."

"This is even worse than you thought. As I said, Jarvis is classified in our computer with a special code, so I can't get into it. He must work for the CIA or for NSA; he's supposed to be one of the good guys," Ken replied. "I suppose there's always the possibility he's a mole."

"You mean he's a double agent?" Bill exclaimed. "Or could he just be a single agent, or whatever you call them, and a shady businessman?"

"To be honest, I don't know what category Jarvis falls in. But I am sure he has high-ranking connections. And that is going to make it tough to nail him." Ken paused and looked at Holly.

"We need as much information on Jarvis as you can remember. Anything, no matter how insignificant it may seem to be, might give us what we can use to make a dent in his armor. So, Holly, tell me about Jarvis."

"Well, I'm not sure where to start; at times it's all so unreal. . . ."

"Ken, this is going to take a while, and in the mean time I'm worried about Holly. While this basement might be safe enough, it lacks for certain amenities. And if Jarvis gets hold of her again he may not take the chance of losing her a third time; he may kill her on sight. At least with me he needs my plans before he can afford to do me in."

"We're going to have to hide you and Holly until we can take care of Jarvis. You're right; he probably isn't going to take a chance on losing her again," Ken said.

"Do you have any ideas?"

Handing Bill a key, he said, "Take her to the Crystal Towers Hotel over in Crystal City. I got a room for you today on the chance you'd need it. Make sure Holly is safe, then come back and meet me in my office at the bureau. I'll leave word at the front desk so you can come in, Mr. Sienna."

"*Sienna?* What kind of a name is Sienna?" Bill queried.

Ken smiled. "It's another word for Brown."

Bill rolled his eyes in a gesture of despair. "All the people in the world, and I get an agent with a warped sense of humor."

They left first, and twenty minutes later they were riding an elevator to the fifteenth floor of a hotel in Crystal City. They entered the room and stared in wonderment. The outside wall was a plate-glass window. With the rain reflecting the thousands of lights from across the Potomac, the world looked like a thousand tiny jewels.

How can there be so much beauty and terror at the same time? Holly wondered.

The red light atop the Washington Monument blinked its warning to the airplanes descending into National Airport. Suddenly the sky lit up in a blinding flash, and the whole room shook from the force of the electrical discharge.

The strain of the last few days flooded over Holly. She grabbed Bill, buried her face against his chest, and began to sob. He picked her up and carried her to the bed, her breath now coming in short gasps as she fought to control the outburst. Gently he laid her down on the bed and removed her shoes. Without a word spoken, he covered her with a blanket and lay down beside her.

Bill held her in his arms for well over a half an hour, and she finally calmed down. He went into the bathroom and washed up. He brushed as much dirt as he could out of his clothes and tried to gain a reasonably respectable appearance for his visit to the Hoover Building. When he came out, Holly was watching the news on the television.

Her damp, muddy blouse and slacks were drying on a chair as she sat in bed with the blanket drawn up over her bare shoulders. Bill admonished her not to go out until he returned and to keep the door locked. Then he left. Twenty minutes later he was at the Hoover Building.

"Agent Jenkins is expecting me," Bill said.

"Mr. Sienna? Sure, he said you would be coming along." The civil servant guard wearily checked him into the ritualistic log.

Bill took the elevator to the third floor and walked down the hall to Ken's office. Ken was busy at his computer terminal.

"What do you have?" he asked.

"I can't get much on Jarvis. It's all classified. But I cross-checked his company, NuStyle Import-Export. It shows offices in New York, Washington, and San Francisco. It also lists property in Tulsa and Carolina Beach. That part of Holly's story checks out. However, there's something strange here," Ken said.

"Oh, what's that?"

"I ran a check on licensed motor vehicles. It shows that NuStyle has a small army of cars, boats, and airplanes. It certainly seems to be too many for a company that specializes in importing trendy clothes from the Orient," Ken said. "I'm going to try one more thing."

Ken punched his keyboard. Suddenly the screen began to print a story.

JARVIS, SIDNEY ELVIN, SSN 456-84-3187, DOB 6-18-39, BORN SHELDON, IOWA, ENLISTED UNITED STATES ARMY 10-1-61. UNIVERSITY OF NEBRASKA 1961, B.S. COMMUNICATION. COMMISSIONED SECOND LT. OCS 1961, SPECIAL-TRAINING

INTELLIGENCE. ASSIGNED FORT BRAGG 12-62 TO 11-64. REASSIGNED TURKEY 11-64 TO 4-7-65. DISAPPEARED 4-7-65 AFTER A WEEK'S LEAVE IN ISTANBUL. DECLARED DEAD 4-7-72. SGLI NOT PAID. NO LIVING RELATIVES. NO WILL.

FURTHER INFORMATION AVAILABLE: GIVE A-I-D CODE.

The cursor blinked several seconds then repeated: GIVE A-I-D CODE.

Ken reached up and shut his terminal off. The screen went blank.

"So, Bill, it looks like your Mr. Jarvis is a dead man." Ken looked up, puzzled.

15

INSIDERS

The Pentagon

"Mr. Secretary, Mr. Jarvis is here to see you."

"Sid, come in, come in. Good to see you again. I didn't know you'd be up this month," Secretary of Defense Randolph Blaine said, holding out his hand.

"Mr. Secretary," Jarvis said, "I appreciate you seeing me on such short notice." The ritual of amenities was for prying eyes and ears.

Jarvis sat down in a leather chair across from the imposing desk used by the defense secretary and all his predecessors since the mid-eighteenth century.

"Can we talk candidly here?" Jarvis asked.

"The office was electronically swept this morning," Blaine assured him.

"I have Chandler and the girl at my place here in Potomac."

"What! I thought he was killed in that fire in North Carolina. What is he doing at your place?"

"It seems we have the good fortune to have the very man we

167

wanted. He was trying to help Holly get away. But now we have both of them!" Jarvis said arrogantly.

"How long will it take to get the Tel-Ray data from him?" Blaine asked. "I don't like the idea of them being up here. It's too close."

"I don't think it'll take long. You know these science types. Besides, we have leverage. We have Holly, and I think he's fallen for her," Jarvis replied. "But I agree with you. I don't like having them up here. It's too risky. So tonight I'm going to have them taken back to Cape Fear. It will be much more private for what we may have to resort to—in case he gets stubborn."

Blaine got up and walked around the room. He paused by the window overlooking downtown Washington. The traffic always fascinated him. The very streets flowed with power. You could walk out in the early-morning fog and sniff it in the air. He loved the city, and he loved the power. Randolph almost had both. The city responded to his wants, and the world would soon respond to his power. Still, he felt troubled.

"I don't like it, Sid. I don't like this operation one bit. Too many things have gone wrong. You know I, or rather we, promised our clients the Tel-Ray project to complete the communications on that last weapons system. I have to deliver so they will sign the non-aggression agreement. Not only that, but they've already made a large deposit in my election fund. We have to deliver on it, and time is of the essence." Blaine's forehead was sweating, and his breathing was coming faster.

"Don't get yourself into a lather, Blaine," Jarvis said. "I'll deliver. I always have before, haven't I? And don't get too hooked on 'Hail to the Chief.' Even with all the money you can raise, the voting public can be fickle!" Jarvis grinned.

"Sid, don't get cocky! We have too much at stake. I've worked too hard for too long to get into a position where I can influence what happens in the world. We who know how to use power must be left in a position where we can take care of the common person, not only in our country, but all over the world. It is—"

"Get off your soapbox, Mr. Secretary. You love the intoxication of power, but you're in it for the money, too, just like I am. Otherwise you would still be a GS 9 and a half. There's another thing. It may not mean much, but one of my sources tells me there's an FBI agent inquiring about me in the computer banks. It may be coincidence, but I don't like it. His name is Ken Jenkins. Why don't you get him out of our way?" Jarvis suggested as he got up to leave.

"Who do you think you are, ordering me to take care of an FBI agent?" Blaine snapped angrily. "I don't take orders from anyone except the president, and soon I won't take them from him either! Do I make myself clear?"

Jarvis slowly walked to the door, stopped, and turned around. Drawing a cigarette out of his pocket, he placed it in his mouth, and with deliberateness, lit it with a gold lighter. Smiling as the blue haze swirled up around his nose and eyes, he said, "Oh, by the way, if something does go wrong with this, you can rest assured a full disclosure of our arrangement will come out. So I'd suggest you take care of that agent. Do I make myself clear?" His voice gave the threat with a honeylike sweetness.

Without waiting for an answer and without looking back, Jarvis walked through the doorway.

Blaine turned and stared out the window once again. He felt tired and angry that Jarvis would come into his office and threaten him. With his office in the "A" ring, he could watch the rush-hour traffic starting to build on the George Washington Parkway below. Again the power of the city was evident; to him it was a pulsating, living being, something to be used and controlled. With his position, he could harness that creature; with his strength, he could control and use the raw force of its innermost spirit. He could have anything he wanted here. That's what he had worked for, the power. *That's what it's all about*, he told himself.

Pondering on all that had happened and the events that had brought him to this point, his thoughts took him back to the time he'd rather forget—when Captain Randolph A. Blaine had been a junior officer in the intelligence division at the Pentagon, an assistant to the undersecretary of weapons research in the Defense Department.

He was young then, just out of college, enthusiastic but not too idealistic. There had been a practical side to him even then. Certainly that was when he first felt the quest for power, but there was more to it than that. Maybe it was because of Vietnam.

Jarvis had been right about one thing. At first, what they did was for the money. But soon, a higher calling wooed them, a calling that makes wrong feel right, even if the mechanisms are not always respectable.

The end justifies the means—always has, and certainly in the cause I lead, it always will, he thought to himself. *Of course, someday I know I'll have to do something about Jarvis, but until then, he is very useful.* Blaine looked down at the deepening shadows of the Washington scene and thought, *There is nowhere in our society I could be the demagogue I am here—that is, until I become president. Then I'll easily be able to deal with Jarvis. Soon it will be time for him to die. And once Jarvis is gone, there will be no trail to me.*

He remembered back to that day in 1973. . . .

• • •

The phone rang in the office of the undersecretary for defense contracts, disturbing Randolph Blaine's thoughts. He was trying to see where his future would go now that the Vietnam War was winding down. It had been an exciting and lucrative time to be in this office. The war effort required supplies and equipment, and no one paid much attention to how and where they came from. Defense contractors were anxious to supply what was—and sometimes was not—needed. His only concerns had been that the goods were delivered and that his personal gratuity could not be traced. Now the character of all that was certainly going to change. He must be able to adapt to a changing situation. The phone buzzed again.

"Blaine here."

"Mr. Blaine, there's a caller on the phone who insists he must talk to you personally. I told him you were in a meeting and could not be disturbed. But he is so persistent I can't get rid of him," Carol Shemp, the undersecretary's receptionist, said.

"I don't want to be bothered now," Blaine said.

"I know, sir, but he has called three times. And this last time he said to tell you Jarvis was coming to Washington the first week of June. And then he said something very strange."

"Yes, what did he say?" Blaine asked.

"He said, 'Tell him that, and I'll bet he'll talk to me.'" She sounded angry and curious at the same time.

Sweat broke out on Blaine's head, and he felt a knot forming in his stomach. His hands began to shake, and an evil blackness began to invade his soul. The nightmare of the news story he had read seven years earlier in London now flooded his consciousness again. After several seconds of silence, he replied, "Oh, all right. I'll take the call, just to get rid of it."

"He's on line one," Miss Shemp said, her disdain for the caller evident in her voice. She had contempt for anyone who would use such a tact to get to her boss.

"Hello, this is Blaine."

"Mr. Blaine, I have a message for you," the voice said.

"Who is this?" Blaine demanded.

"It really doesn't make any difference. I've just been paid to make this call and give you this message. Now listen! Mr. Jarvis will be arriving at National Airport at nine-thirty in the evening on the seventh day of June. He would like you to meet him at the baggage claim area. He'll be wearing a cowboy hat and boots. He's looking forward to seeing you again after all these years." The line went dead.

Blaine slumped back into his chair and stared at the far wall. It had been so long ago he had almost forgotten about it altogether. At first he had lived in fear that somehow he would be tied to the murders and fire in Istanbul. Then, as his conscience was seared, it became like a dream that had never happened. Now the memories began to flood back over his mind. He buzzed Miss Shemp.

"Carol!" he said.

"Yes, Mr. Blaine?"

"I don't feel very well. I'm going home for the rest of the afternoon."

"Yes, Mr. Blaine," she responded. "Do you need anything from me?"

"No, nothing today. By the way, Carol, do I have anything scheduled on the eighth of June?" he asked.

"No, sir," she replied.

"Good. I may not be in that day," he said as he felt the phone shaking in his hand.

"Mr. Blaine, are you sure there isn't anything I can do for you?" she said.

"No . . . no, Carol, not right now."

He walked out of his office into the anteroom that held Carol's desk. She was looking at him with a combination of concern and anxiety on her face. He appreciated the way Carol used her executive-secretary and womanly skills to see to his needs. She would be most valuable as he moved up the power food chain in Washington. He knew he would make it to the top, and he also knew he needed someone like Carol to support him. If only he could tell her the dark secrets that made him tremble when the name Jarvis was mentioned. But how could she ever understand murder and cover-up by a man she so respected? The pedestal she had placed him on was much too high to fall from.

Randolph paused and looked at her. "It's been a troubling day, Carol. I'm going to leave early."

"Mr. Blaine, if there's ever anything you need, or something I can do for you . . ." She smiled a sincere smile, which conveyed the full meaning of her words. "You just have to ask."

"Yes, well . . . ," he stammered. "Uh, yes. Good-night, Carol."

• • •

He had not had the dream for almost four years, but that night the old nightmare returned. He was standing ankle-deep in blood. His shoes and socks were wet; he could feel the gelatinous material seeping through the leather. He stood there with a gun in his hand as people were brought past him on a conveyer belt. He was to shoot them all, one by one, as they came by. The people were screaming and pleading with him to spare them, and he wanted to. Oh, how he wanted to! But beside him stood a man who dominated his will, saying, "SHOOT! SHOOT!" Each time the man shouted he would respond to the order and kill the next victim. The entire time, the pool of blood was growing higher and higher on his legs as the life of each person ebbed out onto the floor in a wave of red liquid. The victims alternated between men and women, and they all looked like Sidney Jarvis and Maria Clifton. In his dream, Blaine knew one day there would be too many killed, and he would drown in the blood of his prey.

He screamed and woke up. His heart was racing, his hands sweating, and the acidic taste of his stomach's contents rising into his throat caused him to bolt out of bed. He raced to the bathroom, got down on his knees, and began to vomit into the toilet.

"Randolph! Are you sick? Do you want me to call the doctor?" his wife asked.

After washing his mouth and gargling, he answered. "No! I'm all right. There was just something at dinner that didn't agree with me."

As he got back into bed, he was still shaking. His wife, in a rare display of affection, pulled him to her, enclosing him safely in her arms. She held him like a small child against her breast until he finally fell back to sleep.

With diminishing intensity, the dream recurred about every third night for a month as Undersecretary Blaine anxiously awaited the arrival of Michael Jardeen, alias Sidney Jarvis. Blaine knew he had the ability to overcome the most grotesque circumstances with time. And the affair in Istanbul had been only an unfortunate circumstance.

• • •

June 7, 1973

"Hello, Randolph."

"Hello," Blaine said without emotion as they shook hands.

"Undersecretary for defense contracts—you've done very well for yourself. Do you have a family?" Jarvis asked.

"Yes, I got married about six years ago, and we have two children. I can't imagine what you've been doing these past years," Blaine said, glaring at Jarvis.

"Well, I've been, I guess you could say, out of sight." Jarvis smiled. "But our other fraternity brother, Michael—you remember Michael Jardeen—?" he asked.

"Yes, I remember Michael," Blaine replied flatly, wondering what Jarvis was hinting at.

"Well, Michael just retired to a little place in Idaho. He was with the Company, you know," Jarvis said.

"I had no idea we still employed people of such caliber in our country's service," Blaine said with a snide tone to his voice.

Jarvis stopped and glared at Blaine. A young couple walked past as Jarvis slowly took out a cigarette, placed it between his lips, and lit it, staring intently at the flame before his eyes. He inhaled deeply and let the pungent blue smoke slowly fill his lungs then exit through his nose. When the couple were safely out of hearing, Jarvis said in a low, well-controlled voice, "Let's get one thing straight right now. There is no statute of limitations on murder.

And you, my dear undersecretary, are as guilty as I am. I'm sure Interpol would still like to solve that case in Turkey. And you're a prime suspect in the disappearance of Jardeen, I'm told. So . . . I trust our relationship in our new business dealings will be . . . let's just say . . . long and profitable."

They walked on a little farther, and Jarvis continued. "I do have some bad news to tell you about Michael."

"Oh? What could possibly have happened to our friend Michael, now that he's retired? In Turkey Michael was able to handle anything and everything. Or so he would tell me."

"There was an unfortunate accident." Jarvis sighed audibly. "He's dead. He had just moved into a small cabin in the mountains when a space heater exploded. It was really terrible. Burned him beyond recognition." Jarvis gave Blaine another chilling smile.

"I can't imagine Michael ever playing with matches," Blaine countered, continuing to play the game but visibly shaken now. He wasn't quite sure what Jarvis was getting at, but this playacting was feeling more and more like a threat.

"Poor fellow," Jarvis went on. "He was so looking forward to his retirement. I sent flowers to his funeral from the both of us." Jarvis laughed at Blaine's growing discomfort. "Oh, by the way. I hope your daughter—that's your oldest, isn't it, your daughter? I believe her name is Ashley. It is Ashley, isn't it?"

"Yes, but how did you know her name?" Blaine demanded.

Without giving an explanation, Jarvis went on. "I hope Ashley enjoys her time at the Kinder Home Nursery School. Of course they are very good there. I don't believe they've had even one accident with any child since they opened."

Blaine fell silent and walked slowly beside Jarvis.

Why was this man threatening him? Or, more specifically, why was he threatening his family? What was he really mixed up in? And now that Michael Jardeen was officially dead—now what? The confusing thoughts swirled in Blaine's head. When would it all end?

The roar of a departing jet made Blaine think of a steamroller coming at him. The noise reached a high-pitched crescendo and then was gone. Why did there have to be any killings? But . . . killing is a part of life, he reasoned. After all, fifty thousand have died in Vietnam, and we're just walking away from that. People die every day in car wrecks and from disease. And, to be quite honest, no one really cares for more than a few minutes or, at the longest, a few days.

As they walked along, Blaine noticed the heat from the early summer day was gone. A fresh breeze had sprung to life from the Potomac just beyond the airport runway. He thought about it. What had happened seven years earlier was done. It would do no good to reopen the murders in Istanbul; it certainly wouldn't help that poor, unfortunate Jarvis or the woman either. And there was no way they could connect him with this new "death." Now he had his family to protect, his future to look out for—and he was considering all his options, since Vietnam would soon be over. A man has to look out for his own welfare.

One thing he was sure of: Jarvis had the ability to carry out his plan, whether it was selling military secrets or killing Blaine's family. Even a member of a high government official's family would not be safe from him. This was sure to be a time of transition for the country. It might as well be a time of transition for him too. Who knew where this might lead?

As the summer breeze blew his tie over his shoulder, he smoothed his hair and felt as free as the breeze. All right. He would follow this new path with an unlimited horizon. After all, a man has the right to protect his family—and his future.

"Ah . . . Mr. Jarvis," Blaine said.

"Yes, Mr. Undersecretary?" Jarvis answered. His stony stare caused Blaine to hesitate.

"Well," Blaine continued after a prolonged pause, "I was wondering what needed to be done at this point to . . . well . . . to facilitate our new venture?"

Jarvis smiled slowly, seemingly pleased by Blaine's question—almost as if he had expected it.

They stopped at Blaine's car parked in the VIP parking lot. As he leaned on the top of it, Jarvis looked across the runway of National Airport toward the spike of the Washington Monument. It thrust its tapering silhouette high into the blue sky, making it the most important structure on the horizon. And to Sidney Jarvis, Blaine thought, it was undoubtedly a symbol of the power the man so craved.

"What I need from you, Blaine, is access to the computer that lists the most top-secret agents. Sid Jarvis needs a clearance, but he can't afford an investigation. Isn't that right?" Jarvis replied with a wink.

"That won't be easy," Blaine said.

"I also need an import-export license for NuStyle Imports. And I want the company to be listed as a longtime defense supplier. Here are several lists of supplies the government has bought from NuStyle and the dates of delivery along with invoice numbers. All of these transactions took place during the last three years."

"I said it won't be easy," Blaine reiterated.

"I have confidence in your abilities," Jarvis responded with a twisted smile.

• • •

Randolph Blaine, secretary of defense for the most powerful country on the planet, was still looking out his window at the rush of traffic as he contemplated all that had happened over the last twenty years. He was proud, immensely proud, of his accomplishments. He had risen to unexpected heights in the government, and he had grown wealthy in the interim. He was winning, and as he had learned long ago, winning was everything. *It's funny*, he thought, *that no one has ever asked how a person could make so much money by being a career civil servant.* The money he'd made during

Vietnam was nothing compared to the money he and Jarvis had made since. Selling off the high technology of the United States had been profitable; after all, only spare parts were sold. What's one computer chip, more or less?

There are certain things common people really don't want to know anyway, Blaine mused. If only this Tel-Ray thing could get finished up, he'd get on with his plans for the presidential election. Soon, very soon, he would achieve the most majestic trophy in the world. He would be the President of the United States.

Randolph thought to himself how easy it had all been. For that matter, life had always been easy for Randolph Blaine. He had been born upper middle class—that's always good for a presidential candidate. He had been well educated in prep and Ivy League schools where he had developed the necessary manners that allowed him to move in the most eminent circles with ease. He served in the army for a short time. Yes, he had all of the qualifications for his most prized trophy, the presidency. But there had been two events that had shaped Randolph Blaine's personality more than anything else because of their reinforcing message.

The first event he readily remembered and would talk about at length. It was a lesson taught to him by his father when he was a young Cub Scout. At a large Cub Scout pack picnic with a lot of food, games, and races, the prize for the footrace was a big trophy. He could still remember how it stood above all the other prizes, its gold gleaming in the afternoon sun. He wanted that trophy more than he could remember wanting anything. He also remembered telling his dad how much he wanted it. His father had replied, "Then do whatever you have to do to get it!" His dad knew he wasn't a strong runner. If he was going to win the race that day— and win in life—he would have to live out those words and win at any cost. He had learned the lesson well; he had used his cunning to overcome the obstacles, and by evening the prized golden trophy was sitting proudly in the family living room. Now years later his father's words still echoed in his mind whenever he faced life's obstacles: "Do whatever you have to do to get it!"

The second personality-shaping event was buried deep within his conscience. Carol Shemp was the only person he had ever trusted with the details; his wife didn't even know. It was a secret so dark he could not share it with himself on most occasions. It had occurred when he was in the sixth grade at prep school. He had been caught cheating on a test in math. After school, Miss Stevens, the teacher, a woman in her mid-thirties, took him into the coatroom and locked the door. He could still see her standing in front of the door. She was tall, probably five feet eight or more. Her hair was dark and pulled back from her face severely, and she held it with an imposing pin. She had been wearing a dark blue blouse buttoned tightly to the collar so that it encircled her neck completely.

"Randolph, you know that was a bad thing to do, don't you?" she questioned.

"Yes, Miss Stevens. I promise I won't ever do that again," he whispered.

"I must inform your parents; you know that, don't you?"

"Please don't!" he blurted out.

"I'm sorry, but it's school policy. I'm afraid it is out of my hands as soon as I report it to the principal." She looked at him sternly.

"Oh, please, Miss Stevens, please . . . I'll do anything. Just don't tell my dad," he pleaded.

What followed would haunt Blaine for the rest of his life. After that day in the coatroom, he suffered recurring nightmares of the smell of her sickening perfume. But his teacher had stuck to her promise . . . his father had never found out about the cheating. As the sixth grader had reluctantly submitted to his teacher's wishes that day, his father's words had echoed in his conscience: "Do what you have to do to win!" It was a defining moment for Randolph Blaine, and it was how he continued to live his life, moving up through the most powerful circles of the country. That he needed a dominating woman would continue to plague Blaine throughout his life. But once Carol Shemp came into his life, she was able to make it an asset of immense proportions.

• • •

The call and visit from Jarvis earlier in the day had disturbed him. He had felt an apprehension from the time he learned that Ed Harris was dead. There had been a bad tenor to the conversation involving Harris, Tel-Ray, and now this scientist and the girl. It just didn't feel right. Jarvis had as much as threatened him here in his own office. He leaned over and pressed the intercom button.

"Carol?"

"Yes, sir?" she answered immediately.

"Come in here, please." He clicked it off and sat back in his lavish chair.

"Mr. Secretary," Carol Shemp said as she walked around his desk and paused behind his chair. Gently, she began to massage the strained muscles of the back of his neck.

"Yes, Carol," he replied, bending his head forward to relax the stress. He breathed deeply and let out a long sigh.

"We'll be working late tonight. . . ." She smiled but seemed to sense his uneasiness. "Won't we?"

"Has everyone else left?" he asked.

"Yes, I sent them all home thirty minutes ago. We're alone. I told the guard you didn't want to be disturbed under any circumstance." Carol stroked his temples with her fingertips. "Maybe I should have told him we didn't want to be disturbed," she murmured as she leaned over the back of the chair and enticingly nipped the corner of his earlobe between her teeth. "Go lock the door, Randolph!" she directed.

He rose from the chair, walked across the room, and locked the door. Walking back toward her, he untied his tie and dropped it on the arm of a chair. She was leaning against the front of his massive desk with her shoulders back. The starched lace of her white collar closed tightly around her long neck. She had removed her pin-striped double-breasted coat and it was folded neatly on the desk. The hem of her straight skirt was rising slightly above her knee. As he approached, she loosened her hair and let the long black strands fall from the matronly updo that had clung to the back of her head all day. The locks cascaded in curving arches down her back; she shook them free and smiled alluringly at Randolph.

Placing one of his imposing arms around her, he drew her close to him in a long embrace, and they walked to the couch on the far side of the room. This couch, where so many weighty matters of the world were discussed and settled, was the same couch on which they had spent many a long, erotic night. But this night, Blaine's mind was not on his mistress.

There was something about this Tel-Ray project that just wasn't right. Jarvis was making a mess of the whole affair. Blaine decided at that point that when he became president, Jarvis would have to go. After all, he would be doing the right thing, since Jarvis was a known murderer. At least Blaine knew he was a murderer. And if he were president, he would certainly have the responsibility of bringing him to justice. Of course, he couldn't let him come to trial. Blaine smiled to himself. You do whatever you have to do to win!

• • •

Carol could always sense Randolph's moods. After all, in her mind, she had made him what he was. She had perceived the potential in him when she first became his secretary. She knew he could become great with the proper cultivation. It had always been her ambition to be someone important. She had felt from the start, however, that she was one generation too early. Though presently only in her mid-forties, Carol had always felt she was too old to be a person of prominence in her own right. However, she was certain she could be someone by making Randolph Blaine someone. She believed all she had to do was determine what his needs were, then supply them. She had studied him as diligently as she would have studied for a college course.

Then, one night, while working late in their office at the Pentagon, Carol had discovered the secret: This most powerful of men needed a woman who could overpower him. It was true that women were finally taking their rightful place in the world, but the world stopped outside the bedroom door. Women were still to be the submissive ones. They were not the ones to commence the voyage, they were the ones who were to be transported into love. Randolph Blaine was in complete control of his public life; what he demanded he got. But when this man of power was alone with Carol, he wanted desperately to be conveyed, to be overpowered, to be used. When fulfilled in this way, he was a power unleashed; he was revitalized and renewed. His ability to work, to persuade, to conquer, reached new heights in all aspects of his life.

She had planned tonight's seduction as carefully as she had planned his schedule for a NATO summit. His needs had been appraised, the gestures had been refined and practiced. With time, even the initial disappointment knowing she could never have him completely had been overcome.

"Randolph, you've had a hard day. Just lie back, and I'll show you how to make the worries of the world disappear," Carol said as she unbuttoned his shirt. Blaine had told her of his storybook marriage, endured for the sake of appearances. He had married well; his wife had produced two children to maintain the image. Even she had expected to do that. However, Carol also knew his wife could not stir his emotions; nor could the proper Mrs. Blaine imagine intercourse to be for anything other than procreation.

Carol knew that every seductive movement she made was drawing Randolph deeper into her authority. She had control of his mind, his emotions, and his body. He was helpless before her, a servant to her every want. Only she could make him react this way.

When their energy was spent, she knew Randolph had been strengthened and renewed. Tomorrow would be a good day.

"Carol, I don't know how I could ever handle this job if it weren't for you," Blaine whispered in her ear.

As she smiled sweetly at her lover, Carol thought to herself, with a mixture of pride and disgust, *Who could have guessed that Randolph Blaine, one of the most powerful men on the planet, is actually a jellyfish. His tentacles can engulf and devour people. He can spread his influence across the world. But in the hands of his mistress, he has no backbone!*

Randolph lay on his back beside the couch—completely exhausted, staring up at the ceiling, with Carol's head resting on his chest. Her hair spilled over his shoulder like a light blanket. He marveled at her lack of embarrassment at their nakedness as he absent-mindedly stroked her spine with his fingertips.

Slowly he felt the guilt starting to creep back into his mind, the guilt that he could not feel this same eroticism with his wife. The sensuous feeling of Carol's nakedness was both satisfaction and guilt, both heaven and hell.

Quietly, like the tranquillity of a lake after a storm, Carol arose and gathered her clothing. Without a word she slipped into the bathroom adjoining Blaine's office.

Minutes passed, and the momentary pleasure of his mistress had worn off. Blaine slowly began to dress, then paced the room as he finished tying his tie. The regret of being unfaithful to his wife began to sear his conscience. He found himself growing angry. He'd stop and get some flowers for her on the way home; she liked flowers. Roses, she liked roses. He knew just where he could get the long-stemmed ones without the thorns.

It's bizaare, he thought, *on the nights I do these things with Carol, I bring my wife the best presents—and she never questions me.*

16

SANCTUARY

The Hoover Building

Ken and Bill sat in silence, entranced by Ken's computer screen, when the phone rang, startling both of them.

"Hello, Agent Jenkins here," Ken said. "Oh, hi honey. . . . The office has been calling me? I don't know why. I've been here off and on most of the day. . . . No, I don't know why he didn't see me. If he calls again, tell him I'll stop by his office on my way home. No, I'll be a while longer. . . . Yes, I love you too. Good-bye." He hung up the phone.

Ken turned to Bill. "I think you'd better get out of here, Bill. Go on back to the hotel. I'll be over in the morning."

"Do you have any idea what's really going on?" Bill asked.

Ken paused in deep thought. "If you want to know the truth, I don't have the vaguest idea. But I have a feeling that either you and Holly are the biggest liars on earth, or judging from the classification of information we just found, you may have stumbled into one of the biggest spy rings ever."

Bill knew the first wasn't true . . . and he didn't like to think about the second.

"Good night, Mr. Sienna," the guard said as Bill signed out at the front desk.

"I hope you have a quiet night," Bill replied, trying to act non-chalant.

The rain had stopped as he headed for the Mall, but the wind had a cold, wet chill to it. Strangely, a sixth sense told him as soon as his foot hit the gravel path that he was being followed. Very few people were out on that rainy fall night, and, at first, he couldn't see anyone suspicious, but he knew someone was there, watching him.

Bill began to sweat in spite of the cold as he walked toward the safety of the underground Metro station. At one end of the Mall, the Capitol was ablaze with lights; ahead of him, the Washington Monument was shrouded in low-hanging clouds. The wind blew his hair and tugged at his coat as he continued down the dark path. Bill's internal clock ticked off the minutes in slow motion, each swing of the giant pendulum increasing the tension in his gut. By now he was sure there were at least two men following.

Turning up his collar against the wind, he glanced back and saw them. The pair maintained a perfect distance across the street. He kept a steady pace until he came to a group of street people huddled around a steam grate. Then, boldly, he moved into the group.

"Who'd like to earn twenty dollars real easy?" he asked.

"Yeah? Who do ya need killed?" asked a surly man, about Bill's size, with a water-soaked cigarette hanging out of the corner of his mouth.

"No one, but I want you to take my coat and walk slowly down to the Lincoln Memorial. Two men will follow you; they won't hurt you. They just want to know where you're going. I need about twenty minutes without them," he replied. "You get twenty bucks—and a bonus. You can keep the coat."

"You got your man," the stranger said. He put on Bill's trench coat over his old, torn army field jacket, threw the cigarette to the ground, and stamped it out with an exaggerated movement of his foot. He walked away as Bill palmed him the twenty-dollar bill.

The group around the steam grate was tightly huddled, which, with any luck, had allowed the switch to be made unnoticed by Bill's shadows. As the man walked off in the direction of the memorial, Bill moved closer into the group, enjoying the warmth of the steam coming from the depths below. His shirt did little to stop the cold night air.

Bill watched the tails follow his coat on down the Mall; then he slipped into the darkness and disappeared down the escalator into the rail system of underground Washington. The rumble of a train filled the dimly lit tunnel. It was a Red Line away from downtown Washington toward Silver Spring. Not the direction he needed to go, but why be choosy? The bell sounded, and the door closed behind him as he bounded aboard.

Shaking almost uncontrollably, he took a seat at one end of the car. He could see the reflection in the glass door of the three other passengers. An elderly black woman with a teenage girl sat several rows behind him, and at the far end of the car was a man. He'd seen him board at the same stop and walk to the opposite end of the car, passing all of the empty seats. Bill could feel the man's eyes on his back. A cold sweat trickled down his neck.

The stations slipped past with fewer and fewer passengers departing from the other cars as the sleek metal train emerged from the depths and entered the outskirts of Washington. Takoma Park station was empty when the train stopped. That was what he'd been waiting for. Bill exited onto the platform and began to walk toward the escalator, quickly glancing over his shoulder. The man stepped off the train also. Bill could hear his footsteps on the tile and picked up his pace. He had intended to cross over the tracks and take a train back downtown; instead, he exited the station and quickly crossed the street, stopping in the shadows of a building to watch.

The man stepped down from the stairs and stopped on the

sidewalk. He slowly scanned the street, then began to walk away from where Bill was standing. Bill slipped from his hiding place and made his way along the sidewalk in the opposite direction at a brisk trot, the light rain whipping at his face. Even without his coat, Bill was unaware of the cold now, feeling only the beating of his heart at the sound of footsteps from behind. Running footsteps.

This part of town had long passed its prime, taken over by derelicts and gangs. The streets were dark and littered with debris, the buildings covered in graffiti. Bill began to run in earnest and almost tripped over a man lying in a doorway with a bottle clutched in his hand, a lit cigarette glowing between his fingers. The drunk grunted and turned away. As Bill rounded the corner he immediately spotted a lighted sign above an old gothic building: *Takoma Park Community Church*. Without a second's hesitation, he bounded up the stone staircase and grasped the wrought-iron doorknob, praying it would open. He pushed inside and closed the door, leaning against it and breathing heavily. He listened for the footsteps outside but heard nothing.

The church sanctuary was dimly lit by a few low-wattage bulbs in sconces along either wall. Bill hurried down the aisle and threw himself under a pew on the cold stone floor. His heart was still racing and he struggled to keep his breath under control as he tried to lie perfectly still. *Oh, God,* he prayed, *I don't know what's happening or why.*

The church door opened. A car went by outside with a screech of tires, followed by the wail of a police siren. He heard heavy footsteps on the stone flooring; quietly he pulled his knees farther in under the pew. A shadow passed by his row and stopped. There was a cough and a wheezing sound. Time seemed to be suspended before the footsteps slowly retreated back up the aisle. Only then did Bill realize that his lungs were burning from holding his breath. After the door slammed shut, he lay on the stone floor for several minutes . . . until no more sounds were heard.

Slowly Bill crawled out from under the pew and sat upright on the wooden bench. He laid his arms on the seat in front of him and put his head down, exhausted. His hands were still shaking. He didn't look up until the tremor had finally subsided. Then he slowly lifted his head and saw a gleaming brass cross above the altar, a single spotlight shining on it.

God, why are you doing this to me? First you took my wife and child . . . and now this! Have I done something wrong? The thoughts ran through his head like a prayer, yet he wasn't sure he was actually praying to anyone. God was too distant, too unknowable. If there was a God, as so many claimed, did he even care to listen to the frantic prayers of humans in trouble? He tried to remember what his mother had said to him after his father's death. *"Billy, we can't know the mind of God. I don't know why he took your daddy to heaven, but He will always be with us no matter what."*

He thought about his mother's words for a few minutes. *She told me that was a promise.*

He looked back up at the lighted cross and boldly said out loud in the empty church, "You promised!" His words echoed off the stone walls. The scientist in him argued that the emptiness of this place was real. It was up to him to survive, that was all. But his heart remembered his mother's words, and he wanted desperately to believe.

"God, I don't understand," he said more quietly this time, "but I *want* to believe that promise. Please don't give up on me . . . no matter what." He put his head back down on his arms and rested, an unexplainable peace calming the inner turmoil he'd felt just moments before. Suddenly he smiled to himself and glanced back up at the lighted cross. *It's funny,* he thought. *I don't remember that light on the cross being on when I came in.*

● ● ●

Twenty minutes later he found the courage to make his way cautiously back to the Metro platform. The man he had run from was nowhere in sight, but he kept a wary eye about him just in case. As soon as the next train came along heading back to town, he boarded it and enjoyed the heat radiating up along the window.

He leaned against the glass on the ride back to Crystal City, somehow lacking the energy to sit up. He felt weary—weary from being on the run, weary from the strain, weary from too little sleep, weary from life. Bill wondered if his tails from the Hoover Building had approached the street person and if they did, what their reaction was.

He smiled inwardly. *Well, Holly and I survived today. Whether we'll survive tomorrow is another question.* Despite his exhaustion, he felt a satisfaction he had not known for many months. Bill now had a purpose for living . . . a purpose that somehow included Holly James. Maybe it was just to help save her life, but he couldn't stop thinking there was more to it than that. Ever since Sandy's death, life had seemed so meaningless. There had been several times he didn't care if he lived. But now he knew he wanted to live. And he wanted Holly to live too. He thought again of the confidence that had come to him just now in that old church . . . and that lighted cross. What did it all mean? Maybe he and Holly *were* being protected in some supernatural way. He felt a sudden pang of anguish at these thoughts. Was he being untrue to Sandy?

The train let him off at Crystal City. No one followed him to the hotel. The lobby was deserted, and the night desk clerk didn't bother to look up from his computer terminal as Bill crossed to the elevator.

He quietly let himself into the room and undressed to his shorts without waking up Holly. He grabbed a pillow and blanket and began arranging himself on the small couch by the picture window. The couch was too short to lie comfortably, however; he would either have to sleep in a fetal position all night, or hang his legs over the hard arm. He looked at Holly sleeping soundly in the queen-size bed. *Maybe she won't mind,* he thought.

Carefully crawling into the bed so he wouldn't disturb her, he felt the heat of her body warming the blankets. She slept soundly, not stirring as he settled down next to her. He felt physically exhausted, but the quietness of her breathing and the nearness of her body aroused his desire for her. This time the yearning was stronger and more natural—more caring. He draped his arm over her shoulders gently and curled up against her back, as if they were two teaspoons in a drawer.

Within seconds, he was lulled into much-needed slumber by the rhythm of her breathing. He didn't hear the rain as it began to beat with renewed ferocity against the exterior glass walls of the hotel.

Day Five

The knock at the door seemed to be a long way off. Bill was dreaming. A boat was heading for a giant vortex. Desperately, two people fought with the wheel, trying to change the boat's direction. They strained frantically at the helm, but it was frozen. The noise he heard was one of them pounding on the wheel with a wrench, trying to get it to move.

The roar of the swirling, gaping pit grew in intensity as the swiftly flowing water propelled the boat forward into oblivion. Finally, the persistent noise penetrated his consciousness, and he realized he was awake. He slowly opened his eyes, then stumbled out of bed.

"Yes?" Bill asked through the closed door.

"Bill, Bill! It's me, Ken."

Relieved, he unbolted the door and let in his friend. Holly was just beginning to stir under the blankets. She looked over at them with wide, blinking eyes.

"Well, you look better. The sleep must have done you some good," Ken said, glancing at the bed with a knowing grin.

"Yeah, well, looks can be deceiving," Bill snapped, annoyed by his friend's insinuation. "What time is it, anyway?"

"About eight-forty," Ken replied. "Bill, we need to talk."

"OK, what about?" Bill hoped Ken had some new revelation that would bring a quick conclusion to the mess they were in.

"Not here. We have to be very careful. I'm not supposed to even be in Washington now. I've been sent on an emergency assignment to western Montana," Ken said. "I think we're on to something big, but unfortunately they may suspect I'm involved."

"You seem to be leaving a lot out, Ken. I'm not sure I like what you're *not* saying."

"Ken?" Both men turned at the sound of Holly's voice. She sat up in the bed and pulled the bedspread over her shoulders.

"Yes, Holly?" Ken replied.

"I have to ask this, and I need an answer. Do you believe now that I'm not a murderer?"

"We have a lot to talk about, and I don't want to talk here, so you two get dressed, and we'll meet where we can have some privacy. I have to make a stop first. Give me about an hour, then meet me at Mount Vernon. Buy a ticket and take the tour; I'll find you. Be careful and watch your back," Ken said as he walked toward the door.

"Ken! You didn't answer my question!" Holly shouted.

Ken turned halfway through the open door and looked at her. "I don't know what your part in all of this is, Holly, but I'm sure you're not a murderer." And then he was gone.

Bill picked up the small suitcase Ken had brought with a change of clothes for them and set it on the bed. Fortunately, Ken and his wife were about the same sizes as Bill and Holly. As they got dressed, Bill laughed and said, "At least this time we get some new clothes without running up my Visa bill. They've probably canceled my card by now anyway."

Ken's wife had sent a red-and-black-plaid skirt, its pleats sewn down over the hips, and a black turtleneck sweater to match. As Holly stepped out of the bathroom, Bill couldn't take his eyes from her. Seeing his approving look, she twirled once and smiled at him.

"Ken advanced me some money last night," Bill said, handing her several hundred dollars of mostly twenties. "Don't spend it all in one place."

"As long as I'm with you, it looks like I'll never be broke," she quipped, tucking the money into the nearly empty purse Ken's wife had sent along.

• • •

"Mr. Jarvis, we followed that FBI agent, like you said. He went to the Crystal Towers in Crystal City. It looks like that's where they are. Should we take them now?"

"Yes, I want them captured as quickly as possible, but don't attract attention." Jarvis hung up the phone with a warm feeling of satisfaction. They would be his again shortly.

"All right, now listen up. Mr. Jarvis wants them taken now. The best place would be as they come out of their room. Get up there! Take the service elevator, and don't make a scene!"

Two men immediately headed for the back of the lobby. "Now, just in case they don't get them, scatter out in the lobby and watch every elevator. Any questions?"

• • •

Bill quietly closed the door behind them, and they headed for the elevator. "By the way," Holly asked, "where's your raincoat?"

"It took a walk on the Mall last night." He laughed.

"I don't understand."

"Just believe Ken and watch your back all the time."

Bill and Holly had no way of knowing that two of Jarvis's men rounded the corner of the hallway just as the elevator doors closed on them.

When they got off the elevator, Bill had the same feeling he had experienced the night before on the Mall. He was certain several people were watching them as they walked through the hotel lobby. He guided Holly into the coffee shop, and they took a table positioned so that he could observe the door.

After ordering breakfast, he asked Holly to go out to the lobby and get a newspaper. As she walked through the door he saw one of the men he suspected of being a tail follow her out. She brought back the paper and sat down at the table again.

"Don't look up or act startled, but we've been spotted."

"What are we going to do?" she asked with a strained effort to conceal the panic welling up inside her.

"I'm not sure . . . yet," he replied. "How about if we eat breakfast?"

"I hope for our sake this is an inspiring meal," she chided.

They tried to eat at a leisurely pace, each holding a section of the paper but not really reading it. After the refill of coffee, Bill excused himself and went to the men's room. Again one of the men followed him in.

As Bill returned to the table, he saw a side door to the kitchen along the same corridor that led to the rest rooms. He had an idea, a plan that sprang up like a desert flower after a rain. He just hoped it wouldn't wilt equally as fast.

"I have an idea," Bill whispered.

"You've been a good knight thus far, so I'll follow your lead. What do we do, run out and jump on your white horse?" Holly quipped.

"If it were only that simple," he replied.

"I'll trust you on this one, especially since I don't have the least idea of what to do," she said in a subdued whisper.

"Go to the ladies' room. The hallway is a dead end, so hopefully you won't be followed. There's a door to the kitchen about halfway back. Go through the kitchen and out the back. Get as far away from here as you can, then take a cab to the meeting with Ken. I think I can lose our friends out in the lobby. By splitting up, we double their problem and halve our own."

The plan had a firm analytical foundation, though Bill was thinking that theory and reality are not always analogous. He knew only too well from his years of research that what looks good on paper doesn't always work out in the laboratory.

"I'll meet you two there, but if I get delayed, tell Ken I'll meet him at the Lincoln Memorial between nine and ten tonight."

"I don't want to leave you." Holly's voice trembled a little at this suggestion and she grabbed his hand.

"I know, but it's just for a little while," he soothed. "Anyway, that's the best I can come up with." Then, taking her hand in both of his, he looked deeply into her eyes. "Holly . . ." He hesitated, searching for the right words.

"Yes?"

"Uh . . . be careful, OK?"

"Be careful yourself, Mr. White Knight." She smiled that disarming smile and gave his hand a gentle squeeze.

"That's *Dr.* White Knight, to you, m'lady." Bill attempted a reassuring smile back, hoping his expression did not betray his inner turmoil.

Holly got up from the table and walked toward the rest room as Bill picked up the newspaper and prepared for a wait. He wanted to give her as much time as possible before their shadows realized she was not coming back. About ten minutes after Holly had left the table, Bill noticed the men starting to fidget and look around nervously. The idea that Holly wasn't coming back was evidently sinking in. She had been in the powder room too long.

Bill decided it was time to make his move. When he got up to pay the check, one member of the surveillance team went over to the hall leading to the rest rooms. The other walked out behind him.

He entered the lobby and angled toward the front entrance. A group of people departed the elevator and he cut in front of them, trying to put distance between himself and his tail. He was in the clear as he left the hotel and turned up the street toward the Metro station. The familiar large white M and the entrance lay just ahead. Once in the shadowy depths it would be easy to disappear.

Before he could reach the entrance, a large black limousine slowly pulled up beside him. A man appeared on his right side and pressured him toward the curb just as the car stopped.

The car door swung open abruptly in front of him, blocking his way. A raspy whisper demanded, "Get in, Dr. Chandler."

All he could see was the cavernous end of a revolver pointed directly at his chest. He looked around for help, but there was none. Reluctantly, he slid into the backseat. The door closed, blocking the morning sunlight. Staring at the black hole of the gun barrel, he wondered momentarily what it would feel like to be shot.

"You've caused Mr. Jarvis a lot of trouble, Doctor. I don't think he's going to be very happy when he sees you. There are many other things he would rather be doing than chasing you around the country," the man sneered.

"Well, he sort of screwed up my vacation too," Bill rebutted.

No one could possibly see in through the blackened windows of the limousine as it nosed its way through traffic and turned up the George Washington Parkway on the Virginia side of the river. He knew they were headed to Potomac, an easy drive from Crystal City. Bill silently prayed Holly had gotten away and was able to meet with Ken.

The day was spectacular. The leaves, still covering most of the trees, displayed a multitude of color. They had been washed clean by the rain the night before, and the droplets of water magnified their pigment. It was the kind of day when he would have enjoyed walking the streets of Georgetown arm in arm with someone he loved.

Suddenly he realized he might never see Georgetown again. Just as abruptly it occurred to him that he had fallen in love with Holly. *I wonder if Sandy somehow knows, and if she knows, does she approve?* he thought.

The car swerved sharply onto the brick drive to the mansion's entrance and brought him back to reality. It was hard to believe that only twenty-four hours had passed since he and Holly had been in this house together; that all seemed like a different world in a different time in a different life.

His escorts pushed him ahead into the great room. If this house was supposed to give the impression of a fortress, it was well designed. Jarvis stood at the far end of the room, watching with an amused grin as Bill was tied into a straight-backed chair and then pummeled several times by one of his thugs.

"Where's Holly, Dr. Chandler?" Jarvis finally asked.

"I don't know," Bill spat out defiantly.

The impact of the back of Jarvis's hand snapped Bill's head sideways. Blood ran from the corner of his mouth.

"Don't make this unpleasant! Where's Holly?" Jarvis demanded again.

Bill licked the blood from the corner of his mouth, smiled slightly, and said nothing.

"Holly, where's Holly?"

"The last time I saw her she was on her way to the ladies' room. Did your thugs try there? Maybe she has a bladder problem." Bill wanted to hurt Jarvis, but all he could do was make bad jokes.

A feeling of dread swept over Bill Chandler as he saw Jarvis step back; one of the escorts from Crystal City methodically began to beat him. Each impact was expertly executed. This was clearly a man who was good at what he did and who enjoyed his work. The blows were not hard enough to break anything vital, and Bill fought to remain conscious. They were delivered and placed hard enough to hurt, but he was determined not to go easily into oblivion. He wondered if they would beat him to death or execute him with a bullet to the brain. Finally, feeling consciousness slipping away, Bill's last thought was that he would probably never wake up.

Who knows? he told himself as another blow landed on the side of his face. *Maybe I'll see Sandy.*

It was late afternoon when he woke up on the floor of the same room in Jarvis's manor house that he and Holly had escaped from earlier. He hurt everywhere. Bill concluded he wasn't dead, since he couldn't imagine being dead and having so much pain. He rolled over, moaning, and felt dried blood caked in the corners of his mouth. He checked his teeth with his tongue; his swollen lips felt rubbery. He thought he knew how a prizefighter felt after losing a fight and couldn't imagine why anyone would want to do that for a living.

There was a dreamlike quality to his orientation. True, he hurt; that was real. But why was he here? Slowly, his memory came back, running through his mind like TV reruns. *I was taken by Jarvis's men as I left the hotel. Holly and I were supposed to meet Ken. . . . I hope Holly made it. I was brought in a limo to Jarvis's house in Potomac, Maryland.*

Jarvis's goons had been very insistent that he tell them where Holly was, which could only mean she got away. As he felt the pain in his face and stomach, he realized just how badly they wanted her. *She must know something or have something they need desperately!*

"This spy business really sucks!" he said out loud as he lay there on the floor.

At least she got away, he thought. He hoped he'd not said anything about the meeting with Ken while they were pounding on him. . . . He shook his head, trying to clear the fog and sharpen his memory.

When the room finally stopped moving, he slowly inched his way to the wall. Grabbing the windowsill, he pulled his way up the wall and looked out. Dusk was settling over the landscape. Painfully, he made his way to the door and checked, but as he suspected, it was locked.

Well, I've missed the meeting at Mount Vernon, and by the looks of it, I'll miss the meeting at the Lincoln Memorial too. He slid down to the floor as his legs became rubbery; the room started to spin, and a new wave of darkness settled over him. Gradually, the pain eased as unconsciousness enveloped him like the embrace of a lover on a dark night, ending his concern and anguish.

17

MEETING PLACE

Holly turned through the kitchen door marked IN. Quickly, she crossed the kitchen, clipping past the large stoves and ovens. Cooks and waiters looked at her inquisitively, but since several were undocumented aliens they said nothing. She went out the back of the hotel, undetected by Jarvis's men standing vigil in the lobby. They had not anticipated one of their prey leaving by the back door. She then walked into and through the kitchen of the Pentagon Place Hotel across the alley. There were some strange glances, but again no one said a word to her as she wound between the steam tables and ovens.

The lobby of the hotel was almost empty at this time of the morning. She paused at the door and carefully surveyed the panorama from the front desk to the entrance, noticing, on her far right, a hallway that led to the meeting rooms, or so a sign indicated.

Just then the elevator doors opened, and a small group of people started across the lobby. She fell in at the rear of the crowd. As they passed the front door on their way to the meeting rooms, she stepped out onto the sidewalk. A large black limousine was parked near the corner on the opposite side. She turned away from it and saw the doorman approaching her.

"Cab, ma'am?"

"Yes, please," she answered quietly, trying to control the quiver in her voice.

The doorman signaled, and almost immediately a taxi pulled to the curb, the back door opened—and she was free.

Holly boarded the cab and within minutes was crossing the Fourteenth Street Bridge into downtown Washington. She wanted to watch out the back window but was afraid to, afraid she might see the black limousine. She was sure it was the one Jarvis had used when he had taken them from Bill's apartment to his house in Potomac.

Now that she was clear of the immediate danger, she had time to think. Bill's name was the first thing that swept into her consciousness, then apprehension and concern flooded her thoughts. If only he could have gone out with her. . . . Did he get clear of the hotel?

She thought about the previous night when he had returned to their room. Though she had said nothing, she had awakened as he had crawled into bed. Remembering, Holly could still feel the security of his arm across her shoulders. And she could still sense the assurance his body had given to hers as he snuggled against her.

She had fully expected him to wake her and make love to her. The fact that he had not done so left her gratified yet longing for him even more. She could not remember ever knowing a man quite like him. He just had to be safe. . . .

The ride around the Mall seemed to take forever, and more than once a black limousine pulled alongside her cab at a stoplight. She kept her head turned the opposite direction as if she were sightseeing. Finally, near the Lincoln Memorial, Holly said, "Pull over here!"

The driver stopped in front of the Lincoln Memorial. Holly paid the driver and cautiously exited the safety of the cab. Quickly, she ran away from the openness of the large marble shrine and found refuge in the cover of the trees surrounding the entrance to the Vietnam Veterans' Memorial.

Shaking with fear, she stopped and looked around. Several people were at the Wall, looking for names. No one seemed interested in her, so she slowly walked down the sloping sidewalk and stopped near the center. In the shadow of the black marble she felt sheltered. The Wall and its thousands of names seemed to shield her with massive arms extending in both directions.

She stayed there for twenty minutes, pretending to look at the names inscribed on the Wall. In reality she was constantly scrutinizing the few people who were coming and going at that hour.

Finally she left the seclusion of the somber memorial and hailed another cab. After telling the driver she was a tourist, she had him circle the Mall and the White House before asking him to take her to Mount Vernon. She joined the short line of people waiting for tickets and then entered the grounds.

Holly had a hard time trying to imagine what the place must have been like when George Washington actually lived there. The view of the house as she walked up the curved brick path was magnificent. She wished it were possible to see carriages arriving at the stately front door to discharge their finely dressed passengers.

The outlying buildings and grounds gave testimony to a time that is revered as a kinder era. But, she thought, how could it have been a kinder time when the slaves who built the grand mansion couldn't leave their master and live—any more than she could leave Jarvis and expect to live?

She glanced at her watch. It was 10:50. If only Ken and Bill would get here. Holly felt very alone and vulnerable. Her thoughts returned to Bill and a smile graced her lips. *Oh, he just has to have gotten away!* she thought again. She entered the mansion and slowly started through the rooms, hoping against hope to find Bill waiting inside the next doorway. Exiting out onto the long porch overlooking the river, she heard, "I think we could use Old George and the Continental Army about now, huh?"

The sound of Ken's voice startled her and she turned to face him.

"Where's Bill?" he asked.

"We were being watched at the hotel. He acted as a diversion to let me get away. He said if he didn't show up here, you were to meet him at the Lincoln Memorial tonight, between nine and ten o'clock," Holly answered. "But, Ken, Jarvis's men were all over the place. How did they know where we were?" she exclaimed.

"I don't know. I didn't think I was followed, but . . ." He paused, looking around. "Bill seems to have been very resourceful up to now. I think he'll be all right," he said, trying to convince himself as much as Holly. "These people"—he searched for the words—"have a lot of knowledge about your movements. They're dangerous and intelligent opponents."

"*Opponents!* Do you think this is some kind of a game?" she asked indignantly.

"No, Holly, it's not a game. However, sometimes it's easier to plan moves and countermoves if we act as if we're playing a game of strategy. Does that make sense?" Ken countered.

"No, it must be some kind of male thing. I just want it to go away!"

Ken and Holly walked down a small path leading away from the house and sat for a while on the grassy slope below the crest of the hill. Ken reclined, leaning on one elbow, and Holly sat with her legs drawn up under her skirt. She smoothed out its edges, just short enough that her bare knees were discreetly exposed. They looked like a couple enjoying the day. The balmy late-fall sun felt warm on her face; the air had lost its chill from the night before.

"We need to talk about your work for Jarvis," Ken said. "If we hope to defeat him, we need to find a kink in his armor. And from what I can learn, which hasn't been much so far, he has well-constructed armor. Tell me everything you know, no matter how trivial or insignificant it may seem."

Holly began to tell Ken of her time with Jarvis and his organization. "I was hired by Jarvis two years ago as an executive secretary for the NuStyle Import-Export Corporation. At first, I worked primarily out of the San Francisco office as the secretary for the branch manager. The company brought in clothes made mostly in Hong Kong, Taiwan, Singapore, and Korea, though we did some business in Europe. Most of the clothes were what you would call trendy—jeans, sportswear, and things like that. We sold to a few large department stores on the West Coast, but mostly we sold to wholesalers."

Holly paused while she gazed across the river at the colorful leaves of the Maryland countryside.

"One interesting thing . . . we did have a very large army contract for some winter coats. That was a very active account. At first I was astonished at the amount of money the army spent on winter coats. One day, Jarvis came to the San Francisco office. It had been announced that he was looking for a private secretary, and I was called in for an interview.

"A few days later, I was contacted and told that Jarvis wanted me to move to the New York office and become his private secretary. It was an unbelievable promotion, and the money was great. For a time it was just routine work, and nothing seemed out of the ordinary.

"Then we started to take frequent trips to North Carolina. Jarvis said he liked the island, that he did his best work at Cape Fear Manor. But his business meetings there were . . . well, unusual."

"Unusual in what way?" Ken asked.

"Well, the people would arrive at strange hours. Most of the meetings were at night, and I wasn't involved until recently. I guess it was this past June before I really understood . . . what was going on. I made the reservations for Jarvis's guests at the local motel, usually at the Sand Dollar. But it was strange, because the guests almost always had some very common name, like Smith or

Jones, yet many of the clients looked foreign, principally European or Asian, but more recently Middle Eastern—you know, Arabs," Holly continued.

Ken straightened up. He knew they'd been in one spot too long; instinct told him it was time to move. He stood up and offered Holly his hand. He pulled her easily upright, and they began to walk down the path to the wharf below. The path descended sharply and then bent into a long, slow incline toward the river. It was tree-lined and covered with a fresh layer of white gravel. The wharf was at least an eighth of a mile from the main house. Ken and Holly were the only people on that part of the grounds.

"Did you ever recognize any of these Smiths or Joneses?" Ken continued as they approached a low wall by the water's edge.

"Not at first. Other than that picture of Mr. Harris that Bill showed me, but . . ." She paused as she sat down and toyed with the hem of the skirt again. "Over the last three or four months one man came down several times. I just saw his picture on the front page of the newspaper this morning." She unfolded the paper that Bill had sent her to buy at the newsstand in the hotel.

The headline over the photo of Randolph W. Blaine said, "Secretary of Defense to Leave for NATO Meeting."

"Holly, you've got to be wrong! That's Secretary Blaine! Certainly *he* didn't visit Jarvis as a 'Mr. Smith'!" Ken said.

"Ken, I'm not lying! He was down there two weeks ago. He and Jarvis met at the house from twelve-fifteen until two in the morning. I sat in on the first half of that meeting. It was then that I decided I had to get away from Jarvis." Holly was speaking softly but earnestly as she watched the swirling water of the Potomac River.

"What did Jarvis and Blaine talk about at that meeting?" Ken asked.

"He wants to kill me to make sure I never tell about those meetings." Holly's voice almost broke. Then she took a breath and smiled wryly. "Since he's probably going to kill me anyway, I might as well tell you. But, you know, then he'll probably kill you too," she added with total resignation in her voice.

Ken put his hand on Holly's shoulder and looked at her. "He isn't the first to try, and he won't succeed if I have anything to say about it. Now, tell me about the meeting."

She stared for a moment at the landscape across the river and then said, "Blaine was asking if the contract was made with Hezbollah. Then he asked if any money had been received. Jarvis said the first payment had been received into the usual account. Then they got into an argument about how they were going to get the information. It was concerning something called a Tel-Ray system. Jarvis said he needed the drawings, and Blaine said the department had not received the blueprints yet from the contractor.

"Blaine asked if a man named Harris could be counted on for the information in time if the plans were not submitted to the department. Jarvis replied that if he—I guess he meant Harris—didn't come through, Jarvis would eliminate him as a supplier from the network. That started an argument. I was asked to leave, but you could hear them yelling at each other from the other room. Finally, Blaine got up and walked out. I was waiting in the hall, and he went right past me. He was saying something about too much killing, but I didn't hear all of it."

"Holly," Ken said, "was any record of these meetings ever kept?" Ken rested his foot on the wall beside Holly and leaned down to her so they could talk in quieter voices.

Holly nodded. "Jarvis has been getting more nervous lately, and about six months ago, he started keeping a record of the meetings he had with certain people. He would give me a tape recording to transcribe after each one," Holly replied.

"Where does he keep the tapes and the transcripts?" Ken questioned.

"I only made one copy of the transcripts, and I gave it to him. I don't know what he did with them. At first I had to give the tapes back to him. Later on, after we were engaged, he told me to just erase the tape, and he would use them over," Holly said.

"Holly, don't you have any idea where Jarvis put the minutes of any of the meetings?" Ken urged.

"No, Ken, I really don't! I just typed the transcription of them and then I gave it to Jarvis!" Holly glanced off into the distance. She was thinking about Bill. Where was he? Was he dead? Why did she ever get mixed up in something like this? And worse yet, why had she dragged someone like Bill into it? She fought to hold back the tears welling up in her eyes as she thought about him. And now, why was she holding back with Ken? She was going to have to trust someone sometime. She did trust Bill. But he wasn't here. There were too many questions and not enough answers.

Ken looked at her and continued. "For what it's worth, I believe what you've told me."

As the water ebbed and flowed against the gray granite wall, Holly felt the river take on a sinister tone. She could feel the brownish liquid pulling her from the shore, closing over her head and cutting off her breath. She began to wish she had drowned in the ocean when she had jumped from the pier. Holly knew it was just a matter of time until Jarvis had them all.

Suddenly there was a rustle of leaves on the path behind them. An elderly couple appeared around the turn at the upper end of the path, apparently engrossed in the multicolored leaves that were making a futile attempt to cling to the branches. Slowly they strolled past Ken and Holly, remarking how the colors of the trees looked like an impressionist's painting. Ken and Holly tried to look unassuming as they lowered their conversation and turned toward the river.

"I think we'd better get out of here," Ken said under his breath.

"Where can we go?" Holly asked.

Just as Ken pulled Holly from her position on the wall he heard the sound of metal on metal. Instinctively he threw Holly to the ground behind a fallen tree. She hit with enough force to momentarily lose her breath. Ken pulled his model 649 Bodyguard .38 Smith & Wesson from under his left arm and dived to cover as a projectile glanced off the exact place Holly had been sitting. His aim was deadly accurate as the first two rounds slammed into the chest of the elderly man, sending him backward into a pile of dead, tangled branches. Another round splintered the fallen tree just in front of him; Ken's arm moved ever so slightly, and he squeezed the trigger again. His years of training and practice at the FBI Academy proved lethal as the woman crumpled onto the river-bank.

It was all over in less than three seconds, but the sounds seemed to echo again and again in Holly's ears while the smell of cordite stung her nostrils. The blue-gray smoke slowly drifted out over the water.

Ken grabbed her and lifted her up. "You all right?"

"I . . . I think so. I can't breathe too well. But I think I'm OK," she stammered.

Ken quickly checked the bodies. Both were dead. There was no identification on either of them, and all the labels had been removed from their clothes. The shock of the bullet had knocked the wig off the woman, revealing that she was much younger than she had appeared. This was, without a doubt, a professional hit. But was it aimed at Holly, or was it someone from the past who wanted him? His years in the bureau had earned him some notable enemies. Unfortunately, the event had happened so fast he did not have time to take the chance on not killing the aggressors. So he would not be able to find out whom they were really after.

"Like I said, we'd better get out of here . . . if we can. There's probably a backup to this pair around somewhere."

Ken and Holly moved cautiously through the trees toward the house, looking for the walkway that would convey them to Ken's car in the parking lot. He avoided the well-worn paths and ducked behind the hedge guarding the entrance. They stopped in a small cluster of trees for a moment to watch Ken's car. It was surrounded by two other cars, and there were at least three men sitting in one of the cars, obviously watching for something or someone. It was evident that the couple back in the woods had not come alone. Several agonizing minutes passed. Eventually the car doors opened, and the men got out. They talked for a short time, then two of them started toward the gate. The third stayed behind, standing beside the car.

"Now what are we going to do?" Holly whispered.

"Why not pray for a miracle?" Ken said curtly.

At that moment a Gray Line tour bus drove up to the entrance gate, stopped, and opened its doors. A horde of people began filing out of the main house and side buildings in a steady stream and headed for the bus. Most were elderly couples, some with canes and walkers. All were talking at once, the noise akin to that from a flock of magpies.

As the tourists approached the hedge where Holly and Ken were hiding, the guide was saying, "This is one of the most visited parks in the D.C. area. However, it's also a nice, quiet place for a picnic or a casual stroll in the woods. I'm sorry we can't spend more time here, but we're late for the luncheon. But please note the tranquil paths, amid scenic woods, where the harmony of nature is unspoiled by the city about it."

It took the tour group about ten minutes to load onto the bus, due to the disabilities of many of the elderly participants. This effectively blocked the entrance to the park. When the last of the assembly of people was past them, Ken pulled Holly from their cover and joined the merry band of senior citizens near the end of the line.

As they mixed into the center of the crowd, they crossed the open entrance and walked casually past one of the observing men. They boarded the tour bus unnoticed, with Ken guiding Holly to a seat at the back where he could watch out the back window. The bus pulled out of the parking lot and headed north up the parkway toward downtown Alexandria and the bridges to Washington. Their escape went unnoticed.

The guide did not notice that two more seats on the bus had been filled until they were well under way.

"Pardon me," he said, looking at the new additions. "Where did you two come from?"

"It seemed like a fine day for a tour," Ken said. "We thought we would join up. Where do we go to next?"

"You can't just join up!" the guide protested. "You have to have reservations. You have to start with the rest of the group. You have to pay! You have to be picked up! You can't just join up!" By now he was screaming. "We don't even know where to drop you off." Ken and Holly's materialization into his tour greatly disturbed his sense of order.

"Well, if that's the way you feel, let us off here. We certainly don't want to be somewhere we're not wanted!" Ken replied with a tone that implied his feelings were hurt.

The tour group was equally divided. Some said, "This nice young couple should be allowed to stay!" while others felt they were infringing on the company's autonomy.

The whole scene was so comical Holly found herself laughing.

The bus pulled to the curb. Ken and Holly got off and quickly disappeared down an alley near the center of Alexandria. Ken found a phone and called his wife.

"Hi, honey." He paused. "Listen carefully, and no questions . . . bring your kit and meet me where we spent our last anniversary. One more thing. Watch out for a tail." He hung up the phone.

He turned to Holly and said, "We need to have you see my boss, but first you need a new look. I think you're too recognizable."

They took a cab to the Holiday Inn in Bethesda and went up to the room reserved by Ken's wife. She met them there with a change of clothes and her beautician supplies. It was only a short time until Holly's dark hair had been changed to auburn and its shoulder-brushing length trimmed to a short feathered cut. New makeup and a different dress, and Holly could pass for almost anyone but herself.

Looking into the mirror, she was amazed at the transformation. "I can't believe it's really me!" she exclaimed as she shook her short hair.

"You look great. I think it will be hard to recognize you now," Ken said. He turned to his wife. "Honey, would you see if you can get us reservations for a couple of cabins up at Skyline Drive in the Big Meadows area? We need a safe house for a while, and I'm not sure there is anywhere in the District that qualifies. Make the reservations under the name Hoffman. Then, I want you to get the kids out of school and take them to your aunt Pat's house. You all stay there until you hear from me. Don't go back home to get anything. Just go get the kids and get out of town."

"Ken, I don't like this. What's going on?" she asked.

"I don't want to tell you now. The less you know, the better. Please just do what I said, and do it very quietly. I love you."

18

A WIDENING WEB

The Hoover Building was an impressive sight to Holly as Ken led her up to his third-floor office. She seemed nervous as he motioned for her to take a seat at his desk, and he picked up the phone.

"I'm sorry," a woman's voice came over the speaker phone, "but Mr. Billings has someone in his office right now, Mr. Jenkins. I'll call you as soon as he's free." Then as an afterthought, the secretary added, "I thought you were in Montana."

"On my way. Just had to take care of one small thing before I left town. Thanks, Evelyn." He hung up the phone.

Holly sat at Ken's desk looking out the glass partition that made up the upper half of the cubicle forming his office. Ken was staring at Holly for no particular reason just as her face suddenly went pale and a gasp escaped her throat. She instinctively brought her hand up to her chest while the other clutched the arm of the chair.

"What's the matter, Holly?"

"Jarvis! It's Jarvis! What's he doing here?" Holly demanded, her voice shaking. "Why the big charade, Ken? If you were going to give me to Jarvis, why didn't you just kill me down by the river

213

like you did those other people?" She looked at him with an icy gaze.

"What are you talking about? Settle down. I'm not going to hand you over to Jarvis," Ken responded.

Holly motioned down the hall as she tried to hide her face without being too noticeable. Two men were talking just outside an open door; then they shook hands warmly, and the taller man slapped the other on the shoulder in a gesture of friendship as they parted. The shorter man turned and went back into the office. The taller of the two walked straight down the hall toward Ken and Holly. He walked right on past without a glance at either of them.

"Then what's Jarvis doing here?" she said under her breath.

"Holly, are you sure that was Jarvis?" Ken asked.

"That was Jarvis! I worked for the man for two years. I was going to be married to him. I may not have known him on the inside, but I certainly knew him on the outside!" Holly answered.

"Well, if that was Jarvis, he was talking to Arthur Billings, my boss," Ken said glumly.

Just then the phone rang.

"Mr. Billings can see you now, Mr. Jenkins," the secretary said.

"Holly, stay here. I think it would be best if no one knows what you've told me. At least, not yet. Not until we can figure out who is on what team. This is beginning to look like we are going to need a scorecard just to keep track of the players. And I don't seem to have a scorecard . . . yet!"

Quickly Ken opened a drawer and pulled out a file. Now he wished he hadn't asked to see Art, but there was no way out. This was going to be especially awkward, since he wasn't supposed to be in town right now. He then began to wonder, if Art and Blaine were involved, who in the FBI, CIA, or anywhere else in the government he could trust.

The meeting with Billings was short and went quite badly, but that was not unusual. He and his boss had not gotten along well since he transferred into the section.

"The fingerprints found at the warehouse . . . I've been study-ing them, and I don't think they add substantially to the case . . . ," he stammered again. "I don't think they will add to the overall impression that he . . ." Ken went on for several minutes, dis-cussing something he would not have normally taken to his super-visor. He was afraid Billings was becoming suspicious of him. But Billings didn't seem too concerned or interested in the discussion; mercifully he cut it short by declaring, "Jenkins, you've worked on this from the beginning. You do what you think best. I don't have time to get involved. Now, make a decision, and get out to Montana where they need you."

"Right, Art. I just wanted to be sure I had these loose ends tied up," he said with relief as he stood up and left the office.

Meanwhile, Holly was sitting at Ken's desk with her head buried in her hands. She felt everyone passing by was sizing her up, and any of them might walk up and say, "FBI! You're under arrest." A wave of relief swept over her as she saw Ken walk back toward her.

"Let's get out of here," he said softly.

"I'll go for that!" Holly replied.

As Ken walked Holly down to the elevator, they sensed that each person they passed was staring at them. Ken was very con-fused. He groped for an answer, knowing he was into something that was so big it could possibly consume them all.

Ken signed out a government van from the motorpool. They drove out of the parking garage and turned west toward Virginia. He needed time to think. After crossing Memorial Bridge, he went to a small Italian restaurant in Arlington. There, as he lifted a beer to his lips, he noticed his hand was shaking.

"Holly, we've got to find Bill. Do you have any idea where they might have taken him?" Ken asked.

"Probably back to Cape Fear, if at all possible."

"How about around here? Does Jarvis have an office or ware-house in the D.C. area?" Ken persisted.

"No, there's nothing like that closer than New York. However, when they picked us up at Bill's apartment, they took us to a house in Potomac. . . . I think that was what Bill called it," she replied. "Anyway, when we escaped, we walked a long way down that old canal beside the river. Bill called it the C & O Canal."

"Could you find that house again?"

"Maybe, but only from the river. We'd have to walk up the path Bill and I came down," she said.

"OK, kid, it's too late this evening, but how about a walk first thing in the morning? I hear exercise is good for one's health." Ken waved the waiter over and ordered a spaghetti dinner for both of them. "Hopefully it will be good for Bill's health."

He kept the appointment at the Lincoln Memorial, but knew beforehand it was a wasted trip. Bill never appeared. Ken arrived at 8:30 and left at 11:30, alone, having spent three hours in the shadow of Abraham Lincoln, trying to sort out the information Holly had supplied.

None of this made any sense. Where did this Jarvis come from, why was he a friend of Billings, and how was Secretary of Defense Blaine involved? It made no sense at all.

They spent the night in the motel in Bethesda where Holly's transformation had taken place. Ken left for several hours to slip into his house to get his camera. The rest of the night he spent wondering who his friends were and who in the government he could trust. Ken knew it was impossible to do all that needed doing alone. He needed help, but all he could see were shadows. He was sure the problem was complex. Just how complex was a mystery at this point.

Ken reviewed the facts: One, the man who was holding Bill and wanted to kill Holly was somehow friends with Billings, Ken's own boss in the FBI. Two, Bill had been followed by agents as he left the Hoover Building the other night—Ken had seen that from his window. Three, Bill and Holly had been spotted at the hotel in Crystal City, or, worse, Ken had been followed there. That would mean they already knew Ken was involved in this. Four, somehow the secretary of defense was heavily involved. That raised more questions. Was the CIA? The National Security Council?

For all he knew this might go right up to the White House. If that was the case they could never win. Ken knew he needed a friend he could trust. Suddenly, all the agents he'd worked with the past ten years seemed like strangers. Finally, at 3:30 in the morning, he decided on a name from the past. John Brandt.

19

BILL'S CAPTIVITY

Potomac, Maryland

W e did find your girlfriend and Jenkins down at Mount Vernon, Mr. Chandler. It was good of you to help us. Oh, yes, you don't remember, do you? My men gave you a drug while you were on your way up here. Of course, you know no one will be coming to your aid, don't you?" Jarvis said.

"I don't believe you," Bill shot back. But privately, he wondered if he had sent his two friends to their deaths.

"You might as well face facts, Dr. Chandler. There is no help. The only chance you have is to cooperate and give me the rest of the schematics on the Tel-Ray system. The offer still goes; you can turn a profit, too, if you so choose. In fact, with Harris out of the way, I can arrange for you to have his old job. I'm sure we can work out an arrangement as profitable as he had."

"There's only one problem, Jarvis," Bill said. "I doubt that I would swim in from your boat any better than Ed did. And my old grandfather had a saying, 'If you mix with the bran, the hogs will eat you.' Jarvis, what I don't know about you is if you are the bran or the hog—or maybe you're both."

"Suit yourself. But, Dr. Chandler, you will eventually give me the information on the system. Whether it is easy or hard for you matters little to me. But rest assured, you will give me the information. What happens after that will be up to you." With a snap of his fingers he motioned his guards to remove Dr. Chandler to his quarters.

• • •

About midmorning of his second day at the Jarvis estate, they brought Bill a drawing board and tools from his office at the plant. It was awesome to realize that in a free country a man like Jarvis had so much power and so many resources. He could literally walk into Bill's office and clean it out. In fact, Bill thought, he probably had the security people help carry the stuff out to his car.

"Mr. Jarvis wants you to finish that drawing for him. I'm supposed to make sure you do," a brawny man said as he stood behind Bill. Though there were no thumbscrews in sight, Bill was certain some could be found if the necessity arose or if the thought occurred to his captor. Bill hoped the man's IQ wasn't high enough to think about using them.

"I'm doing the best I can," he replied as he erased the same line for the third time. "This isn't like drawing a cartoon!" If there was ever a time to act like a spoiled, eccentric professor—as Ed Harris was so fond of calling him—now was the time.

Late that night Jarvis came into his prison room and announced, "The day after tomorrow we're going to take a trip, Dr. Chandler."

"Gee, I'd love to, Jarvis, but I just got back from the beach, and I don't have any vacation time left," Bill replied sarcastically.

"Don't get cute, Professor. I own you now, and I will own you for as long as I want. If I want you to go on a trip, you will go. If I want you to die, you, my dear professor, will die," Jarvis mocked.

"You may have me locked up in your house, and I may have to

work on this drawing for you, but you don't own me. You will never, and I mean never, own me."

"Chandler, if you don't become more cooperative I may have to find someone else to finish the Tel-Ray."

"You're welcome to try. Quite frankly I'm tired of the project anyway. But, before you put an ad in the *Post*, there's probably only one other person in America who could take this project from the point I'm at and finish it. That's Dr. Strong, my old mentor. But, unfortunately, he died last April in a car wreck."

Bill had thought long and hard about those words. They had come to him as he sat in his prison. With Sandy gone and Holly and Ken probably dead also, he had nothing to lose and nothing really left to live for. Jarvis didn't know it, but by telling Bill that Holly and Ken were dead, he had freed the scientist. And, Bill thought, there is nothing more dangerous than a totally free man.

"You will leave for Cape Fear the day after tomorrow. Maybe the solitude of the beach will improve the quality of your work. I hope you understand, Chandler; I will not be patient forever."

Day Six

They looked like tourists out enjoying the fall leaves as they pedaled the rented bikes up the path along the old C & O Canal the next morning. The bright autumn sun quickly warmed the cool night air as Ken stopped occasionally to take a picture of the leaves or of Holly or both to ensure their look of innocence. They had ridden about half an hour when Holly stopped.

"It's that brick house up on the hill," she said without pointing.

Ken backed up a little and raised the camera. He carefully aimed at Holly and adjusted the telephoto lens to capture the background detail. Then he began to photograph the house and grounds.

"Smile," Ken said automatically. As the camera whirred he focused and refocused on the grounds and the yard and the approach. If Bill was being held there, it would not be easy to get him out.

"We'd better move on up the path a ways before we turn around so it doesn't look suspicious." They mounted their bicycles and rode another ten minutes up the trail before returning to their car.

They returned their rented bikes and took the film to a one-hour developing service at the Congressional Mall in Bethesda. As they waited for the film to be processed, Ken and Holly bought an early lunch at a cafeteria. He finished eating before Holly, excused himself, and went to a phone.

"Good morning . . . Commander Brandt's office. This is a non-secure line. Petty Officer Solomon speaking."

"This is Ken Jenkins. Is Commander Brandt in?"

"Just a moment, sir."

"Ken! Hey, I haven't heard from you in a coon's age. Whatcha been up to?" Brandt said.

"John, I need to talk to you about something."

"Sure, ol' buddy. Come on over," John answered.

"No, not there, " Ken countered.

"OK. How about lunch? Say, twelve-fifteen?"

"How about some coffee and a bagel in an hour?"

"Sure, anything you say. Do ya want to go over to the Pentagon?"

"I'd rather meet you at the snack stand outside the Natural History Museum on the Mall," Ken replied.

"Anything you say, my man, but you sure are sounding cloak-and-dagger today. That FBI stuff gone to yer head?" his friend joked.

Back at the table Ken told Holly, "I'll drop you off at the motel. I have to meet someone downtown."

Holly looked at him questioningly.

"Reinforcements," he said.

An hour later John bought his coffee and walked toward the bench where Ken was sitting. He was wearing service dress blues under his bridge coat, and as he walked the sun reflected from the gold of the buttons, the shoulder boards, and the bill of his hat that hid his face. But he had a distinctive swagger that would identify him at any distance. They shook hands and sat down.

Across the Mall, the castle of the original Smithsonian museum loomed into the blue sky. Between it and them stood a group of homeless men, huddled around a steam grate.

"OK, ol' buddy, now that we look like two spies out in the cold, what's up?" John said.

It took a while to explain what he knew about the situation. First NuStyle Imports, then Holly, Bill, Jarvis, and last of all, Secretary of Defense Blaine. There was a long silence when he quit talking. Finally John let out a slow sigh mixed with a whistle.

"Well, my man . . . if what you say is true, you've got a bull by the tail."

"Look, John, I need your help. There is no one else in the country I can trust. I don't know how high this goes; I don't know which agencies are involved. What I do know is where they are probably holding Bill. I need your help getting him out. If you will do that much, then you can walk away from it," Ken pleaded.

John looked across the Mall. The stark blue sky silhouetted the old castle. His mind thought of his twenty-eight years of naval service. Just two more years, and he'd be eligible for fall retirement.

He reflected aloud, "This is no time for me to get mixed up in something that might wreck my whole career. There are a lot of things hanging in the balance—my family, my plans, my retirement. . . . But you do have a problem."

He looked up into the sky for several seconds. "Do ya remember '67 down in the delta?"

"I don't think any of us who were there will ever forget the delta," Ken replied.

"You didn't have to give up your cover to get me after I'd been hit."

"I didn't have great cover anyway, and it seemed like a good idea at the time."

The mention of 'Nam drew the two men into sharing their recollections of those events that now seemed as if they'd happened in another lifetime.

• • •

They had been walking through a rice paddy with water up to their ankles. They had just left the patrol boat on the river and were advancing on the village, the day's objective. Lieutenant Junior Grade John Brandt was on the right flank and slightly ahead of the six others in the patrol. Ensign Ken Jenkins was bringing up the rear, constantly looking back at the canal to be sure they had a clear path back to the boat.

The first mortar round exploded with Lieutenant Brandt just within the explosive radius. A piece of shrapnel tore through his right thigh as the concussion knocked him backward. The patrol members hit the ground and raised their weapons out of the water to return fire. More mortar rounds began to rain on the rice paddy. Ensign Jenkins was behind a small retaining wall between the fields. It was clear that if they stayed in their present position it was only a matter of time until they would all be dead. Ken raised his M-16 and squeezed off a quick burst. In that instant he saw John lying exposed and bleeding.

As the patrol boat began to return fire into the village, Ken rose from his position and ran forward to the place Brandt had fallen. The other members of the squad opened up with cover fire for Ken.

"Let's get out of here!" he yelled at the four others lying scattered in the paddy. Ken lifted John onto his shoulder and began to run back toward the boat. He was crossing the small mound separating the paddy when his foot slipped, throwing them both to the ground and knocking the wind out of him. At that moment another round exploded just ahead of them, sending a torrent of mud and water over them.

Ken's ears were still ringing as he jumped up, hoisting John back onto his shoulder and running again toward the boat. All six members of the patrol returned to the boat, and they sped away back down the river. After the explosion of the first round, the boat had called for air support, and as they pulled away from the bank, three A-7s roared out of the cloudless sky and dropped a full load of bombs onto the village. Ken watched as the bright orange napalm spread its death by fire across the rice paddy and village. The concussions followed the retreating boat down the muddy Mekong River.

Lieutenant Brandt lay on the deck of the boat while a Navy corpsman cut his pant leg to expose the torn flesh mingled with blood and mud.

"Hey, ol' buddy, that was a pretty dumb thing to do out there," Brandt told Ken. "Ya could've got yourself killed. . . . But thanks, pal. I owe ya one."

"Not a problem," Ken replied. "You'da done the same for me."

"Hope we never have the opportunity to find out. Hey, that hurts!" he yelled as the corpsman began to clean the mud out of the wound.

"You're a lucky man, Lieutenant. It just took the top off some of the muscle. Doesn't look like it went too deep."

Following his convalescence at the Naval Hospital in Okinawa, Lt. John Brandt had been selected for SEAL training at the Naval Amphibious Base in Coronado, California. He and Ken never served together again, but that day in the rice paddy was a part of their lives that neither man would ever forget.

● ● ●

The wind blew across the open expanse of the Mall, and as Brandt watched the homeless men move onto the steam grate, he felt the chill of the autumn dampness. Or was it the chill of the story he and Ken had just been talking about? *What would be the best thing to do?* John thought. *I should walk away from this . . . but . . . I'm obligated.*

"Yeah. OK, my man, I'm with ya. I guess I'll grab on to the tail of that bull too," John replied as he turned his gaze away from Ken and toward the Capitol at the far end of the Mall.

Later that afternoon Ken and John met at Holly's room in Bethesda. They spent the rest of the day poring over the pictures Ken and Holly had taken and listening as Holly repeated again and again whatever she could remember from her internment and escape from the house. Then they studied the map of the area repeatedly until a plan began to take shape.

After dark, they assembled the necessary supplies and moved to a staging area along River Road.

At 11:30 that night, Ken and John were walking down the path of the old C & O Canal along the Potomac; Holly was driving a van to the Virginia side of the river, downstream from the objective. There was no moon and no sound along the canal except for the rustling of the leaves still clinging to the trees and the occasional crunch of a stick under their feet.

Ken wondered, *Is this just a move of desperation, this attempt to rescue Bill?*

Then immediately he chided himself for thinking like that. Just as it had been in the jungle so many years ago, once a mission started, you did not think about the why, you just thought about what you had to do. *That's probably why we have the young fight the battles,* he reflected. *They don't stop to think about the why. They just fight.*

John rounded the bend and crouched low behind a bush. He motioned ahead. Silhouetted against the black sky was the house, surrounded by a low brick wall. The house overlooked the canal and river with a clear view except for the upriver side, the area that Ken and John had picked to mount their assault. They waited a full five minutes. Just as they started to move along the wall, a lone figure appeared. He walked slowly by the inside of the wall, carefully surveying the approaches up the hill from the riverbank. As he turned, John could make out the shape of an Uzi slung casually from his shoulder.

"These boys play with the real thing, don't they?" John remarked to Ken in a low whisper.

The man moved on and Ken whispered back, "I'll neutralize him on the next round." He quietly moved off through the thicket they had been hiding in and reached the side of the brick wall several minutes ahead of the guard's next pass. Lying beside the wall, he could feel his heart beating against the cold ground. Sweat beaded on his forehead and he wondered how well camouflaged they really were with the dark face paint. He was thankful that it was a moonless night.

The quiet, safe sounds of the night were shaken by the approach of footsteps. At first John was afraid the man had crossed over the short wall and would step right on him. Then he realized the man had stopped beside the wall just past him. The guard placed one foot on the low brick and leaned down on his knee with an elbow. The Uzi hung at a casual angle, pointed at the ground. Ken crouched like a leopard ready to spring. The leather strap twisted around both his hands with enough slack to easily slide over a man's head. With one quick movement he sprang up, slipping the leather around the neck of the guard and pulling him over the wall.

The move caught the man completely by surprise. He tumbled forward over the wall. Ken was on top of him before he could utter more than a grunt. He quieted the man with a well-placed blow to the head with the butt of his .38, then hurried to gag and tie the unconscious man.

Next, Ken and John rolled over the wall, keeping low profiles, and silently crept up to the back door. There didn't seem to be an electronic security system in place as registered by the hand-held scanner, or if one was present, it was currently disarmed. The door was unlocked. Silently they crossed the threshold into the kitchen. Voices could be heard down a hall to the left. Ken moved in that direction with his 9 mm automatic at the ready.

"Got any beer left in the fridge?" a voice with a thick southern drawl asked.

"Yeah, I think there's a couple left. Git us one, and let's play some cards. I'm ready to git back to the Cape. Met a new gal 'bout a week ago. Like to git back there and see some more of her!" the second voice said, laughing.

Meanwhile, John had found the stairs to the second floor. He started down the hall, waiting and listening at each door before he cautiously opened it. Each door seemed like an Indian basket; he expected a king cobra to spring out at him at any minute. The anticipation at each door grew as he knew sooner or later he would open one and find Jarvis's men. The fourth door was as silent as the rest as he tried the knob. It was locked. Reaching inside his pocket, he produced a lock pick, inserted it into the lock, gave a slight twist, and felt the tumblers fall as easily as if he were using a key.

The room was dark, but he thought he could hear breathing. He stepped into the room out of the highlighted doorway and scanned the blackness. As he scanned the room with his infrared glasses, he saw a figure crumpled into the corner. It wasn't moving. Silently he approached the man and put his gun barrel against the head of the sleeping figure.

"One noise or move, and you're history," John whispered.

"Who . . .who are you?!" Bill asked in a groggy but terrified voice. What he saw was something out of a horror movie. The gun was being pointed at him by a biped with a large helmet and mechanical eyes, like antennae, protruding out of it. It didn't occur to him he was looking at infrared night-vision glasses.

"Makes no matter. I'm looking for Bill Chandler."

"I'm Chandler."

"Let's go!" John said.

"Where?" he demanded.

"To see Ken and Holly," he answered.

"They're dead. Who are you trying to kid? I killed them." Bill slumped back into the corner.

"Ken's downstairs right now and will get his butt blown off if you don't get yours movin'. You didn't make the meeting at the Lincoln Memorial the day you got picked up at the hotel. Now do you believe me?" John was getting nervous. This was taking entirely too long. Their risk of discovery was growing with every second.

Bill looked into the camouflaged face with the strange Martian glasses on and said, "You must be the Marines. I'd prayed they would land."

John helped him stand up. The room spun, and his legs were like rubber.

"I think they drugged me tonight for the trip in the morning," Bill said.

"Can you walk?" John asked.

"I'll crawl like a snake if it gets me out of here," he replied.

With John's help they made their way back to the kitchen and met up with Ken. In spite of the space-age glasses, Bill could recognize him, but at times there seemed to be two or three of him. Bill elected to think the middle one was really Ken. They started out the back door, and a loud voice suddenly came out of nowhere.

"Hey! Where . . . ? What the—?"

The rest of the man's thoughts were lost for an eternity as fire and smoke belched from Ken's gun and a large red hole appeared in the man's chest. Bill's rescuers grabbed him under the arms and half dragged, half carried him across the yard to the wall. He stumbled and fell over the wall, then rolled uncontrollably down the steep embankment into a stagnant pool of water in the old deserted canal. Many shouts and voices, none of which he could make out, arose above him.

His orientation was completely destroyed, and he knew he was about to vomit. He tried to raise himself out of the slimy water, but he had no strength left. Bill felt the acid, rancid taste in the back of his mouth and immediately began to regurgitate. The world spun in ever faster circles as he lost consciousness. John and Ken caught him and dragged him out of the water.

Bill was in a dark, peaceful sleep, oblivious to the mayhem occurring around him. Men crashed through the underbrush just yards behind them. Ken and John threw him into the bottom of a rubber raft and silently pushed it out into the current of the Potomac River. Shouts of, "Which way did they go?" could be heard on the bank as the men slowly glided away from their pursuers.

After a few minutes, the rescuers rowed the raft toward the Virginia side of the river. Bill lay in the bottom in a small pool of cold water but never knew it. Several miles downriver, the raft came to rest on a small sand bar. Ken and John carried Bill up the bank to their van and pushed him into the back.

He regained consciousness again, but his whole perception was distorted. He could see grotesque shadows of people above him; the heads and arms weren't connected, and strange colors flowed through them. Some of them had multiple arms in pairs of twos and threes, all moving around.

There was a voice, but it was a long way off. It sounded familiar, but he couldn't get close enough to it to make it out. It was calling him, and Bill wanted to answer. But he couldn't.

"He's really out of it, ol' buddy," John said.

"We might as well let him sleep until it wears off. I don't think it will do any good to stimulate him," Ken answered.

Holly climbed from the driver's seat into the back of the van and looked at Bill.

"Is he dead?" she asked, stunned at his appearance.

"Nah . . . but tomorrow morning he's going to wish he was," John said.

She sat down on the floor of the van and lifted his head onto her lap. Taking out a handkerchief, she began to wipe the mud and vomit from his face.

"Where to now?" John asked.

"Big Meadows, up on the Skyline Drive. My wife, Sally, has a couple of cabins reserved for us under the name Hoffman. It should be safe enough until we can figure out our next move," Ken answered.

Day Seven

Big Meadows, Virginia

Bill awoke the next morning with the room going about ten revolutions per minute faster than the earth. He seemed to hurt everywhere. However, the worst part was that he had no idea where he was. He lay there trying to orient himself; time and place were a mystery. The room was rustic, with pine walls and ceiling and a large stone fireplace which occupied the entire wall opposite his bed. There were two doors. He was trying to imagine where they led to when one of them opened and Holly walked out. He could see a bathroom in the distance. He tried to rise to get out of the bed and would have fallen to the floor but for the quick work of Holly.

"Am I dead?" Bill asked.

"No, and you're not dreaming either," she replied as she kissed him lightly on the lips.

"That the bathroom?" he asked.

"Yes."

"Pardon me . . ." He began to stagger in that direction. Holly supported him and guided him into it.

He leaned on the sink. "OK, I think I've got it now."

"You sure?" she questioned.

231

"I'll holler if I need help." He wasn't ready to admit he was an invalid yet, his male ego kicking into gear.

After washing and gargling, he swayed and weaved his way back to the bed.

He looked at Holly as he lay down. "I thought you were dead," he mumbled.

She pressed her mouth against his in a long and promising kiss. Then she replied, "If that feels like I'm dead, that's the last one of those you'll ever get!" Her eyes sparkled.

She took his hand and put it up to her cheek. He felt the warm softness of her flesh and watched her close her eyes. She seemed to be praying.

"Does this feel like I'm dead? Now don't be an idiot. You didn't save me in North Carolina to have me die in Washington." She laughed.

"But, but Jarvis said he killed you and Ken!" he protested.

"He tried. But, your friend Ken . . . he's good," she responded.

"Where are we?" Bill said.

"Ken and John brought us up to a cabin on the Skyline Drive. We're safe here, at least for a little while. Now you get some rest," she ordered. Holly dropped his hand and walked slowly across the room. Bill drank in the sight of her as she walked across the room, picked up a desk chair, and returned to the bedside. Taking his hand in hers after she sat down, she brought his fingers to her lips and kissed them. He soon fell into a deep sleep, his last memory her gentle eyes smiling at him.

He slept most of that day and all of the night. His sleep was interrupted by dreams of being chased. The chase was erratic and disconnected, though it felt very real. Holly woke him once to eat, but he fell back to sleep between bites. Those twenty hours would be forever lost to him.

20

DAY EIGHT:
HOLLY'S SECRET

Well, are you really awake this time?" Ken said.

Bill sat up and quipped, "It's noisy enough around here that a person couldn't get any sleep even if he wanted to."

John walked in the door of the cabin carrying some breakfast. The smell of coffee and eggs filled the room, and he suddenly realized how hungry he really was. Introductions were made between John and Bill as he ate breakfast.

"I vaguely remember you coming in and getting me out of the room I was in, but I thought you had big bug eyes sticking out of the side of your head. The rest seems to be pretty well lost," he told John.

His descriptions brought hysterics from Ken and Holly.

"But anyway, thanks. I don't think I had much of a future with that outfit."

"No, I doubt very seriously if you did. Judging by our introduction to Jarvis and company at Mount Vernon, they like to keep a tidy office. We had a shootout at a very public place, and there has been nothing in the news about it," Ken added.

John spoke up and said, "I don't think any of you have much of a future at this point if we don't find some way to stop Jarvis and Blaine. And I'll tell you, they seem to have a lot more resources than we do."

"Yes, they do," Holly inserted. "But there is one thing that we have that they don't know we have."

"Oh, what's that?" John coaxed.

"Ken, you know when we talked about Jarvis while we were at Mount Vernon?"

"Yeah?"

"Well . . . Bill had just been taken."

"Right, but what's this getting at?"

"You asked me to tell you everything I knew about Jarvis and his business," Holly said.

"Yes, and you seemed to give me a lot of information," Ken answered. "Though most of it won't do us much good."

"Well, I held one thing back. I guess I was afraid to trust you completely. At least, I was afraid to since Bill wasn't around." She stopped, took a breath, and then continued. "Do you recall that I said I typed transcripts of the meetings Jarvis had?"

"Yes, and I asked if you knew where we could get a copy of one," Ken responded.

"I told you I didn't know where Jarvis kept the copies. That is true. However, what I didn't tell you . . ."—she paused—". . . was that I have one of the original tapes." She spoke softly, as if making a confession. Her eyes fell to the floor to avoid any disapproval she might encounter for having held back this piece of information.

The silence in the room lasted a full thirty seconds as the information that Holly had just laid before them worked its way through the synaptic connections of the men's consciousnesses.

Ken was the first to speak. "Holly, you mean you have Jarvis and one of his business deals on tape?" He was jubilant. "Do you know who he was talking to? Who the meeting was with?"

"Yes, it was with the one you all call Blaine," she calmly answered.

Bill looked at Ken for an explanation. "I hate to sound ignorant, and I realize I've missed some of the last few days, but this started out to be my rescue, and now I don't even know all the participants. Does anyone have a program? Who is this guy Blaine you're talking about?"

"Bill, you're going to find this hard to believe," Ken began, "but the company that fronts for a spy ring—the people you and Holly have been running from—has Secretary of Defense Randolph Blaine as one of its major stockholders, or possibly a member of its board of directors."

Bill looked helplessly around the room. Finally, after several moments, he asked, "Who else is involved? The president?"

"That's the problem," John added. "We don't know for sure. We do know that Ken's boss is probably involved, and the way they were able to monitor your movements, I suspect several other people in very high places in the government are involved too."

"Well, we have Holly's and my testimonies, don't we? Won't that be good enough?" he asked.

"It might be if you two weren't felons on the run from every law enforcement agency in the free world. The news is still carrying stories about you planting the bomb at Carolina Beach and killing someone. I'm afraid your credibility is a little short," Ken answered. "And anyway, there is nothing to tie Blaine into the whole mess."

"Well, the answer seems easy enough; let's get the tape," Bill said. "Where is it, Holly?"

"It's in my safety deposit box in a bank at Carolina Beach."

"Sorry I asked," he mumbled.

Cape Fear

"What do you mean, they've disappeared? You have the resources of the entire government to find them! Listen, Blaine, they have enough on all of us to not only send us to jail but probably to the gas chamber. I want you to find them and find them now!"

Jarvis was shaking as he hung up the phone. He walked around his desk and looked out over the ocean. He had immense wealth and power. The power he didn't control himself he could commandeer from those who were subject to him. Yes, that was a good word—*subject*. He saw everyone as subject to his wishes. Now, if his subjects weren't so incompetent in what they did, he would not have to deal with these problems.

He had had the originator of the Tel-Ray project in his hands, the very man who had created this last piece of the communications system they needed. Now, it seemed, they were back to square one. And worse yet, Holly had not been found.

Jarvis put on a leather jacket, turned the fur collar up to guard against the breeze, and walked up the beach from his mansion. The salt spray in the air mixed with the cold wind was invigorating. It seemed to clear his head. He was beginning to think that maybe the best answer was to eliminate Holly, Chandler, and whoever was helping them, forget the Tel-Ray project, and take the loss. Sometimes it's better just to cut and run.

He would give Blaine one more day to find them. Then he would impose his own solution. One of these days he would probably have to impose a solution on Blaine, too, when his usefulness was gone. It would be simple enough. Blaine was actually a weakling; even worse than a weakling, he was impotent . . . a toad. However, he'd been a useful toad until now.

The sun was casting long shadows across the uneven dunes when Jarvis returned to the house. He sensed in himself a feeling of growing hostility and rage. He feared not being able to deliver the plans for the Tel-Ray system, not only for the loss of money, but, more important, for the loss of his reputation.

Losing Chandler had been careless, and he didn't want anyone to ever get the idea he was careless. In his business, that could be a fatal flaw. And something else was bothering him: Holly was gone.

He was frustrated, knowing he had to kill Holly but also wanting her . . . sincerely wanting her.

Jarvis had wanted to sleep with her from the day he first saw her in San Francisco. She was the kind of woman fantasies are built around. But now, she was gone. Worse yet, Chandler had probably already slept with her. Jarvis had been unable to possess her during the one opportunity he'd had; now he couldn't stand the thought that a powerless, unarmed professor might be sleeping with her. The thought of the two of them together, locked in a passionate embrace, fueled his anger.

A sharp rap sounded on the door, startling him out of his vengeful reverie.

"Mr. Jarvis!"

"Yes!" he spat in disgust at the interruption.

"It's a telephone call, sir. The caller says he may have located your missing property," James responded.

As he picked up the telephone, Jarvis observed that his heart was starting to pound, and he felt a tightness in his chest, making his breathing more noticeable.

"Hello, this is Jarvis!" he said in a hurried, authoritative voice.

"Mr. Jarvis, I'm a janitor with the parks department out here on the Skyline Drive. We got word you were looking for a man and a woman. I think they may be staying in one of the cabins at Big Meadows," he said.

"Why do you think I'm looking for them?" Jarvis asked.

"Well, sir, the word was passed from a very high source. These folks seem to fit the ones you're lookin' for. And I was told to call this number. If I got the wrong number, I'm sorry I bothered you. I'll be glad to hang up."

"No! Don't! You have the right number. If this is accurate, there is some money available for you. Now, slowly, why do you think the people I'm looking for are there?" Jarvis asked.

"Well, it was kind of strange, but two nights ago a woman with a couple of kids checked in and rented two cabins, units 14 and 15.

But, well, ya see, she left right after that, an' I ain't seen her since. And then the next night, this other van arrives with two men and a woman, and they carried a third man into the cabin. I saw all this 'cause I was workin' the night shift that night." The man paused.

"What did these four, the three men and the woman, look like?"

"Well, the woman, she was a looker. 'Bout five-four or so, short reddish hair, nice shape, ya know what I mean?"

"Yes."

"The men, well, both of them was wearing camouflage gear the night they arrived. One of the men is a big fellow, looks like a football player. The other is kind of average."

"What about the one who was carried in?"

"I didn't see him too well. I was back in the shadows, ya know. But I did hear them call him *Bill*, and they mentioned your name too."

"My name?"

"Yeah, they was laughing and one of 'em said, 'I'll bet ol' Jarvis is gonna croak when he finds Bill gone.' That's why I called you, sir." There was a long silence. "Now I've seen the woman and two of the men, but that third one that got carried in, well . . . I ain't seen him out of the cabin yet. But they, the others, well, they keep buying food after they've eaten an' take it back to one of the cabins," he concluded.

"Is that all?" Jarvis pressed.

"Well, ya see, the only reason for coming up here this time of the year is to see the leaves. An' these folks don't come out for nothing but to eat. Now, don't you think that's kinda strange? An' the word we got was you were looking for some people who might be acting kinda strange." The line went quiet in Jarvis's ear.

"OK, where is this Big Meadows place?" Jarvis asked.

"It's on the Skyline Drive about forty miles from Laray, Virginia," the janitor replied.

"Now listen," Jarvis said. "Some of my people will be there in a couple of hours. If what you say is true, you will be well paid for your effort. And one more thing: Keep an eye on them."

Jarvis hung up the phone and looked at the darkness of the beach in front of his window. "Get in here!" he roared.

"Yes, sir, Mr. Jarvis," came the quick reply.

"They've been located, I think. Someplace called Big Meadows on the Skyline Drive, cabin 14 or 15. I want some men up there now, and I want them taken. I don't want any of them terminated, but if they're hurt some . . . well, that's OK," Jarvis barked.

"Even Holly?"

"*Especially* Holly!" Jarvis added with vengeance, and the man quickly retreated from the room to carry out his boss's wishes.

Jarvis could feel the excitement of the chase again. He was almost certain his prey had been located. Now it was his turn to inflict pain. Because of this business with Holly and Chandler . . . well, this whole Tel-Ray affair had become very painful to him. He felt as if he had been robbed. Chandler had been stolen from him and with him, Tel-Ray. Holly had stolen from him the pleasure of having her. In many ways she was just like Maria; he burned with anger at the memory. And now to think that spineless scientist might be satisfying Holly this very minute. Not only that, but this was costing him a lot of money.

Now, at last, it would be time to inflict a little misery on someone else. Soon, Holly and Chandler would know their own world of agony.

Big Meadows

"When do we leave for Cape Fear?" John asked.

"You know," Ken said, "I told you you could bail out after we rescued Bill."

"Yeah, ol' buddy, but I've never been to Cape Fear," John replied.

"Isn't that going to be like Daniel going into the lion's den?"

Bill interjected. "If you guys knew the trouble Holly and I had getting out of there . . . well, couldn't we try to think of some other way?"

"I'm afraid the only chance any of us have now is Holly getting the tape from her bank box," Ken said. "And she's really the only one who can. If I tried to get it with a court order, I'm sure Art Billings would intercept it and keep it out of sight forever."

"Along with all of us," Holly added.

"Unless you can come up with a better plan, I think this is what we have to go with. If you'll excuse me, I'm going down to the lodge for a snack. All this excitement has made me hungry. It's sort of like when we were out in the bush in 'Nam. You never knew what was coming. Eating is a great way to hide anxiety." He laughed as he left the cabin.

"John, I don't like the idea of Holly going back to Cape Fear. Even with her looks changed she still might be recognized. Don't you think it's too risky?"

Holly spoke up on her own behalf. "I understand, Bill, and believe me, I don't want to go either . . . but like Ken said, what other chance do we have?" There was an assurance in her voice that she had thought about the risks and felt the effort was worth it.

Bill was still recovering from his captivity and had no ambition to repeat it or to see Holly fall into Jarvis's hands. It was difficult to know when to be cautious and when not to.

Ken had walked down to the restaurant at the lodge while they discussed the merits of the trip to Cape Fear. He had just started back up the dark path through the trees when he spotted a figure crouched in the bushes near the two cabins he and the others occupied. He stopped and blended into the nearby trees. Years of training had taught him to be patient. He controlled his breathing to slow his heart, which had responded to the adrenaline rush as his mind comprehended the menace ahead. Minutes passed. Maybe it was just shadows; maybe he had not seen anything. Then suddenly it moved; the figure adjusted its position. Ken remained motionless. His time in the jungle had taught him that no matter how uncomfortable he was, survival depended on control. Now that lesson was being reinforced.

Someone was watching the cabins. Creeping slowly, Ken advanced, staying low, using the shadows for cover and moving only when the quarter moon was behind a cloud. There must be no broken twigs to give away his approach. Silently he placed one foot after another on the ground. His heartbeat now was well controlled by his breathing, but he knew his target's wasn't. He could hear the man wheezing and panting as he approached. *This is not a professional*, he thought.

The wind was blowing from the west, and the smoke from a distant fire filled his nostrils. Under ordinary circumstances it would have been cold on the mountaintop, but as Ken neared the crouching figure, he felt sweat trickling down the back of his neck. He had crept to within five feet of his target when he suddenly leaped on the man like a lion in an attack. As the weight of his body hit the prowler from behind, Ken wrapped his powerful arms around him, pinning his opponent and taking him completely off balance.

The two men rolled wildly out of the cover. Ken kicked at the ground as he felt their momentum failing to bring him up on top of his target. In a lightninglike move, he hit the body under him along the side of the face and felt the bone of the man's maxilla crumble under the force of his blow. The man yelled in pain.

Quickly, Ken reached under his coat and drew his gun from its shoulder holster.

"Don't say a word, and don't move unless you want to depart this planet!" Ken warned. "Now, carefully, get up!"

Ken walked the spy into the cabin. The man was holding his cheekbone, which was obviously broken. Leaves and broken twigs were hanging from both men.

"Look at what I found on my way back," Ken stated matter-of-factly.

"Who are you?" John asked.

No answer.

"We don't have a lot of time, mister. Who are you, and what were you doing out there?" he asked again.

"Nothin'," the man mumbled, still holding his face.

"What exactly . . . ," Ken reiterated slowly, "were you doing, watching our cabin?"

"Nothin', I told ya. I wasn't doin' nothin'. Jes' mindin' my own business and you jumped me—"

"You were hiding in the bushes watching this cabin," John said. "Now either you're some kind of sick Peeping Tom or else you're trying to keep an eye on us. Either way, I don't like it." John started across the room toward the man, who cowered in a defensive posture.

Ken spoke up. "Look, friend. My partner has a bad temper, and I can't get him to cooperate very well these days, so why don't you tell me what you were doing out there before he loses his temper?"

"You all's the ones, ain't ya?" he said.

"Which ones, friend?" Ken soothed.

"The ones Mr. Jarvis wants," he stated.

The silence in the room was deafening. Ken, Bill, John, and Holly all looked at one another in amazement. In a matter of only thirty-six hours Jarvis had tracked them down. They were well hidden here; there should have been no way for him to have found them. But he had. Suddenly they realized they had seriously underestimated what they were up against.

"How do you know Jarvis?" Bill asked.

"He takes care of folks. We take care of him," the man replied.

"Let's get out of here—now!" Ken stated emphatically. He motioned at John to leave the room. They walked out onto the porch, and Ken said, "Take the van and head back to the District. Here's a number to call tomorrow night at seven. Find yourself a safe house. They probably don't know you, but don't take a chance by going home."

John nodded and walked into the darkness toward the van.

Ken returned to the cabin. "Bill, tie and gag our friend here. Holly, get the coats, and then let's go. I don't know how much time we have, but my bet is it isn't much."

As Bill finished putting the last knots on the ropes they heard John drive out of the parking lot. Ken stuck his head in the door and whispered coarsely, "Let's go!"

Turning off the lights, Bill and Holly went out the door, following Ken into the darkness of the dense forest. A narrow, steep path began a few feet from the cabin and progressed upward in a serpentine fashion toward the area called Black Rock. They paused about five hundred yards up the trail and looked back. They had a clear view of the parking lot and the cabins.

Suddenly, several cars descended on the area where their van had been parked only moments before. The doors opened, and they could hear the sound of men running over the fallen leaves and sticks. The clamor of wood splintering shattered the silence of the night as the door of the cabin was broken down. Holly gave out a frightened whimper.

"Follow me, and watch your step," Ken whispered.

Painfully, they picked their way along the ridge of the mountain in the blackness of that terrible night. Most of the time, Bill couldn't even tell if they were going in a straight line or in circles. He still hurt from the beating, and his legs felt weak. But the instinct for survival kept him going.

"I've got to rest a minute!" Holly protested. They had been walking for more than an hour through rugged terrain.

"All right. I guess we have enough distance between them and us for the time being," Ken replied.

"Ken, what are we going to do? They know we're on this mountain now. Come morning, are we really going to be that hard to find?" Bill asked.

"I took a precaution against this eventuality," he responded.

"A precaution?" he questioned.

"I had Sally stash an RV about an hour from here. If we can get to it before daylight, I think we can get down off this hill."

"We have to make it," Holly asserted. "I have to go to Cape Fear and get that tape. We have to stop Jarvis and all of them!"

"If we don't stop them, we're as good as dead," Ken answered, nodding grimly.

Bill's silence was complete agreement.

Just as the sun was starting to lighten the eastern sky, they came upon a camping area, deserted except for a lone RV with Maine license plates. Ken crossed over to it and unlocked the door while Holly and Bill hid at the edge of the clearing. They were tired, dirty, sweating, and scratched from branches. But they were alive. Ken quickly searched the vehicle, then beckoned toward them.

As they entered the camper, Ken was plugging in a coffeepot.

"We all need some of this after last night," he said. "You two get in the back and pull the shades. There's some security in the cupboard over the bed," Ken said, motioning as he slid into the driver's seat. "I suspect there will be some kind of roadblock. I hope I can get us through it. Do I sound like a leaf peeper?" he said in a phony New England accent.

Holly and Bill closed themselves up in the back bedroom of the RV. Bill opened the cupboard and found the gun, then checked to be sure that it was loaded.

The drive out of the Big Meadows area was uneventful until they reached the exit from the Skyline park. Then Bill and Holly felt the camper slowing to a stop.

"What's the trouble, Officer?" they heard Ken ask.

"Just a routine check. You traveling alone?" the voice outside the camper responded.

"Jest me an' the missus," Ken stated confidently. "She's asleep in the back. Wanted to git an early start on the day. Rollin' on down to Florida. Winter's coming up north. Know what I mean?"

"Yeah, it'll be here before long. I'm afraid I'll have to take a look in the back," Bill and Holly heard the voice say.

"Yeah, sure thing. Jest a minute. Let me git the door of this contraption open. This is the first year we've had this thing. Sometimes I git trapped inside. Need a can opener to git out, know what I mean?" Ken laughed.

He fumbled at the lock, delaying as long as he could before he let the trooper in. Ken watched as he looked around the inside of the RV.

"What ya lookin' for?" Ken asked.

"There was some trouble up at Big Meadows last night. A couple of guys and a woman beat and killed one of the park workers."

"Goodness!" Ken responded. "We were camped at Big Meadows in the campground. Sure didn't see anything like that."

"This happened over at one of the cabins," the officer stated.

"Say, it's kinda cool this morning. Would you like a cup a coffee? I made a fresh pot 'fore I started driving," Ken said, trying to delay the search of the back of the camper.

"Sure. But I got to take a look in the back. You understand," the trooper replied.

Ken poured a cup of black coffee into a Styrofoam cup and handed it to the officer. "Cream or sugar?"

"No, thanks, just black."

"Ya kin look back there, but be careful," Ken said, pointing toward the closed door. "The missus, well . . . ya never know how she'll be first thing in the morning. Gotta git her face on, ya know what I mean?" Ken stalled.

The officer walked to the back of the camper and opened the door to the bedroom. Ken held his breath. Suddenly there was a shriek. Ken tensed and put his hand on his gun under his jacket.

"Sorry, ma'am . . . I apologize. I'm real sorry to have bothered ya."

Holly sat on the bed clad only in her panties, calmly painting her fingernails. She had quickly wrapped a towel around her head, to give the appearance that she had just finished a shower. Bill sat out of sight in the bathroom, holding the clothes she had tossed to him.

The officer backed away, looking embarrassed and wiping the hot coffee from his hand onto his pants.

"Is everything all right?" Ken asked with a smile on his face. "Can I git ya some more coffee?"

"No . . . no, thank you. You can go. Sorry for the trouble." The officer was in a hurry to leave the RV.

Ken slid into the driver's seat and pulled away from the roadblock, chuckling about the embarrassed look on the officer's face. He was wondering what Holly had done when she suddenly appeared at his side.

"What in the world did you do to that poor guy back there?" Ken asked.

"I'd rather not say," she responded, still somewhat embarrassed.

Bill joined them in the front of the camper as they drove down the western side of the mountains into the mist rising from the floor of the Shenandoah Valley.

"I'm going to get cleaned up!" Holly announced with resolve and departed for the bathroom.

"I think you looked great a few minutes ago," Bill teased.

She punched him in the stomach unexpectedly, and he doubled over, grabbing the side of the dinette to keep from falling.

"You deserved that," she announced and walked off.

"Well, friend. Where to?" Ken said.

"It won't be long before they have our fingerprints from the cabin, and we'll have another murder to answer for," Bill replied.

"What are our options?" Ken urged.

"We really only have one option—to nail Jarvis," he answered.

"And there's only one way to do that, isn't there?"

"I guess we'd better go to Cape Fear and get that tape." There was a long pause. "I just pray the discussion Jarvis and Blaine had will be worth it."

The passing trees and fields flashed past the window like a surrealistic painting falling from the wall. Bill's whole life was on a roller coaster, and it seemed to be going faster and faster. He knew intellectually it would end sooner or later. Either the ride would end or the car would leave the track and they'd be killed. Somehow they had to get the car to stop, and it had to stop someplace where they could get off in one piece. Now it appeared the only way was to go down the first big drop on the roller-coaster track. They had to go back to Cape Fear.

Day Nine

They headed toward North Carolina by picking up Interstate 95 at Richmond then turning south. Ken drove, Bill rode shotgun, and Holly retired to the back.

After she had cleaned up, she put on a pair of jeans and a plaid blouse, leaving the top two buttons open so a slight hint of her roundness and the lace from her camisole were exposed, ever so discreetly.

Holly called, "Bill! I'm done in the bath if you want it."

He retreated from the front and stepped into the back of the camper.

"You're gorgeous!" he exclaimed. Lying on the bed, propped up by several pillows, she smiled coyly at his reaction.

"I wonder if this comes equipped with a razor?" he thought out loud as he rubbed the stubble on his face. He turned to face the mirror so she would not see how very much he desired her just now.

"Top shelf on the right," she answered. "All the comforts of home."

He stripped off his shirt with his back to Holly. Turning around, he started to speak, but the horror on her face stopped him cold.

"What happened!" she cried.

Her reaction came from seeing the bruises that extended from his shoulders to his beltline. Bill shrugged. "Can't be a good white

247

knight without a bruise here and there." Then he added, "Though maybe you'll have to call me your *purple* knight instead."

Holly's smile brightened once again, and she laughed. "That's dumb," she said, throwing a pillow at him as he ducked out of the way.

He washed and shaved, feeling her eyes appraising him all the while. Then he stepped into the shower and closed the door.

"Hey, what're you doing?" she shouted through the closed door.

"Changing my pants," he retorted.

"Well, I'll have you know, Mr. Chandler . . ."

He stuck his head out the door. "That's *Dr.* Chandler," he corrected with a smirk in his voice.

"I'll have you know, Dr. Chandler, when we arrived at the cabin you were a mess! I undressed you, I washed you, and I bound up your wounds," she said, emphasizing the *I* each time. "You can be relieved to know," she continued, "that you have nothing different from what I already know about. And, no—I repeat, *no* impropriety took place."

Bill stepped from the shower stall with just his slacks on and gently threw a towel at her. It landed on her face. She pulled it off and shook out her short hair the way a playful colt shakes its mane.

"I guess I deserved that, huh?" she said.

He lay down beside her, tenderly drew her head over, and rested it on his shoulder. The curtains swayed rhythmically above them with the motion of the camper. Bolts of bright light from the morning sun skipped around the room as the curtains parted and met in a syncopated promenade. With her head cradled next to his, he kissed her. There was a pulsating rhythm transmitting between them as Holly instinctively brought her leg over his. The sensation of her closeness stirred an aching to have her.

"I . . . want you so much . . . ," he said, his hand tracing the hollow of her back.

"I know, and I . . ."

He reluctantly brought his hand from her back and placed his finger to her lips to stop her from completing her sentence. If he heard the words, he would give in. The desire to know her intimately burned with an intensity that was almost out of control.

"Holly, I love you!" he blurted out and then quickly added, "I love you, and I want you, but . . . not now, not yet."

"Bill!" she responded in a provocative whisper, "Oh . . ."

They lay there, secure and private for the moment. He felt the softness of her body against his and her warm tears of joy spilling from her eyes onto his bruised chest.

21

TEL-RAY'S TRIAL

They reached the North Carolina border in the late afternoon. At the first exit that advertised a campground, they turned in. Ken took a call on a special phone in the van at seven. This was the prearranged call from John. He learned that John had no problems getting away from Big Meadows. John said he had arranged to meet them at the airport in Charleston, South Carolina, by noon tomorrow. All seemed to be going as planned, considering they really didn't have much of a plan formulated yet.

"Bill, I want to go over a few things with you and Holly," Ken said.

"Such as?" he questioned.

He reached into a small closet beside the couch in the RV. "This is a .38 caliber Smith & Wesson model 14-SA six-shot police special. It weighs two pounds, six and a half ounces, and is eleven and a quarter inches long with a six-inch rifled barrel. The load is 170 grain. I want you to get used to it."

"Ken, you know I'm a research scientist, not Dirty Harry," Bill chided.

"If you are half as smart as I think you are, this should be child's play. Then look at this one, a Browning MK-3, takes a 9 mm and carries thirteen rounds per magazine. Now listen. In a fight, the one who wins isn't the fastest one to shoot. It's whoever has the nerve to take enough time to hit his target. And Bill, if it comes to that . . . remember . . . it is your target and your enemy. The opposition has only one purpose: to kill you. Don't be foolish and think you can wound or disable him. If you have to shoot, shoot to kill!

"There are a few other things," Ken continued, pulling out the next item. "This is a semiautomatic 16-gauge shotgun. It holds six rounds, and at close range and in tight spaces, it can be quite helpful."

For the next two hours Ken went down his arsenal of weapons, both offensive and defensive. He concluded by saying, "A defensive action is akin to losing. The last defensive action an American unit did well was at the Alamo, and you know how that turned out. The Marines have a saying, 'Hey diddle-diddle, right up the middle.' That may be the only option we have left before this is over."

He gave Holly a small Smith & Wesson .22 sport semiautomatic handgun she could conceal without difficulty. She acted uncomfortable with it at first, but after loading and unloading it several times, she began to get the feel of having it in her hand. She then placed it in her purse.

"This is kind of a ragtag army you've assembled here, General," Bill teased Ken. "By the way, do you have any electronic listening stuff stashed in this wreck?"

"I have a little. Why?"

"Well, who knows what might come in useful, but you do know that is what I do for a living," Bill reminded him.

Ken showed Bill the electronic gear on board, and Bill began to play with some of it. Several hours later he said, "Ken, wouldn't it be helpful if we could monitor some of Jarvis's conversations? Then maybe we wouldn't have to play our trump card, Holly's tape."

"Sure, I'd love to slip right into his bedroom and know what he talks about in his sleep, let alone know what he's talking about on the phone or in his office tonight. But I think it might be kind of tough to plant a bug. I suspect he has beefed up his security system over the past few days."

"If we could, though, Holly wouldn't have to risk going to the bank in Jarvis's backyard," Bill insisted.

"You're right, but do you have a plan short of knocking on the door and asking if we might come in, look around, and plant a bug?"

"How about if we use Tel-Ray?" Bill asked.

"I thought that wasn't finished yet," he responded.

"It isn't—or rather, it wasn't. But while Jarvis had me tied up in Potomac, I think I figured out what was wrong with the final program. If you can get John to pick up some of my equipment at the plant before he comes down to meet us, I might have a shot at it. Who knows? With a little luck, maybe I can let you hear not only what Jarvis talks about in his sleep but every word that slime bucket says!" He was excited.

"Give me your shopping list and go on to bed. I'll see what I can do." Ken grinned.

Bill hurriedly made out a list of the essential things he needed from the lab. After that he took Holly by the hand and got up from the table in the van.

"We're going to give this our best shot, aren't we?" Bill said.

"If we can't do it, I have an awful feeling it is not going to get done. The one big problem is that we don't know everyone who is involved. I just hope we can find out who all the players are before they find us. Now, you two get out of here. I have a shopping list to work on," he said, laughing.

Holly and Bill put on their coats and left the RV. They walked across the deserted campground, looking up at the millions of stars. There was some small comfort to the pinpoint of light each star gave off. No matter how black the night sky was, the darkness could not blot out the twinkling lights. Maybe the three of them would be like those stars; if so, then Jarvis's blackness wouldn't blot them out either.

They stopped by a picnic table. Bill put his hands on Holly's waist and lifted her up so she could sit facing him. The steam from her breath was warm against his face. He kissed her, and she kissed him back.

"I love you, Dr. Bill Chandler," she said as she drew him close to her. "No matter what happens, no matter how this ends, I want you to know I love you more than I have ever loved anyone."

That night Holly slept in the bedroom, Ken in the bunk over the driver's seat, and Bill slept wretchedly on the dinette bench.

Day Ten

The next morning Bill drove the RV to Charleston to meet John while Ken caught up on his sleep in the back. They waited in the parking lot at the airport to keep their exposure to a minimum.

John's plane was late, which added to their anxiety, but he finally arrived and casually strolled out into the parking lot to meet them. He had procured almost all of the Tel-Ray equipment Bill needed except a small computer. Bill made Ken stop at a Radio Shack, where the clerk was delighted when he completed the easiest computer sale he'd ever made.

The only condition of the sale was that there would be immediate delivery and that the computer had an auxiliary battery power source. The clerk said it would take him about forty-five minutes to locate the necessary hardware, so they had time for a leisurely lunch. The salesman recommended a restaurant on the Ashley River, where they assessed the food as awful, the view spectacular.

"John, did you hear any news up in Washington?" Bill queried.

"There was nothing at all about you and Holly or about any trouble along the C & O Canal—no major stuff like that," he replied.

"Jarvis sure has a way of keeping things quiet, doesn't he?" Ken added.

"I tried to tell you how much power Jarvis has," Holly said. "It's real scary. It's so hard to believe it could happen here in the United States," she said with a shudder.

"There was one interesting rumor, as rumors go in that town," John related.

"Oh," Ken groaned, "what is the great rumor mill sending up now? Let me guess: Senator Smuckfelt is having a tryst with the latest Hollywood starlet, right?"

"Not quite that good, ol' buddy, but it might be important to us if this thing drags out too long."

He was decidedly more serious than Bill would have liked. Creature of habit that he was, he leaned forward to hear John's words better.

John looked at each one of them to assure himself he had their attention, then he continued. "The hot rumor of the week is that the president is not going to seek a second term in the next election, and he will probably put his weight behind Secretary of Defense Blaine. Blaine is expected to announce his plans to run within the next two weeks, or at the latest, when he gets back from that NATO meeting after Christmas."

Bill sat back in his chair, letting the gravity of what John had said sink in. It was no secret in Washington that the president and his vice president had had a falling out over the arms negotiations with the Chinese and over how much emphasis to put on the defense budget. But to throw his weight this early toward Secretary Blaine spoke volumes about the powerful men they were up against.

Ken whistled through his front teeth, and they all fell quiet.

"Want to steal a boat and go to South America?" Bill said finally, breaking the staggering silence that had enveloped their table. He pointed at the marina across the river with its multitude of yachts moored in rows. "I've done that once. I can probably do it again." He chuckled.

"Hey!" Holly interjected. "I helped, remember?"

"OK, guys, we're taking this much too seriously. What the heck? It's only our lives. Tell ya what. Let's go pick up that computer for Bill, head up the road to Cape Fear, and get the information to put this little company of cutthroats, thieves, and murderers behind bars," Ken declared.

"Right," John dragged out the word, emphasizing his southern accent. "And if that doesn't work? What then?"

"We'll take a gun and blow the creeps off the face of the earth," Ken retorted.

• • •

During the drive to Wilmington from Charleston, Bill was busy putting the finishing touches on the Tel-Ray system, interfacing it with the new computer, and touching up the program necessary to make the system function. In theory, it was for battlefield situations, so it had to be able to work from small PC-type systems.

Holly spent most of the trip telling Ken everything she knew or could remember about Cape Fear Manor and Jarvis.

As they were passing through Myrtle Beach and approaching the state line into North Carolina, John came back to the makeshift workshop Bill had set up. "Just what does that contraption do?" John asked.

"Well, it's supposed to provide instant communication of high-volume information to a drone, an AWAC surveillance plane, or a guided missile while in flight. In addition, it reports on the area it is approaching by monitoring all the electronic and microwave signals in the target zone. The final phase is to intercept telephone-line communications or commandeer any broadcast frequency and lock out the home signal. In other words, it can transmit and receive simultaneously from any form of communication it is directed at. It can be used to give a visual target like the fiberoptic tank rockets, it can sense a target such as a heat-seeking device, or, in our case, it can tap into all of Jarvis's communications, including monitoring his bedroom antics, if we so desire," Bill stated proudly.

"That's the Tel part; the Ray function makes it dominant," he continued. "If so used, it would override any electronic signal and substitute its own." Bill paused to give John time to sort out what he had said before going on. "It would be very useful for slipping into enemy territory and spreading propaganda to the locals." He opened the back of the ceramic antenna. "See this?" He pointed to a small circuit board.

"Yeah, looks like a card for a modem or something in my computer," John said.

"Well, this is a wavelet dichromatizer and integration board."

"A what?" John frowned as he peered into the back of the antenna.

"It takes the incoming signals and sorts them out. That's the short answer. Then it passes the information into the digitizer." He pointed at another small board. "This encodes each of the separated inputs with a specific signature. When it reaches the computer it's very simple for the computer to identify and reconstruct and display it in any format you want."

"Hey, ol' buddy, that's fantastic! Does it work?" John challenged.

"I don't know for sure," Bill responded. "This is the first one ever made."

John looked at him, rolled his eyes, and laughed. "Okay, so you do the electronic mumbo jumbo to listen with this. Just how does it take over someone else's communications?"

"Once the unit has the signal, say of a radio station, and it finds its frequency, it's like a magnet and locks on. Then it reverses the flow at that frequency, blocking out what's being sent, and sends its own signal." Bill looked at John and saw a puzzled expression. "Not with me, right?"

"Right," John answered.

"Well look at it this way. When the Tel-Ray transmits it has the dominant flow of information. It overpowers the transmitter originating the signal. It makes the transmitter feel like it's trying to drink from a fire hose, so all the transmitter can do is send out what ever it gets from Tel-Ray."

"Maybe I understand, Doc. But tell ya what. If it does the trick and we can get out of here, then go for it!" John gave Bill a slap on the shoulder and walked toward the front of the RV.

The field test of the Tel-Ray began on the south end of Pleasure Island. They parked the RV on a slight rise in a small group of coastal pines. John climbed into one of the trees to anchor the antenna. From that vantage point they had a direct line of sight to Jarvis's compound, Cape Fear Manor. It was an impressive-looking southern-style mansion featuring tall white columns with a large porch that wrapped around three sides on the ground level. The top floor had a porch along the ocean side. Two outbuildings were visible on the compound. One was obviously a garage, and the other looked like a barracks. *If they need a building that large to house the hired help, we are certainly outgunned,* John thought.

A ten-foot white stucco wall surrounded the entire grounds, and the massive iron gate looked like something out of a Hollywood movie set. The approach to the house was open on the front, where it bordered the beach. The remainder of the property appeared to be as tightly controlled as Fort Knox.

The next two hours were tense as Bill worked out some of the minor obstacles that had resulted from a hurriedly adapted setup. Ken said nothing but several times stood looking over his shoulder in anticipation of the results. Finally, Bill turned around and said, "I think we're ready to go."

Ken looked around the RV at the three of them. "If you know any good prayers, this might be the time for them. We need all the help we can get."

Bill adjusted the volume and tones as the system warmed up and went through the programmed checklist. The computer screen flashed a message and went into listen mode as he typed in the correct code. Suddenly the dreadful silence was broken. They heard, "Mr. Jarvis wants his supper served in the study. He said he's expecting a call and wants it transferred to him as soon as it comes in!"

"Holly!" Bill whispered coarsely, "where is the study?"

"First floor on the front corner of the house . . . on this side here," she answered and pointed to a rough sketch she and Ken had drawn.

"Which side?" he asked.

"This side. It's on this corner, facing the ocean," she said as she held up the drawing in front of him.

"Thanks," he mumbled. He adjusted the controls to concentrate the power on the portion of the antenna that should be monitoring that segment of the house. The tape machines were rolling as they heard the footsteps of the man bringing supper come through the study door.

"Your supper, Mr. Jarvis."

"Put it on the table, and I don't want to be disturbed until my call comes in."

"Yes, sir."

Quite clearly, they could hear the sound of the door closing.

"This thing does a pretty good job!" John said enthusiastically.

Bill beamed as he spoke, "It's more than pretty good."

"John, this may take a while. Let's set up a protective perimeter and let Holly watch Mr. Wizard."

"That's Dr. Wizard. He already corrected me on that one." Holly's temperament was light at the expectation of their ultimate success.

They listened to Jarvis walk around the room and eat his supper. They could even hear him shuffle some papers. Bill was amazed at the clarity of the sound Tel-Ray produced. Then the phone rang, and he knew Tel-Ray would get its first true test.

Bill changed the reception sequence and typed the code into the computer. The result was exhilarating.

"This is Jarvis." He came through crystal clear. It sounded like they had picked up another extension phone in the same room.

"Jarvis! Blaine here. What happened? I gave you the location of the property. Why didn't you pick it up?" Blaine was conspicuously irritated.

"The property in question must have been tipped. It was not there when the messengers arrived. Do you have any more information in regard to its new location?"

"Jarvis, this has gotten out of hand! I think we should call off all the transactions at this time. I think it would be a good time for a vacation. Why don't you take one?" It sounded like Blaine was trying to give Jarvis an order.

"Randolph," Jarvis said smoothly, "your difficulty is that you think too much. For years you haven't had to think; you just enjoyed the money. Now, just because you are going to run for the noble office, you surmise that you should start thinking. Do us all a favor. Provide the requested information when I need it, and don't think. Now, in regard to our East—"

Abruptly the transmission went dead. "What happened?" Holly asked.

The door of the RV opened, and John jumped in with Ken closely behind.

"Holly, do the people that work for Jarvis wear jackets like this?" Ken said, pointing to a blue jacket John was holding.

"Yes. Where did you get it?" Holly asked.

"Well, the guy who was wearing it won't need it for quite a while. But let's get out of here!" Ken answered.

"Where is the antenna?" Bill demanded. "And why did our signal quit?"

"I pulled out the wire; we have to get going. There are a lot of this fellow's friends around here!" John said as he held up the blue garment. "They don't seem to like the idea of us hangin' around."

Bill jumped up from his chair as Ken started the RV. "I'm not leaving without the antenna!" he shouted angrily as he rushed out the door. He grabbed the lowest branch of the tree that held the priceless ceramic object. Pulling himself up branch over branch, he fought for footing at each level. He reached the antenna and carefully inspected it for damage caused by John pulling out the wire. It seemed to be intact. He had started back down the tree when he heard two men approaching the RV from the riverbank. They walked up to the driver's side of the van and tapped on the window.

"Hey, you—you in there!" the larger one shouted.

Ken slid the window open slightly. "Yes, what can I do for you?"

"You're on private property! You can't park that thing here. What are you doing here anyway?" he said in a threatening voice.

"Uh . . . I'm sorry, what did ya say, I'm a little hard of hearing. Got hurt in the war, ya know," Ken answered, stalling for time.

The man repeated himself.

Bill had worked his way down to the lowest branch, and he saw the second man moving around to the back of the motor home. He was right below Bill, reaching for the door, when Bill noticed the sun gleam from the barrel of a gun. Without a second thought, Bill jumped onto the man's back, pushing his head forward into the side of the vehicle. The commotion disturbed the conversation on the driver's side.

"Bob! What the hell's going on!" the man talking to Ken shouted, pulling his weapon from under the blue jacket he was wearing. He looked up at where Ken had been, but there was no one in the driver's seat. Slowly he started to back away from the vehicle toward the cover of the bushes. His head swung to his right and left. He shouted once more, "Bob . . . Bob, are you OK?" Still no reply. He turned and ran into the underbrush.

John burst out of the RV and started after him but stopped when he saw that the man had too big a lead. He halted and looked down at the man lying on the sand. Bill turned him over and removed his gun from his hand. The man's head was twisted at a bizarre angle. John felt his neck.

"Well . . . we won't have to worry about this one. Nice job, Doc!" he complimented Bill.

"What do you mean?" he asked.

"He's dead."

Bill gazed at the body, stunned. This lifeless shape, merely seconds ago, had been a walking, talking human being named Bob. Now whatever had been life for him was gone. Just like that. But intensifying the horror for Bill was the realization that he had caused that life to leave. *I killed him!* The thought erupted in his head like a high-powered explosive. He felt like he was going to vomit. He had actually killed someone. He was paralyzed, unable to move. The blood was pounding in his ears, and his eyes were riveted on the corpse. All he had done was jump on his back from the tree. He shouldn't be dead.

"There wasn't anything else that could be done. Come on, get in!" John shouted. He shoved Bill in the door as Ken roared down the sand road to the main highway.

On the way off the island, Bill sat in dazed silence. How rudimentary it had been. One minute, a man was alive, preparing to break into the RV, and the next minute, he was dead. And he, Bill, had been the instrument. It had been incredibly easy. He looked at his hands. There was blood on them; why couldn't he see it? Holly just sat beside him and said nothing. Bill wondered if she could see it. He prayed for forgiveness, then he prayed that Holly would still love him. It was a selfish prayer; he wasn't even sure at that point in time that he could love himself.

Minutes later, after the shock had worn off, Bill felt a strange sensation in his chest. He put his hand inside his coat. "Oh, no!" he screamed.

"What's the matter?" Holly asked, alarmed.

"It's broken! I can't believe it's broken!" He was frantic.

"Bill! Calm down! What's broken? Are you hurt?"

"No, worse than that. The antenna for the Tel-Ray system is broken. I had it inside my coat. When I jumped on that guy it must have been smashed." *What else can go wrong now?* he wondered.

"Can't we get a new antenna?" Ken asked.

"No . . . the whole principle of the system operates on the antenna. It's made out of a special ceramic-titanium alloy. It's irreplaceable. Only one other exists in the world, and it's in my lab in Maryland." Bill sat in numbed silence, staring at the floor, watching small bits of the precious ceramic and metal particles fall from the bottom of his jacket.

"We could find a place to hole up for a few days, and I could go up to your lab and pick up the other one," John said.

"I'm afraid we don't have a few days," Ken said. "As easily as they found us up in the mountains . . . I don't think there is anywhere we could hole up safely."

"I'm afraid Tel-Ray is out of the picture . . . for now," Bill replied slowly.

The mood in the van fell into a canyon of depression that seemed to dwarf the Grand Canyon. Bill could not even take pleasure in the fact that Tel-Ray had worked—and worked even better than he had hoped.

Finally, as they neared the motel, Holly spoke up. "Well, I guess I'd better go to the bank tomorrow, huh, guys?"

Holly and Bill went up to one of the rooms they'd rented. After the door was closed, he took her in his arms and held her . . . tight.

Too much had happened for one day. Those days happen now and then, and Bill had just had such a day. He was depleted, physically depleted. Living on the run for eight days had exhausted him. He was also psychologically depleted after having the Tel-Ray work and then coming so close to getting the evidence they needed. Finally, he was emotionally depleted, having killed for the first time in his life. He paced the room like a caged animal for several minutes while Holly sat on the bed, watching.

He thought a hot shower would help wash some of the exasperation from him. But as he glanced at Holly sitting on the bed, her beautiful eyes watching his every move, he opted for a cold shower instead.

22

DAY ELEVEN: SURVIVAL AT ALL COSTS

Bill awoke the next morning to find he'd spent the night alone, again. There were two double beds in the motel room; Holly was asleep across the room in the other.

Bill slipped quietly over to Holly's bed and sat down next to her sleeping form. Tenderly, he kissed her soft cheek. She groaned and pushed him away as she awoke from a deep sleep, then rolled over and buried her head in the pillow.

"Good morning," he whispered, trying to sound as jubilant as possible, defying the fear in his chest. Today Holly would place her head into the mouth of the lion on Cape Fear. He wanted desperately to shield her from the danger.

Holly peeked out from beneath the pillow. "Hi," she said sleepily. Glancing over his shoulder, she remarked, "You certainly tore your bed apart last night."

The bed was a reminder of the violent dreams that had kept him tossing and turning all night. But he was awake now, and Holly was still there; they were still alive. "Yeah," he said. "Mind if I visit yours for a while?" She laughed as he lay down next to her and took her in his arms. When she wrapped herself in his embrace and looked into his eyes, the playful lightness vanished and he found himself becoming serious, overwhelmed with longing for this woman he had come to love.

"Holly . . . ," he murmured. No other words could fight their way to the surface. He drew her close and gently kissed her. As he embraced her lovingly, she whispered in his ear, "I love you, Bill."

"And I love you," he said, then he lay back, releasing her. Looking up at the ceiling without really seeing anything, he thought, *This is not the time or place.*

"Penny for your thoughts," Holly said.

"I, . . . oh, it's hard to say—you know, to put into words." Would she understand? How could she? He barely understood himself. "I was just thinking how much I want you." He paused as the thought hung in the air. "But, I can't—we can't. Not now, not like this. It just wouldn't be right."

Bill looked into Holly's eyes and could see that, yes, she understood. With relief he realized that she wanted him, too, but that his willingness to wait was worth more to her than giving in to the passion of the moment. "I know what you mean. No more words. Just hold me."

Abruptly, there came a knock at the door.

"Oh no," he groaned. The knock grew more persistent. Bill rolled over onto his back, releasing his grasp of her. The knocking echoed in the room.

"Bill! Holly! You folks awake yet?" Ken's voice was the last thing either of them wanted to hear.

"One of us should answer the door," she said, not trying to hide her frustration over the ill-timed interruption.

Muttering incoherently, Bill crawled out of bed and went to the door. Ken's arrival had eliminated any hint of Bill's former fervor. He fumbled with the night latch and cracked the door. The blazing sun caused him to squint, and he could just perceive the silhouette of their uninvited guest.

"What?" he grumbled.

"You two up yet? Rise an' shine. We have to go catch some crooks today, remember?" Ken was behaving entirely too jovially. Bill could have wrung his neck.

"Your timing rivals only the navigation of the *Titanic*," Bill responded.

"Huh?" Ken asked with a puzzled expression.

"Nothing. Yeah, we're awake. Give us fifteen minutes to get dressed."

"Meet you at the camper," Ken said as Bill shut the door more firmly than he intended to.

Holly had gotten up and was in the bathroom. Bill could hear her humming in the shower. He wondered how the day would go. For those few brief moments in each other's arms, he had forgotten what the plans were for this day . . . and what she was going to have to attempt. He pondered how she could act so casual in the shadow of the encounter before her. Holly was truly an extraordinary woman.

Bill paced the room and ground his teeth together as he thought of just how much he loved Holly. Yet at the same time he couldn't help feeling he was betraying Sandy. His feelings for Holly were not unlike the love he'd had for Sandy, though Holly was a different woman and he experienced love for her in a new way.

"Bill, darling, your shower is ready," Holly called as she left the bath and began to rummage through the suitcase for some clothes. She was wearing one of his shirts as a bathrobe, and he averted his eyes as she prepared to get dressed.

Bill sat on the edge of the bed, rubbing his face and wondering if they really were crazy. No, it was right to wait. But wait for what? He stumbled to the shower, trying to sort through his feelings. He thought about Holly; he loved her and he knew it without any reservation. And clearly she loved him too. But he was also sure that they were faced with the worst predicament they could imagine. Was it bad timing?

After a few minutes in the hot, steamy water, he stepped out of the shower and peered into the clouded mirror. He took a towel and started to wipe it off, then stopped. As he looked at his own foggy reflection, he felt a very real peace come over him—as though Sandy were there with him and she knew. She not only knew, but he was certain she understood . . . and was releasing him at that very moment to go on with his life, to accept his deep need and longing for the wonderful woman in whose company he'd been thrown so unexpectedly these last few days. With his finger he carefully wrote a message on the wet glass.

Then he cracked the door open. Holly was dressed and waiting.

"Could you find me some clothes and throw them in here?" he asked, sticking his head into the room.

"Sure. Are all men this helpless?"

"Only us official knights!" he replied, grinning.

Holly gathered underwear, socks, pants, and a shirt out of their bag. She handed them to him, and he closed the door and quickly dressed, leaving his belt hanging on the back of the door. One last check to make sure the message was still visible and he stepped into the room.

"Have you seen my belt?" he asked.

"I gave it to you," she answered.

"I don't think so," he countered, rummaging through the suitcase.

She walked through the bathroom door, saying, "I'll prove it to you!" It was quiet for several seconds. For Bill time stood still.

The next moment the door flew open and Holly's eyes glistened with ecstasy.

"Yes! Oh, Bill, yes! I'll marry you!"

Laughing, she threw herself into his arms. "My knight," she whispered through her tears. "My gallant knight." He could hardly believe the joy he felt as he held her, and he knew without a doubt that now they had to survive.

John rented a new van and left the RV several miles outside Wilmington in a deserted farmyard. They felt fairly safe as they drove over the Intracoastal Waterway onto the island, pondering the irony that this island that held Holly's bank and Jarvis's home was known as Pleasure Island.

Over breakfast they discussed the probability that Jarvis would be waiting for them. It was agreed that the likelihood was low. First, they hoped Jarvis did not know Holly had a tape in her safety deposit box. Second, while he might have suspected the incident yesterday was related to them after what had happened, who would be stupid enough to come back the next day? Also, they were reasonably certain he had enough enemies that he couldn't be sure they were the ones there. Third, and most important, there was nothing else to do.

Bill looked out the window and watched a sport cruiser heading out to sea. It was similar to the one Jarvis owned. He wondered if it truly was a fishing party or if Jarvis was getting rid of another business associate. His paranoia level was extremely high.

Ken parked the van in the parking lot of McDonald's, beside the bank. "Let me go with Holly," Bill said.

"No, it would be better if she went alone. Fewer people to attract attention," John answered.

Holly stepped nervously from the van and walked toward the bank. She hesitated once and looked back at them. Watching her walk away, Bill relived the scene at Heathrow Airport. He had watched Sandy walk down the corridor, out of sight, into eternity.

Holly's figure grew smaller in the distance. She put her hand on the door. Suddenly, flashing before his vision, he could see Sandy reaching in her purse for the money with which to buy the magazine. As the door of the bank slammed shut behind Holly, he saw the magazine rack exploding, ripping his wife and unborn child from his life. *That will never happen to me again!* Bill bolted from the van and ran toward the bank. He would not relinquish Holly the way he'd lost Sandy.

"Bill!" John's words were lost in the salt air of the morning.

Holly entered the bank and paused. Her hands were sweaty, her heart was pounding perceptibly against her breastbone, and her stomach churned. She took a deep breath and walked up to the assistant manager. "I need to get into my safety deposit box, please." Her lips tensed against her teeth.

"Certainly, please fill out the card," he replied.

Holly was filling out the card as Bill entered the bank.

"I have a small problem. I've lost my key." Holly smiled a warm, friendly smile.

"Well, if you'll sign here, let's see, yes, your signature matches, we can have the lock drilled." He then looked up at her and continued, "It will, unfortunately, cost you fifty-five dollars. Are you sure you don't know where the key is?" he questioned.

"I've looked everywhere. You don't know what I've gone through the last few days! I hoped I wouldn't need to get into it before I found the key." She looked helpless.

He looked down at her identification again. "It's a shame to have to go to the trouble and expense, but, when ya got it, ya got it, and when ya don't, ya don't." He chuckled and picked up the phone to call the local locksmith.

When Bill entered the bank he stopped at a large sign at the entrance that advertised the current IRA rates. During the exchange between Holly and the manager, he read and reread the sign. Slowly, he became aware of two cold, steel-gray eyes watching him. His stomach sank to the level of his knees.

"May I help you?" asked a middle-aged woman who looked like Our Miss Brooks. She scrutinized him over the top of her half-glasses.

"Uh . . . yes . . . I guess I want to open an account," he stammered. "I just haven't decided on the terms, considering all these different signs and rates," Bill said, stalling.

She rose from her desk and walked over to him. She was in her early to mid-forties but dressed as if she were sixty. Her back was as straight as a flagpole. She wore a charcoal-gray pinstriped business suit padded at the shoulders and cut to mask any trace of curvature she might have. She walked with an air of authority and dominance. Had this been a nunnery, Bill was sure she would have been the mother superior.

She took him over to a desk that had a sign reading, Ms. Hinsen, branch manager. "Sit down, here," she ordered.

He obeyed.

"Now, what type of account would you like to open?" she began.

Bill pointed at the sign and replied, "One of those IRAs." He looked down into his lap and said, "Do you think that's a good idea?"

"Young man, if you don't plan for your future, when you're old and gray the working people of this country will have to support you. Is it a good idea? Why, of course it's a good idea, and it shows fiscal maturity."

"Well, ma'am," Bill stammered, "how do they work?"

Ms. Hinsen began to explain the rates and bank policies to him. It was an eternity waiting for the locksmith to arrive. He halted her oration frequently with pointless questions, stalling for time. Meanwhile, Holly paced nervously in front of the vault.

Ultimately the locksmith arrived and began to drill the lock from the box. Holly waited just outside the vault door.

By this time, Bill had agreed to open an IRA for twenty-four months with a minimum five hundred dollars. This was after he had been admonished two more times to make yearly contributions so he would not become a burden to his children or to society in his old age. He assumed Ms. Hinsen had an outstanding record of contributions.

He needed more time; he couldn't leave Holly in here alone.

"What about a checking account?" he blurted out.

Ms. Hinsen peered at him over the glasses again as she drew

her chin back, merging it imperceptibly into the wrinkles of her neck.

"A checking account? You don't have a checking account?" She was astounded.

Not so patiently she began to explain to him about the different colors of checks and the imitation alligator checkbooks. He saw the assistant manager return to his desk.

The assistant manager picked up the phone and turned away from the direction of the vault. He was facing toward Bill, so he dropped his gaze as he dialed, but Bill was close enough to hear him say, "I need to speak to Jarvis."

"She's here in the bank, Mr. Jarvis. . . . Yes, I'm sure. . . . She's getting into her safety deposit box. . . . Yes, I'll do what I can to keep her here. . . . No, I didn't see anyone come in with her. . . . Yes, sir. You're welcome." He hung up the phone as the lock fell off of the box.

The locksmith swung the door open.

Holly had prepaid the fee; she took the box to a small room and opened it. The tape was on top as she cleaned out the contents and put them into a briefcase. She quickly thanked the assistant manager and walked toward the front door.

Ms. Hinsen was in the middle of typing Bill's application for the new account when he sprang out of the chair and followed Holly through the door. Ms. Hinsen stared after him with a look of disgust. He had not given her the money for the IRA account.

A car was sitting in front of the door of the bank as Holly went out. The right-hand door opened and a man emerged. He was six feet tall with broad, muscular shoulders and a pockmarked face. The expression on his face said volumes about the score he wanted to settle with Holly.

"Get in!" he ordered.

Holly looked like a fox with its foot caught in a trap. She looked right and left. *There must be a way out!* she thought. Panic seized her, and terror was written on her face. He grabbed her arm, attempting to pull her into the car. Bill was ten paces behind, running out of the bank, as the man pulled Holly toward the car. Bill reached for his gun in the shoulder holster; noiselessly, Ken walked up to the driver's side of the car. The sun gleamed from the barrel of his .44 magnum. He placed the barrel at the side of the driver's head and cocked the hammer.

"Everyone stay real quiet, and no one has to get hurt," he said calmly. "Now listen close; I'm not going to repeat. Let go of Holly first."

The man holding her looked at his partner for instructions.

"Do you see that gray van over there?" Ken said. Without waiting for a reply he went on. "There is a guy who has a rifle with an incendiary round in the chamber. It's aimed at your gas tank. Do you know how large an explosion that will make?"

Ken paused. They indisputably had the advantage of the moment, so Bill walked up to the man holding Holly and removed his hand from her arm. Bill flashed the man a view of the gun in his right hand. The man didn't resist. Bill whispered, "I killed one of your buddies yesterday. I'll kill you, too, if you even breathe." Bill hoped the man couldn't sense his own ambivalence and fear. He had wrestled all night with the accidental death at Pleasure Island. While he still felt that what he'd done was wrong, he knew larger wrongs in the world—one of which would be letting this guy take Holly back to Jarvis. He knew he couldn't allow that to happen.

Ken said, "Now, get on that two-way radio and tell all your buddies around here we are leaving quietly and none of you—and I mean none of you—are going to follow us."

"If you blow the car, you'll die too," the driver said, trying desperately to regain the edge.

"I don't think you're dumb; don't be stupid either. I think you know that as far as Jarvis is concerned, we're already dead anyway. So the choice is yours. You'd better make it quick!" Ken replied.

As Ken was talking, Bill gripped Holly's arm and escorted her away from the car. They walked briskly across the parking lot to the waiting van. Holly got into the front seat on the right; Bill slid the side door open and climbed in, trembling with an adrenaline rush. He didn't have time to be afraid, not yet anyway.

Ken was still standing by the car. He continued, "Here's a message for Jarvis: Tell him we have him where it hurts. Tell him when we're done he'll be lucky if he can even sing low enough to be a soprano. Do you understand?"

The man nodded.

"Now, I'm going to walk away, and if your hands move off the steering wheel, this car will come down somewhere between here and Bermuda." Ken bent down by the back tire and punctured the sidewall with a knife. "Just to keep you honest," he said.

Bill steadied the door as Ken rolled into the already moving van. They rocketed out of the parking lot, bumping wildly as they hit the street. The tires frantically dug into the sand-slick asphalt, looking for traction. Their momentum pitched them forward as they raced toward the bridge and the mainland. The bridge was around the next curve. They had accelerated to seventy miles an hour and were still gaining speed.

"Here they come!" John shouted as he looked in the mirror.

"I just hope they haven't blocked the bridge this time," Bill said.

Ken pushed the back door of the van open as they headed up and over the channel. At least two cars were starting to gain on them. At the bottom of the bridge, John made a hard left turn across traffic, narrowly missing a BMW. He rocketed down River Road. It was a narrow, winding stretch of pavement that paralleled the Cape Fear River. The road's sandy shoulders quickly gave way to forests of the slender eastern pines of North Carolina. As they picked up speed, the passing trees became a blur of green and brown.

The cars in pursuit drew closer. A flash from the passenger side of the lead car was immediately followed by an explosion of the rear window and the splintering of the wood in the overhead. Holly screamed. Small splinters rained down inside the car. Ken raised the rifle he was holding to his shoulder and fired. The lead car jerked suddenly to the right, went into a skid as its tires dropped into the soft sand, and rolled over and over in the air. It ended its flight in eternity abruptly. The car exploded in a ball of flame. The occupants, if not killed in the crash, were immediately incinerated as the flames devoured the vehicle.

The second car slowed as it passed the burning wreckage. For several miles after that, it kept a respectable distance. Everyone in the car held on tightly as they swayed and swerved over the road toward Wilmington.

"We don't seem to be losing them," John commented as he looked in the mirror.

"They're too far back to get a clean shot," Ken yelled.

"Maybe when we get closer to town, and as the traffic increases, we'll have a better chance," Bill answered.

"I think we should divest ourselves of them before we get too many people around," Ken said. "Stop around the next corner and let me out!"

When the pursuing car dropped from sight, John stomped on the brakes and skidded sideways to a stop. Bill slammed his shoulder against the front seat as the van bucked like an unbroken stallion.

Ken quickly jumped out of the van as it slid to a stop, then John jammed the gas pedal to the floor once more. Smoke and sand formed a storm in the air behind the van as it accelerated up the road, the rear end fishtailing with a rhythm that would make a disco dancer envious. Ken ran for cover, diving to the ground and rolling into firing position as the pursuit car came into view.

The rifle was snug against his shoulder, the leather strap wrapped on his forearm, his finger poised on the graceful curve of the trigger. He sighted on the driver. Almost by instinct, his tours in Vietnam and his years of training made these movements as spontaneous as walking in the park. When the distance was right, he applied pressure with his index finger and squeezed off two quick bursts from the automatic rifle. The windshield of the car exploded with the first burst. Glass flew in all directions. One round hit the driver in the right side of the neck. The projectile split the skin and muscle. The carotid artery was partially severed, and blood spewed all over the inside of the car.

Its velocity unchanged, the bullet then shattered one of the bones in the neck and transected the spinal cord. The driver was dead by the time the hot metal exited his body and plunged into the vehicle's roof. The car swerved out of control to the left and impacted a tree, splitting off the right front fender. Then it was silent.

Ken slowly arose from his position and cautiously approached the wreck. He swept the rifle back and forth as he approached the twisted metal, looking for any movement. The smell of oil, a hot engine, and blood gave off a peculiar odor that Ken knew he would never forget. Killing was something he never became used to. True, in Vietnam he had participated in his share of battles and the slaughter on the battlefield was something he had seen before. Now there it was again, the killing. *Why did they have to follow us?* he thought.

He alertly approached the left side and looked in. The sight was one of carnage, which, in all of his years in Vietnam, he had never grown accustomed to. The passenger had been thrown forward with his head impacting the windshield support. His skull had been split, and the whiteness of the frontal lobe of the brain could be seen on the vinyl of the roof. Blood was still running slowly from the neck wound of the driver, but he was obviously dead. "I didn't want to kill you. Why did you follow me!" he said aloud to the corpse. The man in the backseat still had a pulse but was unconscious. As Ken began to examine him, he heard a car approaching. Hastily he crouched in the trees.

The van rolled slowly to a stop on the soft sand twenty feet from the wreck.

"Do you see Ken?" Bill asked.

"No, but I think he got them," came the response from John.

Just then Ken ran out from the trees to meet them. Holly had opened the front door of the van and moved into the back with Bill.

Ken jumped in.

"Get out of here!" he yelled.

They rapidly spun around and continued toward Wilmington. Bill kept watch out the broken back window for any more of Jarvis's men. He was now trembling, but not with the adrenaline rush he'd experienced at the bank. This time it was fear. Somehow, they had gone into the lion's den, pried open its mouth, and lived. At least for the moment.

• • •

Jarvis was walking on the beach when his lieutenants, James and Howard, ran up to him. "They got away," James said.

"Don't tell me that!" Jarvis screamed. "Bring me those incompetent slobs you call men!"

"They're dead," he answered.

"They let a woman and a couple of amateurs get away from them and got killed in the process? Well, it probably serves them right."

"Mr. Jarvis, these guys aren't acting like amateurs. I think the doc and the girl have some pros with them," Howard said. "And, sir, one of them sent you a message from the bank. . . ."

"Yes, what's the message?" Jarvis asked.

"Uh . . . well . . . ," he stammered.

"Out with it, Howard!"

"He said to tell you that when they're through you'll sing soprano." Howard looked away as he said it.

Jarvis strode away from his house and up the beach, toward the burned-out villa that now dominated the landscape of the lower end of the island. This was now more than an operation that had gone awry. This was now a personal vendetta. Chandler, a mere nothing of a person, had invaded Sidney Jarvis's world and had taken his possessions. He had taken Holly. He had taken the opportunity to sell the Tel-Ray system, and now he had taken his reputation as well. *No one interferes with Sidney Jarvis and lives to tell about it,* he fumed. "This scientist will pay, and pay dearly!" He spat out the words loudly as a group of sea gulls screeched overhead.

Returning to his house, he called James again.

"I'm going back to Washington—tonight!"

"Sir . . . Mr. Jarvis, we don't know where they've gone. We don't have any idea if they headed back up there or not."

"Oh, they went back to D.C.," he sneered. "By the way, did you clean up any mess that might have been left from the misadventure this morning?"

"Yes, sir. There is no trace of the men, and it is impossible to trace the cars to you. Shall I order the plane?"

"Of course! And James, bring me my Beretta and plenty of ammunition." Jarvis looked in the mirror and smiled. He had never wanted to personally kill anyone the way he now wanted to kill Dr. Chandler. It reminded him of that slut Maria, back in Turkey. That's how much he wanted to kill Chandler.

If Maria had only realized how much he had wanted her. How much he had loved her . . . back when he was a young CIA agent named Michael Jardeen. In Istanbul he had lived his life on the edge, and he wanted his women with as much passion and danger. That is why he had coveted her to be his and his alone. But no, she fell for that schmuck Lt. Jarvis. She had even slept with him. And she had made fun of Michael only nights before. He could still remember the pain as she had laughed at him.

They had dined and drunk expensive wine on her patio overlooking Istanbul. She had been beautifully seductive that night. Her white teeth had sparkled as she talked. She was a smuggler; he knew that. She had been taught the trade and given her connections by her father, who had also been a smuggler, like his father before him. Maria was very good at it, and she represented an influential force in the Mideast. He was enamored by the way she laughed at his jokes. When dinner was over she invited him into her private chamber. He had heard rumors that men had to be very special to be invited into her private chamber. Michael had always considered himself special, and Maria's invitation proved it.

There she had clung to him with her hands locked behind his neck, and she had swayed her hips enticingly in front of him. When he reached out to pull her to himself, she had danced lithely away.

"Michael, why don't you disrobe and lie down. I'll be right back," she taunted him with a revealing kiss.

But the night had turned out to be an amorous disaster, and Maria had laughed at him, eventually asking him to leave. That was why killing her had been so satisfying.

Until Dr. Chandler, she was the only one who had ever laughed at him. And she didn't get away with it. No one laughs at Michael Jardeen. It was a shame that Maria didn't appreciate the potential and the power that would have been available to her if only she had cooperated with the original plan. *But she learned,* Jarvis thought smugly. *She didn't laugh at me long, and Chandler won't laugh at me long either. People who steal from me don't get away with it for very long.*

• • •

The plane left the ground in a blinding rain, and the lights of the beach disappeared from sight almost immediately. Jarvis stared out the window into nothingness. There had been only two women in the world he had ever really wanted to possess. The first had been Maria. The second was Holly.

He couldn't endure Maria's laughing at him. Now he wouldn't permit Holly to laugh at him. But, Jarvis vowed, he would not kill

Holly until she understood and until she had begged for him and for her life. Then he would kill her . . . slowly.

As the plane roared through the stormy night, he felt the same surge building up in his body that he had felt as he smashed his fist into the soft flesh of Maria's body. When he was in control, the excitement was just below the surface; the throbbing of the engines of the plane resonated with his emotional awareness as the aircraft dug its way through the night sky. Yes, he was in control again.

Jarvis was at his stronghold in Potomac hours before the car carrying the tape was out of North Carolina. He called Blaine.

"Blaine residence," the maid answered the phone.

"Is Secretary Blaine in? This is Sidney Jarvis."

"Why no, Mr. Jarvis, he isn't. He and Mrs. Blaine went to a meeting down in the city. They should be home soon. May I give him a message?" she asked.

"No, I'll call back later. Do you have any idea what time he is expected?"

"Mrs. Blaine said she thought they would be home by ten o'clock."

Jarvis hung the phone back on its cradle. He didn't like to be kept waiting when there were things to do. But he was sure time was on his side.

• • •

Secretary and Mrs. Randolph W. Blaine sat at the head table in the State Dining Room at the White House. The affair was the brainchild of the president. He had decided against a second term. He had been diagnosed with lymphoma and feared the strain of a campaign would aggrevate the illness. "Things are going so well, it's best to quit when you're ahead," he had told Blaine. "I want you to be my successor and carry forth our plans. The country needs you." The president and Blaine had been friends since college, and after the philosophical break with the vice president,

Blaine had become his most trusted adviser. In the president's mind, having Randolph succeed him was the most natural order of things.

This night was chosen to call the party's top leaders and supporters together for an informal banquet. The central theme was to lay the groundwork for Randolph's announcement of his intent to run in the upcoming primary for the presidential candidate of their party. They thought it a good idea to determine the internal opposition, if any.

The affair was attended by a select group of twenty-five men and their wives, the president and first lady, Secretary and Mrs. Blaine, and Carol Shemp.

The presidential couple and the Blaines sat near the center of the head table, and the presidential press secretary sat nearer to the end to the president's right. The Speaker of the House sat on the opposite end; Carol sat next to him. His wife was a patient at the Naval Hospital in Bethesda, recovering from a small stroke.

The night had been specifically arranged when the vice president was out of the country representing the president at an economic meeting in Tokyo. The rest of the tables were filled by the president's supporters in the order of their importance politically, or their ability to give or raise money. Dinner was served on gold-trimmed china with the presidential sterling.

After dinner the president tapped his glass politely and stood up as the murmuring conversations around the tables ceased.

"Gentlemen, we have a most distinguished guest to hear from tonight, but first a toast." He elevated his wine glass. "To the lovely and talented ladies who grace our table tonight, and a special remembrance to the Speaker's wife, Kathy. May her recovery be swift and complete."

The men stood, raised their glasses, and said together, "To our wives." They drank from the glasses as the women smiled and bowed their heads in a slight and demure manner. The Speaker acknowledged the president's consideration.

The President continued, "As you all know, I will not be seeking re-election. I've asked my friend, Secretary of Defense Randolph Blaine, to address you tonight. Randolph," he said as he turned and offered his hand in a gesture to focus attention toward Blaine.

Blaine stood and surveyed the group. Before him, the power and the wealth of the nation waited expectantly. These men could control or buy whatever they wanted. He was proud; he would be their candidate.

"Mr. President, distinguished guests, ladies." He glanced down at Carol, sitting near the end of the table. "You all know the effective job this man"—pointing to the president—"has done for our country." Applause. "I am here tonight to ask your advice about continuing his programs—programs that have pulled us from the edge of disaster economically, militarily, and morally. . . ." He paused for effect. "Of course they should continue, and I am here to say, if you will give me your support, I will run in the next presidential election, I will win the next presidential election, and those programs will continue."

There was an immediate response. Applause and shouts of "Hear, hear!" echoed throughout the room. Randolph knew without a shadow of a doubt that he had arrived. *I belong here,* he thought. *I'm one of them. I will win, whatever it takes.* He smiled, dutifully took his wife's hand, and helped her stand up. She beamed. Randolph looked again at Carol and felt the torrent that only she could provide.

Carol sat clapping and cheering as she contemplated the meaning of the night. This was where she had been headed when she set out so many years ago—when she, and she alone, had seen the untapped potential buried deep in that midlevel bureaucrat, Randolph W. Blaine. With the others she stood and cheered, secure in the knowledge that she solely was responsible for him. She had done and would continue to do whatever was necessary, to him or for him, so that his full and rightful place would be reached. And, more important, she would be there beside him. She was the luckiest person on earth.

The function ended about 9:30. There was unanimous agreement that Blaine was the person to take the banner from the president and carry it forward to new frontiers, to borrow a phrase from the past.

The Blaines and Carol were the last to leave.

"I'm sorry, but I'll have to have someone take you home," Randolph said to his wife. "I received a message, before the dinner, and I have to go to a meeting over at the Pentagon. Something fairly urgent has come up."

"Oh, Randolph," she sighed. "OK, but you've been putting in such long hours this month. Please get some rest tonight." Mrs. Blaine was the perfect and dutiful wife. She kissed him lightly on the cheek and left.

"I have my car," Carol said. "Can I drop you?"

"That would be helpful; I may have something for you to do anyway," Blaine replied, letting his eyes begin at her feet and wander in a lustful fashion up to her waist.

They drove off the White House grounds and directed the car toward Georgetown.

"You were magnificent tonight!" Carol bubbled. "You had us all eating out of your hand. You emanated strength and power as you spoke. Oh, Randolph, you will make the best president we've ever had."

Randolph felt the intoxication of authority. It was pumping though every vessel and fiber of his body. His goal of winning was coming to fulfillment. He had the power, power to do whatever he wanted to do, power to do whatever he had to do.

They arrived at Carol's townhouse, then parked in the garage and entered unseen.

• • •

Randolph and Carol reclined on her bed of satin sheets, propped up on large pillows covered in gigantic flowers of every color. Carol's bedroom was the ultimate in femininity. Draperies matching the bedspread graced the windows, and fresh-cut flowers were delicately displayed on the dresser. A large Oriental rug covered polished hardwood floors. The room appeared considerably larger, enhanced by the large mirrored closet doors that reflected the elegance of the arrangement.

The evening had started off peculiarly for a night of love. Blaine had been uncommonly assertive as they drank wine. While sitting on the floor by the crackling fire, he had initiated their excursion into intimacy. His forwardness inflamed her with an arousing and terrifying hunger; it seized Carol with surprise and destroyed the predesigned evening she had planned.

He had touched her in a way that was foreign for him. He was bold, insistent. Carol was at a loss. Her control was gone. Ever since the speech and the acclamation of the audience Blaine had taken on a different personality. When he drove them to her house, he was aggressive. Now he had swept her off of her feet and carried her to the bedroom. Things were out of hand. She was scared. His forcefulness, his control, his will over hers were all things she had yearned for for years. Now that she had it from him she was overwhelmed. Her mind was spinning as her heart raced. This was the man she always knew he could be. The man she always wanted. When he was president it would be magnificent! Her orderly mind was in a tailspin. As they gave themselves over to a passionate embrace, the telephone rang.

Ordinarily it would have been ignored, but this was a phone line known only to a select few, to be used only in extreme emergencies. The only other time it had ever rung, the president himself had dialed the number from his private office.

"Hello," Carol answered on the second ring. Her voice trembled slightly. The interruption was akin to a dive into an icy pond.

"Let me talk to Blaine. This is Jarvis."

She covered the phone with a pillow. "Randolph! It's that awful Jarvis fellow. Do you want me to tell him you're not here?"

Blaine propped himself up on one elbow and looked down at the exposed body of his mistress. Oh, how he wanted to be rid of Jarvis!

"No, I'll talk to him," he said, reaching under the pillow to take the phone in his hand. "Jarvis, I thought I told you never to call me here unless it was an emergency. Now, what's the trouble?"

"We have a problem," Jarvis said.

"Can't it wait until morning?" Blaine asked.

"No, it can't! Our friends, the ones troubling the current project, visited down south this morning. They got something out of a safety deposit box, caused real pain to some of my people, and then left. I have a feeling whatever they got out of the bank is not in our best interests. Now, get your butt out of the sack, kiss your sweetie good-night, and get over to my place in Maryland!" Jarvis hung up abruptly.

Blaine listened to the dial tone for several seconds and then slowly hung up the receiver. He was going to be the next president of the United States, and Jarvis was still ordering him around. He seethed with anger.

Randolph threw back the sheet and stood up. He caught the reflection of himself in the mirror. "No, he won't get away with it this time," he said out loud.

"Get away with what?" Carol looked up questioningly.

"I'll go when I'm good and ready."

She looked at him questioningly.

He lay back down on the silk sheets and rested his head on Carol's softness, listening to her heart beat rhythmically in his ear. He wanted to stay. He didn't want to go see Jarvis tonight or ever again. He would go eventually, of course. But for now, he decided, he would stay and listen to her heart; it was safe and secure, provocative.

"What's wrong, Randolph? Why does that horrible man call you at this time of night?" She pressed his head against her breast and caressed his temple. Carol was paralyzed with fear, worried that disaster was overtaking them again.

"Oh, just business. Nothing to concern yourself with. I'm going to have to meet him tonight; something has come up," he said, smiling at her reflection in the mirror.

Randolph then gently lifted Carol's hand from his temple and kissed her fingertips. "But not just yet, my love . . . not yet."

He pulled her close and Carol's heart began to throb.

• • •

Later, Carol lay satisfied, truly satisfied. Randolph had not left immediately afterward, as she suspected would happen. He lingered. She was expended. Her body had never experienced the magnitude of such an encounter before. After years of leading him, tonight she could only be led. She had lost all perception of time and place, and could only accommodate and oblige him as he gently ravished her.

Randolph sat with his feet swinging from the side of the bed. His victory had been complete, his lifelong struggle against his sexual inadequacy conquered. It was time to go; now he would see Jarvis. As he stood up, Carol clutched at his leg. She did not want him to leave her, not tonight. True, Jarvis was a dangerous man; she was sure of that. But there was something new and strong in Randolph, and she wanted to lie in its shadow.

When he was dressed, she got out of bed and wrapped herself in a sheet. Putting her arms around him from behind, she laid her cheek against his back and whispered, "If only we could leave the rest of the world behind. If only we could have a life together. . . ."

• • •

Twenty minutes later, Blaine was driving Carol's Porsche toward Jarvis's Potomac manor house. He felt uneasy and antagonistic. He and Jarvis were meeting much too often. After this affair was over, they would not see each other as frequently. In fact, he thought, it would be best if they had no communication until after the presidential election. Jarvis would certainly understand how much more valuable Blaine would be then.

As he drove up the driveway, the outside lights were blazing, making it difficult to see. He parked the car in front of the house and walked in as the door opened without a command.

"Blaine, how nice to see you again!" Jarvis remarked.

"Cut the crap, Jarvis! What is so all-fired important that you had to get me out here tonight?" Blaine was indignant as he walked briskly past Jarvis without shaking the outstretched hand.

"I had a visit from Chandler and Holly. They have some new friends now, too. They ran a very smooth operation, in and out in minutes. Whatever they were after they got. I'm not sure why they were down there, but it appears there was something in the bank at Carolina Beach. Holly cleaned out her safety deposit box."

"Do you have any idea what they were after?" Blaine was alarmed.

"I have a hunch, but I'm not certain," Jarvis replied.

"Didn't you stop them?" Blaine responded in dismay.

"If I had, do you think I'd be here now, bothering you with this?"

"Well . . . well . . . ," Blaine sputtered. "What do you think I can do to help? Every time I've located them for you, you . . ." He was searching for the right word but couldn't find it. He finally blurted out, "You screwed things up!"

Jarvis didn't like this new forcefulness Blaine seemed to be displaying. Maybe he had miscalculated having asked Blaine over to assist in finding them. Well, it was too late now, and he did need the resources Blaine had available. He hoped Blaine's aspirations for the presidency would not make him too hard to handle. Blaine appeared to be vacillating somewhere between his usual wimpiness and a newfound formidable personality. This could spell problems in the future. Killing a national figure was always messy. Occasionally necessary, but messy.

"Look, Mr. Secretary," Jarvis said coolly, hoping to soothe

Blaine's fury, "this is a problem that affects both of us. Now, I admit there have been some difficulties encountered in the situation, but we need to work together to resolve it."

"Difficulties!" Blaine screeched. "One woman and a man—how much trouble can there be for you and your people to take care of one lousy woman and some yellow-livered scientist?"

Unruffled, Jarvis continued. "In spite of our most recent setback, we can do so by working together to find them. Then we have a second question to ask, concerning whether we can still deliver on the Tel-Ray project or whether it's in our best interests to forget Tel-Ray and eliminate all concerned."

"This mess needs to be settled. If necessary, I can handle our Eastern clients. . . . At this point, I'd, er, we'd all be better off if it was over. . . . Yes, yes! Just get it over with." Blaine sensed, somehow, he might later regret the decision. But it furthered his resolve to eventually rid himself of Jarvis.

"Blaine, I need your people to find out where they are hiding. It's my guess they will try to take whatever they obtained this morning to some authority. We must . . . must locate them. Once they are located, I'll take over. It must be done quickly, though, before they find someone to go to."

Blaine went to the telephone and dialed a number. "Hello, Billings, this is Blaine. Sorry to bother you so late. I need your assistance in locating some people. . . . Yes, the same ones. . . . That's right, Holly James and William Chandler." Their names were becoming too familiar to Blaine. "No! I don't want you or any of your people to do anything but find them. That is an order. Oh, and Billings, use whatever resources you need to, do you understand?" He hung up the phone and turned to Jarvis.

"We'll find them one more time for you. But I'm warning you, this is the last time I am going to do this. Is that clear?"

"Mr. Secretary," Jarvis said coolly, "there's no reason for us to argue. I'm sure Holly has enough on the both of us to bring the house down around our ears. You and I will both do whatever we have to for as long as we have to! Don't let this presidential thing go to your head. We started out together, we have grown rich together, and we will end together. Is that clear?"

Blaine scrutinized Jarvis carefully. The thought that they might be two of the same kind was repugnant. He turned abruptly and proceeded toward the door. "Jarvis!" he yelled over his shoulder. "Don't screw it up again!" He slammed the door as he left.

Now what? Should he go home or back to Carol?

23

LOSING IT

The four occupants of the motel room sat in silence as they prepared to listen to the small magnetic tape. The cost had been high; five men had died trying to take the tape from them. Bill wondered whether the information it contained would be worth the price. It had to be.

He pressed a button on the recorder.

The conversation developed from the informal niceties of the greeting to its chilling climax and was punctuated by a very businesslike cordiality that sounded more like a board meeting of a Fortune 500 company than what it really was.

Blaine: "What was the final figure proposed for the plans?"

Jarvis: "With a working model, the agreed price was 3.2 million. If it was only the plans, with or without a working copy of the computer program, 2.7."

Blaine: "How much of the down payment has been received?"

Jarvis: "The usual from a Middle Eastern country, half in advance, the rest COD."

They listened, awestruck, as two men conspired to sell out their country's secrets, one the secretary of defense, the other a name, someone who had died years before, at least officially. For Bill it was like sitting in a house of horrors.

The remainder of the two men's conversation was a discussion of the network and the routing necessary for transportation of the final plans for the Tel-Ray system to the Middle Eastern buyer. It was obvious that not only were members of Jarvis's organization to be used, but startling enough, elements of the Defense Department also were in the plans. It appeared from their conversation that Air Force MAC transport planes would be used to take the hardware from Washington, from Bill's own laboratory, to Germany. The excursion from Germany to the Middle East would be handled by members of a NATO unit that guarded a specific border crossing. This sounded like a well-used pathway. Listening to the ease with which they discussed the transfer, Bill thought they might as well have been using Acme Van Lines.

The business ended with a promise by Jarvis that the final plans would be brought to Cape Fear no later than the first of November by Ed Harris, Bill's former boss and friend.

Then Jarvis said, "I see you brought your secretary along this time. Is there anything special we can provide for you? When did you start mixing business with pleasure, Randolph?"

"Well, we have some work that has to be finished. And anyway, a man is entitled to a little recreation now and then. We'll just spend the night down at the Sand Dollar. Please don't expect us for dinner."

They sat in stunned silence as the tape clicked off, lost in their own thoughts of what this really meant. Ken was the first to speak.

"Well, Holly, I must say, your tape was more than I ever expected to hear."

John mumbled, "This is too much for us to handle. Who knows who all is involved with these people? We don't know who the enemy is. The next person we talk to may be in on this thing. We don't even have a clue who to take this information to. . . ."

Not being familiar with the inner workings of the government,

Bill took a different view of the situation. "If too many small people are involved, the word would have leaked out before now. I think there are surely some big names implicated. They're the ones we have to avoid being trapped by. And I agree, there seems to be a lot of people working for them. But I'll bet most of the middle men don't know what's going on."

"I don't see what you're driving at," Holly responded.

"We need not fear the average agent in the government if we can keep from getting caught."

"That's a big *if*, buddy boy," John interrupted.

Bill continued, "But we also know they can't do us much good. Therefore, what we need to do is get as high up as we can on the first try with this tape."

"I have a hunch we're not too safe here in North Carolina right now," Ken said. "Let's head out of state as soon as we've made some copies of the tape."

Within the hour, they were heading north on Route 17, thinking it was in their best interest to avoid Interstate 95. There was very little talk in the car. This time they traded off drivers and tried to reach Washington as soon as they could. Bill took over at Norfolk. It seemed that every approaching set of headlights was a menace. There was no comfort or safety in the usual traffic in northern Virginia.

They reached the outskirts of Washington late in the evening. In Alexandria Bill pulled into a small motel that once had been nice, but that had been many years ago. Now it was used by no-name people with little money and little future. They had money. But the question was, did they have a future? The next few days would decide.

Day Twelve

The next morning they all slept late. John bought breakfast at a fast-food drive-through, insisting on bringing something to the motel for all of them to avoid the exposure. He reasoned the less they were on the streets, the less the likelihood one of them would be recognized. So far, he was the only one who had not been positively identified in the little band of marauders. It was nice to have him in the assembly.

Several hours were spent discussing alternatives, but none of them, when pushed to their ultimate conclusion, were workable. Finally Bill spoke up. "I have an idea. It may be a long shot, but I'd like to try it," he said.

"What is it?" Ken asked.

"Without going into details . . . I thought I might take the tape to the president."

"To the president?" Holly queried.

Not a word was spoken for several seconds. Then John declared, "Are you going to ride up on ol' Paint and knock on the door? Or did you think you might call for an appointment?" he asked sarcastically.

"I know it sounds crazy, but I have a plan. I'd like to keep the details to myself; I think it would be safer for all concerned. Maybe . . . it might work. And if it does, we're home free. But, like I said, on the outside chance it doesn't . . . if you don't know, it will reduce your danger. Is there someplace you all can go where I can get hold of you on a short notice? Somewhere that's safe?"

"I don't like it!" Holly said.

"I think I know a place," Ken said.

"I want to go with you," Holly protested, glaring at Bill.

"No! I think it best if I do this alone. If something happens and it doesn't work out, then you'll have to come up with a better plan. In that case, Ken and John will need you as a witness."

"We've all been in this together since you called me a week ago. We have the right to know!" Ken was adamant.

"All right . . . all right, here it is in a nutshell. An old friend of mine is a newscaster on one of the local TV stations. I'm going to see if, in exchange for the exclusive story, he would arrange a meeting with the president's press secretary."

"Why don't you just call him from here?" John asked.

"Because if he turns on me and calls the police, I don't want any of us to be in a position to be cornered. That's why I think it best if I do it myself."

Bill looked at each of them in turn; their silence constituted the agreement he was looking for. Without a word he got up and walked out of the room, pausing just long enough to kiss Holly on the cheek. He stopped at the door. "Come on, guys. We only have one vehicle. If I take the van, you won't have any wheels. This motel is not in the most convenient place in town."

He drove to Washington's National Airport and left the car in the farthest corner of one of the long-term parking lots after he had dropped the others at the terminal. They planned on taking the Metro back to Alexandria. Bill had a phone number where he could reach them. They all thought it best if he didn't know the exact location.

He caught the shuttle from the lot to the Metro station. The darkness of the underground was pleasant as he rode to Cleveland Park. Exiting the train, he walked up the hill to the Cleveland House Inn. When checking in, Bill blamed his lack of luggage on United Airlines and made the bell captain promise to bring it to his room as soon as it arrived. As near as he could tell, he had not been followed or spotted on his way from the airport. But, he kept reminding himself, he was a research engineer, not a spy. Anything was possible.

By the time he settled into the room, it was 10:30 in the evening. He knew he had to make a phone call, but he wanted to sleep in the worst way. Sleep won out as he lay down on the bed. The next thing Bill knew the sun was coming in the window; he had neglected to pull the drapes.

Day Thirteen

Bill rolled out of bed with a headache from fatigue. After washing away the stupor with a cool shower, he picked up the phone in the room and dialed a number he had written down the evening before. The paranoia began to surface again. He slammed the receiver down as it began to ring. His heart was picking up speed, and his forehead broke out in a sweat. He ran into the bathroom and twisted the cold-water faucet. Splashing the water on his face, he regained some control. Bill decided to go down to the lobby and use a pay phone.

"WQAP-TV," the voice at the other end of the line said.

"Robert Owens, please," he almost whispered.

"I'm sorry, I couldn't quite hear you," she replied.

He cleared his throat and looked around. No one was watching him. "Robert Owens, please!" he said louder and more deliberately.

"Just a moment."

"Hello, this is Bob Owens."

"Bob, if you recognize my voice don't say anything but *yes*," Bill said into the phone.

"Yes," he responded.

"I need to see you."

"OK. Where and when?" he answered.

"Go shopping at White Flint Mall from eleven until two today. I'll find you."

"OK, but . . ."

"Don't say anything to anyone, and Bob, come alone! Please!"

"This sounds crazy . . ." Bill didn't hear the rest of Owens's sentence; he'd broken the connection.

It was only 8:30 in the morning. Bill bought a paper and went back up to his room. He ordered a razor and breakfast from room service. An article buried deep in the first section reported the two cars found in North Carolina. The devastation was described, but strangely enough, there was no mention of fatalities. There was speculation the bodies had been removed since a lot of blood was noted in one of the wrecks. But the mystery surrounding the event persisted.

Bill arrived at the mall at 10:30 and mingled with the crowd of morning shoppers and store clerks. The very crowds that a few short weeks ago had seemed to be such a nuisance in the Washington area now offered the only protection he could find. He momentarily wondered what had happened to his life.

He saw Bob Owens walking toward Bloomingdale's on the second level. Bill followed the reporter at a distance for twenty minutes as he browsed his way through several stores looking very bored. Finally, at least to his untrained eye, Bill felt certain he had come alone and was not being followed, except by him. He walked up behind him.

"Bob, don't turn around or acknowledge I'm here. Just walk to your car. We'll talk there," Bill said.

"I hope you're not as dangerous as the FBI says you are, or I'm a real fool for being with you," was his only reply.

Five minutes later they were heading down Wisconsin Avenue.

"Get on the Beltway and drive," Bill instructed.

He took the entrance ramp to the eastbound lanes in silence.

"First off, thanks," Bill said to break the tension building between them.

"Bill, just what is going on?" he demanded. "You went away for a vacation for a few weeks, and then you were reported to have been killed in an explosion. But Joan saw you leave your apartment in a limo a few days later, and now the FBI has put you and some unknown female on the ten most-wanted list. You set up this meeting with me like a CIA agent. What's going on?" Owens asked.

"Bob, I know I owe you an explanation, and I'll give you one, but first I need a favor."

"Like what?"

They were just passing Georgia Avenue. The sun had broken through the dull, gray clouds; as it reflected off the leaves, it gave a brilliance to the trees that Bill had never noticed before. He began to wonder if his idea was even worthwhile or had a chance of success. Momentarily, he was lost in his own thoughts. But they disappeared with Owens's next question, asked in a raw, harsh voice.

"What kind of favor do you need? Or did you just want me to give you a ride around the Beltway?" he demanded.

Bill took a long, deep breath as Bob's words shocked him back to reality. "I need for you to arrange for me to see the president," Bill said.

The car drifted out of its lane as the request penetrated Bob's thoughts. A horn screamed its warning as a car swerved to avoid hitting them, and the other driver shook his fist at them.

"You're not only one of the most wanted human beings on earth today, you're one of the craziest!" he shouted.

He drove along in silence.

"Well?" Bill questioned.

"Well, what?" Owens retorted.

"Will you get me in to see the president?"

"How can I get you in to see him? And even if—and I say *if*—I could, why in heaven's name should I?"

"All right, listen. First, I am not crazy. Second, I am not a murderer. Third, it would be a lot safer for you and your family if you don't know why I need to see him. And fourth, I'll have the best story of your life for you and you alone to break—when it can be broken, or whatever you say in your business."

The conversation continued in variations of that theme as they circumnavigated the Beltway surrounding Washington. After forty minutes, Owens concluded that Bill was definitely crazy, though probably not dangerous. The best he could do, he said, was to talk to the president's press secretary. If he could get Bill in that far, Bill would have to make his own case, whatever it was.

He let Bill out at a place called Rent-A-Wreck in Silver Spring.

"This probably won't work. I hope you know that up front."

Bill picked up a car and soon was back in his hotel room. Not knowing where the others were staying, he had to wait until evening before he went out to call the number he'd been given.

Bill had not felt so alone since the bombing in London. The only people in the world he could trust were at an unknown location, and he was sitting in a hotel waiting for a meeting that could end his life. Less than two weeks ago, he had been a despondent and angry man with few friends and no vision of a future worth living. Now he was a wanted man with two brothers in arms, he was fleeing for his life from Jarvis, and he was engaged to be married. It was enough to stagger the most analytical mind. The good news was, he was no longer despondent.

Late that evening, he went down the hill from the hotel to a small Italian restaurant on the street below. He ordered the pasta special, then proceeded to the pay phone in the corner.

While dialing Bob's number, the smell from the kitchen brought a flashback of the Atlantic House Restaurant in Carolina Beach, the greasy spoon where Cookie had worked. *He tried to help me, and now he's dead. Will the same thing happen to my former neighbor and friend?* That thought had not occurred to Bill until he was calling Owens. Maybe, he thought, he should hang up and walk away. The urge was so strong he found himself looking at the black receiver he held in his hand. Bill hadn't even heard it being answered. Surely his mind was playing tricks on him.

"Hello . . . hello . . . is anyone there?" Joan Owens's voice finally snapped him back to reality.

"Hello . . . ," he stammered. "Is Bob there?"

The voice grew cold. "Yes, Bill, he's here."

A silence enveloped him that seemed to last for an eternity.

"This is Bob."

"How did you do?" he asked.

"There wasn't a lot of enthusiasm to see you except behind bars. My friend wants more information."

"It's a matter of national security!" Bill protested, trying not to attract attention.

"If you will trust the press secretary, I can get you in to talk to him. That's the best I can do."

"Let me think . . . ," Bill said. Nervously, he glanced around the restaurant. No one was paying the slightest attention to him. "It will have to be a private meeting . . . and I name the time and the place." He was getting scared. What if the press secretary was in with Blaine? Ken and John had said almost anyone could be involved. His stomach was tied up in knots, and he'd been on this phone too long. "I'll call you back in the morning." Bill hung up.

The waiter had just brought his food to the table. Bill grabbed the check and walked to the counter. The cashier gave him a very peculiar look as Bill paid for the meal he didn't eat, but that did not stop him from taking Bill's money.

Bill was afraid Bob Owens might already have talked to the police; he did not want to run the risk of being caught in this part of town. He was certain he had been on the phone long enough to be traced. A new and definite apprehension now seemed to govern all aspects of his life. He didn't know why, but he was having a difficult time thinking.

It was raining hard as he retrieved his rental car from the hotel's underground lot and headed down Wisconsin Avenue toward Georgetown. He drove aimlessly for several hours before the fear of being alone overpowered him. Suddenly his thoughts felt confused; it was impossible for him to form whole sentences in his mind. The oncoming lights from passing cars twisted into bizarre and unearthly shapes as they pierced his windshield. Faces materialized, then exploded into rainbows of colors that ran in rivulets of paint along his dashboard and dripped into pools of blood on the floor of the car. The explosion of a horn sounding in the next lane echoed through his head with an ear-shattering blast. Bill knew he needed help. He wasn't sure why, but he knew he needed help now.

He steered the car into a darkened service station. An isolated phone booth sat on the edge of the blacktop, its light casting an eerie luminescence in the forlorn rain. Stumbling from the car, he warily approached it, pulling from his pocket the number of the safe house. Oblivious to the drenching rain, he leaned against the side of the booth. He was afraid to stand inside it; he wasn't sure it wasn't some kind of a monster that would open its mouth and swallow him whole. Inside his head, lights continued to flash like fireworks. . . .

The phone rang three times . . . then four . . . five . . . as his anxiety escalated to a new high. Six . . . seven . . . finally someone lifted the receiver.

"Hello?" It was a strange voice. To him it sounded like a 45 rpm record set on 33 rpms.

"Uh . . . uh . . . a friend of mine . . ." He fought for the words. "Uh . . . told me to . . . call this number and I could find him."

A surreal vision flashed through his mind: John and Ken lying on the ground in crimson pools of blood, their lifeless eyes staring up at him.

And Holly! He could see her tied to a table, one extremity lashed to each corner. He could see her pleading eyes, her clenched jaw, as Jarvis held a huge knife to her throat, demanding to know where Bill was hiding. As the images flashed vividly in his mind, panic ran rampant throughout his being. An explosion of color rained down on him as the thunder crashed.

The voice sounded again. "Can you tell me anything about this friend?"

"We . . . we have traveled a lot together recently," he stammered.

"Where did you travel?" the voice asked smoothly.

"Uh . . . we were in . . . North Carolina, yes, . . . we were traveling up from North Carolina," he answered.

"One moment please." Silence.

The rain fell harder, now blown by the wind. He was getting soaked. The chill of the night made him ache right down to his feet. The pain of the cold erased the last trace of the nightmare. He was back in touch with reality again. *The whole world must be mad,* he thought, *and me along with it.*

"Hello, Bill?" Ken's voice rang in his ear.

"Ken!" Bill couldn't talk. "Ken . . ." His words trailed off.

Ken realized Bill was on the verge of hysteria. He said, "Where are you?"

"I . . . I don't know." He felt like he was falling. He was caught in a whirlpool that was pulling him down. He couldn't fight it any longer. He wanted to lie back and let it take him wherever it was destined to go.

"Bill!" Ken pronounced his name with deliberateness. "Bill, look around. Tell me what you see!"

"I'm at a gas station. There are streets . . . yes . . . lots of streets, one, two, three, four, five . . . ," he counted. "And cars . . ." His mind was losing contact with reality again. All he could see was dead bodies. Sandy's, Ken's, John's, Holly's—and hundreds of others with no faces, circling their bodies with torches and knives.

"Bill! What else do you see?" Ken urged.

"The lights are pretty . . . and . . ." He began to laugh hysterically. "I like the bear. It blinks." Bill hung up the phone, stumbled back to his car, and sat down in the front seat on the passenger side. The rain beating down on the roof sounded like an approaching freight train. He wondered what it would feel like when it hit him. Then there were no more thoughts in his head. . . .

● ● ●

"Where in the world is he? And what's happened to him?" Holly anxiously asked.

"I'm not sure . . ." Ken hesitated. "I didn't even recognize his voice at first."

"OK, we've got to try to put it together. Exactly what did he say?" John queried.

"First he said he was looking for his friend. Then he said he saw a lot of roads. He started to count them, one, two, three, up to five. I don't know if he only saw five roads or if he just quit counting . . . and cars; he saw cars," Ken went on. "Then it was the strangest thing. He talked about a blinking bear. He said he liked it. Oh yes, he also said he was in a gas station."

"Was he hallucinating, or did he really see those things?" Holly wondered aloud.

"I think we have to assume he saw them, though he was probably hallucinating; it's the only chance we have. Does a blinking bear make any sense to anyone?" John asked.

"They have bears at the zoo, but I don't think any of them blink," Ken replied.

"How about a restaurant or some kind of a store?" Holly said, reaching for the phone book. She looked under restaurants for bears and animal names but found nothing. They looked at one another in silence for some time. Holly looked down at the floor and sat quietly with her hands clasped in her lap. She was thinking of Bill; she was praying for Bill. *Oh, God,* she thought. *You just gave me this man. Please don't take him now!*

Suddenly John said, "Give me the phone book!"

He looked up motels. Rapidly, he ran his finger down the page. "Here, look at this."

There in the Yellow Pages was an ad for the TraveLodge Motels. The little box contained the "sleepy bear logo" on the advertisement.

"Now, if—and I repeat, *if*—that is the bear Bill saw, which TraveLodge is it? There must be thirty of them in the D.C. area," John said.

Ken scanned the listing of motel addresses. Then he exclaimed excitedly, "Here, listen to this: 'TraveLodge: Seven Corners, Arlington, Virginia.'"

"That has to be it! Oh, dear God, that *has* to be the one!" Holly exclaimed.

It took thirty minutes to drive to Seven Corners, an area so named for the intersection where seven roads came together. The tension in the car was high. Ken drove while Holly gazed, expressionless, out the side window at the falling rain and the blackness of the night.

There were several gas stations, the motel, a grocery store with a small strip mall, and a shopping center surrounding the intersection. They had driven through the parking lots of all but the shopping center and the Exxon station when they spotted a car parked in the shadows by a pay phone.

Ken switched off his lights and allowed the car to roll quietly to a stop with the engine off. Cautiously, he approached the darkened car. He opened the door on the passenger's side and found Bill sitting like a zombie, staring blankly out the window at the rain. He didn't respond when Ken began to question him, but he obeyed when told to get out of the car.

"Has he been hurt?" Holly questioned.

"I don't think so. He looks more like he's on drugs," Ken responded.

"No! Not Bill!" Holly retorted forcefully.

"I mean, he looks like he has had a flashback reaction. Probably from the drugs Jarvis gave him," Ken said. "It sometimes happens to people under stress."

Holly led him to their car and helped him into the backseat. She slid in beside him and cradled his head on her lap. Then she tenderly and delicately stroked his hair and cheeks the entire trip back to the safe house. Bill neither moved nor spoke.

He was completely unconscious by the time they returned to Alexandria and the safe house. John and Ken carried him in and laid him on a bed. Holly sat quietly in his room for the next three hours. She told him later he had short bursts of agitated tremors followed by thrashing and moaning, then silence. Holly had checked his pulse and placed her hand on his chest to feel his breathing after each episode. Finally, he lapsed into quiet sleep.

Day Fourteen

Bill slept for most of the next twelve hours without convulsing. Finally he awoke and stumbled into the kitchen. His hair radiated wildly in all directions, and his growth of beard made him resemble a wino.

"My head feels like a train ran over it," Bill said, falling into a chair. "What happened?"

Holly immediately poured a cup of coffee and set it on the table in front of him. "Welcome back, Sir Knight."

"You were in pretty bad shape when we found you. I think you had a flashback reaction to the drugs Jarvis gave you last week," Ken answered.

"If that ever happens again, do me a favor," he said.

"Yeah, what's that, ol' buddy?" John responded.

"Shoot me before I wake up," he muttered, rubbing his throbbing head. The coffee was hot and rich, and he wasn't at all sure he could keep it down. But it did taste good.

"Where are we?" He finally felt like he could carry on a conversation.

"We're at a safe house in Alexandria," Holly answered as she started massaging his neck. Her adept kneading of the muscles at the base of his neck soon loosened the knots; he had started his comeback to the human race.

Ken and John brought him up to date about his phone call and how they had found him. Then they asked, "When you left two days ago, where did you go? What were you trying to arrange?"

Suddenly he remembered. "What time is it?"

"About one-thirty," Holly replied.

"I have to call someone. Is there a phone I can use?"

"Not here. We'll go out and use a pay phone over in Maryland," Ken answered.

They drove across the river on the Beltway and exited at Upper Marlborough. Ken found a pay phone in a gas station.

"Hello, let me speak to Bob Owens, please," Bill said into the receiver. "Hello, Bob, it's me. . . . I know I was going to call earlier, but I've been indisposed the last few hours. . . . Well, it couldn't be helped. . . . Good, you're sure he'll come alone? Have him meet me at the Teddy Roosevelt Memorial at seven-thirty tonight." Bill hung up the phone and took a deep breath. The air smelled good today.

Walking back to the car, Bill wondered what the press secretary's reaction would be to the revelation he would have for him. He slipped into the backseat.

"Bill, sooner or later you have to tell us what you've been up to," Holly insisted.

Ken and John turned to look at him, their expressions conveying absolute agreement with Holly.

"You're right, and since it's all set up, we have plans to make," Bill announced. "I'm going to meet with the press secretary to the president. I want to play the tape for him. If he or the president is not involved, I think he will take me to see the big guy. It's the only way we will ever get both Jarvis and Blaine and extract ourselves from the middle. Even if we could kill Jarvis, there would be little consolation if we spent the rest of our lives running from the law."

Ken wheeled the car around and headed back toward Alexandria; they began to finalize the strategy for tonight's meeting. Bill would be at the meeting on the island, and Ken and Holly would have a boat just offshore in case of trouble. It seemed deceptively simple.

Bill was at the meeting place thirty minutes early. John was lying under a tree on the Virginia side of the river with an old overcoat and a bottle of Pepsi in a brown bag, looking like a wino. That way he could watch the approach to the bridge without being noticed.

Holly and Ken had rented a boat and were slowly cruising just off the island.

Bill watched a man approach the memorial. There were no

other people on the island as far as he knew, so this had to be the press secretary, he hoped. The man walked slowly up to Bill.

"Dr. Chandler?"

"Who wants to know?" Bill asked.

"Frederick Johnston," he replied.

"May I see some identification?"

"I could say the same to you," he said.

"You're right. I have to trust someone sometime." Bill's hands were starting to shake, and he felt his nerves at the breaking point. If he had another reaction to the drugs he'd been given, it would end everything for everyone. This meeting with the president's press secretary was their last hope of ever terminating this night-mare.

"Look, Dr. Chandler, I owed Bob Owens a big favor. I'm paying that debt by meeting with you. You are on the ten most wanted list, it's getting late, and we're standing in the rain getting wet and cold. Now, either you tell me why you had to see me, or I turn and walk." He was getting angry.

"I need to see the president," Bill blurted out.

"Well, so do two-thirds of the people in this country. And they don't have criminal charges against them like you do. They don't get to see him except on television, and neither do you. I'm sorry; I can't walk you in to see him. I think you need a good lawyer, or maybe a psychiatrist, or possibly both." He turned on his heel and started to walk away.

"Mr. Johnston!"

"Yes, Dr. Chandler," he said without turning around.

"I have some information . . . information he, the president, needs to know. His secretary of defense is selling the country out to the Arabs—or anyone else—to make a profit," Bill said with some hesitation. "And I will probably be killed shortly, so someone has to warn him before it is too late."

Johnston spun sharply around. "Preposterous!" he hissed. "Secretary Blaine is one of the most trusted and respected men in modern politics. He will probably be the *next president!*" he said with emphasis. "Just who are you, a deranged scientist, a wanted murderer? The papers have likened you and your girlfriend to Bonnie and Clyde. Are you trying to create some kind of elaborate smoke screen to cover up what you've done or to justify this little crime spree you've been on?"

In the dim light of that rainy November evening, Johnston's face was clearly flushed, and his eyes were enraged with the thought that Bill was accusing the president's right-hand man.

Had he not been personally involved in this drama, Bill reluctantly conceded, he would probably have agreed with Johnston's assessment.

Johnston turned again and started down the path leading to the woods and off the island.

Bill shouted, "Wait! Wait . . ."

"I'd leave this area soon if you don't want to be apprehended. My debt to Owens doesn't include not turning you in!" he shouted back.

Bill sat down on a low wall surrounding the moat. Staring blankly at the ground, he thought, *I've blown it. Now there's nowhere to go, no one left to turn to.* . . . The rain beat harder on his back, and a chill ran up his spine. The silence enveloped him.

"Dr. Chandler."

He looked up, puzzled. There stood Press Secretary Johnston.

"Dr. Chandler, I acted a little hastily. I was annoyed at having to pay the debt to Owens, and this clandestine meeting was not what I had planned for this evening. I would like to hear what you have to say. Please." His voice and demeanor were conspicuously subdued.

"Why . . . why did you come back?" Bill asked.

"Well, I thought it over and realized I had acted rashly, and well, to be truthful, I was a newspaperman before getting mixed up in the politics of the presidency. There's a part of that journalist's curiosity that never leaves you, I guess. Bob Owens has been a good friend for years, and he said you were credible and that I should listen to you. I do think maybe you're crazy; however, I don't think you mean to hurt me. So, if you don't mind, I'd really like to listen to what you have to say," he said apologetically.

Bill smiled. The rain seemed to be letting up somewhat.

"Please sir, sit down and listen to this." Bill turned on the small portable tape player. As he adjusted the volume, Jarvis's voice penetrated the darkness of the night. "Ah, Secretary Blaine, nice to see you again," Jarvis started.

"Mr. Jarvis, it's always a pleasure to come down to Cape Fear and see you. Tell me, what news do you have of our Eastern friends?"

The look on Johnston's face made it obvious that he recognized Blaine's voice. The tape continued.

"Let's get down to business, Blaine," Jarvis said. "We delivered the initial plans on the new communications system, but without the Tel-Ray component, they are useless. Now, you need to apply some pressure on that company to get the rest of the schematics to the Defense Department so we can make good on the delivery. . . ."

The tape ran on for forty-five minutes as they sat in the cold night air, listening. When it ended, Bill clicked off the tape player.

Several seconds of silence passed. Finally, Johnston spoke.

"Who knows about this?"

"I'd rather not say. It's a small group of reliable people," Bill answered.

"How many people in the government are involved? What other levels and departments?"

"I don't know for sure. Besides the ones mentioned in the tape, there is one supervisor in the FBI for sure."

"Are there any more tapes than this one?" he asked.

"This is the only one, though there are several copies of it in a safe place," Bill answered.

Just then there was a noise from the walkie-talkie on his belt.

"This is Pigeon. Over," Bill said into the microphone.

"Three duck hunters have set up a blind. Over."

"Roger. We'll exit stage left. Over," Bill answered.

"What's happening?" Johnston asked.

"Either you brought someone with you, or the enemy is getting closer. We have to get out of here, now! Come on!" Bill grabbed his arm.

They ran down the path leading to the river. It was dark, and the footing was slippery from the evening rain and the fallen leaves. Johnston stumbled more than once, but Bill maintained a firm grip on his arm. He had come too far to lose him now. Rounding the bend, he could hear the boat idling offshore. Bill urged the press secretary out onto a rock jutting into the rapidly moving Potomac River and signaled the boat with a small flashlight. Ken carefully eased the bow of the boat in, coming as near the rocks as he could.

Bill was positive he could hear heavy footsteps drawing ever closer toward them.

"Jump!" he shouted over the sound of the motor.

"I can't! I'll fall! I can't swim!" Johnston yelled back.

"Jump, fool! You have a better chance of learning how to swim than you do living with bullets in you!" Bill shouted.

Johnston jumped, landing squarely on the deck of the small boat. He grasped a wooden handhold to steady himself.

"Back here!" Ken urged.

Holly assisted him along the slippery side of the narrow fiberglass walkway and down to safety in the stern cockpit. The current had carried the boat downriver despite Ken's best efforts to hold his position. It was clearly too far for Bill to jump. Bill threw the tape player to Holly as a small piece of the rock suddenly splintered off near his foot. The sound of the shot arrived a half-second later.

Bill dived from the rock into the thick, wet underbrush; he lost his footing as he hit the ground. The thin stalks of bushes and weeds broke under the strain of his grasp, and he frantically grabbed at the wet earth as he slid toward the river. A rotted log the river had deposited years previously stopped him just inches from the water.

Above him there was the clamor of approaching footsteps. He scrambled up the bank and began to run recklessly toward the center of the island. Branches tore at his face and clothes. He reached under his coat and felt the gun Ken had given him several days ago. He drew it out of its holster. It no longer had an awkward feel. The hardness of the grip molded itself to his hand, and the coldness of the metal gave him a feeling of security. He ran on.

When he neared the memorial, he slowed his pace. Each step took on a new deliberateness. There were voices; he couldn't understand any discrete words, but there were voices. Silently, stealthily, he crept forward. A small group of men stood near the statue. They had high-powered lanterns. Bill knelt in the bushes and studied the gathering. Out of the seven men he could count, he recognized two: Sid Jarvis and John. They were talking, and John was not acting like a prisoner.

The moat surrounding the central park area was full of water, and Bill slid into it, the intensity of the cold stealing his breath away. He silently glided down toward the assembled group, staying in the shadow of the wall.

"Are you sure they have the tape?" Jarvis asked.

"Yeah, I've heard it. Not only that, he played it for the press secretary," John answered.

"Is that the only copy, or has it been reproduced?"

"We made several copies, but I know where all of them are," John said. "I don't like it. I think I should just take care of them all now!"

"Don't get in a hurry," Jarvis responded. "We need to find out how much they all know and if there are any more surprises that dear little Holly might have."

"Yeah, but now they've brought Johnston into it. It looks like that just complicates things more."

"Not really. Johnston works for me. So there's no problem. We just need to find out if they have any more damaging information." Jarvis laughed. "They don't really think I have spent all this time and effort to be brought down by a couple of amateurs, do they?"

"Just remember, Jarvis. Ken is not an amateur and Chandler is nobody's dummy," John cautioned.

"You sound as if you like him," Jarvis retorted.

"He's not such a bad guy and all . . . but what I am sayin' is, he's smart!"

Bill should have enjoyed the compliment, but he could feel the cold water of the moat sapping his vitality. And the realization that John was one of them chilled him almost as much. He knew he had to get to Ken and Holly as soon as possible. Slowly he began to drift away from the lighted group and toward a bridge. His feet were numb, and he was afraid they would be frostbitten soon.

There was a lot of activity on the island; it was getting crowded. The men who had shot at him were combing the underbrush, looking for his trail. Bill slowly made his way to the far side of the circular mall and climbed out of the water. He was shivering so much he was unsure he could walk. As difficult as it was, the activity of walking helped to warm him slightly.

The bridge was completely sealed off by Jarvis's men. Bill knew if he waited until they were gone he would probably die of exposure or, worse yet, he would be found. He moved down to the southernmost tip of the island and walked into the cold Potomac River.

24

CLOSING IN

When the shooting started, Ken pivoted the boat and roared down the river. The white wake sparkled from the lights of National Airport on the Virginia side and the Jefferson Memorial on the D.C. side. There was no pursuit. Jarvis's men were evidently not prepared for an escape down the river.

"We've got to help Bill!" Holly screamed above the sound of the boat's engines and the rushing wind.

"We can't right now!" Ken responded.

"We have to! Can't we go back? Can't we just take this to the police?" she persisted. "Can't we do *something*?"

"No! Going to the police wouldn't be good. Not yet," Johnston spoke up. "This is too big and involves too many people. I'm afraid it would be your word against Jarvis and Blaine. And from reading the newspapers, I don't think they would have any trouble discrediting you. No, I think it would be best if we kept this to ourselves until we find Dr. Chandler and can present a complete story."

"Holly, as much as I hate to admit it, I think he's right," Ken added.

"But . . . but . . . !" Holly was pleading. "What about the tape?"

"The tape is damaging, but with the power they seem to have, they can probably get it suppressed," Johnston said.

"Believe me, Holly, if there was something I thought we could do for Bill right now, I'd do it," Ken added. "Unfortunately, he's going to have to take care of himself . . . at least for the moment. He knew the risk going in."

The boat slowed as it neared the marina. Holly sat on a seat near the transom, staring longingly at the cold, dark river. Tears ran down her cheeks as she reflected on how Bill had looked standing helplessly on the rock, his arms outstretched, as the boat had slid away from him. Why had he let Johnston jump first? She didn't even like that man.

She saw Bill jump back into the bushes as a shot rang out. At least she *thought* he jumped. What if he fell because he was wounded? What if they had killed him? They might as well kill her too.

She tried to feel the love she had experienced when he had held her in his arms. She longed to sense his touch. She was in love with him, but he might already be dead. It wasn't fair. Her shoulders shook as the spasms of grief poured out of her innermost self. An emptiness gripped her entire being, and she experienced the cold, icy grip of hopelessness.

Ken affectionately put his arm around her after tying up the boat.

"Where do we go now?" she asked weakly.

"Back to the safe house," he replied.

"What can we do there?"

"Wait!" he said emphatically.

"Where are you going to be so I can get in touch with you?" Press Secretary Johnston asked.

"I'd rather not say just yet," Ken responded. "Give me a number where we can reach you. We'll stay in touch."

"I'm not used to being kept in the dark!" Johnston said curtly.

"Well, sir, *get* used to it until this thing is over." Ken turned and stuffed the paper with Johnston's phone number on it into his pocket. He then took Holly's arm and walked down the dock toward the shadows of the darkened yacht club.

• • •

Later that night, the phone rang at the estate of Sidney Jarvis in Maryland.

"Jarvis here."

"Are you some kind of crazy?" Johnston said.

"What seems to be the problem, Mr. Johnston?"

"You nearly got me killed this evening! What do you and your cowboys think you're doing? I've already heard the tape, so I know what we're up against. It would have been easy enough to take care of them later. But no! You had to ride in like Custer at the Little Big Horn. At least I hope you got that Chandler out of the way. With him gone, there won't be any problem taking care of the girl and that FBI agent."

"We haven't found the body yet. It's pretty dark out there. But I can assure you, it's just a matter of time. Now, about the tape. What's on it?"

"Jarvis, you have to be some kind of a fool. No one since Watergate has kept tapes of their meetings. What in the world were you thinking of?"

"Just tell me what was on it! Could it cause damage to any of the interested parties?"

"It could probably put you and Blaine in the electric chair tomorrow if it became public knowledge. That is, if there wasn't a lynch mob that took you for a public hanging first!"

"Do you have the tape?" Jarvis asked.

"No, but it wouldn't make any difference. I was assured that it was only a copy. I don't know where the original is. Jarvis, I'm worried. Do you have any idea how many people could be pulled in peripherally if this thing is not silenced?"

"One more question: Is that the only tape?"

"As far as Chandler knows, it's the only one she kept. But Jarvis, I don't like the way this whole thing is going. Do something about it, and do it quick!" Johnston said.

"Don't worry. As long as we're sure that's the only one she kept, I know how to get the principals and the tape, no matter how many copies. Good-night, Mr. Johnston." Jarvis hung up the phone. Now he knew for sure what he was after. The beginning of control is to know the objective. It would be easy now that he knew the objective. He would get the tape, and with any kind of luck, still get Tel-Ray, and more important . . . he'd get Holly! Jarvis's guts twisted with rage and passion.

• • •

Ken and Holly sat in the dark at the safe house in Alexandria. It had been two hours since they'd left the press secretary on the dock of the Washington Yacht Club. John was not back, and Bill was who knew where and in what condition. The stillness of the night was broken by a siren a long way off. Both Ken and Holly were lost in their innermost thoughts. Suddenly, Ken straightened and tensed.

"What is it?" Holly whispered.

"Quiet!" he said as he moved silently out of his chair and slowly felt his way through the darkened room to the wall near the door. He placed his back up against the wall with his right shoulder toward the door frame. Sliding his gun out of the shoulder holster, he brought it up to the ready position and eased back on the hammer. There still was no noise from outside the room. Holly sat still, almost unable to breathe. She listened intently.

Ken edged closer to the door frame. The doorknob began to turn ever so slowly, and there was a faint sound as the tumbler fell. The door came free of the casing and cracked open. Ken remained motionless; Holly's heart pounded in her ears. The smell of danger was everywhere. Slowly the door swung noiselessly into the room.

A dark figure stepped inside, his arm extended. The rays from the streetlight gave a flicker of light reflecting from the barrel of the gun in his hand. He stepped forward, his knees flexed, his weight balanced on the balls of his feet. Slowly he swung his shoulders and waist from the right toward the left. As he came in the direction of Ken, Holly let out a small, barely imperceptible gasp. The noise was inaudible, but to the trained ear it caused a reaction. The figure spun in her direction. At that instant Ken moved from his place behind the door. He impacted the figure at the level of the twelfth rib on his left side; the force was transmitted to the left kidney, causing extreme pain. As the unknown invader fell to his knees, he fired. The silencer on his gun effectively muffled the sound, but the wood of the window frame split just behind Holly's head. She screamed.

Though stunned by the ferocity of Ken's attack, the unknown figure recovered, thanks to the adrenaline pumping through his system. He rolled to his left and, almost without effort, sprang up to his feet. As he brought his arm into position to fire, he was hit again, but this time it was a glancing blow that did little damage. The gun was almost an extension of his hand, and his aim was only deflected slightly. The bullet tore a hole through the top of Ken's shoulder, fracturing the clavicle and tearing the artery beneath. Ken hit the assailant in the face and felt the bone break as it absorbed the blow. He tried vainly to reach his opponent's neck, but the loss of blood was starting to take its toll. Ken felt the world starting to weave and spin. Darkness began to settle over him. He knew instinctively this would be a fight lost, and there would be no more fights for him.

"Holly, run!" were the last words Ken said as he lost consciousness, collapsing to the floor. A large pool of blood spread like a sticky red river under his shoulder. The darkness Ken entered became eternity for the FBI agent as his attacker leveled the gun at his head. There was a muffled crack, some smoke, and Ken was dead.

Holly raced for the door as a hand reached out and grabbed her, throwing her to the floor. She screamed again as she lay against the couch, bruised from the fall. She watched as the dark figure slowly walked to the door and pushed it shut. A hand reached out and turned on the light switch. Holly looked up in horror and thought, *Oh, dear God, anyone but him!*

25

LAST RITES

Bill emerged from the river about three-quarters of a mile downstream from the island. He was almost dead from exposure and had lost the gun that had come to represent the only security he knew these days. But at least he was off the island that had threatened to become his grave.

Cars flew by on the George Washington Parkway, all heading home in the darkness of the autumn night. He stumbled up the slippery slope toward the lights of Crystal City. He stepped inside a gas station that was doing a brisk business of self-serve gas and carry-out beer, and immediately he became dizzy from the heat. In typical big-city fashion, he received several unusual stares, but no one asked why he was dripping wet.

A pay phone was nestled between the beer cooler and bread rack on the back wall of the shop. Bill put in a quarter and dialed a number. He hoped to reach Holly and Ken and tell them of his suspicion that they had been set up by Johnston, and he hoped to warn them that he'd learned of John's betrayal. The phone rang incessantly. The sound in his ear became louder and louder until his head pounded with the knowledge that something was very wrong. As he hung up the receiver, his hand was shaking, not from the wet and cold, but from the fear that was racing through every fiber of his body.

He rushed out of the shop and flagged down a taxi. The driver looked at Bill with suspicion and said, "You got the fare to go that far, buddy?"

Bill reached in his pocket and handed him a twenty-dollar bill.

"Put that on my account. When it runs out, tell me. I got more," he said sarcastically. "Now move it, OK?"

Bill had the cab drop him about a block from the safe house they were using. The street was quiet, not even a dog barking. He approached the yard slowly, trying not to be backlit by the street-light. There was a lamp on in the living room, and from the side window, he could see a lone male figure sitting in a chair. From the back, the silhouette resembled Ken.

The fear that had been haunting him from the time of the phone call began to dissipate. But where was Holly? He went to the back of the house and surveyed the vicinity. The car was parked in the yard. Again his level of suspicion dropped another degree. As he turned from the car, he laid his hand on the hood. It was cold.

He stood for a minute like a department store mannequin. His mind was rebelling against reason. If the car was cold, then Ken and Holly had been back for some time. But if they were there when he called, why hadn't they answered the phone? Unless . . . unless they couldn't. He opened the driver's door cautiously. Ken had taken the precaution of removing the dome light so they could get in and out at night without attracting attention. As he sat there, the light in the living room suddenly went out. His body tensed.

Carefully, he slid his hand under the front seat. His fingers closed around the cold metal barrel of a Smith & Wesson 9 mm model 900. He pulled it out, and, as he had been taught several days before, ejected the clip and made sure it was loaded. He snapped the clip back in place and chambered a round. He slid out of the car and let his arm drop to his side. The weight of the gun in his hand felt good. Now it was time to see who or what was in the house. For an instant, he felt foolishly paranoid taking these precautions.

Silently, he approached the back door. Ken had agreed to leave it open for an easy return in case they thought they were being followed. It opened without effort. Bill had dried sufficiently that his shoes didn't squeak as he walked. Taking great pains not to bump against anything, he crept across the kitchen. Each step was calculated and executed like a dancer. He placed his heel slowly on the floor and gradually let his weight come down on the ball of that foot before he started to raise the other. At the far side of the kitchen was a short hall to the living room. He paused to let his senses take in the sounds and vibrations of the night. It was then that he heard, or perceived, the quiet breathing in the darkness of the hall before him. He could feel his heart rate increasing, and he tightened the grip on the gun. He felt the sweat in his palm. Nervously, he placed his index finger on the trigger. He consciously controlled his breathing to slow his heart and gain some command of his reflexes.

When his mind had been loaded, primed, and cocked, he took a deep breath and dropped his shoulder slightly. Then, with all the force he could muster, he took two running steps and threw his weight against the form. The weight and force of his blow landed in the same spot that Ken had damaged earlier. With a loud grunt, the unknown man fell into the lighted living room and rolled helplessly across the floor. A black metal object flew out of his hand and skidded under a low table. The man knocked over a floor lamp, and a loud snap sounded as the bulb broke when the lamp shattered against the wall. He lay dazed, his head against the coffee table and a small trickle of blood running down the bridge of his nose.

"Turn over, but don't get up!" Bill yelled as he regained his footing from his planned encounter. He didn't move.

"Turn over NOW if you ever want to move again!"

Slowly the man rolled over, bracing his arms on the floor to gain an advantage to attack.

"You move those arms a fraction more and it will be the last move you ever make," Bill cautioned. "Put your hands behind your head and look at me."

The man on the floor looked up.

"Hey, ol' buddy, what's the matter?"

It was John. Bill stood motionless, lost in time and space. His mind didn't comprehend or want to think of the possibilities of this moment. He looked over at Ken sitting in the chair. He was in the same position as when he saw him through the window. Only now, Bill's stomach revolted as he saw the gaping hole in the side of Ken's head and the cavern where his frontal bone had formed his forehead in life. The moment crashed around him as he heard John moving on the floor, trying to take advantage of Bill's shock.

Bill swung the gun toward him; the hammer was already cocked back.

"You traitor! Who are you, Judas?" he demanded.

John lay back, helpless. "Bill, I'm sorry. I had to do it. He was going to turn us all in to Jarvis. He was working with Jarvis! I couldn't let him do that."

"Yeah, convince me. And do it good, because that's all that stands between you and a plot in Arlington."

"I'm telling you the truth," he pleaded.

"Then where's Holly? Did you put a bullet in her head too?" Bill asked. "I saw you tonight . . . on the island!"

John looked down and said nothing.

Bill readjusted his aim and said, "I'll tell you what. You tell me the truth, and I won't put the first shot through your knee. I'll let you die fast. I saw you with Jarvis on the island tonight."

Still he said nothing.

Bill reached down and tore some light cord loose from a nearby lamp and threw it to him. "Tie your feet together and tie them tight." He then used another cord to tie John's hands to the doorknob. Without ceremony, he stuffed a gag into his mouth. Bill could tell John was favoring his left side. He reached down and ripped his shirt.

When he had him securely fastened, he kicked him in a bruise he saw growing on his flank. After the third kick in the same spot, John indicated he wanted to talk. Bill took the gag out of his mouth.

"You can guess the questions. Give me the answers!" Bill demanded.

"OK, ol' buddy," he panted. "I work for Jarvis. He and I go back to the days when he was with the company. Obviously, I work for Blaine too. But that only makes sense, him being the Secretary of Defense and all. Don't you see? This thing is so big and so many important people are involved, you can't win. You'll never win. I know I can make a deal with Jarvis for you. What do you say?"

"Keep talking. Where's Holly?"

"Ah, ol' buddy, she doesn't count. There's a thousand like her—probably better than her, and working with Jarvis. They're easy to come by."

"You 'ol' buddy' me once more and I'll blow your tongue out of your filthy mouth. Now . . . where's . . . Holly?" Bill repeated the question slowly and with as much savagery in his voice as possible. He leaned down and placed the barrel of the gun into John's mouth. "Right now, it would feel awfully good to blow a hole out the back of your head." He smiled at John. "I've killed once. My bet is it's a lot easier the second time, especially if you have a reason. And, *ol' buddy,* I have a reason."

"Jarvis took her. He figured that if he has her you won't do anything with the tape."

"Why didn't you just eliminate us earlier? Why did you wait until now?"

"We had to be sure there was only one tape. Couldn't take a

chance on another one showing up after Holly and you and Ken were dead."

"Now tell me about Big Meadows," demanded Bill.

"I tipped the man to call Jarvis," John replied.

"So, now what's the plan? What were you to do with me?" Bill demanded.

"Blaine wants you dead. But Jarvis, well, he has a head for business, so he wants you to finish your work on the Tel-Ray project. If I can, I'm supposed to talk you into that and maybe even have you join up with us," he answered.

"And if you can't?"

"Then I'm to eliminate you."

"Sounds simple enough."

"Yeah, well, Jarvis is holding Holly as insurance so you don't go public."

"Where does he have her?" Bill asked.

"Don't know for sure, but I think he's having her taken back to Cape Fear. He's more comfortable there. Easier to keep things quiet."

"I guess you were the one who told Jarvis about the meeting with Johnston?"

"No! Heck, ol' buddy, Johnston works for Jarvis too." John laughed.

"I want you to call Jarvis," Bill said. "I want you to tell him I'm coming to see him. Tell him not to hurt Holly, and I'll come and talk."

"Now, that sounds more reasonable. How 'bout untying me?" he asked.

He looked over at the chair that held the earthly remains of his friend. Bill felt cold inside, but not with fear. Cold with rage . . . rage that so many people could be involved in Jarvis's web of iniquity . . . rage that so many people could care so little about another's life . . . rage that Ken was dead.

Bill thought about the man he had killed when he jumped from the tree. He had not meant to kill him; he had been truly sorry it had happened. He did care about the man's life. He may have been the first, but Bill suspected he wouldn't be the last. The last would be Jarvis. *And to be sure,* Bill thought, *I care about his life a great deal. I want it!*

Bill untied one of John's hands and handed him the phone. "Call Jarvis. Tell him I want to talk. He's a businessman; tell him I want to negotiate."

John dialed a number. "Hello, this is John. Let me speak to Jarvis."

Several minutes of silence.

"Hello, Mr. Jarvis. John. . . . Yes, sir, I found Chandler. . . . Yes, sir, he's right here. . . . Well, no, not exactly. . . . He wants to talk to you."

John handed Bill the phone. He took it and stepped back from him as if he were some sort of dangerous reptile.

"Jarvis, where's Holly? . . . How do I know she's all right? . . . Not good enough. Let me talk to her. . . . I don't care if it takes all night to get her to the phone, this conversation stops right here, right now, if I don't hear her voice. You wanted to negotiate—well, that's the first term! . . . I'll wait."

Several minutes passed. Bill was no longer in a hurry. Finally he could hear footsteps in the background.

"Bill!" Her voice was weak and overflowing with emotion.

"Holly! Holly, are you all right?"

"She's fine; you heard her voice, now let's talk." Jarvis was back on the phone.

"OK, Jarvis, it seems we both have something the other wants. It would make good business sense if we worked out some kind of a deal. . . . No, I don't want to meet you here. I'll meet you at Cape Fear. . . . No, two days from now; I'm tired, I want to rest. I'll let you know the time and place later. And Jarvis, don't let anything happen to Holly. If I don't see her at the beginning of the meeting, you won't even be a memory to most people, let alone have the plans for Tel-Ray. I hope I make myself clear. I don't have anything to lose if you touch Holly."

He hung up without waiting for an answer. Bill looked down at John, still tied up and lying on the floor. *OK, Jarvis, hey-diddle, diddle, right up the middle!* he thought.

Now Bill had two days to get what he needed. It was time to meet Jarvis face to face. Cape Fear might be his territory, but he knew they would meet on Bill's terms.

• • •

It was raining as Randolph Blaine walked out of Jarvis's house after their confrontation. He turned up his collar against the downpour as it pelted his head and shoulders. There was an occasional clap of thunder after lightning split the night air.

He walked toward the waiting Porsche he had driven from Carol's. Blaine opened the door and slid under the wheel. The aroma of the interior smelled of her scent; it was more powerful than just her fragrance. It flooded his mind with the memories of hours he had just spent with her.

This latest problem with the Tel-Ray was disturbing. He began to wonder just who this Bill Chandler and the girl really were. Maybe they were plants, or agents from some other branch of the government out to get him. Paranoia was something he was used to, but it was getting worse in all of the government personnel he met recently.

"I'm tired," he said out loud as he started the engine of the Porsche. He savored the sound of the engine and drove it whenever he could. It was especially useful when he did not want to be recognized or spotted by the news media. It was registered and licensed in Carol's name. However, as with many of the finer things she had, he had paid for it. It never occurred to him that in her own way, she also had paid for it. If Blaine could have been honest with himself, he would have admitted she had paid more dearly than he had.

He turned the key, and the powerful engine roared to life. Blaine adeptly dropped it into gear and gunned the engine as he let out the clutch. The tires spun momentarily on the rain-slick asphalt, then gained traction and powered the car down the drive toward the lane leading to River Road. The back of the car swerved slightly as the momentum of the tires was transmitted to the entire machine, giving it an almost lifelike quality.

The energy under his control was exhilarating—the thrusting of the gears, the smooth acceleration, the whine of the massive engine. It gave him a sense of power he had never before enjoyed in quite this way. The potency transmitted from the gas pedal sent a tingling up his leg. He began to daydream about Carol. He wanted to feel again her warmth and closeness, her passion. He decided to go back to her townhouse. He accelerated slightly.

Blaine didn't stop where the lane entered onto River Road. Instead, he downshifted and turned the wheel hard to the right, pushing the gas pedal almost to the floor as the rpm's climbed toward the red line. The car shot forward, sliding slightly to the left as the tires dug fiercely for traction. The rain increased in intensity as he headed south along the Potomac River toward the Beltway.

There was a light film of oil on the window creating small rainbows around the drops of water when a light flashed by. Blaine knew he should go home. Any more delay would not be explained by a late meeting. But he had to see Carol again.

The road took a sharp bend to the right just before Seven Locks Road. Blaine was pushing the sports car to its limits as he neared the intersection. The rain was now coming faster. As he approached the turn, a car came from the opposite direction. The glare from the advancing headlights was intensified by the millions of droplets on the window, shooting a burst of light into Blaine's face. He instinctively put his left hand up in front of his eyes. The right front tire drifted toward the right-hand side of the road and slipped off. The weight of the car sank into the rain-softened shoulder. The car pulled hard to the right, ripping the wheel from Blaine's other hand.

Desperately, he grabbed the steering wheel and yanked it back to the left; the maneuver was too sudden and too severe. He instinctively took his foot off the gas and pressed the brake pedal hard to the floor. This exaggerated the sliding of the car sideways. Now both wheels were off in the soft mud, and the car was starting to lift up onto its side. The night air was broken with the sound of the engine screaming past the red line as both back wheels came off the ground and the car started to roll.

The last thing Secretary of Defense Randolph Blaine saw was an upside-down light pole. His brain was still trying to reason out the position of the pole when the impact occurred.

The vehicle collided with the pole about three feet above the ground, shearing it off. The front end then crashed into a small bank of sandstone and dirt. The sudden deceleration threw Blaine forward against the steering wheel. In his haste to leave Jarvis's place, he had neglected to buckle up. The force broke his breastbone and several ribs. One of the broken bones punctured a lung and caused a large bruise to develop in the heart muscle. His mind never fully comprehended the severity of the accident; instead, a pleasant shade descended over him.

By the time paramedics arrived, Randolph Blaine was in a coma. He was transported to the trauma center with life-support attached.

Mrs. Blaine was notified by the Capitol police and escorted to the hospital. She called Carol Shemp as she was leaving the house.

"Hello, Carol?" her voice was guarded.

"Uh . . . yes, this is she," Carol replied, having been snatched out of a deep and restful sleep. "Oh, hi, Mrs. Blaine."

"There's been an accident. Can you meet me at the trauma center?" The edge of her voice quivered slightly. "Thank you, Carol, and please hurry."

Mrs. Blaine was standing at her husband's bedside in the intensive care unit as Carol approached. The click of her heels on the hard, sterile surface of the floor startled the grieving wife. She turned and saw Carol approaching at a rapid walk, her hair disheveled, her makeup smeared and streaked. She looked gaunt.

Randolph was lying on crisp, white sheets. A plastic tube snaked its way into each arm, one tube protruded from his nose, and another tube protruded from his chest wall and descended into a container that bubbled with blue water, trying to keep his lung expanded. Oxygen was flowing through a mask, and the constant beep in the background was the only indication that he was still alive.

As Carol advanced, Mrs. Blaine turned. "Oh, thank God you've come." They took each other's hands in greeting. Both women's hands were wet and clammy; they hugged awkwardly.

"How is he? What happened? Oh, my God!" Carol gasped as she looked at him.

"They haven't told me much yet; they just brought him here from surgery," Mrs. Blaine said, choking back tears.

Suddenly the beep stopped. It was followed by a split second of silence punctuated by the ear-shattering scream of the alarm. Nurses and doctors rushed past the two women and began a frantic ritual following cardiac arrest protocol, all to no avail.

As Randolph W. Blaine died, his wife unknowingly hugged and wept with his mistress.

The next morning the headlines of the *Washington Post* read, "Secretary of Defense Killed in Accident." The story reported that Randolph Blaine was killed in a car crash on River Road in Montgomery County, Maryland, when his car slipped off the road during a heavy downpour. The president expressed shock and sorrow for the nation and ordered flags flown at half-staff for three days.

Jarvis was back in North Carolina before he heard the news, and Bill Chandler was too busy to read the paper or listen to the radio.

Cape Fear

Jarvis hung the phone up after his conversation with Bill, then turned to Holly and slapped her across the face with the back of his hand. The force of the blow sent her reeling back into a chair.

"Sid, why did you bring me back here?" Holly screamed.

"Oh, my dear child, I have use for you. You are the bait with which I am going to catch a very special fish," Jarvis sneered.

"You have the tape; there isn't anything more I can do to try to stop you, so why not just kill me and get it over with?" She placed the back of her hand against the painful welt rising on her cheek.

"Make no mistake about it, Holly, I am going to kill you. You have cost me a great deal in the past few weeks. However, before I do kill you, dear Holly, you will beg . . . you will beg me for your life." He laughed. "And you will beg me for your death."

Holly sat expressionless.

Jarvis continued, "But for the present, I still have use for you. It seems our Dr. Chandler has fallen in love with you, and he is coming down the day after tomorrow to rescue you. But of course, you didn't know that, did you?" he chided.

When she heard his voice on the phone and knew for certain Bill was still alive, Holly's heart had begun to race. Since leaving Washington, she had been petrified that he had been killed on the island. Now she knew he was alive. But he must not try to get to her. Surely he knew that. Cape Fear could not be taken by one man.

"You're lying! Bill wouldn't be dumb enough to come here alone."

"Oh, you underestimate the resolve of your Dr. Chandler. Our conversation confirmed not only that he is coming but also when he is going to show up. Would you like to hear the tape?" Jarvis laughed mockingly. "You seem very good at playing with tapes!"

Imprisoned fury boiled to the surface. Jarvis clenched his jaw and snarled through his teeth, "Were you as good at playing with Chandler?"

As he said that, he hit Holly again on the right side of the face with the side of his hand. The force of the blow knocked her off the chair she was sitting on and opened a small but deep laceration on her lip.

She looked up at Jarvis standing over her. Her tongue licked the salty, wet blood from her mouth. She felt tears fighting their way up in her eyes but was determined not to cry in front of him. Even though she was completely at his mercy, he no longer looked so menacing. In fact, at that point in time, he looked like a pathetic little figure.

Her voice started low and soft, then increased in intensity as she said, "I'll tell you what I have learned about Bill. He is a very resourceful and courageous person. And if he is coming down here, I'll spit on your grave!" she shouted.

Jarvis grabbed her off the floor, shaking her with both hands as if she were a rag doll. He then threw her into a chair and with a clenched fist hit her hard in the face. Holly lost consciousness after that and did not feel the rest of the beating. Jarvis's pent-up rage was partially quieted by the time two men carried Holly's badly beaten body out of the room and into a bedroom on the second floor of the mansion.

She awoke several hours later, hurting everywhere. Her eyes were almost swollen shut, and blood was caked on her puffy lips. She felt her teeth with her tongue; they all seemed to be in place. A funny thought went through her head. In spite of the pain, she gave a small laugh. She mused that it was good that her teeth were all right, since her parents had spent so much money on braces when she was a young girl.

Her hands and feet were tied to the corners of the bed, and she desperately wanted to move but couldn't. The pain was excruciating, but finally, with tears running down her swollen cheeks, she drifted into the peaceful oblivion that covers all the evils of the conscious world.

One of the guards looked in to make sure she was still breathing. He just shook his head as he looked at her battered body tied to the bed. He saw the tear-stained face and felt pity for this unfortunate creature. Certainly if it had been an animal he would have put it out of its misery.

"James, get in here!" Jarvis shouted loud enough to be heard on the second floor.

"Yes, sir?" the servant responded.

"Dr. Chandler is coming down to pay us his last visit. I want everything to be ready so it's a memorable occasion. . . ." He walked slowly around the room. "How's Holly?"

"She's awake but that's about all," he answered.

"Get someone to look at her and get her something to eat. She and Dr. Chandler have become lovebirds, so I want to be sure they go to the grave together." He talked slowly and deliberately as he paced the room, like a lion circling its prey. He could smell the victory and the blood of the kill.

• • •

"So what are you going to do with me?" John asked as he looked at Bill with concern for his welfare.

"The easiest thing would be to kill you right now and leave you here with Ken. It would be easy enough to make it look like a fight to the finish. But I have other plans for you. So I guess you're going with me."

John thrashed like a serpent as Bill put a gag in his mouth and carried him out to the car at the back of the house. It was still dark and quiet in the neighborhood. After making sure there was nothing on the seat he could use to get loose with, Bill returned to the house. Inside he found the weapons Ken had stored in the basement. There were two Uzi machine pistols with ten clips of ammunition. While that would have been more than sufficient for quail hunting, he knew he did not have enough firepower or friends to start a war with Jarvis. He wrapped the weapons carefully in a blanket and carried them to the trunk of the car, wishing for more. Then he returned to the living room. His friend Ken, or what was left of him, was still sitting in the chair. He got a wet towel and wiped his friend's face of the dried blood and bone fragments. Then he lifted him out of the chair and carefully laid him on the couch. Bill was panting and sweating when he finished.

Sitting down on the floor beside Ken's body, he looked at it and wept. "I'm sorry I got you into this," he said aloud. Then he remembered Holly saying the same thing to him and how he had chided her for it. Bill knew Ken would have chided him the same way. It was a full hour before he could get off the floor and say his last good-bye to his friend. However, he had now figured out a plan to finally bring down Jarvis and his organization. And he had two days to get ready. Friday would either be the end of Sidney Jarvis or the end of William Chandler, Ph.D.

26

NEW BEGINNINGS

Bill drove at the speed of the traffic coming out of Alexandria, not wanting to attract any attention. The streets were still dark and the rain had stopped. There was a cold wind blowing from the northwest as he headed the car counterclockwise around the Beltway. He wanted to avoid at all costs passing the island where he had last seen Ken and Holly alive.

His eyes were damp with tears as he headed into Maryland toward the plant where he used to work. Somehow his Tel-Ray project had been a part of this whole tragedy from the beginning. Now he knew he would use the very thing Jarvis wanted to bring the monster down.

He quietly pulled up to the gate. The plant was primarily for research, so there was no night shift. Security was on the basis of obscurity, and the three drab brick buildings certainly supplied that. Otherwise, there was only a tall fence, one gate, and no night watchman. His key still worked the lock, and after opening the gate, he parked the car at the back of the middle building. As he stood fumbling for the lock to his old laboratory, the wind reminded him that he did not have a heavy enough coat for the coming winter. He was shivering as much from the cold as from

335

the fact that he was breaking into a building to steal equipment that was considered top secret.

It was dark inside, and he used his foreknowledge of where things were and a minimum of light to locate the items he wanted. Tel-Ray had been his project from its inception. He had always wondered how well it would work. After the field test at Jarvis's place several days ago, he now knew.

The plan was relatively simple. Use the Tel-Ray device to transmit a video and audio signal of the meeting between Jarvis and himself. The only hard part was deciding whom to transmit the signal to.

Bill carried the electronic equipment he needed out to the car. Then he brought John into the laboratory.

"Who else in the government is on Jarvis's payroll?" Bill asked.

"How do I know? And anyway, if I did, why should I tell you?"

"One reason might be to save your life."

"You're not a killer, ol' buddy. You told me that yourself." John laughed.

"Oh, but John, I've already killed one man. Remember?" With Holly's life hanging on the next forty-eight hours, Bill wasn't exactly sure what he was capable of. Killing John in cold blood was probably beyond what he could do. However, he knew he had to rescue Holly or die trying.

Bill pushed him into a chair and tied him into it with a rope he'd brought along. Next he got a wire with a lead exposed and hooked it to John's wrist. The second wire he placed in a bottle of water. John watched with growing apprehension as Bill began to strip the ends of both wires. Bill stood in front of him as he carefully twisted the gleaming copper strands together. "John, you might be right. I might not be a killer like you are."

"You wouldn't really do anything stupid with those wires, would you?" he asked.

"Now, John, you know I'm an electrical engineer by trade—I

even have a Ph.D. You can rest assured I won't do anything stupid with them. But what I might do with them could be very unpleasant for you. Designing something to produce the desired information is not really difficult. Even the Gestapo in World War II were able to do that," Bill answered in a flat tone.

John watched Bill as he went about the lab, gathering up the things he needed for the procedure. Sweat beaded up on John's forehead, and he began to lick his lips with increasing frequency.

"You know, John, this whole thing is about to come crashing down around Jarvis's head. You can either be on his side and fall with him, or be with me and have a chance for survival. The choice is yours. Now, what is it going to be?" Bill asked the question while he dropped the end of the wire he was holding onto a metal plate lying on the table in front of him. There was a tremendous flash followed by a burning sound as the wire melted into the steel plate. The smell of hot metal and ozone permeated the laboratory.

John wrenched back in his chair. The corners of his mouth drew tight and his lips were pressed white against his teeth.

"You can't bring Jarvis and the organization down by yourself. Even some countries have tried and failed, and you're just one man," he snarled in a false bravado.

"Yes, well, maybe so. However, for you that is a moot point. You see, if I don't hear from you what I want to hear, well, for you, it won't make any difference," Bill replied emotionlessly.

"Yeah, ol' buddy? Why not?" John asked.

"Well, ol' buddy, I've decided not to kill you. As you said earlier, I may not be a born killer, though it appears I could learn to be. No, I've decided to leave you with no functioning intellect. You, sir, are going to become a vegetable. You'll spend the rest of your days in a nursing home. It's great at one of those places. They feed you several times a day, and I hear, if you go to a good one, they even change your diaper from time to time."

Bill looked at John intently. "Now, one last time, who in the government is involved with Jarvis?"

John's eyes darted from side to side; he chewed on his tongue and cheek. "I didn't bargain for this!" he shouted.

"I really don't care what kind of a bargain you thought you bought into. I need the information. Without it, you are of little use to me. . . ." Bill waited a full minute. "John, I'm really sorry, but I have to go. Now this may hurt a bit, but, then, you won't remember it—or anything else, so I guess it won't make a whole lot of difference." He stepped toward him, holding out like a serpent the wire he had dropped onto the metal plate.

"Stop!" John pleaded. "OK, I'll tell you. You know about Blaine. There's Fred Johnston, the president's press secretary, and Art Billings in the FBI." He was starting to babble.

"I know all of those names already. Tell me something I don't know," Bill said, moving closer.

"Jim Shaw, director of Mideast Operations, CIA . . ."

For the next fifteen minutes John gave Bill more names than Bill cared to remember. But he carefully wrote down each one. As the list grew, it became obvious that many levels of the government were involved. John assured him he didn't know all of them, and in fact, most of the people didn't know any of the others. Jarvis had an intriguing game of keeping most of the people in the dark except for the top few, the so-called board of directors.

Bill dropped the wire onto the floor and sat down facing John, who by now was a whimpering, broken man. The cocky assurance of the former jungle fighter was gone. He looked fifty years old. His flesh seemed to hang from small supports on his face like an old curtain in an abandoned theater.

In some ways, Bill wanted to feel pity for John, but the image of Ken sitting in that chair with his forehead blown off kept coming back to his mind.

"I told you what you wanted to know. Now what are you going to do with me?" John asked.

"I think I'll take you along. If I get Jarvis, I'll let you give yourself up to the police. If Jarvis gets me . . . well, he'll probably figure out that you talked. I suppose he'll kill you. You can spend the next few days trying to decide which option is the best," Bill replied rather matter-of-factly.

He looked out the window and noted the first hint of light coming through the trees. The car was loaded with everything for his assault, so he herded John into the car and headed south.

Exhaustion overtook him in northern North Carolina. He pulled into a motel at four in the afternoon and slept until three in the morning, making sure John was securely tied while he slept. He completed the trip to Carolina Beach in three more hours, and at 6 A.M. he was ready to set the trap.

The Last Day

The boardwalk area of Carolina Beach was a fugitive from the 1950s. Most of the stores had gone out of business, and the ones that hadn't looked as if survival was not the better alternative.

There was a fun house with a fading green dragon on the front. At some point in its existence, electric cars had operated on a rail and carried passengers through the maze of plastic goblins and witches. It probably never scared anyone but was one of the few places on the old boardwalk where the teens of yesterday could neck without the prying eyes of a parent. It looked like it had not been used in years, but it still had electricity since it was up for sale.

On the second floor was a large dance hall with a layer of dust an inch thick. The front windows looked out onto the beach and the ocean beyond. There were two staircases leading to the second floor. The back stairs had been for the employees only, or so the sign read. The front stairs came from the beach side. They were twice as wide as the back ones and entered the center of the dance floor.

Bill backed up to the employee stairway door and unloaded his supplies, including John, whom he carefully laid in the corner, still tied up like a sack with his mouth gagged. Then he nailed the door shut to slow down Jarvis's men. The explosives he rigged to an infrared trigger were to stop them. He had no other way to cover his back.

John had told Bill enough to know that almost every level of government was somehow involved with Jarvis or Blaine. At first he thought his plan was doomed, as there was no sure agency to receive his signal. Then it occurred to him that if he was going to use the Tel-Ray to trap Jarvis, he might as well do it on prime-time television.

He set up the antenna on the roof inside an old air-conditioner housing and aimed it at the sky. Soon he had the signal from one of the commercial television and communication satellites locked in. With Tel-Ray, he could receive or send with equal ease.

He then took a video camera and placed it in the old jukebox at the far end of the dance floor. Ordinarily, the backlighting from the windows would have been a problem, but the walls were lined with mirrors that gave all the light necessary for his production. He installed a device to block the normal signal from the satellite to the Tel-Ray and rigged a makeshift remote control.

With microphones placed in the false ceiling, Bill was ready for his meeting with Jarvis. He only had one concern. Would it work? He knew the theory was good; he was a theorist by profession. He also knew the system had worked when they eavesdropped on Jarvis. But this was a much more ambitious project. Bill just hoped the first test of the system was all it needed; he knew he would only get one chance.

He walked downstairs and out onto the boardwalk leading to the beach. There was a phone booth at the end of the block. He dropped a quarter into it and dialed Jarvis's number.

"Hello."

"Let me speak to Jarvis."

"I'm sorry, Mr. Jarvis is not available at this time."

"This is Chandler. Put Jarvis on the phone now!"

A few seconds later, he heard, "Ah, Dr. Chandler, good to hear from you. I was afraid you might have had an accident since we last talked."

"Cut the crap, Jarvis," Bill said. "You have something I want; I have something you want. It's time to do business."

"You seem much more direct these days. I think we may learn to get along yet," Jarvis answered smoothly.

"Bring Holly to the old dance hall over the fun house at the Carolina Beach boardwalk in twenty minutes. . . . And Jarvis, come alone; this is between you and me." He hung up.

Quickly, he dialed a second number. The phone rang and rang; it seemed an eternity before it was answered.

"North Carolina Highway Patrol, second district, Sergeant Wayne speaking. May I help you?"

"Do you have a TV at your headquarters?" Bill asked.

"Why . . . er . . . well, yes. Why do you want to know?"

"Turn it on in twenty minutes to the local NBC affiliate station." He hung up and walked back down the street to the dance hall.

Up in the building, he sat at an old table he had placed in the middle of the dance floor, waiting. John was carefully tied and sitting in the corner. As much as he could be, Bill was ready for Jarvis.

It was not long before Bill heard a noise and some cursing in low voices at the back door. The back entrance was being forced open. Time stopped momentarily as he listened. There was a footstep on the first step, then the second. When the man's leg descended onto the third step, the infrared beam was broken. The electronic trigger released the pin from the explosive device. The noise of the explosion echoed up the stairway and across the dance floor. A light shower of dust fell onto the table where Bill sat. There was a crash of falling bodies on the back stairs. He smiled.

Several seconds later the sound of footsteps on the front stairs could be heard. One set walked with deliberateness, the other shuffled or stumbled. As Bill had anticipated, Jarvis and Holly crossed the threshold into the dance room. He pressed a tiny button mounted under the table where he was sitting.

The response was instantaneous.

"Get ready to cut to satellite feed," the engineer at NBC's main control room in New York commanded.

Suddenly, the entire network went blank.

"What is this? What happened?" he screamed. "Hit the override!" the chief engineer shouted.

"I did. Nothing happened!"

Puzzlement and denial of any wrongdoing swept the room. Tel-Ray had captured NBC's signal. The transmission from Bill's remote camera began. The signal was clear and obviously an amateur production.

"Jake! What's that?" the supervisor shouted as the camera with a motion sensor zoomed in on Jarvis and Holly. Jarvis was dressed in a blue pinstriped suit. Holly's clothes were torn and bloodstained, her face swollen, her left eye blackened, and she could barely walk as she dragged her right leg slightly. Jarvis led her over to a chair and dropped her into it. The video camera had a remote motion control; it had followed Holly and Jarvis's entry and progression to the table in perfect focus.

The supervisor was alert enough to know he was on to something big. "Where's that signal coming from?" he demanded.

"I don't know, but I'm trying to kill it," came the response.

"No! Don't!" the supervisor shouted.

"I'm glad you said that, because we can't kill it. Whoever or wherever it's coming from has control of the entire network through our satellite hookup. We'd have to shut the entire satellite down to lose this."

"OK, then, just ride with it. I'll take the flack," the supervisor said.

• • •

"Sit down, Jarvis," Bill said calmly.

Jarvis sat down across the table from Bill and laid down an

automatic pistol. He carefully eyed the Uzi lying in front of Bill. "Holly said it would be precarious to meet you, Dr. Chandler. Somehow, sitting there by yourself, you don't look so threatening. You have a gun; I have a gun. However, I can assure you that does not make us equal," he mocked.

"I may not look dangerous, Jarvis, but you have some men on the back stairs that might give you some argument about what is equal. If they're still alive, I suspect they have one heck of a headache. By the way, you don't have much for a backup, either, now." Without emotion, he continued. "I thought we negotiated for you and Holly to come alone. You didn't bargain in good faith."

"I must have misunderstood," he replied.

"That misunderstanding will cost you."

"Dr. Chandler, I doubt that you really realize what you're up against."

"Oh, to the contrary! In the last few weeks I've learned a lot about you and your friends, Mr. Jarvis. Let me tell you some history; you can add a few details, I'm sure. I've learned that you seem to be able to get whatever you want and kill whomever you want without a great deal of difficulty, and no one seems to care. It would be stupid for me to think I could come in here like the cavalry and defeat you, wouldn't it?"

"Dr. Chandler, you are a much more reasonable man today, quite a change from the deranged killer we've been reading about in the news. Does my having Holly mean that much to you?"

"Jarvis, I came here to deal. This is the deal. I have the completed plans for Tel-Ray; you have Holly. Let's trade," Bill said.

"Is that all?" Jarvis asked accusingly.

"No, we get out of this town alive, and we get a twenty-four-hour head start before you send your goons after us."

"Don't you think I'll leave you alone after I have Tel-Ray?"

"Don't play with me, Jarvis. You and your organization have too much at stake. You have to protect Secretary of Defense Blaine, as well as many others I know about in the government. You have to eliminate us eventually. Like I said, I've gotten to know you better lately. And Holly knows you even better than I do. I believe it was your bungled attempt to kill her that started this whole mess, wasn't it?" Bill chided.

"Alas, Dr. Chandler, that is true. What should have been a straightforward elimination of one meddling female has turned into a rather messy affair. Though there is one bright spot. I guess you didn't hear that Secretary Blaine's dead. Had a car wreck, poor fellow. So, I don't have to protect him any longer."

"Another of your convenient accidents? Like Ed Harris's accidental drowning?" he queried.

"No, strange as it may seem, it was an accident—though I always knew someday I would have to dispose of my junior partner," he said sarcastically.

As they sat there in the dusty dance hall overlooking the Atlantic Ocean, everybody in America who was watching NBC television was a witness to the unfolding drama.

"Jarvis, tell me something. What is it you are involved in anyway? I know the tape I played for Press Secretary Johnston indicated that you and Blaine were selling U.S. military secrets to the communists or whoever would pay, but what is it that you're really doing?" Bill goaded him.

"First, let's talk about your offer. I will let you and Holly leave, with a head start of twelve hours, if I can have the Tel-Ray plans now. And I'll tell you what you stepped into, since I doubt that you'll live long enough to tell anyone." Jarvis's arrogance was growing with his confidence.

"Since 1973, I have been building an organization to supply whatever is needed by anyone with the money to pay the price," Jarvis said.

"Yes, I understand that, but you seem to have so many people in the government who work for you. I mean, there's Blaine and Johnston, the president's press secretary, and Billings in the FBI.

There's John back there in the corner from the NIS division of the navy, and there's Jim Shaw of the CIA, and who knows how many others. How did slime like you get these people to do your dirty work?"

"Usually it was money; occasionally it was sex. In Blaine's case, for instance, it was both money and power. I used whatever it took. When it gets right down to it, most people don't have much love or patriotism for the country. They do whatever is easiest and produces the most profit. My organization provides what people want most: power, sex, or tax-free income. It is very simple." Jarvis sat back and laughed.

"OK, but I would like to tie up a few loose ends that involved me. First, what about Cookie?"

"Cookie? I'm afraid I don't know anyone by that name."

"He was the unfortunate fellow killed when the condominium complex was bombed."

"Oh, that. That was an accident. Some of my boys got a little rambunctious. That was also sloppy. Again, they were just trying to eliminate Holly."

"I suppose, then, you can rationalize your elimination of Ken the same way—sloppy work, just trying to get rid of Holly?" he taunted.

"Chandler, you are so provincial. Small things like that don't really matter. The world is much too complex to let little people and their problems concern you."

"Am I one of those little people also?" Bill was trying to control his emotions; he wanted this confession to continue as long as possible. "Jarvis, I am very curious about the man up at Big Meadows."

"Who?"

"The man who tipped you off when we were hiding up on the Skyline Drive. He was alive when we left that cabin."

"Oh yes, him," he sneered. "I thought it would add some pressure to the hunt if you and Holly had committed another murder.

Just added some realism to your crime spree." He laughed. "Dr. Chandler, let me see if I can sum up all of your questions this way. I like to think of some of us as special people. We have a duty—no, more than a duty, a trust or a mandate, to guide certain things in the world. You do it by inventing; I do it by assuring the balance of power. . . ."

• • •

In the second division of the North Carolina Highway Patrol, the watch commander was glued to the TV. "Do you recognize where that's coming from?"

"No, sir. The caller just said watch the NBC station."

"I keep thinking it has to be in our area."

The watch commander was staring intently at the screen for a hint of the location. In New York, the shift supervisor at NBC was frantically trying to put some perspective on this nonscheduled program. And all over America, people from the farmhouses of Iowa to the yuppie complexes of the West Coast were wondering why they were using real people's names on a television program. The president of the country was reaching for his phone as it was ringing. Thirty seconds later, he would be turning on the television in the anteroom to watch the conclusion.

"Look, Jarvis, that's a bunch of bull. You're a hood and a slime. You're what's left on the sidewalk after a snail has been stepped on. Now, I do know you operate out of your house here at Carolina Beach. . . ."

"That's it!" the watch commander shouted. "Get some cars rolling to Pleasure Island on the double! And keep watching. Call me on the radio when you pinpoint their location," he called to the radio dispatcher as he ran out the door.

"But how do you have all the cargo, guns, and equipment come and go through the ports without anyone catching on?" Bill asked.

"Most of it goes out under my export license. From my legitimate company, you know. And"—he laughed—"a bribe in the right place helps from time to time. The most help comes from the Defense Department."

In the distance Bill heard a siren. He hoped everything had worked as planned. He knew there was little use in postponing the inevitable.

"Jarvis, do you remember when you held me prisoner at your house in Maryland?" Bill asked.

"Yes," he replied.

"I told you then that someday I would crush you, that you had best kill me then. Well, now's the time."

"You're crazy, Professor. You are in no position to crush anyone!" he responded.

"Look, Jarvis, I know this isn't what you had in mind, but I'm going to take Holly and leave now." The wail of the approaching cars was increasing. "You might as well wait here in the dance hall; the police will be up shortly."

"Where are the plans, Chandler? I'll kill her right now!" Jarvis grabbed Holly with his left hand while waving the gun wildly in his right.

Bill knew the end was in sight one way or the other. Jarvis would kill Holly, or if the police arrived in time, he would be arrested shortly and they would at last be free. He had to keep Jarvis's attention.

"First, Jarvis, I want to tell you, Tel-Ray does indeed work. You see, I have been using it to transmit this little meeting we have just had."

"You're lying!" he shouted.

"No," Bill said calmly. "I preempted whatever was showing on NBC this morning. Hear the sirens? They're coming for you, not me." Bill looked into his eyes, and the fear he saw in the once-proud man told him that Jarvis knew the truth.

"It's over, Jarvis. The police are downstairs. This whole little

347

drama today was witnessed by everyone watching NBC. You see, the idea behind Tel-Ray is not only to provide instant communication of a lot of information, but also to commandeer the enemy's own communications and use them for whatever is needed. In this case, I took over the satellite signal of NBC, and ever since you walked in here, we have gone into millions of homes and offices across the country. I took the liberty of calling the local highway patrol and told them to tune in. I suspect the noise outside the dance hall is the boys in blue. So Jarvis, this is the end of the line for you."

Jarvis pushed the table over, grabbing his gun. He scanned the room carefully then aimed at Bill. Bill dived for cover behind the overturned table and frantically looked for his weapon as Jarvis began to spray the mirrored walls of the dance hall.

The air was heavy with blue cordite as fragmented splinters of glass skyrocketed in Brownian motion across the room. The old jukebox exploded as a spray of bullets splintered the wood and plastic. The camera was left untouched, staring at Jarvis like a primeval animal.

"You know, Professor, our deal is off!" he snarled. "Get Holly and stand over by that wall!" He motioned with the barrel of the gun.

Bill shoved the table at Jarvis, catching him at the waist. The impact caused him to lose his balance; he dropped Holly and fired a shot wildly at Bill again. Bill dived for him, his shoulder burrowing into Jarvis's midsection. They crashed to the floor, wrestling for the gun. He slammed a fist into Bill's back; the pain shot through him like a knife. Bill had one hand on Jarvis's wrist that held the gun; his other hand tried desperately to ward off blows from Jarvis's left hand.

As they grappled, the gun was slowly turning toward Bill. He locked his leg over Jarvis's like a lever; they rolled several times. Bill then brought his knee into Jarvis's groin and lifted him off. The big man lost his breath when he hit the floor; the gun slipped from his grasp and skidded across the floor. Bill lunged for it, but Jarvis caught his pant leg and pulled him back.

They clenched and struggled, rolling over several times, neither of them gaining the advantage. Bill glanced up and saw they had come near the top of the stairs leading to the boardwalk.

With all his strength he rolled to the edge, gripping Jarvis as close to him as he could. Jarvis's inability to move his arms meant the blows he tried to deliver were falling harmlessly on Bill's back. With one last burst of effort, Bill rolled them both off the top step.

They broke apart on the third revolution and crashed into a twisted heap at the bottom of the stairwell, their contorted bodies forcing the glass doors open. Bill was dazed, dizzy, and disorientated. Slowly, his eyes began to focus, and he was looking at the circular opening of a gun barrel. He expected to feel the impact instantly.

"Freeze!" the voice said. "Which one of you is Dr. Chandler?" A state police lieutenant was standing over them.

"I'm . . . I . . . Bill Chandler. . . ." He raised his free arm slightly.

Another man in uniform began to untangle them. Jarvis was out cold, or dead. At that moment, Bill didn't care which.

Slowly and with difficulty, Bill stood up. Leaning on the handrail, he began a painful climb up the stairs. He still wasn't sure if he had broken anything. But he wanted to get to Holly. A third policeman grabbed his free arm and helped him walk to the top.

Holly had not moved from the place where she had fallen when Bill had shoved the table at Jarvis. She still lay in a crumpled heap in the middle of the dance floor. He knelt beside her and felt for her pulse in her neck. It was strong. Gently he rolled her to her back and straightened out her legs. Sitting down beside her, he stroked her hair and watched her breathe. He was trying to reassure himself that she would live.

"We have an ambulance here for the woman, sir. I don't understand what's been going on, but that was quite a show you put on!"

"Thanks," Bill said.

The paramedics gently lifted Holly onto the stretcher and covered her bruised body with a clean sheet and blanket. The white sheet accentuated the purplish green bruises on her face. Her eyes were swelled almost completely shut.

The ambulance attendant told Bill the name of the hospital where they would take Holly. He thanked them and said he would be along shortly.

Meanwhile, Jarvis had come to and was sitting against the wall outside the dance hall. His brain was trying to sift through what had just happened. He had always thought things would end in a hail of gunfire—maybe like in the movie *Butch Cassidy and the Sundance Kid*. As it turned out, he was sabotaged by electronics, the very thing he was trying to sell. He looked up at Bill with all of the hatred he could muster.

"Jarvis?" Bill smiled.

"Huh," he grunted with a dazed look in his eyes.

"I gotcha."

Other police were rounding up the rest of Jarvis's men, taking their guns and handcuffing them. A young officer with a sergeant patch on his sleeve walked up to Bill and said, "Dr. Chandler?"

"Yes?"

"There's a call for you on the radio in the lieutenant's car." Bill followed him to the side of the building. He noticed he had acquired a limp after his battle with Jarvis. As the adrenaline wore off, he was starting to feel pain everywhere.

"Here, Dr. Chandler," the officer instructed. "Just press this button to talk; let up to listen."

"This is Bill Chandler."

"Dr. Chandler, wait one minute for the president," a staccato voice said.

He swallowed hard and sat down on the edge of the car seat to take the weight from his throbbing ankle.

"Dr. Chandler?"

"Yes, Mr. President."

"I saw part of your program on television. Good lighting, interesting script."

"Yes, sir. The unfortunate thing is, it wasn't fiction."

"Yes, I understand that. I want you and the young lady, she is . . . uh, she's . . ."

"No, sir, she's not dead," Bill interjected.

"Ah, good. I want you and her to brief me on this situation as soon as it's feasible."

"We'd be happy to."

"My people will be in touch with you to make the arrangements."

Bill hesitated. "Mr. President, it's not that I doubt that most of the people who work for you are OK, but sir, let me call your office to make the arrangements."

There was a long pause. "Given your last few days, I think I understand your hesitancy. That will be fine. Call when the lady is feeling up to it. The switchboard will put you through."

"Thank you, sir." Radio static punctuated the end of the conversation.

The state police lieutenant took the microphone from his hand. "We'll need a statement, sir. Looks like this is going to be complicated," he said.

"Yeah, it is. I'm not sure I understand it all." Bill sat in silence for several minutes. "Do you mind if I go to the hospital first? I want to see how Holly's doing. We have a wedding to plan."

The lieutenant's face lit up in a grin.

"Yes, sir! How about if I have someone drive you?" he asked.

"Yeah . . . that would be nice."